BLACKHEART MAN

Also by
Nalo Hopkinson

Novels

Sister Mine

The Chaos

The New Moon's Arms

The Salt Roads

Under Glass

Midnight Robber

Brown Girl in the Ring

Collections

Jamaica Ginger and Other Concoctions (forthcoming)

Falling in Love with Hominids

Report from Planet Midnight

Skin Folk

Comics

The Sandman Universe: House of Whispers

BLACKHEART MAN

A Novel

NALO HOPKINSON

SAGA PRESS

LONDON SYDNEY **NEW YORK** TORONTO NEW DELHI

SAGA))) PRESS

AN IMPRINT OF SIMON & SCHUSTER, LLC

1230 AVENUE OF THE AMERICAS, NEW YORK, NEW YORK 10020

First Saga Press hardcover edition August 2024

SAGA PRESS and colophon are trademarks of Simon & Schuster LLC

Simon & Schuster: Celebrating 100 Years of Publishing in 2024

For information about special discounts for bulk purchases, please contact Simon & Schuster Special Sales at 1-866-506-1949 or business@simonandschuster.com.

The Simon & Schuster Speakers Bureau can bring authors to your live event. For more information or to book an event, contact the Simon & Schuster Speakers Bureau at 1-866-248-3049 or visit our website at www.simonspeakers.com.

Interior design by Lewelin Polanco

Manufactured in the United States of America

1   3   5   7   9   10   8   6   4   2

Library of Congress Cataloging-in-Publication Data is available.

ISBN 978-1-6680-0510-1
ISBN 978-1-6680-0512-5 (ebook)

To David, my rock, as ever.

BLACKHEART MAN

Chapter 1

HERE AT THE TOP of Cullybree Heights, the stone statue honouring the twin goddess Mamacona loomed out over the ocean. She was carved in the form of two caimans, standing back to back on their hind legs, clawed front legs reaching out to embrace or to scourge. The caiman facing seawards was Mamagua, her jewelled eyes and pointed teeth the deep blue of lapis. Facing inland was Mamapiche, eyes and teeth a gleaming black obsidian. Each sister had a powerful caiman tail curled around her feet.

The fore-day morning sea was a deep, cold blue. Mama Sea was cheerful on the surface of Her vast, shifting self; whitecaps dancing towards the port in fishscale recursives, like slatterns kicking up their skirts to show their knickers. But beneath those knickers, ah, what? Salty depths that had swallowed many a somebody who surfaced changed, or surfaced not at all. What might be down there in the deep? You didn't need to sink too far into the water before the sombre blue shaded even darker to navy, then deep night, then full, cold blackness.

Veycosi shuddered. Best to let women be the fishers. Take to their rudders to ride the sea. They understood Her better.

Straddling the wide clay outlet pipe that took fresh water from the Cullybree Heights reservoir to the south side of Carenage Town, he scooted a little farther along it. He had to be quick. As soon as the sun was fully up, other people would start visiting Carenage Town's big reservoir, whether maintenance workers, people hunting the iguanas that were plentiful in the brush up here, or people fishing the reservoir for frogs and mullet. Every so often, Veycosi knocked on the pipe. Each thump netted him a juddering thud, as when you knocked on the green rind of a watermillion to test its ripeness. He'd been right, then; there was water in this pipe, too, as in the other five he'd tested. That was well. But he could also tell that the water wasn't moving; when he'd done this same procedure a few minutes ago with the five other massive pipes that fed the other areas of Carenage Town, he hadn't even needed to thump on them. The water filling them was running so strong that when he straddled each pipe, he could feel the powerful thrum of the flow against his haunches, like the stroke of a masterful lover. In this sixth pipe, however, the water was still; there must be a blockage somewhere farther down.

Stale water made for ill humours. Every day the town elders didn't let him act, they risked an outbreak of cholera or bottle leg disease in Carenage. And if South Carenage sickened, it could spread to North, West, and East Carenage, Blueing, and Cassava Downs.

Veycosi kept knocking against the pipe, advancing as he went. *Thud. Thud. Thud.*

Thump.

A flat sound, with no answering resonance. Was that the blockage?

He moved forwards a little more, knocking the while. He hadn't gone more than thirty handsbreadths when his knock fetched a third sound; a low, hollow clang. The quality of the sound told him that from that section onwards, the pipe was empty. And as he'd suspected, the blockage was right at the point where the pipe turned to begin its gentle dip down to Carenage Town's south side. Likely a build-up of matter blown into the reservoir during Chynchin's long dry season. Council members were addlepates, every last one of them. Refusing his petition to try out his idea for getting the water flowing again. Instead, they wanted to wait until the rainy season, which should arrive in a few sennights. The council hoped that the weight of extra water from the rains would flush the pipe clear. The histories sang of only a few times pipes from the reservoir had become blocked, and each time, the weight of water pressing against the blockage had quickly cleared it. But this time, it had been going on for months. In the meantime, South Carenage, the bustling centre of town, had to fetch water from the river in buckets. And there was an ever-present smell of rot from still sewers. Next it'd be mosquitos breeding, their larvae wiggling in the putrid water. Then sickness. Thandy, his and Gombey's fiancée, lived there, in the centre of town. This thing had to be fixed, and now. He would make the air down there sweet again, make the water flow. Thandy would be proud and show him favour once more, as she used to. She'd seemed cool towards him for some weeks now. He had no idea why. He was training to be a chanter of knowledge that others might employ it. The council had reminded him he was a chantwell, and a student one at that. Said he was not an ingenieur. Said he shouldn't be meddling in the business of builders.

Fuck that. He could reckon instructions as well as anyone with a brain. Could chant the first five chapters of Mauretaine's book *Of Divers Matters on Constructing Wells, Pipes, and Sewers,* beginning to end and back again, the full tenor main part. He and his classmates had studied its song last year. But he hadn't had to memorize the section on clearing blocked pipes; that part was for the sopranos of his line.

Veycosi was beginning to slaver around the selfsame book he'd brought out onto the pipe with him, clenched between his teeth. He released it into his hand and opened it to the place he'd marked by slipping a z'avocade leaf in between the pages. The vellum binding creaked as the book opened. The ancient handmade paper of the pages gave off the usual dusty library smell, so sweet and exciting to his nose, it nearly made him hard every time he scented it. The book's handwritten ink was fading; good thing he and his line at the Colloquium were committing it to memory, setting it to music so the song might spread on the winds like Mamacona's breath. That way, the knowledge the book contained might never be forgotten.

He reread the instructions on the page. Yes, rap on the pipes for soundness. He'd already done that and verified that it wasn't cracked. Open the sluice of the blocked pipe. He'd done that before he'd mounted the pipe. Drop some dye into the reservoir water now, very near the inlet of the suspect pipe. Thence he must watch and see where it did and didn't flow. Ingenious, that. He pulled the bottle of indigo out of his sleeve pocket, removed the cork, and emptied the bottle into the reservoir water, as close to the pipe as possible. Slowly, a thread of it began to spiral downwards, away from the spreading circle of blue on the surface and towards the inlet below. So the pipe wasn't completely blocked. Presently, though, he saw his mistake in using indigo. Blue dye, blue water, sombre morning light. The thinner the indigo spread, the less he could see it, until he couldn't make out the dye at all.

No matter. He'd learned what it had to tell him. Time for the next part of the instructions.

Veycosi humped back along the pipe, towards the service steps from the reservoir to the ground below. He refused to think on how his movement resembled that of a cat with a wormy behind. Good thing Thandy couldn't see his undignified dismount from his water pipe steed.

Standing on the top step, he looked around. Still no one up here but him and the birds. Half-seen flashes of iridescence laced with brown and green, the cullybrees flitted around him in their endless, wheeling flight. Truth was, the council had another reason for waiting till rainy season to think about the blocked pipe. They didn't want to risk disrupting the cullybree eggs and ruining the annual Cullybree Festival. The cullybree chicks would hatch soon as the season turned fully from dry to rainy. Already they'd had a slight drizzle or two this month, but it was tapu to disturb the cullybree nests. Laying cullybrees tipped their eggs onto moss-lined crags on the northeastern face of the Heights, a furlong or so farther off. The foolish had a way to say that touching a cullybree nest would bring the world to an end. Chuh. Credulous gullwits. Any road, he was nowhere near the nests. He would get this thing done, then be off tomorrow on the ship to Ifanmwe, where the Colloquium's book trader was holding a copy of the Alamat *Book of Light* for him. That tome hadn't been seen for near on five centaines! The Colloquium had thought it long gone, lost to the sea when the siege of Ifanmwe had seen that country's fine library put to the torch. Seventeen hundred books and scrolls burned. The histories sang that the clouds above the burned shell of the Ifanmwe library had been black for three days with paper ash. Knowledge destroyed. It was abominable to even think on.

Veycosi had heard that in the mountains above Ifanmwe, two oceans away, it was so cold in their wet season that rain hardened in midair and fell to the ground as a fine white powder. He'd always longed to see that. And to taste it. Steli said they creamed the stuff with yak's milk and honey to make a divine confection. Veycosi was soon to become a fully fledged Fellow of the Colloquium of the nation of Chynchin. He had only to fetch a rare book for the Colloquium Council. The Alamat book was the prize that would bring him closer to that fellowship. Bring it home, take the dreaming draught that would give him a Reverie, and then he would be a full chantwell. Once he was a Fellow, he would be free to travel the world, collecting and preserving the written knowledge of history. To be on the sea! He'd only done so once, as a youngboy. He still remembered standing at the bow, the tang of salt spray on his lips.

Back at the reservoir wall, he tucked the book into his sleeve, which was turned and hemmed to form a deep pocket. From the foot of the reservoir steps he fetched the three unfired clay jars he'd brought with him from the market, each about the size of a baby's head. He had calculated it all, based on Mauretaine's figures. Five measures of phosphorus powder in each jar. The water would seep in, react with the phosphorus, and explode. He was going to create a swell of water within the reservoir, perhaps five handspans high. The extra pressure would push more water through the pipes and hopefully clear the blocked one. It would take some little while for the water to dissolve the jars' raw clay and ignite the phosphorus. That would give him time to get down off the cliff—briskly, mind!

Not that there was much danger. He had tried a version of this at one-fiftieth size. Based on that experiment, he had perhaps nine minutes to get down from Cullybree Hill. Add one minute for margin of error, and he still had plenty time. He might make it all the way down into Carenage Town before the thing blew, so no one would know he had caused it.

He grinned to himself. Of course they would suspect who was

responsible. After all, when mischief came at the run to Carenage Town, wasn't it usually he, Veycosi, nipping at its heels? But by then the water would be running again, and they would be grateful. And if they weren't; well, he'd be long gone on a ship bound for Ifanmwe, headed for the marvels of iced cream and the Alamat *Book of Light*. He'd return with his standing well secure at the Colloquium, and his little jackanape forgotten.

Flush with the righteousness of doing a needful thing, no matter who would gainsay it, Veycosi rose to his feet on the large bole of the pipe. He dropped the three sealed jars into the reservoir. They bobbed on the surface of the water, which would soon begin to dissolve the clay. The jars began at once to darken with wetness. Now he'd best be gone down the hill. It was all safe, but prudence, valour, et cetera. Quick as he could, he minced along the pipe.

The sun was just about risen. Something in the ocean caught the corner of Veycosi's eye.

There was a fleet heading briskly for the bay below. Some fifteen galleons; and flying Ymisen colours! Veycosi startled and nearly lost his balance. He daren't fall into the bombed water! His arms pinwheeled, sending his squared sleeve flaps semaphoring around his body. His smooth leather slippers slid on the clay pipe. He tilted. Desperately righted himself as Mauretaine's ancient book *Of Divers Matters* slipped from his sleeve, tumbled into the water, and disappeared from view. It was the only copy in existence! He shouldn't even have removed it from the library. For a Colloquium student to actually destroy one of its precious tomes! He could well be drummed out of the Colloquium for this. His adventure had just progressed from jackanape to infamy.

Jittering in shock on the pipe, he considered for an instant diving after the book. Its parchment pages would remain intact, but even now, the inked words inside would be dissolving into the water.

The water into which he had just introduced three bombs. It would be folly to leap in.

The fleet would soon enter the bay. Its foremasts, mains, and mizzens rose like spears from the ships' decks. Veycosi's scalp prickled. Ymisen. The country that had stolen his Cibonn' ancestors' lands and press-ganged them into slavery, along with people from Ilife and some unfortunates from Ymisen itself. But the ships were flying trade flags. Since when had Ymisen decided to quit its sanctions on Chynchin?

Home! After so many years, to be home. Standing on the deck of the Ymisen ship the Empire Star, *Androu couldn't still his traitor heart from leaping in his breast at the sight of the graceful sweep of Carenage Bay, the cocoanut and gru-gru bef palms blowing in a gentle breeze, the cullybree birds circling on the drafts in the air above. So long since he had set foot on Chynchin soil.*

The captain gave the order for the sailor to run up the flags that would signal to the rest of the fleet to break away. Those ships would put in at deserted Boar Island a short distance away. They would load up with fresh water, hunt boar and dry the meat, and wait until they were sent for. Then they would arrive in force and take this wretched island of Chynchin. Turn it back into Ymisen territory, of sorts. That is, if the new Ymisen regime would acknowledge Tierce's right to succeed to the throne, now that it had deposed Tierce's father.

The steersman longingly eyed the bay. They had been weeks at full sail. Standing nearby with the captain, Advisor Gunderson stared at the bay too, and grunted his relief.

Well he might. They would get their precious passenger safely to their destination after all. All this for a book. But the trip would bring Androu, finally, his revenge.

The captain called out, "Full ahead!" to the steersman.

So busy were Androu's eyes taking in the sight of Chynchin Island that he nearly overlooked the small spinning swirls of foam a scant few ells in front of them. Two smaller circles lay in a line pointing at them, leading to the largest one, which was closest to the bay. When Androu did notice them, the back of his neck prickled. "Hard to!" he yelled at the steersman. "Now!" Gods blast it, they were about to run up on Mamagua's Pearls!

The steersman squinted at him but looked to the captain for his orders. The captain and Gunderson gave Androu a suspicious glare. Damned Ymisen prigs like Gunderson would never trust him, for all that he had blood such as theirs running in his veins. "Heave to!" Androu barked. "You'll have us run aground!" Fearsweat crawled beneath his collar.

———

Datiao drew breath! At last! But straitway he met the blockage; no air to fill his lungs, no way for his chest to expand even had there been air in it. All he got for his pains was a hot honey-trickle of black piche sliding into his nose and tickling down the back of his throat. His body spasmed, but there was no way to cough so as to expel the piche. How long he had been embalmed this way in sludgy blackness?

Long enough for him to unlearn the habit of breathing. But it had come back to him just now. All it needed was air for him to practise the skill proper. Then the three bitches would rue their borning days.

———

Veycosi realised he had been standing still on the pipe, transfixed in shock at the sight of the Ymisen ships. He'd lost track of how much time he had before the water dissolved the clay jars. Nine minutes, fifty seconds? Nine thirty-eight? His heart swelled his throat near shut. Teetering a little, he hotfooted it to the end of the pipe, jumped down, and broke into a pounding run down the path. Nine minutes, twenty-two seconds? Twenty-one? The foot of the hill was looking farther away than it had on his way up here.

Eight minutes, fifty-eight seconds, fifty-seven . . . Soon, he was scurrying down the part of the footpath along the very edge of Cullybree Hill that led down to the town. Eight thirty-two . . . He glanced up to the top of the ridge, where the jars in the reservoir were surely dissolving.

There was going to be hell to pay for losing the book. Maybe he'd be able to fish it out once this was all over. Perhaps some of the words would have survived.

"'Ware ships!" he yelled to the town below. Not that they could hear him at this distance. He leapt over a patch of prickly scrub that was barring his way. He skidded on slippery moss on the other side. His feet slipped out from under him. He landed hard on one hip, the breath exploding from his lungs. Before he could brace himself, he slid out over the edge of the cliff. His legs kicked air. He scrabbled at the ground, at the skittering rockstones his fall had dislodged, at anything, anything!

He managed to grab a sapling. It whipped through his hands, skinning his palms. Frantic, he tightened his grip. The greenstick sapling cracked, but didn't break. He blinked dirt out of his eyes and looked up at it. Its roots were starting to pull free. He dug his elbows into the lip of rock and paddled his feet around, feeling for purchase. But there was only air.

He twisted his body to look down over his shoulder. Red dirt cliffside all the way to the water. The black, deep water.

Rocks dislodged by his fall were bouncing at speed down the cliff. One of the rockstones sprang away from the hillside. He was up so high, he didn't hear the splash when it hit the sea surface. Sweat trickled down the back of his neck. His shoulders burned with the strain of carrying his own weight. If he let go, he would fall into the bay, likely crack his spine like a twig when he hit the water from such a great height.

There! One foot had found a solid place. He jammed the foot into a shallow crevice in the rock. A breeze ran chilly fingers up under his robe. He still couldn't lever himself up. And he'd lost complete track of how much time had passed. "Help!" he bellowed, into the echoing bell of flesh made by his chest and arms pressed against the cliff face. A gusty updraft plucked at his hair and at the hem of his robe. His hands were slipping down the length of the sapling. Six minutes, forty-seven seconds left? Forty-six?

"Help!"

Androu clutched at the polished wooden shell he always kept on a thong around his neck, hidden beneath his shirts; his soul case. It had been with him from birth. Mama-ji willing, it would be with him when he died. Which might be this very morning, if they didn't listen to him now. He cursed himself for forgetting about the Pearls.

He pointed to the left of the peaceful bay, to a narrow, muddy outlet of the Iguaca River. The river mouth had more twists and turns than Mamagua's tail. "We mun go that way!" he yelled at the captain, over the sound of the creaking ropes. "North by north-west, fifteen degrees! Quick, man! Else we'll founder on the rocks under us!" He indicated the line of eddying whirlpools. The sharp, hidden rocks of Mamagua's Pearls had torn the hull out of many a would-be marauder ship. What appeared to be the easiest way to approach Carenage Town by water was in fact the most deadly. "And run up the trade flags, sharp now!"

Advisor Gunderson nodded his permission. The captain peered through his spyglass. "North by northwest, fifteen degrees!" he bellowed at the steersman, who hung hard over. No time to measure out their course change. His face lined with doubt, the steersman set the ship leaping past the bay on a course towards the narrow inlet.

Androu threw his own weight onto the wheel to help them hold their course. They swept past the Pearls, so close that the ship's starboard side was almost in the first eddy before she turned. Androu could feel the drag on the wheel, feel her struggling to break free of the whirlpool. "Come along now, old girl," he muttered to her as he and the steersman held the wheel to. "Ye'd make poor firewood, all soaked with salt as ye are. Take me home, girl."

The ship shuddered and leapt free of the whirlpool. Androu blew out a breath, let his shoulders creep down from around his ears. He stepped back from the wheel. The steersman muttered a grudging thanks. Androu wiped his brow with his sleeve. "Put her into the bay, there," he said.

Androu stood on the deck of the ship and watched as the place he'd fled in anger some two decades before drew him in again.

Home.

Datiao tried to close his thoughts to the old memory of being mired, still on his donkey, in hot, suddenly liquid piche where there had been a flat road instants before. Of the screams and the sucking noises around him as the others were bucking up upon the same fate. Of sinking chest-deep before he could even think to fight his way free. The manic dying struggles of the donkey below him, between his thighs. One of those thighs, pressed between the kicking beast and the engulfing piche, being snapped like a stick of sugarcane. The howl of agony that had filled his mouth with black, tarry ooze as the piche closed over his head. And then the desperate sucking and sucking for breath—

No. It was done. He had died, and now air was no longer sovereign to him. He would have wept, if he could.

But though he couldn't cry tears, he could and did curse himself for losing his nerve as he'd ridden out with the foreign soldiers that day, disguised as one of them, to march upon his own fellows. Had he only kept muttering the witches' protective chantson as he had planned, the road might have stayed solid under them and he might not be in this simmering hell, surrounded by the bodies of the defeated. By reflex, he snarled.

And the very corner of his upper lip twitched. Such a tiny movement that he might have imagined it. Still, he strained again to repeat it.

And did.

Would that he could smile fully, laugh, caper about with glee for the joy of it! He could not; not yet. But his mouth was beginning to move!

Not just his mouth; the slow return of sensation brought with it a steady ache to Datiao's forcibly outstretched arm, its palm splayed open. But he blessed even that feeling. Against the sullen shifting of the piche, he had been moving his fingers, agonizing increments at a time, to grasp at the source of the object he could not see; the thing that had woken him again to this horror. The thing that was bringing life back to him, radiating from his outstretched hand to the rest of his body. Some while ago, three of his fingertips had just barely touched the edges of something solid. The power emanating from the object was glorious and terrifying in its strength. He had been reaching, straining to grasp it for oh, how long? He needed to curl his hand around the thing, whatever it was, to draw it closer to him. And in between, he never ceased trying to move the rest of him. He went on and on trying. Soon he would be able to form the words of the life-preserving chantson again, and when the thing for which he was reaching brought him back full to his capacities, the chantson would help him remain hale. If chance was with him finally, there were three blasted women he would show the meaning of rue in all its fullest. Not to mention that backwards piece of rock the escapees were pleased to call Chynchin. Running away with his fellow enslaved had eventually cost him his life, and for what?

He tried not to think on all the times before that life had returned to him, only to be wrested away again by the engulfing tar that still held him trapped as he died again, in the same agony of suffocation as the first time. He died, and died, and died. He supposed he'd been enduring like this for hours. This morning, his biggest worry had been whether he would survive the day. Now he feared he would be trapped for days, perhaps weeks!

He more felt than heard the deep sound that went gonging through the treacly piche, setting it to vibrating. What had happened above? Who was winning the skirmish between the soldiers and the village with its three witches?

There must be a particularly hot day's sun shining down on the piche from above, melting it some. The shuddering of the slowly liquefying piche made his position change, just a mite.

He found he could stretch his reaching arm a little bit farther. Good. Good. He strained and stretched his fingers till he felt sure their sinews would part from their joints.

And he touched it, first with scrabbling fingertips. And then he managed to curl his fingers around it until he was clutching it tightly in his fist.

Now, up. He didn't have much time. If he didn't reach air soon, he only had minutes of this unlife left. Without air, he would spend those minutes suffocating, as he had the first time. Already he could feel his death agonies creeping up on him again. With a mighty heave, he clawed a gobbet of softened piche to one side. Desperation lent him strength. Slow as justice and as blind, he began to claw his way up to the surface of doomed Chynchin.

The uprooted sapling slid a bit, then caught between two rockstones, held by its root ball. Veycosi tested the strength of it. It seemed solid, for now. Six minutes, nineteen seconds. Perhaps.

There. A bit higher up the cliff face and a little to the right was a place he might jam his foot, if he could reach it. Praying to Mamagua in wordless terror, he pulled himself up by the sapling. His arms were trembling so from fatigue that he feared he wouldn't be able to keep hold of it. But he had to. He started swinging his body side to side. He'd heard it sung that a pendulum would achieve a wider arc if a greater force were applied anywhere along its length. The force came from his body, from his determination not to fall and burst himself apart on the rocks below.

It took four sweeping tries before he was able to set his foot into the toehold, keep it there, and roll his body back onto the path.

Five minutes, thirty-nine seconds left? Thirty-eight? He couldn't lie there. He had to warn Chynchin. He pushed himself to his feet with arms whose muscles screamed for mercy. He began staggering down the hill again. He kept moving until he was in the valley. The buildings of Carenage Town were only a few yards in front of him. There was a street-side alarm bell right around that corner. Lungs screaming, legs trembling, he staggered on. "Ymisen," he wheezed.

Carenage Town's grey sand high road stretched out in front of Veycosi now, far as the eye could see. The street was busy, as it ever was: shops and businesses receiving custom all along the sides; covered stalls down the middle, dispensing bootlaces, boiled sweeties, and the like; and horse, camel, tricycle, and donkey traffic clattering along the twin lanes. Everywhere, people going about their business. He wove through it all like a drunken man. Nearly got stepped on by a camel. His lungpipes burned like they'd been washed with acid. His vision was blurred and the street sounds were getting muffled in his ears. He feared he might faint before he accomplished his duty. He could see the emergency bell on its pole, only a few yards away. Just a few more steps.

He was nearly to the other side of the street when a hand on his shoulder neatly moved him out of the way. It was a guard in his official garb of gold-embroidered red buba on top and matching sokoto trousers. Veycosi could have collapsed with relief. He started to croak out his warning.

"Stand back," the man said, his voice pitched to carry. Chuh. A chantwell with a phthisic could speak louder. Not Veycosi at the moment, though. He tried to insist, but his voice had shrunk to scarce the hiss of a piss in the wind. The guard chivvied him to the roadside, just as seven more guards, muskets at the ready, came in lockstep down the road. They flanked perhaps fifteen oddly dressed men they were marching in the direction of the city hall. They were moving slowly through the gathering crowd of curious Carenage Town citizens.

Veycosi made to stumble in the direction of the guards. "But there are ships," he wheezed. He'd been trying for a shout, but that was all he could manage. And the crowd was too thick.

A younggirl tugged at the sleeve of his robe. "Just one ship, mestre," she piped up. "A trade ship, from Ymisen."

He shook his head. "No, picken. A whole fleet, full armed."

From the fast-forming crowd on the sidewalk, a woman in a cobbler's apron said, "The other ships gone due west, maybe for Port Royal. So the lookout said. Only one ship made port."

The lookout, in the tower beside the Upper Piche. In his haste, he had forgotten about it. The lookout would have seen the ships and sent the news a-pigeon wing to Carenage while he was still dashing like a fool down the hill. And it was news, but maybe not danger. The trade ship would have travelled with the fleet for protection from pirates.

To put the cap on his ignominy, it looked like his plan for bringing water back to the town centre had failed. If the water had started running again, he would have heard the rumbling from the pipe as he came down the hill. For truth to tell, he had to admit to himself that his headlong dash down to the valley had taken at least three times longer than the clay flasks should have needed to dissolve. Chagrined, Veycosi kissed his teeth. He would just have to go up there tonight and try again. It was the only way to justify the loss of the Mauretaine. The way his arms and legs were trembling with fatigue, he wasn't sure how he would make that trek again. But he would. He couldn't delay; on the morrow he would be away from Chynchin.

The crowd carried Veycosi along. He wasn't far from the guards and the comess they were guarding. A band of foreign strangers, and they were well tall. Their skins were pinker even than those of Chynchin's Deserter Mirmeki people, whom they resembled. The demeanour of the pale ones was different, too, in a way difficult to name. They carried themselves with a swinging confidence, more like the men from the pirate ships that often came to Carenage Town to take their ease and give Chynchin their coin. Five of the strangers were apparently soldiers of some kind, fancy in red-and-blue uniforms—a blue lighter than indigo—their hands held carefully away from their weapons. Three-four of the rest were tanned from the sun and had the rolling walk of people of the sea. Those fellows wore sailors' canvas britches and shirts. The others were strangely dressed. Their kilts were familiar; they looked like the ones Deserter men wore. But the pantalons beneath, the straight, braided hair coiled into loops, the patterns inked onto some of their faces; those Veycosi had never seen. Those men must all be from the Ymisen ship. There were no women among them. Had they left the capitaine and crewe on board, then?

A tall, fat Ymisen man was at the front of their party. His cheeks were red and he was all in a sweat. Beside him walked some other fellows, and bringing up the rear, the shabbier-dressed ones Veycosi had marked as men who spent much of their lives on ships. They would be under the command of the capitaine of the ship. He supposed it made sense for her to remain aboard her vessel. She was responsible for it, after all.

The Ymisen men looked all around them as they went, pointing and chattering with each other.

"'Ey, banna!" a woman from the crowd called out. "You in the fancy hat!" She was hailing the man Veycosi had reckoned to be one of the capitaine's husbands. His hat was a sight, for true. Its grey brim cupped his head like a pair of hands and jutted out a good two handsbreadths all around. Its green crown was shaped like three mountains. The furry tail of some small beast or other was affixed to the crown, and hung flapping around his left ear. Such a confection would bake his head in Chynchin heat right quick.

The woman continued, "That ratshorn piece of sintin is the latest fashion in Ymisen these days?" People near her laughed, but the capitaine's dox never looked her way. Likely he couldn't understand her. Chynchin's tongue was cousin to theirs, but changed

by the two centaines that separated Chynchin from ownership by
Ymisen. It had been that long since any from Ymisen had openly
set foot on this shore. Last thing Veycosi had expected to see was
their old enemy, sailing into port as merry as you please. Two hundred years before, a small band of escaped slaves from the nearby
Ymisen colonies had managed to defeat a troop of Ymisen soldiers
and kill off most of them. From then, Ymisen had left Chynchin
Island alone. Ymisen called it "embargo," but truth was, they were
'fraid of Chynchin. 'Fraid of the obeah that had routed Ymisen that
day, at the hands of three escaped witch women, former slaves. For
two hundred years Ymisen hadn't ventured onto Chynchin soil, for
fear Chynchin would sic the piche on them again. "Mama-ji," Veycosi muttered, not exactly to the statue on the hill, "is what trouble
come for we now?"

One of the party held irself a little apart from the others. Smooth
features, clean-shaven. Ee had big, veined hands. Body of middling
size. Ee could have been a shortish man or a tallish woman; Veycosi
couldn't rightly tell. Ymisen clothing was so strange that what the
person wore gave few clues. Ee looked around calmly, ir eyes curious. Ee was sweating a river, but didn't seem to pay it any mind.
The sailing men hung back little bit from ir. Veycosi would have
sworn they feared ir. And ee was carrying a book. A volume so
small that ir hands mostly concealed it. Veycosi glimpsed a brown
cover, perhaps of wood, but nothing more.

The person's two eyes made four with Veycosi's. Ee grinned,
joy bursting like sunshine forth from ir face. Ee waved at Veycosi
like the two of them were lifelong bannas. Ee pointed at Veycosi,
indicating his robe, the plain tan of an aspirant to the Colloquium.
So catching ir merriness was that Veycosi found his hand creeping
up to return the wave.

"You know that one?" asked a man standing near Veycosi. His

tone was suspicious. He had bronzed Cibonn' features like Vey-cosi's. His linen buba and the hems of his sokoto were embroi-dered with the sibidi of some respectable establishment. He was a slow market agent, then, shilling the products of a market supplier whose goods he endorsed.

"Not me," Veycosi replied. He jerked his chin in the direction of the people from the ship. "What a-go on with those fellows?"

The man shrugged. "Nobody really know yet. Pigeons come down from the lookout little bit ago with a message that they were arriving. After that, the excitement start."

Come the second bells of the afternoon, the giant clay water tubes that ringed Chynchin would carry the news all around the island, to every town and village.

The man said, "Seem they from Ymisen!"

Veycosi sighed. "I know."

A plump dame on his other side leaned over. "Those men come from off it?" she asked. "Off the Ymisen ship?" Her eyes were avid. She waved a delicate fan at her face. Even from where he was standing, Veycosi could smell the oversweet perfume scenting it.

"Is true," he said. His breathing was finally beginning to slow after his dash down the hill.

"Flying trading colours, they say," the man told them. "What a thing! Ymisen seeking trade with us!"

The guard marched the lot of the Ymisen farther along the street. The crowd closed in behind them.

But Veycosi had other business. To the man and woman, he said, "Good walk, goodman, siani." He turned on his heel to take his leave of them. The effect would have had more grace if he hadn't stumbled over the alpagat strap he'd torn in his rush down the hill.

A *thoom!* sound like thunder shoved at Veycosi's ears. Reflex-ively, he ducked. Someone near him gasped. A startled bicycle rider lost control of his machine and spun out in the dusty street, colliding with two others and bringing them clattering down, too. A man squealed in alarm. A passing camel twitched its ears back, in the direction of Cullybree Heights. A youngboy riding on a man's shoulders pointed up at the Heights. "Da!" he cried out. "Water, Da!" Alarmed cullybrees were winging away from the hill, screeching their fear.

Another explosion slapped the air, then a third hard upon it. From his squatting position, Veycosi saw it; the water in the reservoir rose above its containing wall and slammed back down again, with a reverberating crash like Mamagua slapping her caiman tail against the surface of a river.

"To rass," muttered Veycosi. "Too much phosphorus, I think." Still, he wagered the south side was getting good and plenty fresh water now. He stood, smiling, and raised his arms. "You see, all-you?" he called to those nearby him. "That's all we needed to do. Two-three little flasks of a certain powder, and the reservoir fix up good-good."

With a bang, the cistern atop a nearby spectacles shop blew its lid. Veycosi's neck-back goose-bumped as he watched the big clay plate that was the cistern lid wing a glittery flurry of hazel green-brown in the air. A cullybree! Was it injured?

There were voices screaming and shouting, people running out of the spectacles shop. A suspicious brown ooze sludged about their ankles. The alarmed voices came to Veycosi as though there were stout walls between them and him. The explosion had closed up his ears. He looked around frantically. Had a small, sacred bird body fallen to the ground?

Whipping edge over edge, the cistern lid sailed down to break itself over the spine of a donkey tied nearby. Veycosi threw his arm over his face to protect himself from flying clay shards. The donkey grunted and dropped to its knees. Water from the cistern cascaded down over the roof of the shop and crashed into the street. Pieces of something wet and fleshy smacked Veycosi in the face and stuck against his cheek. He put his hand to his face to brush it clear, and felt small, sharpish scales. He pulled his hand away, shuddering as he shook off the thing that had stuck to it. The piece fell into the folds of the scarf around his neck. Frantically, Veycosi clawed it away until it fell to the wet dirt at his feet. A lengthwise half of a fish, neatly filleted. Just a fish. Not a sacred cullybree. Despite the comess around him, Veycosi felt he could breathe again.

All along the high street, cisterns and shit-holes were leaking, some of them erupting. People got lazy during dry season, didn't take care to close cisterns properly or keep their pipe filters clean. Then the first day of rainy season would come, and of course there were overflows just like this, though belike less explosive.

Veycosi had brought a taste of rainy season to Carenage Town, is all. Wasn't as though the world's waters had risen up to swallow the earth. Everything would be all right. It was only a fish the cistern lid had killed.

A siani over there was struggling with two damp, bawling pickens, trying to hustle them out of the muck. Veycosi took a step forwards to help her. His sandaled foot landed on a small something that rolled and gave beneath his sole.

Veycosi lifted his foot and looked down. A fat frog writhed in the mud at his feet, one leg trailing, broken either by the cistern lid or his heedless foot. Its mouth opened and closed soundlessly.

The siani with the pickens was closer now. "I heard you just now," she said, her voice angry. "You say is you cause this?"

She wasn't the only one who had heard. Other people were looking at him, their faces screwed up in suspicion. Someone tugged on a guard's sleeve and pointed in Veycosi's direction. The guard tucked her tanned bull-cod cudgel under her arm and started running his way. She called out, "Mestre? A word?"

Damn and blast. For the second time that day, a weary Veycosi took to his heels, pushing through the crowd as he went. Behind him, he could hear people calling for him to stop.

As they neared the inlet, the sailors began to mutter nervously at the sight of all the toothy, snouted caimans sunning themselves out of the water. But Androu knew the beasts were lazy to attack anything less small and helpless than a squawking hen. As a boy, he'd played dares with his bannas to see how many crocs sunning on the riverbank they could punch on the snout before running away again.

The timing of their arrival was well. It was late in the morning, but a few of the fisherfolk's boats were on the water. They would witness Ymisen's triumphant arrival. Two or three had already spotted them. Some had slowed and turned about to watch their progress. He could imagine the astonishment on the faces of the women in their boats, and of the one or two men some of them had with them as crew. He wished there had been more fisherwomen. As well to begin with them, out of all those in Chynchin who had ever stood in his way. He wished he could take the helm of this grand ship. That would show the fisher-bitches that a man of Chynchin could steer the seas as well as any woman. He was good for more than a hand on deck to pull at the sails and bail out the bilge.

He could smell the sullen river water now, and threaded through it, the sulphur stench of the nearby lake of piche. He hadn't realised it afore this, but his nose had missed that pungent assault.

The ship leapt forwards on a swelling wave. Androu closed his eyes, the better to take in the scents of home. He smiled. He was coming back to the land that had exiled him. He was going to bring his homeland to its knees and make it beg; see if he wouldn't.

A bang came from the top of the hill. The sailors flinched and ran to man the cannon, even as the captain was ordering them to. What, was the game up already? If Chynchin captured their lead ship with their regent in it, the rest of the fleet would never gain the advantage.

A liquid flash of silver on top of the hill caught Androu's eye. The reservoir. What was happening up there? Androu practically snatched the spyglass from the captain's hand. He could see nothing wrong. He trained the spyglass on Carenage Town at the foot of the hill. Wet streets, and all that running about. He muttered to himself, "Is what a-gwan?"

He shrugged and handed the spyglass back to the captain. They would soon be docked. Then they'd see what was what.

Veycosi could hear the guards yelling for him as they gave chase. They were coming up fast. Panicked, he looked around. He was in Surgeon's Row. It backed onto the river. He'd be able to mongoose himself out that way.

The closest establishment had the symbol for "tooth" in its window. He yanked the door open and threw himself inside. He blundered through a waiting room. A few faces turned startled gazes 'pon him; the rest were too busy nursing sore jaws. Some poor soul must have been having a tooth pulled right that minute; the screams hid the commotion of his blundering through the building, though that wouldn't help him if the guards had seen which way he'd gone.

The back doors of Surgeon's Row's establishments let out right onto the river. Easier for getting rid of offal. This toothdoctor's door was no different. In fact, it was so close to the bank that as Veycosi pushed through the door, he nearly fell into the water. There was scarcely enough room for him to stand on the narrow lip of riverbank. One more step, and he'd have taken a six-foot plunge into the river below. The water was low, and brown, churned up from the caimans massed in it, deadly twin tails waving lazily to and fro, hoping for scraps from the surgeons' doings. Usually they slept the days away and hunted in the cool of night. The surgeons must be busy today.

Veycosi flattened himself against the outside wall as his stones tried to climb back up inside his body. His sweaty hand closed tighter on his fish-gut-soaked scarf. It made a squelching sound. The meat smell issuing forth from it was potent, sweetish.

Every caiman floating in the water turned to fix its eyes upon him. They fanned out, their noseholes open wide, he the focus of their gaze.

No, not him.

The scarf. They could smell the fish that had tangled in it.

His hands shaking, he unwrapped the scarf from around his neck. The scent came on stronger, making him retch. The caimans grew more eager. They began to urge forwards. Could they climb a six-foot sheer drop? With those powerful claws, he didn't doubt it. They had no care for their fellows. They could easily clamber upon each other until some of them were able to reach the riverbank.

Someone from inside the toothdoctor's was yelling for the guards.

Veycosi cried out and thrust the scarf from him, towards the river. The caimans raised their heads en masse, the farthest ones out attempting to get over the others to get closer to the scarf as it arced out over the water and went flapping down to be snapped up by the nearest caiman. That beast was immediately swamped by the others. Then it was all snapping jaws and caiman blood and writhing and tearing.

He could hear the guards entering the toothdoctor's place. They clattered out the back door, yelping and warning each other as they were faced with the toothy frenzy not far below them. While they were distracted, Veycosi swallowed his gorge and edged along the wall until he found himself in the side yard of the building. He ran out onto the street and doubled back the way he'd come. A few more twists and turns of streets, and he was in the market, sweaty and gasping for air. He looked back. The guards weren't following. He'd lost them. Perhaps. They would know these streets as well as he, if not better. But it would be easier to lose himself here.

He was tired, and too disoriented to mark exactly where he was. He took what felt like a score of turns and got even more turned around. He ducked behind a dried-meat tent to catch his bearings.

The market, being a put-up-and-take-down affair, didn't have much running water, only a few standpipes. The flooding was less here. Unaware of the comess Veycosi had caused in Carenage Town, the market continued about its daily business of trading in tokens of merit. Free agents were standing or sitting or pacing up and down outside each stall, calling out the wares of the people whose offerings they were endorsing. Like that man over there, whose thin nose, pale eyes, and flowing yellow hair marked him as Deserter-kind. He wore the boiled leather vest of a pitch worker, with the characteristic smears of tar on the left side. He called out to passersby: "Look, Mam; look over here! This siani have nice otaheites, fresh as any strumpet, sweet as the milk from Mama-ji's nipples. And the juice from them, Mama! Lawdamassy! Come, Papi, come get you some, nuh? I wouldn't lie to you! Not to someone so fine. The first taste I ever get of this siani's otaheite apples, I convert to her skills one time. Had to come here to the market to confess it. Confess how I never like no otaheites before this. Come, picken; come try one, nuh? She grow them herself on her own plot. Raise up every sapling with a kiss come sunup and a caress come sundown. She even self wake up fore-day morning to come out in the fresh dark air to sing blessings to them. Take her seven years to raise the trees-them, till them was standing tall and straight, pointing to the sky. Yes, picken; take some home. Here, don't fill your robe; take a string bag. Made by that gentleman over there. I know his wares, too. Soft, strong string with knots that hold true. Tender enough to carry five egg without breaking a one. Strong enough to carry a picken-baby in a shoulder sling. Yes, picken; take. But only what you need, mind!"

The siani's otaheite apples, piled in neat pyramids of pear-shaped fruit on her table, did look tasty; ruby-red, fat, and healthy. The trade book beside her was thick as a plank with her week's endorsements. Veycosi was parched from all the running. To bite into one of the otaheites, expose the tender white flesh, feel the sweet juice running down his throat . . . He started towards the fruit stand to join the people helping themselves, tasting, then reaching for her trade book to sign their approval.

All on a sudden, hunger and thirst washed over Veycosi. The noise of the market crashed in his ears:

"*Goodman, is who make these alpagats? A-you? But how you going to come to the market flogging your own wares? Where your agent? Where your endorsements? Who going trust your goods if no one will speak for you?*"

"*Fish, fish, fresh fish! I'm speaking out today for the Siani Kolumbai, the wise Siani Kolumbai, the skillful Siani Kolumbai, the fisherwoman Kolumbai. I am a mathematician of the Distinguished Colloquium of Fellows. My family's youngest picken-girl had sickened with the flux. Our wife was in despair. My co-husband fed the child fish tea made from Siani Kolumbai's fresh snapper, and she was well again by the next day. And the taste of that restorative snapper brew, my gentle friends! The richness, the umami! These were fish that had lived happy. Fish that leapt eager into Siani Kolumbai's nets with tender purpose, so their souls would fly straight to Mama-ji's loving arms. Fish, fresh fish!"*

The racket had Veycosi bassourdie. He turned and turned in circles, unable to choose a way forwards. He froze as three guards strode briskly into the area. They looked around, scrutinizing everyone.

Something tugged at his hip. He whirled. A round, mischievous face was peeking from behind the snapper stall. Kaïra. Thandiwe's girl child, and his stepdaughter-to-be. "Picken!" Veycosi hissed. "Why you mixing yourself up into my troubles? Get away from here!"

Instead, Kaïra put finger to lips for silence and waved for Veycosi to follow her quietly. The guards hadn't noticed them yet. So he went where Kaïra was leading. It was the quickest way to get the girl away from this mess.

Veycosi thought he knew the market inside out. Hadn't he spent so many days of his youth running around inside here with his bannas? But Kaïra took him by routes he had never spied in all his born days. They zigzagged through a storage tent piled high with sacks of cornmeal. A young man stacking the sacks greeted Kaïra with a whispering of her name. Grinning, the lad let them out through a tent flap hidden behind one of the piles. Crouched low, they crab-walked into a small paddock filled with indifferent sheep. A woman with biceps like hams winked at Kaïra, then pretended not to see the two of them as she threw a fleece over each of their shoulders and let the sheep out to run free. Veycosi and Kaïra, scrambling on all fours, ran with the flock until they came to a narrow back alley where a circle of pickens egged on two of their number who were deep in a marbles tournament. To the cheers of the crowded pickens they threw off the fleeces and their oily stench; a younggirl handed Veycosi a roast chicken leg as they passed through that place. He ate it so fast he scarcely chewed. The spicy flesh was ecstasy. Thence they slid beneath the belly of a camel drawing a cart stacked high with corn. At one point, Kaïra pulled him to the ground beside the feet of a marketeer just as the guards were tromping that way. The marketeer winked down at the two of them, picked up the hems of the three layered kirtles ee was wearing—calico beige, brick brown, and dirt brown—and threw the fabric over both their backs. Over the beat of Veycosi's heart, he heard the retreating steps of the guards. When they crawled out from under ir kirtles, the marketeer gave them each a sugar candy and clapped Veycosi on the back. "Your young mistress looks after you well," ee said to Veycosi. Veycosi didn't bother to explain that he was the one looking after Kaïra by keeping her safe.

By this roundabout way, Kaïra brought them near the fisheries, which Thandiwe managed. A cart rattled by, piled high with delicately curlicued bamboo cages, each one with a large batti mamzelle perched on a twig inside, its four rainbow-prism wings thrumming, a live jewel.

The guards were nowhere to be seen. "Cosi!" exclaimed Kaïra finally, rushing to embrace Veycosi, nearly toppling him in her enthusiasm.

Laughing, Veycosi recovered his balance and returned the embrace. "Ai, picken, I swear you could tire a body out just by being joyous to see them." Kaïra's bird-boned body stiffened. The jest had hit too close to home. People were always telling Kaïra to slow down, take time, stop being so *much*.

Veycosi took the child by the shoulders and leaned down closer to look into the unsure young face. "Never you mind. I'm only making mock. The truth is, you just saved me from a little piece of bother. That was well done. Thank you."

Kaïra's expression brightened at the praise. She could never stay down-at-mouth for long. "The guards won't find you now, Cosi. Is what you do this time?" Kaïra grinned at him, doubtless expecting wondrous tales of mischief.

"I tell you later. Where Thandy-dey?" Veycosi draped a companionable arm across Kaïra's shoulders, and the two of them continued walking.

People in the market looked twice when they spotted Kaïra. Some of them pointed and whispered to one another. She ignored it. She was used to it. She jigged with glee as she accompanied Veycosi. "You hear the news?" she piped up, already moving to a new subject. "A ship! A whole ship full of Deserters!"

"Don't call them that," Veycosi told her. "Is not mannerly."

Kaïra grinned. "You call them that. When none of them around to hear you."

"Just because I do it doesn't make it well."

Kaïra pouted. "They tried to blow up the reservoir!" she said.

They? "They who? And who said so?"

"Nobody. Everybody. Mousa tell me he hear Saviat's mother's uncle talking with a guard who tell him so. One set of pink people come out of the big ship, and the portmaster call the guards to escort them! They have to talk to Cacique Macu!" No one knew he was the one responsible, then. Maybe there was a way out of this brangle after all. Veycosi felt a smile return to his lips. By the time the truth came out, he would be far gone, sailing the ocean.

They resumed their walk through the market. Veycosi noticed Kaïra rubbing her lower belly and grimacing. "Bellyache?"

She nodded. "I think I ate too much fufu at dinner last night." Then she asked, "Cosi, what would happen if you set lamp oil on fire and toss it into water?"

Veycosi chuckled. "Mamapiche Festival coming, nah true?"

"Yes, and me and—" She stopped. "But I mustn't tell you."

"Best not. You know the Blackheart Man will come for tattle-tale pickens," he teased.

Kaïra rolled her eyes. "I not a picken anymore," she said.

Kaïra and her young bannas were probably planning a Mamapiche float. They wouldn't thank her if she let their secrets slip to an adult. Even if Kaïra was about to bypass them all in status come Mamapiche.

"Kaïra! Over here!" A hearty old man was hailing Kaïra from a small open-air table surrounded by stone benches. He was playing Trade Winds with his bannas. They'd stopped in the middle of their game and were looking at Kaïra, their visages open and expectant as though someone were about to tell them a joke.

Kaïra frowned and stayed where she was. The man called out, "You japing in the market today? Some pre-Mamapiche jests for us?"

Kaïra pressed her lips together, shook her head, and stared at her feet. Veycosi nudged her. "Talk to the man, picken. You know you planning something."

Kaïra stuck out her bottom lip. She whispered, "For the festival, not for today." She moved away from Veycosi's nudging elbow.

Veycosi sighed. She was lively enough when running around with her bannas, but the minute anyone tried to treat her as the next Mamacona, she withdrew into herself, became shy and sullen.

Looked like she wasn't going to reply to the man. Up to Veycosi to smooth this over. Affably as he might, he called out, "Time enough for chicaneries after she become the twin goddess, nah true? Let the picken enjoy her remaining time as a picken."

The men shrugged and returned to their game. Kaïra threw Vey-cosi a grateful glance as they moved on. He swallowed his irritation at her reticence.

As though to underscore the problem, they'd only gone a few more steps when someone touched the shoulder of Kaïra's boubou. "Young mistress?" The woman withdrew her hand, clutched it to her bosom as though afraid she'd caused offense.

Kaïra turned to her. "Yes, siani?"

"You're Kaïra, nah true?"

Kaïra's face went carefully still. She nodded.

"Oh," the woman said, a small note of wonder in her voice. She pursed her lips before she dared speak again. "Me just want to know, young mistress; you could give me one blessing, please? My husband taking a trip today over to Cumbia Island, and I always so frightened when he on the water. Men don't belong on the sea, young mistress. Suppose the boat capsize? He can't swim for nothing. Please, if you could ask Mamapiche to speak to her sister, implore Mamagua to take care of him . . ." She trailed off.

Kaïra looked embarrassed and a mickle irritated. "Siani, she don't listen to me more than you," she said.

"Oh . . ."

"And when last you know a Chynchin sailoress to capsize a boat?"

The woman's face became even more drawn. "So sorry, young mistress. I didn't mean to disturb you."

Stern-faced, Kaïra stared at the woman as she fidgeted in shame. Then her visage softened. She instructed the woman, "Get three white eggs and throw them into the water for Her. For Mamagua. Tell Her your desire."

Paying no mind to the woman's shy thanks, Kaïra threaded her arm through the crook of Veycosi's elbow. "Come. Mama working at the fishery today." She led Veycosi away.

"That's more like it," Veycosi told her approvingly. "You acted like the official representative of the goddess sisters there. You were firm, but kind."

Kaïra cast him a sidewise glance, but said nothing, merely rubbed her sore belly. It would be all right. After Veycosi returned from his trip overseas, he would be wed to Kaïra's mother. And Kaïra would have officially become the human representative of Mamacona, embodied as Mamapiche. Her duties would become more important then, and Veycosi would be there to provide fatherly guidance.

When Thandy had found herself pregnant some twelve years before, she had been young, scarcely begun her courses. Her belly was swelling with life, but she swore there had been no baby father. She was having a twinning child, she felt sure; an exact copy of herself. That meant the bokors must needs become involved.

The second Kaïra was born, they whisked the baby away, before even Thandiwe could clap eyes properly on her. Hours went by as Thandiwe and her mother fretted about the new member of their family. Was she sickly? Was she a twinning child, or not?

Eventually, the bokors returned Kaïra to her mother's arms. As Thandiwe struggled to get the knack of giving suckle to Kaïra, one of the bokors pointed out the baby's features. She had the same moles as her mother, in the exact same places. The whorls on her fingertips were the exact same pattern as Thandiwe's. She was identical to Thandy in every way. The bokors proclaimed that Kaïra was indeed that rare thing, a twinning child. As such, she would become the next representative of the twin Mamacona goddesses. Since she'd been born during Mamapiche season, she would be dedicated to Mamapiche—the twin deity's dark half—at festival time of her twelfth birthday. She would be expected to be forever playing tricks, as the tar deity Mamapiche did. Veycosi wasn't the only one to think it would have been better if Kaïra had been born in Mamagua season. The goddess Mamagua was associated with the blue of the life-giving waters and the sky. Yes, she could be terrible when she was angry. But mostly she was loving and friendly towards the nation of Chynchin, flowing tenderly around her and keeping her refreshed with plenty. That would have suited Kaïra's lively but gentle nature better. Better yet, of course, if Thandiwe and her mother hadn't indulged themselves in this fancy of goddesses and a twinning child. Then Kaïra would be growing up without this burden on her.

Still, Veycosi was sure the child would adapt. She had a swift mind, like his.

They had reached the fish cultivation ponds in the market. Kaïra pointed with her chin; "Koo Mama Thandy there."

Thandiwe was waist-deep in the water of the outermost pond, conferring with another woman over the steel workings that stirred the pond water. Both women had stripped down to breechclouts. Their outer clothes were piled on the side. As ever, Veycosi's blood softened and flowed warm at the sight of his betrothed. Gombey said he should be patient, that Thandiwe would let him and Gombey both know when she was ready to take them as husbands. In the meantime, he said, life was brief. Take all the joy this life could give. Veycosi had taken his banna's counsel to heart; had since they were youngboys. Life was sweet, and held many pleasures. But he was impatient to begin his married life.

He slipped his arm out from the crook of Kaïra's. "Picken, I don't know what allyou planning for your float, but don't mix hot oil with water. Hot oil flying into your face is no joke."

Kaïra nodded, her face fallen in disappointment. The Mamapiche Festival was the last time for a long time that she would be able to run free with her bannas. Once she became Mamapiche, her time wouldn't be hers until the next twinning child to be born had turned twelve and could take her place. Kaïra would have to appear at ceremonies to bless this and that, dressed all in Mamapiche black, wearing a grinning wire-and-paper caiman head over her own and sporting a cured caiman tail tied secured with leather straps around her waist. The costume looked ridiculous. It was meant to. Wherever she went, costume or no, she would be expected as the earthly incarnation of the trickster Mamapiche to make sport constantly; pinching the bums of old sianis, thieving washing off people's lines, and the like.

Thandy saw the two of them and smiled. She took the short set of stone stairs out of the water, the other woman following behind her. "The fish were too crowded, is all," Thandy told her worker. "Just take out all the new-hatched fingerlings and put them in the other pool."

"Yes, siani."

Both women picked up their robes and drew them on. Kaïra ran to fetch her mama's straw satchel. She handed it to Thandiwe as her head emerged from her robe.

"Thank you, little sister," Thandy said, affectionately stroking her child's head.

Kaïra beamed. "My pleasure, big sister," she replied.

True they looked as alike as marassas, but Veycosi really wished she wouldn't overindulge Kaïra in this fantasy of being her twinning child. It was too late for that, though. The whole country had taken up the tale since Kaïra's birth. And it was young Kaïra who was bearing the burden of Thandiwe's story-making. Kaïra's twelfth birthday would be this year. The season was changing. Over the past few months, Mamagua's rains had trickled away into the annual false drought, when no rain fell for many weeks. But

Mamagua had one last gift left for her children before she ceded to her sister, Mamapiche, the Black Lady; soon there would be a thunderous monsoon. The sky would open up and drench the land for a couple of days. The Iguaca River would run high and leap its banks. Then the Feast of Eggs would happen. Then, a feverish month of final preparations later, would be the festival to welcome Mamapiche. Because after that there would be no more rain for half the year, until Mamapiche tired of her reign and once more gave sway to her watery sister. At the Mamapiche Festival, Kaïra was going to be given to Mamapiche. Or, as some would have it, *become* Mamapiche. She would ritually descend into the Mother Lake, the always-molten piche at the centre of the Upper Piche Lake. Once she ascended thence, she would in some wise be considered to be the full aspect of Mamacona: Mamapiche as well as that of Mamagua. As far as the general populace was concerned, Kaïra was the closest thing to a living god. If she took a sea bath off the shores of Carenage Town in the morning, the least guard in Maroon village on the farthest side of the island would be singing about it by evening. More disturbing to Veycosi, Thandy had convinced herself that her story was true, that her child had sprung from her without a man planting her with seed. She had chosen this life for her child before Kaïra could have any say in the doing of it.

What would happen to her when she made the same descent into the Mother Lake? Common sense told Veycosi that Kaïra would reap nothing more dangerous than a slight burn or two. She'd been instructed that she would descend encased in a watertight stone coffin; inside it, she would be fully wrapped in wet coir. And the second the coffin had sunk completely below the piche, a bokor would give the signal to winch it back out again. Kaïra should be safe. But Chynchin had a way to be uncanny. Concern for his daughter-to-be had been scraping at the back of Veycosi's brain more and more as the time drew closer. Thandy had told him that Kaïra had begun waking some nights, screaming to be let out. She refused to tell her mother what her nightmares were, but Thandy supposed she was afraid of the box in which she'd be lowered into the hot piche of the Mother Lake during her transformation ceremony.

Thandy took a handful of crabstones out of her satchel and slipped the satchel inside her sleeve. She popped the chalky stones into her mouth and crunched down on them. How the blast she managed to eat chalk like it was sweetmeat, he would never understand. "Cosi," she said warmly. "My dear chirping cricket, always raising a ruckus."

"Sweetling, you know I don't love that name." As a picken, Veycosi had been given the nickname because he asked so many questions so unrelentingly.

"I'll try to remember." She came and grasped his hands with both of hers. As she did, she stepped foot in a puddle of reservoir mud. Her smile changed to a frown. "Cosi, be honest; you have anything to do with events this morning?"

He put on a nonchalant face. "You mean, a ship from Ymisen arriving and blowing up the reservoir? You not glad to have your water running again? You were telling me you were afraid the tilapia fish would sicken in the breeding ponds."

Her eyes narrowed farther. "How the ship arrive and blow up the reservoir same time?"

He shrugged. "Is so people saying. Nah true, Kaïra?"

"A-true," the picken piped up.

"Kaïra," said Thandy, "go and fetch me a cooling drink, please? Mobby." When she was gone, Thandy put her hands on her hips and regarded Veycosi skeptically. "Cricket, I know you had something to do with the reservoir."

The nickname again. Veycosi shrugged, avoiding her gaze. She tutted. "How you can be own-way so all the time? What kind of example you setting for your future daughter?"

"I know, I know." He glanced over at Kaïra, whose eyes were only for the trays of fresh, sweet halwah balls being laid out at a stall not far off. "But maybe I'm just showing Kaïra how to think for herself."

"She too young for that." *Crunch, crunch* on the crabstones. Made Veycosi's own tongue dry just watching her.

"Too young?" Veycosi reached out to brush a white smear of chalk from her upper lip. She saw where his hand was tending, caught it, and drew it to her face. She smiled at him. They stood an instant or two like that, her cheek warm against his palm. Veycosi said, "She's about to become Mamapiche. She will cease being a youth very soon now. She will have to have a mind of her own, or custom and ceremony will wear her spirits down."

Gently, she pushed his hand away. Her face had gone sombre. "We should act proper in public," she said. "Kaïra can see us."

Said holy get was at the halwah stall. She looked to be taking one of each kind. "She already have her own desires, Thandy. Just like you as a picken. Now, if I'm to believe you and Kaïra, she and Mamagua palaver all the time?"

She gave a soft, warm smile at that. "Yes."

Veycosi managed not to roll his eyes. After all, it was just a game that Thandy and Kaïra amused each other with. Didn't youngboy him used to tell tales about being able to fly with the cullybrees? Let the picken's imagination roam free as long as it could. "So you see, then," Veycosi replied, "I can't have any kind of bad influence on Kaïra. If she only make one wayward step, I bet you Mamagua would come tromping right up out of the water and slap some sense broadside her face with her tails."

Thandy giggled. "You have no reverence, you know that?"

"And ain't is that why you love me?"

This banter; he had missed it. It was the most warmth Thandiwe had shown him in months.

She lowered her eyes to the ground. "I think I going to miss you while you're away, Cosi."

"You *think*?"

But Thandy wasn't listening to him. She was watching Kaïra, who was absent-mindedly rubbing her stomach. Thandy smiled. "She going to get her courses soon. Koo how her belly panging her."

Veycosi startled. He hadn't considered that. "She told me she eat too much last night."

Thandy shook her head. "I don't think is that. She's the right age for her blood to start."

In another minute, Kaïra was back from the halwah stall. She handed her mother a calabash of mobby. For herself, Kaïra had gotten four big balls of halwah and a small calabash of watered hill beer. "The Ymisen people are whiter even than Deserters!" she burst out. She took a swig of beer, bit off some of the halwah, and chewed. Her face was alive with fascination. "Ma, they use *money*!"

Her mother smiled at her adoringly. "You have a jest ready to play while you're here in the market, picken? The last one you played was a sennight ago."

Kaïra looked crestfallen. "No one laughed at that one."

Thandy sighed. "You pulled a face at a babe in arms. There's no art in that. No spectacle."

Veycosi said, "Next time, you dress up as a baby. Get into a pram and have one of your bannas push you around and pretend to be nursing you."

Thandiwe chuckled. "Yes, that would work."

Kaïra merely looked stubborn. Veycosi sighed. The child had

a ready-made audience, people prepared to be entertained by her, and she was wasting it.

Five Ymisen sailormen came strolling into the fishery. People working there paused to stare at them. Ymisen stared back. A couple of the Ymisen men went over to one of the ponds, where two men and a woman, stripped to breechclouts, worked knee-deep in the water, using wood-framed nets to dredge the bottom for any refuse that had fallen in. "What's in there?" asked one of the sailors, pointing at the water. His speech sounded warped to Veycosi's ear. It was like Chynchin's, but not. One fellow only stared hungrily at the woman in the water.

"It's fish," she replied with a shrug, and went back to work.

The silent sailor nudged his banna and indicated the woman with his chin. Gesturing with his hands, he mimed her tetas and full hips. The others laughed and pulled him back to join them. "Come away," said one of them. "You'd think they would magic the fish fresh from the sea instead of enclosing them like this. Stinks in here."

It didn't. But with that insult they left, though even as he walked, the man still leered over his shoulder at the worker. She scowled and kept her eyes on the water. One of his bannas asked the others, "What's that big, ugly pack animal they have everywhere here? The ones that smell like damp socks?"

Thandy shook her head. "Mannerless lot. Ymisen sailors walking round the market," she said, "gawking everywhere like monkey. Especially at the women. Principe's guild of companions going to have plenty custom today."

"They take us for the fairy folk!" said Kaïra.

Veycosi burst out laughing. "You mean, they're just as craven as their Mirmeki cousins?"

In every country that Ymisen captured, it enslaved people. Some of these were put forcibly into service as frontline foot soldiers; always the first to die in battle. They were human shields. Chynchin's Mirmeki were descended from these; the Mirmeki who had deserted the Ymisen army the day that three witches had supposedly drowned an army of Mirmeki in piche. Chynchin's Mirmeki were forever putting bowls of milk and beer out front their doors at night to woo favour from the fey. Your cow only was giving turned milk? They would tell you a hob was doing it. One of them turned up late for work? It was because a jack mulateer had merry-led him through the bush and made him lose his way, and he didn't have the slightest idea how he'd ended up in the rum shop instead. "Ymisen people believe in the fey, too? You're making sport, picken!"

"No, is true!"

Thandy nodded. "True thing she's talking. Principe heard one of them tell another one not to eat any of our food, lest he return home again to find a centaine of years passed, and all his fellows dead."

Veycosi shook his head. "What a thing."

"I want a kilt like those men from the ship were wearing," said Kaïra. "Only in purple. With silver trim."

"Red and gold would suit you better," Veycosi told her. "Like the guard colours."

Kaïra's eyes lit up. "Yes, like that! Ma, I could get a kilt like that?"

Thandy sighed and shook her head. "Kilt is man clothes. Too besides, the bokors will give you a new wardrobe, all in Mamapiche black. You will like that, nah true?"

The child nodded uncertainly. In a small voice, she said, "Yes, Mama."

Thandy hugged Kaïra to her bosom and said, "Cosi, what you want to go and encourage the girl for?"

"You know is only jest I making."

Time to pack. Veycosi made his goodbyes to Thandiwe and Kaïra. Still looking back at his betrothed, he turned in the direction of the southern exit from the market. So intent he was on Thandiwe, he didn't notice the three guards till they had him practically surrounded. He made to flee, but they pulled in tighter around him. He was penned in. "Mestre," said one of them, a stout, corn-coloured youth with broad shoulders, "you will come with us, please."

Veycosi nodded at the other two. "Morning, Taibo, Philomena." They nodded warily. They knew him well, from similar circumstances. The fire in the Colloquium's kitchen. The experiment with the half-tonne of soursop seeds. The failed steam-drawn cart. He couldn't help it. If one of the Colloquium's books gave him an idea, he had to try it. "On what charge you come to take me today?"

Broad Shoulders replied, "Nothing specific at the moment, mestre. Council just have some questions for you."

Thandiwe and Kaïra had scurried over to them. "Oh, Cosi," said Thandy, "is what mischief you gone and done now?"

He winked at her and Kaïra, all the while protesting that he was—nearly—a Fellow of the Colloquium, and he had an important appointment to keep down at the docks tomorrow morning on the ship to Ifanmwe. "And I didn't have nothing to do with the explosion at the reservoir. I was just boasting when I said that."

"Never said aught about the reservoir, maas'." Ignoring his protestations of innocence, they marched him away for questioning, and Veycosi well knew it was with regards to the sudden, intemperate flooding of the south side of the town. He waved at his bride- and daughter-to-be as he went. He called out, "Tell Gombey I will bring him some wool from Ifanmwe! I will see oonuh in three months' time!" People were staring as the guards took him away. Over Philomena's shoulder, he stuck his tongue out at a gaping picken-girl leading a black-and-grey guinea fowl by a string knotted around its neck.

Philomena grasped his shoulder. Gently for her, but still, her fingers felt as though they could leave dents. "Mestre, please behave."

He gave her his best smile. "Very well, my fulsome Philomena. For sake of your pretty brown eyes, I will behave."

She didn't reply, simply shifted her hand until it was at his neckback and pressed a little, urging him onwards.

Datiao's arm punched through into the air. He knew it only because the arm met no more resistance. He fought the other arm up as well, then his head. For the first time since the gods only knew how long, he felt the outside world on what was left of his skin again. He'd been crawling upwards through the Mother Piche, the tarry semi-solid at the core of the piche lake, clutching in one hand the prize that kept reviving him. He'd died, smothered and furious at his own folly, three more times since he'd managed to clutch the thing some while ago.

Now he lay with his head and arms exposed to the sweet night air and the rest of him still mired in the sticky Mother Piche. It was dark, and quiet. Was the skirmish over, then? Had the Ymisen soldiers taken the day, or had his compong won out? Datiao sucked in a breath. Air, so, so sweet. He spluttered as he spat black liquified piche out his mouth and nose. The agitation of his body made him sink a little way into the piche again. His mouth dipped below its surface. With a pang of terror, he realised he must fight his whole self free at once, else drown once more amongst the dead Mirmeki soldiers.

He pushed and swam and kicked, and managed to squirm through the sticky, over-warm Mother Piche to a place at its edges

where the stuff was hardened. All around him, drowned soldiers
and their steeds were doing the same, raised back to life by the
pull of the thing in his hand. Because of being a spy for his village,
he'd still been among the Ymisen soldiers when they went to their
deaths. He'd as lief have died amongst his own. But here he was,
with his compong's enemies.

He rolled out onto the hard piche, tried to clamber to his feet,
but his broken leg gave way like rotten kindling, and down he
went. He hit the ground with a dull, wet splat. He cursed, his voice
hoarse from lack of practise.

Some of the Ymisen Mirmeki had injuries worse than his. A
sticky horse crawled forwards on the stumps of forelegs, its rump
in the air. Its screaming was awful.

Datiao rolled over onto his side to try again. He was moving
more slowly, having to strain to bend and unbend his arms. He
swore in fury as he realised what was happening. The very air he'd
been trying so hard to reach was hardening the piche that imbued
his body. He should be chanting the spell! He tried to open his lips
to speak, but the piche had already solidified over his mouth.

He and the others lay there helplessly the rest of the night,
slowly hardening into coal-like lumps.

Chapter 2

VEYCOSI STUMBLED, SWEARING, OVER a small pile of muskets and swords just inside the entrance to the Palavera. Philomena put a hand on his forearm to steady him. He thanked her, though with less grace than he would have liked. Feeling abashed never brought out the best in him. The carriage ride through the streets of southern Carenage Town had rubbed his face in the extent of the damage he'd done. He'd heard a seamster wailing that his two sewing machines were like to seize with rust, and he would have to requisition money from council to purchase new ones from a-foreign. A goat tied up tight near a gutter had drowned when the gutter overflowed, spewing a torrent of rushing water from which the beast had been unable to escape. He saw a youngboy using any dry clothes he could lay hands on to wrap his damp hens in, lest they take the croup and perish. Broken wares, flooded homes, a myriad cuts and scrapes as people waded through muddy water that hid rockstones, spilled implements, shards of pottery. All through the trip to the Palavera, Veycosi had kept trying to convince himself that it was all to the good, that they would thank him later. The carriage had had to detour around the worst of it. He'd tried not to imagine the rest of the damage he wasn't seeing.

As the party drew closer to the main council hall, murmurs from a gathering inside spilled out, echoing and bouncing amongst the tall, bicolor lignum vitae wood columns that upheld the bowed roof of the Palavera. Veycosi, trying for jollity, said, "Look like the whole council seeking audience with me, or what?"

Broad Shoulders replied, "You are small news today, mestre."

"Not a mestre yet, goodman."

Broad Shoulders shrugged. "I'm only saying, Ymisen a-come. That's more important than you today." He nodded a greeting at the guards stationed at the entrance to the Great Hall. More guards! In two hundred years, when had Chynchin ever needed such an ostentatious show of strength?

Once Veycosi was inside the proscenium of the Great Hall, it was easy enough to see the reason for the weapons that had tripped him. Macu, Chynchin's chief cacique, didn't brook a show of arms inside the Palavera. The Carenage guards were doubtless capoeira mestres, trained to subdue bodily and, when necessary, with their staffs. Whereas the soldiers from the Ymisen ship had had to leave their only means of defense outside. Those soldiers, dressed to puss-foot in identical uniforms of red wool jackets and puffy beige pantalons, were all standing to attention at the bottom of the stepped bowl that was the proscenium, behind the same large, fancy-dress Ymisen man who had been among the ones being marched off the ship by the guards. He must be some kind of functionary. And important, by the looks of it; five soldiers to watch over he one, their arms hanging long by their sides for lack of a sword pommel or a musket butt to rest their hands on.

The functionary had been given a humble wooden stool for seating, while on the other side of the podium, Cacique Macu and her advisors reclined in comfort on sturdy lignum vitae chairs with backs and armrests. Even the scribe's wooden desk and padded chair were more comfortable than what the functionary had been given to sit upon.

At the moment, Macu was conferring in whispers and hand signs with her advisors. The Ymisen functionary man looked none too pleased with the delay.

He was girthy and tall, that man, like plenty of his kind. His bulk overflowed the stool. And what an extravagance of frips and frills to his costume! Draped britches of soft hide, tan in colour. The britches were gathered in tight around his knees. Heavy hose sheathed his calves. His feet were shod with stout leather shoes, dark brown, each with a toe that curled over back on itself, held in place with a chain around the ankle. The brogues had a strap with a brass buckle that ran across the top of the foot. A blouse of crisp white linen, extravagantly ruffled down the front, peeked out from the neck of a bronze silk tunic embroidered with gold thread-dragons. The tunic was slit at the sides and long down to his knees. Some kind of cummerbund at the waist, matching the britches and elaborately wrapped. A fat bone hoop thrust through one nostril. It looked to be inlaid with gold. His head was topped by that same ridiculous hat Veycosi had seen earlier. Eh. The man was easily as decorated as the Carenage Town elders' council. He even outshone advisor Komnan little bit, and that was saying plenty. His face was Deserter-pale, his nose long and thin, his eyes blue. That face was beaded with sweat and pinked from the heat. His garments were not made for Chynchin climes. But it looked like that wasn't the only reason he was sweating. For all the arrogance of his posture, any picken could see the man was nervous. Every movement in the room drew his eye. His soldiers were just as skittish.

How long was this going to take? Veycosi sucked on the wafer

of Reverie he had tucked into his cheek. The fragrant bitterness
of it made his mouth spring water. Reverie would keep him alert
through the long hours of conferring with the elders' council. He
made a mental note to tuck some of it into his bags for travel. It
was fashioned out of nutmeg and other ingredients known only to
the apothecaries of the Colloquium, and was not available in other
countries. It was supposed to be used only for a postulant's Reverie ceremony, but Veycosi was not the first Colloquium student
to avail himself of a sliver of it from time to time; nor would he be
the last.

Taibo, Philomena, and Broad Shoulders, their task accomplished, stepped back to leave Veycosi to sit where he would. He
descended to the lowest rows of benches, closest to the goings-on.
His oldest friend and soon-to-be co-husband, Gombey, was there,
in the middle of one of the foremost rows. He waved Veycosi over.
Veycosi made his way along the row, mumbling his pardons to the
citizens whose feet he had to step over. The functionary man practically twitched at the disturbance. His soldiers all reached for their
empty scabbards. "Pardon, pardon," Veycosi said loudly, mocking
meekness. Gombey flashed an amused look at him. Veycosi nudged
himself a place beside Gombey and sat. He leaned forwards and
whispered into Gombey's ear, "They think all of we are witches."

Gombey whispered back, "Too loud, Cosi."

Ah. Veycosi saw that people were staring at him. Reverie had
a way to make you careless like that. He closed his eyes. In the
dark behind his lids, whirling pinwheels of green light signalled
the Reverie beginning to work. Just enough Reverie sharpened
the senses; too much, and Reverie made you its horse. Veycosi
tongued what remained of the wafer into his hand, dropped it to
the floor, and crushed it beneath the heel of the new alpagats he'd
just picked up at the market to replace his broken ones. "I will

hold my tongue," he reassured Gombey. Clearly still too loudly, for this time, his mestre Steli glared at him from his place on the podium beside Macu. Gombey shook his head and cast his eyes to the sky. Veycosi hushed, setting his mind to behave appropriately.

With propriety restored, the Ymisen functionary boomed at Komnan, "Well, fellow; shall we get to the matter at hand?"

Komnan raised an eyebrow at being addressed so forward. He nodded at Steli, who stood and moved slowly to the centre of those gathered on the dais. The functionary took a sweat-stained kerchief from out his sleeve and mopped his brow. Steli began the chants of lineage which would serve as introduction to all seven of their elders, oldest to youngest, that made up the town's governing body. He was in fine voice this afternoon, but Veycosi was already restless. He couldn't make himself study all this pomp. His mind was on the high seas. On a long-lost book found, and on iced cream, sweetened with honey.

Keeping his hands occupied would keep his mind from wandering. He reached into his robe sleeve pocket and pulled out his crooking, still attached to the ball of soft wool twine from which he was making it. Stuck into the piece was the small hooked wand his da Kola had whittled for him from supple mamapom wood when he had had scarcely six years. Then, the wand had been the same peeled twig colour as the twine he was using at the moment. From years of handling, it was now a rich, polished brown.

He found the unfinished end of the piece, stuck his hook through the loop, pulled on the yarn to tighten the loop to the wand, and considered. All around him, other men also sat with pieces of incomplete crooking, the yarn woven through the fingers of one hand, the hook in the other, using it to pull the yarn through divers knots and loops to make whatever they fancied; perhaps a shawl against cool evenings, a friendship cap for a banna, or a doll to be stuffed with straw for one of their pickens to play with. Their crooking marched on in stolid rows or circles. Regular, even predictable. But Veycosi couldn't bear such sameness. He preferred to discover what he was making by making it, varying the stitches and shapes as whimsy took him. As Steli continued to chant their elders' histories, Veycosi did a few tours of double knot, in the fashion they called "wheel and turn." Some he worked through the back loops only. Some he repeated in the same loop till he could no longer force the hook in.

He held the unfinished piece of crooking up. It was a raggedy shape, uneven as a cloud. Maybe it would serve as a string bag for fetching produce home? A gift for Thandiwe, perhaps?

He sighed. She could get her a better-looking string bag in the market. Why bother crooking one? He pouted and stuck the work back into his sleeve. Steli had finished his chanting. Now Ymisen and Chynchin officials commenced to mutter through the empty politesse of mutual greetings.

Veycosi turned his head. A trail of green light followed his gaze. Too much Reverie? That could lead to belly-runnings and dizziness. Not the best way to begin a trip over water.

The green trail of Reverie light seemed to settle around the head and shoulders of a man Veycosi hadn't noticed before. Then it dissipated.

Another of the Ymisen delegation, that man was. He stood quiet, so still he scarce seemed to breathe, like a cat stalking prey. His face was of an unremarkable handsomeness. His clothing was fine of fabric, but dull in colour and plainly styled. Height betwixt and between. Shoulders neither broad nor narrow. He didn't speak, but Veycosi saw where his eyes looked. At Cacique Macu. That man knew where the power in the room lay. The sweating functionary kept addressing his greetings to Komnan, likely dazzled by

Komnan's gaudiments; an agbada suit of indigo cloth: awotele shirt on top, matching sokoto trousers, and over the whole, an awosoke arranged in beautiful folds. The matching neck opening and the brimless cap were heavily embroidered in a spiderweb pattern with thick gold thread.

Just then, the plain man moved towards Macu, silent and swift as a mongoose. The Palavera guards went immediately alert. They and the two elders closest to Macu moved in, ready to protect her if need be. But the unremarkable man held out his open hands, bowed to her, and simply said, "Dama—siani—your cup is empty. May I refill it?"

"To rass," Veycosi murmured. Speaking like a high-flown Ymisen, he was, but his accent was pure Deserter. And he knew to call a mature woman "siani."

Gombey nodded, his eyes calculating. "He from Chynchin, that one."

Veycosi grunted in assent. "Turncoat."

Macu barely shifted her expression; only nodded in the man's direction and held out her empty cup. She was used to Deserters who served to table. Some said it was in their nature. More like their station, though; pickens laboured at what their parents had done before them. They grew up and had pickens of their own, and taught those pickens the same labours.

Why anyone would want to leave Chynchin for good? You heard of people who did it, but they were usually mad. Or, if not, they returned back again very soon. But it looked as though the unremarkable man had stayed away a long while. His skin was unbrowned from lack of sun. Veycosi had heard tell it was cold in Ymisen; cold enough that they had to huddle in the dark by their hearths for warmth the livelong day.

The functionary, probably irritated at the further delay while the man fetched water for Macu, screwed his eyebrows together. Abruptly, he said to Komnan, "We're offering wheat and barley in return for regular shipments of indigo cloth and pitch to Ymisen." Seemed he'd decided the niceties were over.

Komnan didn't reply. The functionary's frown deepened. Chynchin produced some of the finest indigo fabric in the world, and its piche was in high demand for all manner of caulking and paving. Clearly, Ymisen knew that the country didn't use actual money within its borders, but only to trade with the outside world. In Chynchin, standing had worth, not coin.

Macu nodded at Gombey. Gombey whispered, "My turn."

Veycosi said, "Make swift work of them, banna."

Gombey patted his shoulder, then stood and made his way to the front. Macu handed him her cane, the golden one crowned by a cullybree bird carved of camel bone. "Gombey going to be our negotiator with you," said Komnan. Macu liked to keep her counsel in negotiations, hear as much as she could before she spoke.

Gombey said to the functionary, "Ymisen grains not useful to us. They get the weevil too easily."

The assembled crowd chuckled.

Gombey continued, "We prefer our own manioc and yams."

With a patronizing false smile, the functionary replied, "And rum, no doubt. It is known how much your people like your strong drink."

Gombey frowned and continued, "Gold would be a more suitable means of exchange with a foreign nation, think you not? Or if you wanted to give us steel ingots . . ."

A good ask. Chynchin lacked the raw materials for mining iron to craft into steel.

The functionary reared back. "*Steel*? You want *steel*? But I thought . . ." He gave the plain man an astonished look. The corner of that one's mouth twitched very slightly. Only that. Veycosi suppressed a giggle. Surely the functionary didn't also believe that Chynchin people were fey, unable to bear the touch of iron?

The functionary resumed talking to Gombey. "Well, ah, I'm sure we can arrange steel for you. Will have to send word back to make sure." He apparently intended to sidestep any talk of gold. He continued, "And of course we would maintain a presence on the island to, ahm, ensure the smooth traffic of commerce between our two nations."

A mutter went through the crowd. But seeya! *Presence* on *the island*. Not even *in* the island. Like Chynchin was some flitty little perch to light on. And any koonoomunu could understand that that "presence" would be an Ymisen force put in place to rule Chynchin.

"Also," said the functionary, raising his voice, "in order to ensure our continued goodwill, we will require an annual tribute to Ymisen of five hundred hoppers of bitumen."

At Gombey's confused look, the plain grey man stepped in. "He mean 'piche,'" he told Gombey. "Ymisen demands five hundred hoppers of piche every year."

"And the nutmeg, too," the functionary interjected. "One hundred hoppers of the spice annually."

A shocked silence fell over those present. Into the quiet, the functionary delivered the killing blow. "If these terms aren't met, I am empowered by Ymisen to employ such force as is deemed necessary to ensure our requirements are met. You have two sennights to comply."

The crowd erupted in an angry commotion. The functionary mopped his brow on his sleeve. His guards drew closer to him, their eyes darting every which way.

Veycosi's mouth dropped open. It was worse than most in the audience knew. Nutmeg was the key ingredient in Reverie! They couldn't afford to have a tax levied on it. Who had been talking the Colloquium's secrets?

Gombey raised one brow when he heard the terms, and the threat behind them. He looked to Macu. Macu raised her hand for quiet. When the whispering and the exclamations of outrage had died down, she said to the functionary, "You want us to make this decision in haste. Why?"

The functionary seemed to see her for the first time.

Macu continued, "A-true what they say about oonuh Ymisen people. You don't make sport to keep your manners brief." The other elders murmured in agreement. The functionary glanced at the plain man, who had taken Macu's cup to the sideboard to be cleared away. The plain man blinked once, slowly, and inclined his head ever so slightly in Macu's direction. He was telling the functionary whom to address.

The functionary looked a mite startled. Then he sighed and cleared his throat—an affronted sound—and turned his attention finally to Macu. "Dama," he said, "please accept my apologies if my manner is not what you expect. Yet it is so important for our two countries to come to peace, is't not?" He glanced again at the plain man, who nodded very slightly.

So. The functionary was a bauble meant to distract. That meek-acting grey man was the one they should really be minding.

The functionary continued, "Do comprehend your situation, and that of this island. Ymisen wishes to come to terms, and that quickly. The fleet is waiting a mere thirteen knots away, to take the good news to Ymisen that we have a trade agreement."

And if the agreement was not to their liking, that fleet would swiftly become an invading army. Ymisen had lost Chynchin two hundred years before to a handful of slaves and outcasts. Now they had come to stake their claim again.

"They gone?" Macu called out to Gombey as he reentered the Great Hall. Gombey had accompanied the Ymisen delegation out of the building, where an armed escort was waiting to make sure they all went directly back to their ship.

"Yes, siani." Gombey descended the stairs and handed Macu back the staff of office.

Macu screwed up her face. "Chuh. What an ugly strain of wretches. Ymisen faces favour pig fat. Not," she added hastily, "like our own handsome Mirmeki citizens." She gave a caiman smile in the direction of a group of old Mirmeki men in camels' wool kilts and piche-smeared leather blackheart vests, all sitting together in the audience, their ruddy faces tanned and weathered.

The Mirmeki men eyed her warily. Whenever there was something being debated by the elders' council, you could lay odds those old bannas would be there, listening in and mumbling to each other about the way the palaver was going. They were retired from hard labour in the piche lake and considered this their reward, Veycosi supposed. Some old people played Trade Winds all day at the rum shop, whereas these ones here preferred the tomfooleries of politricks. One of them glanced at his fellows and gave a quick, solemn nod back to Macu. She beamed like a farmwife counting the heads of her cows. Then, her face stern again, she asked her council, "What oonuh have feh say?"

Komnan replied, "Whatever they call it, this is an invasion."

Someone in the crowd yelled out, "They gwine to lose!"

"Yes!" shouted a next somebody. "Call down Mamapiche 'pon them!"

Macu banged the tip of her cane on the floor for quiet.

But no sooner had they shushed than Siani Yaaya, from where

she was sitting with the other elders of the council, gave a loud cuss-teeth. "It don't make sense, Macu. If they meant to offer force from the outset, why send their fighting ships away to wait for how we would respond? Why not show up one time with all their power in evidence?"

She was right. There was more going on here than the Ymisen delegation wanted the council to know. Someone yelled, "We must take a posse of fighters out to their ships tonight tonight, and murder every last man jack of them in their sleep!"

The commotion erupted again. "I don't want us to fight!" burst out a child from the audience. He stood. He looked to be about twelve, his face intense and sad both all two. Slowly, the quarreling around him ceased. Macu nodded for him to continue. Shyly, he said, "It's so my mam died. Machete fight. Fighting only make your enemies fight back harder." He looked around and saw everyone watching at him. With a gulp, he sat back down.

"The little youth is right," said Macu. "Might draws might. Too besides, when we fight, if we fight, we must do it with planning, not with recklessness."

"What mek you think we have time for all this palaver?" challenged an old Mirmeki man, whose kilt hung like drapery around his meager shanks. "We going to just let them take us like guinea fowl on the nest?" He waved his crooking wand in the air to make his point.

A woman nursing a baby burst in, "You-all don't see you playing with fire? You picking the wrong choices! Strike a treaty with them, and we end up back in bondage. Strike them down, and Ymisen go take umbrage, and send an even bigger army for us the next time."

An old man laughed. "They didn't do that last time we routed Ymisen! I say we set the piche 'pon them again!"

Veycosi muttered to his neighbour to the right, "But that didn't happen. It's just old people story." The man glanced his way doubtfully.

A younggirl spoke up. She had maybe eleven years. She looked fierce. "They going to hurt us no matter what we decide. So we might as well try to defend ourselves."

"Too right!" shouted a woman. "After all, it's fighting that freed us in the first place! We *have* to defend ourselves. Raise the piche again, do whatever we must to get those monkeys off our backs."

Many of the elders nodded. People in the crowd were clicking their fingers to show they agreed.

Macu held her staff up. The racket stilled. She pursed her lips. "This is a pretty brangle," she said. "Is not like we have three witches anymore with strong science to magic the Ymisen army into the ground." One or two joined in with her bitter chuckle.

The kilted old man shouted, "A musket is plenty strong science!"

"The witches' magic was no miracle, though," Veycosi muttered. Macu looked in his direction. Other people turned to stare at him. The look on Steli's face was rage, plain and simple. The council knew what he had done today, then.

"You're shouting again, banna," whispered Gombey.

To rass. "Beg pardon," Veycosi said.

From her place amongst the council, Siani Yaaya glared at him.

By a jerk of her chin, Macu indicated that Veycosi should come forwards. He stood and picked his way through those sitting.

"What," said Macu, "was your point about the witches' miracle?"

"Those women," Veycosi replied, "if they even self existed, were more canny than uncanny. You don't feel so? There was no miracle to what they did."

People in the audience started to murmur. This wasn't a popular view of the obeah that had set Chynchin free.

"But I wager there was nuff science to it. Battle science, ingenieuring. They must have used the resources they had and their wits to dispatch those soldiers." What was the point of talking fairy stories right now? Chynchin was about to be invaded again. He had to get his ma, his das, on that ship with him tomorrow morning. And his family-to-be, too. Thandiwe and her mother. Kaïra, and to hell with the Mamacona ceremony. Gombey and his parents.

Macu was still staring expectantly at him, so he found more to say. "Or it could be nothing but fairy stories to entertain: you know the way these stories go, Elder. 'The Crab-Back Woman'; 'The Blackheart Man'; 'How Chynchin Came to Be.' They take a sand-grain of truth, and they invent, they embellish. For all we know, a lucky flash flood came down and drowned the Ymisen-soldiers-them." Too late, Veycosi realised the one word he shouldn't have said.

"You mean," said Steli, deadly calm, "a flood like the one you deluged Carenage with this morning?" He was holding out a book, or the waterlogged remnants of one. Half the pages had been torn away, and its damp cover was ruined with mud and worse, but Veycosi recognized it. He swallowed. It was Mauretaine's *Of Divers Matters*.

"We could drown them in shit this time!" bellowed a voice from the crowd. "And mud!" Others joined in with his laughter. Someone yelled, "Dead fish!" Another: "Exploded frogs!"

Macu held her staff up for quiet. She leaned forwards in her chair. "Maas' Veycosi, postulant to the Colloquium of Fellows of Chynchin, what we going to do with you any at all? You don't see we have more serious business at hand than cleaning up after your mischief? You know how much damage you cause today?"

Veycosi stammered, "I— I just wanted to—"

Steli, his face closed and hard as a nut, said, "Hush." So Veycosi hushed. Through clenched teeth, Steli said, "Into the bargain, you removed a precious unsung volume from the Colloquium without permission. You know that's tapu. We could drum you out of the Colloquium for that alone."

The bottom fell out from Veycosi's belly. "Mestre, please!"

"Not satisfied with that, you went and tossed the book away into the reservoir to be destroyed."

"It fell from me! I didn't—"

Macu interrupted, "On purpose or by mischance, it don't make no never mind. Is you set up the circumstance that allowed these unfortunate events to happen."

In a small voice, Veycosi replied, "But at least the south quarter have water again now."

Steli slammed the destroyed book down on the flat wooden armrest of his chair. The wet, hollow clap shivered through Veycosi, brought the hairs on his arms to attention.

Macu was watching him, measuring. Caiman eyes. She said, "Go back and sit down. And stay there. The council have two decisions to make this afternoon."

"Yes, Elder."

"In a little more time," she announced to the crowd, "I will tell allyou what we decide." She looked around at the other elders. They all gathered around her, put their heads together, and began to debate.

Nothing for Veycosi but to sit and seethe and worry whether the ship on which he'd booked passage would take a few more people without notice. Keep him and his family somewhere safe till this mess was over. Gombey gave Veycosi a sympathetic look, but put a finger to his lips when Veycosi leaned over to whisper his plan into his friend's ear.

Four in the crowd went over to the dais to listen in on the elders' discussion. People stood, stretched their legs, helped themselves to water from the jugs on the dais. Some wandered away to get about their own business. Three little girls started up a marbles game. One of them was the youth girl who'd counselled fighting back. They sat right at Macu's feet. Macu, never ceasing to debate, occasionally took time to show the smallest one how to hold her fist to better pitch the marble with her thumb.

He had to get word to the capitaine of the ship he was leaving on tomorrow; weh she name? Yes, Capitaine Kamla. And he had to send word to Ma and his das and Thandy, right away. Veycosi tried again to whisper his plan in Gombey's ear, but Gombey, looking irritated, shook him off.

So Veycosi waited. His bladder was fulling up, but he didn't dare leave until the council had told him its mind with respect to his transgressions.

After a bit, Steli and his cousin began a side argument about whether hill beer was better than city beer. Elder Komnan picked up one of the marble-playing girls—his granddaughter—and slung her giggling body over his shoulder. "Come," he said. "Your daddy probably have fish waiting on the coals at home." He nodded at Macu and left.

And Veycosi waited. For a time, he continued with his hooking and Gombey with his. Gombey was making a neat series of god's-eye squares in gradated sizes. Veycosi tired of his own hooking pretty soon. He sat on the floor with his back against a wall and tried to doze as his bladder sent him more and more urgent messages.

Little time more, the remaining elders straightened up. Yaaya helped Macu to get to her feet. Macu leaned on her cane. "Gombey," she said, "you going to continue your negotiations with the delegate— what him name?—Gunderson. Make half promises, show him the sights, keep him as out of the way as best you can; stall. You know how it go, nuh?"

Gombey nodded.

"Good man. We need time to alert all the provinces and send word to the other islands, see if they stand ready to help us. Yaaya, Veycosi: the two of you going to play fool to catch wise. You going to be Chynchin's official hosts to the delegation."

Yaaya sighed. "Oi. You want me to act the wittering, fluff-headed granny."

"Yes, Sister Elder, beg you please."

Veycosi lurched to his feet, squeezing internal muscles against the twinging of his bladder. "But how I going to do that? I going to be in Ifanmwe. I leave tomorrow for my procuration!" Best not to tell them of his plans to abscond with his whole family.

Macu shook her head. "You not going anywhere. This is your punishment for blowing out the reservoir, and for destroying the only existing copy of that book. Steli says you going to replace the book."

"How? I never finished memorizing it."

Macu's smile was a tired one. "You going to write one, Maas' Cosi. You been talking about the truths woven into our old tales? Well, you going to find out every version you can of the story of the witches, and you going to write it down, and puzzle it out, and tell the council if you find any suggestions in it to get Chynchin out of these hot waters she land up in. That and any other tale you find." Her smile was more a sneer. "Just in case you spy any wisdom in them. And in the meantime, the Colloquium demoting your standing to naught. For the time being, you are not allowed to practise with your line of fellow postulants."

"But . . . Ifanmwe . . ." This was outrageous. It was a make-work project, and Macu knew it. The council was making him a laughingstock. They had just dropped a boulderstone right down 'pon the head of his career and his standing. He stood, gape-mouthed, scarcely believing it.

Macu ignored his shock. She turned to Yaaya again. "As I said, take tamarind balls for the sailors, shite like that. Wear talcum and vanilla like the old biddies we are, and ask after their families. You know the kind of thing I mean. And keep an eye on young Maas' Hothead here." She jutted her chin at Veycosi. "Maas' Veycosi, just try please to not bring this task to rack and ruin. Maybe some good can come of it. This is Chynchin, after all, and not a day of my life she don't find some way to surprise me." She leaned on her cane, groaning. "I expect you to carry out your charge with all that passion you have, and to follow Siani Yaaya's lead."

Veycosi swallowed. Found his voice. "And when am I going to be allowed to continue with my avocation? When I going to have my standing back?"

Yaaya made a *tsk* sound between her teeth. "Like you not listening, lad. Time soon to come, you might not have a Chynchin to study in."

She thought he was lackwitted, or what? He had been right here in the same hall, seen the same drama play out that they all had. Veycosi and Siani Yaaya faced off like fighters in a roda.

Macu sighed, then looked around at the rest of the elders. "Time for good people to be in their homes. But any news, send word for me, any hour of the day or night. And we meeting here, every day, till we decide how to deal with Ymisen." She nodded to all and left, leaning on a guard's shoulder for support.

Veycosi scowled at Yaaya, and she at him. Why the rass Macu had to go and saddle his back with that sour old siani? And for Mestre Steli to thief away his standing! Too besides, how he was going to get his betrotheds and all their families out of the way of harm now?

Cogitating and vexating 'pon it all, Veycosi left the Palavera. He looked for Gombey, but it seemed his banna had already taken a carriage. Veycosi ducked round the side and had a long, luxurious piss into the drain running along the back street. A drain that now flowed with water, thanks to him. But he was receiving no gratitude for his efforts, only spite.

He went round to the front again and waved for one of the carriages waiting outside. As he was settling in, Yaaya came out of the Palavera. To Veycosi's dismay, she hailed down the same carriage he was in. The driver pulled his horse up alongside her. "Evening, siani!" he said. "Room for one more."

"Evening, Thomas. How do?" She put her hand on the railing to the cab. She said to Veycosi, "I'm going to ride with you, maas', if you don't mind."

He nodded and mumbled a graceless agreement. Pointedly, she held out her hand. Veycosi sighed and helped her into the cab. Chuh. Not like she needed the assistance. Never mind how many years she had, her grip was strong and her step spry.

"The council has moved me into an inn not too far from here," she told Veycosi as she settled in beside him. "The rest of my compong gone to stay with relatives and friends. Just until our homes can be dried out." When Veycosi didn't reply, she underscored, "Because of the flooding, you know."

Veycosi had a student's apartment in the Colloquium, a way off from the part of town that had taken the brunt of the reservoir explosion. His rooms would likely have remained dry. Veycosi tapped on the side of the cab to let the driver know they were ready. The driver called down, "Siani, tha wishes the Jamun Avenue Inn, I'll warrant?"

"Yes, Thomas, thank you."

"And the mestre?"

"I'm not a mestre yet, goodman." And might never be one now. Veycosi gave him the address of his apartment on Boriken Lane, just on the edge of the Colloquium. The man clicked at his horse, and they set off.

"Such a botheration," said Yaaya, "for me and my good friends in our compong to have to be dehoused like this."

Mama-ji! Were they still talking about this? "I know it must be hard, siani."

"I been living there twenty-three years, you know that?"

"And gods willing," he replied politely, "you'll be there twenty and thrice twenty years more."

Yaaya only grunted. She had been on the council some years before Macu took office. Hard to tell how much older she was than Macu; she was the type of old woman who didn't shrink, but got solider and smaller with each passing year, like a hardwood.

She stared around her into the streets. They were busy with the close of market day. Led by their owners, camels trudged home, weighed down with untaken produce: yams, coconuts, timepieces, bicycles. There was something a little bit mournful in the weary solemnity of the parade. The carriage had to stop for a herd of cows crossing the road on the way back to their barns.

Veycosi supposed he needs must make some small chat with the nana.

"That man," he said, "the one with the Ymisen delegate."

"The sly one?" she replied, her voice high with disdain. "All over grey?"

"Him self. Anyone said his name?"

"Never heard it, but I marked his ways. Oily. Whatever he calls himself, I think his real name must be 'Trouble.'"

Veycosi nodded.

"Deserter twice over, that one," muttered Yaaya. "Beg pardon, Thomas!" she called out.

Thomas, who sported the traditional Mirmeki tattoos on his knuckles, replied, "Is all right, siani."

Veycosi grasped his soul case where it hung from a leather thong around his neck; two hinged cowrie shells the size of a kola nut, with his obi bag locked inside. A birth gift from an auntie, one of his da Kola's sisters. He slid his thumb over the brass hinge. He'd been doing that for calm from since he was a youngboy. The hinge was polished to a shine from him rubbing it all the while. Well, sith he and the siani were talking, he might as well start in on this insulting project of collecting tales about the Three. "Siani Yaaya, what you know about the drowning of the Ymisen army of Mirmeki two centaines ago?"

"I know that after getting my hamaca soaked in liquid shite while I lay in it this morning, I may be able to imagine more about being drowned in piche than I like."

"It shouldn't have happened that way," Veycosi growled, a hedge against welling shame. "I double-checked my calculations, even did a smaller trial first in a tub of water."

She regarded him coolly for a long, uncomfortable moment. What a way this woman could make him feel sheepish! Then she said, "Earlier, you told the council you don't believe the tale about the three witches?"

Veycosi nodded. "Something likely happened, for us to still be telling tales about it now. I just want to know which version you heard, is all."

The cows were past. Thomas clicked to the horse. The carriage continued on its way.

Yaaya threw Veycosi a sidewise glance. In the falling dusk, he couldn't quite read her expression. "My favourite grandda was the first one to tell it me," she said.

Veycosi listened as she recounted the story. He would eventually use his own wording, imagining how the persons might have spoken and what their senses might have recked on the day. He would keep close as he could to Yaaya's description of events, and render the tale thusly:

The Making of Chynchin: Being a Book of Fanciful Tales of the Founding of This Great Land, Collected from the Recountings of Divers Citizens of Chynchin

THE THREE WITCHES

AS TOLD TO MESTRE VEYCOSI OF THE COLLOQUIUM BY COUNCILWOMAN YAAYA

Moments after the sun's bottom lip cleared the horizon, the brigade charged down the hill. They'd made camp up on the barren heights, the better to survey the community of escaped slaves they'd come to reclaim for their crown. Kima stood with the rest of the halest members of their compong of defiant runaways, ready to give back blow for blow.

The Ymisen pistoleers advanced upon the waiting village compong. Their silence unnerved. Only the paddy thump of the camels' wide feet made any sound. Compong people murmured, stepped back. But Mother Letty gestured to the compong's defenders to stand still. So they did. Kima felt her palm slippery on her sharpened hoe. She'd known this day would come, but she didn't feel ready. Who could really make ready for something like this?

The pistoleers advanced upon them in five rows; some tens of soldiers posting up and down in unison on their camels. Each row but the last comprised seven gangly camels, each camel ridden by a bonded Mirmeki soldier, each soldier kitted out in identical and pristine red jackets with light brown pantalons. Near on four muskets for each of them, and powder, carried by a small boy running beside each camel.

There were only twelve muskets in the village compong.

Now the first rows of camels stepped onto the pitch road that led into the village. The road was easily wide enough for seven camels across. The cool morning sun had not yet made the surface of the pitch sticky. The camels didn't even break stride. Kima made a noise of dismay. Where was the strong science that the three witches had promised them? Weeks and weeks they'd had them carting reeking black pitch from the deep sink of it that lay in the gully, rewarming it on fires, mixing it with stones, and spreading it into this road that led from nowhere to the entrance of the compong, and stopped abruptly there. Had they done nothing but create a smooth paved surface by which the army could enter and destroy them?

From her position at the head of the freedom fighters, the Ilife witch, the Obe Acotiren, showed no doubt. She only pursed her lips and grunted, once. Standing beside her, white Mother Letty and the Cibonn' witch Maridowa did not even that.

Kima fretted. The three witches should have been behind the village fighters, where they could be protected. If the villagers lost them and their knowledge, they would be at the mercy of the whites' fish magic. Yet there the three stood and watched. Acotiren even had her grandson cotched on her hip. So the fighters took their cue from the three women. Like them, they kept their ground, ready but still.

"Twice five," whispered Mother Letty. "Twice six." She was counting the soldiers as their camels stepped onto the black road!

Kima thought it little comfort to know exactly how many Mirmeki Ymisen had sent to kill them, but she found herself counting silently along with Mother Letty.

The leading edge of the army was almost upon them, scant yards from the entrance to the compong. Camels covered almost the full length of the road. A few of the village fighters made ready to charge. "Hold," said Mother Letty. Her voice cut through the pounding of the camels' feet.

They held.

Maridowa turned her wide brown face to the fighters and grinned. She was merry at strange times, the young Cibonn' witch was. "We have almost no chance," she said. "But we going to take the chance we have, yes?"

True, they would. There was nothing else to do. They all stood, suspended between fates, ready as they could make themselves.

The soldiers had their muskets at the ready. The barrels gleamed in the sun. The villagers' muskets were dull and scorched. "So many of them," whispered Kima. She raised her hoe, cocked it ready to strike. Beside her, the white boy Carter whimpered, but clutched his cutlass at the ready, a grim look on his face. He'd said he would rather die than be press-ganged onto the ships once more as a sailor. He had fourteen years. He had spent the last three of them in brutal labour on board the ship that had taken him from his mam, da, and sisters.

Taunted by the sweetish smell of the curious liquid the witches had had them heat and mix into the piche, a tiny hummingbird hovered, shimmering black and green, just above the road.

Thrice six . . .

The man in the first row, in the middle—Datiao! But he was from the compong! "Bastard turned against us," muttered Kima. She spat onto the hard-packed road. She wasn't to know that the

*witches had secretly sent Datiao to the Ymisen army to claim he
had switched to their side. He was spying out any advantage the
new settlement might have and reporting back to them. Now that
it had come to battle, he was to rejoin his compong fellows.*

*Acotiren signalled to Datiao to hie himself off the piche road.
She had no idea what the result of their prayers and spells might be,
if anything. Yet she feared for Datiao, riding out onto that piche.*

*He, however, shook his head. He would wait until it was less
obvious that he was abandoning the Ymisen army.*

*Acotiren shrugged. Datiao had been learning the ways of their
enemy. Best he make his own judgment about when it was safe to
return to his own side.*

*The thrice seventh haughty camel stepped smartly onto the
road, a little ahead of its fellows. "That will do it," pronounced the
Obe Acotiren. It wasn't quite a question.*

*Nothing happened, save that the hummingbird alighted onto
the road. Maridowa hissed in disappointment.*

*Kima blinked. Something in her eye? It seemed the world had
just . . . jumped, and slowed. When it started again, it was somehow different.*

*Then the pitch went liquid. It was that quick. It swallowed the
hummingbird in the blink of an eye. Camels began to flounder,
then to sink. The villagers gasped, talked excitedly to each other.
They had laid the pitch only four fingers deep! How then was it
swallowing entire camels and riders?*

*The pitch swamp had not a care for what was possible and what
not. It sucked the brigade into its greedy gullet like a pig gobbling
slops. Camels mawed in dismay, the pitch snapping their narrow
ankles as they tried to clamber out. Soldier men and women clawed
at each other, stepped on each other's heads and shoulders to fight
free of the melted pitch. To no avail. The last hoarse scream was*

swallowed by the pitch in scarce the time it took the Obe Acotiren's
fifth grandchild—the fat brown boy just past his toddling age, his
older sisters and brothers having long since joined the band of compong freedom fighters—to slip from her arms and go running for
his favourite mango tree.

The black face of the road of tar was smooth and flat again, as
though the army had never been.

One meager row of uniformed soldiers stared at the compong
fighters from the back edge of the pitch road. Their weapons hung
unused from their hands. Then, together, they slapped their camels
into a turn, and galloped hard for the foot of the hill.

All but one, who remained a-camelback at the bank of the river
of pitch.

The pistoleer slid off her beast. She stood on the edge of where
her fellows, suffocated, were slowly hardening. She bent her knees
slightly, curling her upper body around her belly. Fists held out in
front of her, she screamed full throat at the villagers; a raw howl of
grief that used all the air in her lungs, and that went on long after
she should have had none remaining. She seemed like to spit those
very lungs up. Her camel watched her disinterestedly for a while,
then began to wander up the hill. It stopped to crop yellow hog
plums from a scraggly tree.

On the hill above, the Ymisen general sounded the retreat. In
vain; most of the surviving Mirmeki had already dispersed. (Over the
next few weeks, many of them would straggle into the compong—
some with their camels—begging asylum. This was their chance to
be free of bondage to Ymisen. Asylum they would be granted. It was
a good land, but mostly harsh scrub. It needed many to tend it.)

Some few of the compong fighters probed the pitch with their
weapons, which did not penetrate. Cautiously, the fighters stepped
onto the pitch. It was hard once more, and held them easily. They

began to dance and laugh, to call for their friends and their families to join them. Soon there was a celebration on the flat pitch road. An old matron tried to show Carter the steps of her dance. He did his best to follow her, laughing at his own clumsiness.

They had bested their enemy! Kima gave silent thanks to the carved stone Mamacona statue that stood on one of the peaks. Mamacona, she had been told, was the collective name for the twin caiman-headed sisters Mamagua and Mamapiche.

(Write this: "If Kima thought it odd that she couldn't remember the statue having been there before, the feeling soon faded.")

(You can tell him to write that all you want. You know he won't hear you.)

(I know. Ironic. People believe they follow the dictates of their gods, yet they never truly hear us.)

Tempted by the sweetish smell of the strange potion the witches had had them stir into the heated piche, a fat cullybree bird with its iridescent black feathers hovered just above the road. For an instant, the bird looked like a new thing to Kima, as though she'd never seen one before. So much else had happened today that was new. The cullybree stretched its feet down towards the road and Kima's heart was in her mouth, fearing it would land. They said a cullybree would die if its feet ever touched the ground. But it pulled its feet in again and flew upwards to join its fellows above in their endless, circling flight.

"What," Veycosi asked Yaaya, "is a hummingbird?"

She shrugged. "A-so my grandda tell me the story. He always said 'hummingbird.'"

"A bird that hums?" Veycosi set his mind to remember that detail. He'd best start carrying a table-book. And a stylus.

They were pulling up to the inn. "I never heard the actual tale before," he told Yaaya. "Just heard tell of it. Thought it was a big wave of piche the soldiers drowned in. People always say how the piche 'rose up.'"

"Not the way my grandda tell it."

The carriage stopped. Siani Yaaya climbed down. As she was stamping her mark of approval in Thomas's book, she said to Veycosi, "My girl and I going to come collect you tomorrow."

"Collect me for what?"

"To visit the Ymisen ship, young maas'. You forget so soon?"

"Of course not, siani." What a way the old woman was sour! Sour like pickle. Veycosi bade her a falsely cheery, "Good walk!" and rapped on the side of the carriage for Thomas to move on.

Once inside his apartment, Veycosi struck tinder and lit the two kerosene lamps that stood on his study table and on the window ledge. He could scarce bear to look at the open trunk in the middle of the floor, with clothing and books tossed haphazard into it. He'd figured on finishing his packing tonight.

But he wasn't going to Ifanmwe. He was to stay here and scribe down old people's stories. He muttered, "Might as well get me to collect tales of the Blackheart Man."

There was a bottle of killdevil in his cupboard. He took it out. Wiped his mug out with a fistful of his robe. He slung said robe off and threw it over one of the supporting ropes of his hamaca. He climbed into the hamaca and poured himself the first mug of kill-devil. He steadied the bottle between his knees. The popular cure for someone taken ill with the phthisic was to keep drinking until they saw three of everything. Veycosi wasn't sick, but he was ill of spirit just now. Morosely, he tossed back the mug of burning spirit, coughed, and poured himself another. Then a third. And possibly a fourth. The last thing he remembered of the sorry day he'd had was hefting back still more rum and bellowing out the ball-tossing rhyme from his youngboy days:

> Pitch it fast,
> Pitch it slow,
> Turn the pitch quick,
> And down you go.

Down and down, to two days earlier . . .

It was a pleasantly warm night in Carenage Town. All around them in the student apartments of the Colloquium of Fellows of Chynchin, other students and their bannas were outside on their own porches and balconies, making the most of the cool night breeze. Some had strung their hamacas there for the night. Some sat on the ground or on stools, happily a-palaver with each other. Candlelight, laughter, and friendly quarrels danced between friends and lovers. Veycosi had brought out and lit his brazier. He and his intendeds had long since eaten the fish he had cooked on it. Now the banked coals gave off a red glow, popping occasionally when a mosquito flew too close and fell sizzling into the brazier.

"And when you pointed out to Kaïra that it was only an eelfish,

not the goddess Mamagua?" Veycosi asked Thandiwe. From the pitcher he poured her another mug of killdevil mixed with mobby.

"'Ey," said Gombey, holding out his mug, "more of that for me, too!"

Thandy replied to Veycosi's question: "Kaïra said, 'No, Mama. It's an apprentice Mamagua!'" She sipped from her mug, watching coyly at both Veycosi and Gombey as they laughed at the antics of her daughter when she was younger.

Veycosi sat back to take in the perfect moment; it would be months before he had any more such with his best friend and the woman who had agreed to take them both as husbands. He would be off on the ship in two days.

Gombey looked well, as he always did. He was still wearing the khaki sokoto and white buba he'd worn to work that day. It was the uniform expected of an aide to the township's cacique. But it suited his Ilife features and dark skin quite some fine.

Thandy was resplendent in a loose cotton kaftan dyed a vibrant cochineal red. It brought out the warm tones of her olive skin. It was embroidered in black thread around the neckline, in the pattern called "tamarind seed." Her tightly curled black-brown hair—hers and Gombey's were such a contrast to Veycosi's own shoulder-length hanks of straight, coal-black Cibonn' hair—was cane-rowed into an upswept crown, one of her favourite hairstyles. She said it was because it kept her hair out of the salt water when she had to clamber down into the ponds at the fishery she managed. And so it did. But more to the point, it complemented the graceful prow of her nose and lent her height. Thandy had always wanted to be tall.

Gombey said, "Cosi, banna; are you packed for your trip yet?"

Before replying, Veycosi took a long slurp of his killdevil and mobby, savouring the bitter, spicy sweetness of the blood-cooling mobby. "After I'm only going to collect one book and then catch the ship back home? How many clothes so I going to need?"

Gombey shook his head. "You never been away from Chynchin. You will want to take a few days to explore."

(Veycosi's dreaming mind then recollected that Steli had told him about the extravagant, evanescent confection that was iced cream, sweetened with honey and sprinkled atop with crushed pistachios. Veycosi had revised his idea of what Ifanmwe might have to offer him, other than the bookshop that was currently holding for him the book he'd sourced, which was going to be the means of his ascension to full mestre.)

Thandiwe looked downcast. "If you stop aside for merriments, it will be that much longer before you return home to me and Gombey."

The sadness on her face tugged at Veycosi's heartstrings. "Well, I don't have to—"

Thandy smiled. "Nah, sweet. Do as seems best to you. I'm just craving for you to return in glory so we three can have our nuptials."

Gombey raised his mug in a toast to Veycosi. "Yes, banna; I'm so proud of you. I misdoubted me you'd get this far."

That had been Gombey's requirement since the outset: that Veycosi be a full mestre before their marriage. Back then, a couple of years ago, when Thandiwe had proposed that the three of them wed, Veycosi had been set to announce their marriage right then and there. Gombey had been just as eager—like Veycosi, he'd been making mooncalf eyes at Thandy from since they'd first met her. "But, Veycosi," he'd said, "you only just began studying at the Colloquium. Me and Thandy, we have equal standing. You won't until you complete your studies, and I know you, banna; you likely to find some diversion or get into some trouble that will delay you from your aim." When Veycosi had looked hurt, Gombey had taken *him by the shoulders and looked frankly into his eyes. "Is not the fact of standing, you comprehend, brother. In terms of your prowess and your promise, you are more than equal to either of us. I know this. But wouldn't you like to show our bride-to-be that you are capable of following through on your aims?"*

Seeing Thandy's thoughtful nod, Veycosi had had to admit Gombey's point. They had been friends since smallboy days. Gombey had seen Veycosi's plans to become a master dyer fall to naught when Veycosi discovered the joys of working with yeast and resolved instead to open a bakery. Then it was the profession of surgeon, until he discovered he couldn't abide the blood and raw flesh smell of dissected cadavers. But in the world of the chantwell, Veycosi had found a place to feed forever his hunger for divers forms of knowledge; in the Colloquium's archives of the Hall of Records were books and scrolls on every subject imaginable, and more coming all the time. Veycosi was confident he'd finally found his métier. So he had agreed to Gombey's requirement, sith it had seemed well to Thandiwe, too.

Veycosi was jerked awake next morning by someone banging on his front door. "Inside?" the person shouted.

His heart was slamming with that fright you get when a loud sound wakes you. He shouted, "I coming!" He threw his legs over the side of the hamaca. Its swinging made the world spin, and he nearly toppled himself out of it. He picked up the robe—he marked he was still seeing it tripled—that he'd thrown over the hamaca's rope. Got tangled up in it at first and couldn't find the armholes.

"Inside?" came the voice again. A woman's.

"A moment!" he shouted. He finally wrestled his robe on. He shuffled into his alpagats. Ran and opened the door.

The sun struck his eyes like lime juice squeezed into them. He blinked, squinted at the woman standing there. Her skin was a tan light brown, a smidgeon more olive than his golden Cibonn' tones. She wore a buba of green cloth and a matching abosuwo. The wrapped skirt was green with a winding pattern of yellow lizards. The cloth wrapped around her middle was light blue with streaks of a darker blue only an impudent hair away from being cacique indigo. The whole suited her shapely form something fine. "Mestre Veycosi?" she said.

"At your service, maidell." The green of those eyes and the freckles dotted across her prow of a nose were bewitching; the symbols tattooed across her knuckles proclaimed her Deserter.

"Siani Yaaya waiting outside for you. In a carriage."

The world went spinning again. His eyes wouldn't focus. "Siani Yaaya?"

"We going to the Ymisen ship, she say."

Shite. Of course. "You're a friend of Siani Yaaya's, then?" Though if a friend, a young one; she seemed closer to Veycosi's age than Yaaya's.

"Her chatelaine."

She looked down, but not before Veycosi spied a hint of merriment playing about her lips.

"Something sweeting you?" he asked grumpily. His mouth tasted bitter and sour. His eyes felt like they had sand in them.

"Your robe's inside out."

Veycosi looked down at himself. Sure enough, the raw seams were to the outside, his still-full sleeve pockets bulging like a donkey's panniers. "Swive me."

"Beg pardon, mestre?" the woman asked frostily.

"Oh, not you. I wouldn't ask so lovely a maidell as you to endure my attentions," Veycosi joked. "At least, not in the sorry state I find myself."

She looked taken aback at that; even more so when he pulled off the robe, and turned it to the right side, put it back on again. "Better now, you don't think?" he asked her. Oh, the pounding of his head! He needed water. And some food to hold his stomach down.

She smirked. "Siani said you had a way to be flighty, and likely wouldn't be ready yet."

"Siani is wise."

"Siani says for you to meet us then, down by the Ymisen ship. We have an audience at two."

"What o'clock it is now?"

She raised one eyebrow. "The quattie-past-one bell tolled just before I reached your door."

"Mama's tits. Oh, don't screw up your face at me like that, maidell. I sure you know a blue word or two."

"And learned a few more by coming here today," the haughty bit replied. Amusement leavened his queasy stomach for a second. A slight smile played over her face, too. Seemed she was more enjoying the banter than being affronted by it.

Affably, he said, "You and Yaaya go 'long. I soon come."

He bade her good walk and closed his door, but not before watching her comely form depart to the waiting carriage. Then he struggled into a fresh awotele and sokoto. Transferred his things into the pocket of a clean awosoke. Snatched up a johnnycake he'd taken from breakfast at the Colloquium yesterday. It was stale, but he washed it down with some water from his jug. Made to run out the door. Remembered that the Colloquium had tasked him with a project, so went weaving back to put table-book and stylus in his pockets. Stood still a little minute until the dizziness passed. Finally stepped outside.

The sun was hot on the top of his poor head, but he didn't have time to turn back for a topee. He whistled for a carriage that was waiting across the street. The driver nodded and clicked at the horse. They started crossing the street to fetch him. "Turn the pitch quick," Veycosi muttered under his breath.

And stopped still, right where he stood. If he said the children's rhyme as "Turn the *piche*," not the pitch, the song wasn't about pelting the ball at your bannas in a game of dodge. It was about the drowning of the Chynchin soldiers! Turn the piche liquid, and down you go. Just like in Yaaya's version of the story.

Rassa. He took out his table-book and scribbled it down. As the carriage pulled up alongside him, the bell in Carenage Town's high tower started chiming half past one. "The docks," he said as he climbed in. "By where they have the ship from Ymisen."

"Them people bringing nothing but trouble," growled the driver, a young Deserter girl. She flicked the reins to get her horse going.

"Never mind. We going to pitch them down." The Mirmeki had no more reason to love Ymisen than anyone else in Chynchin. They were descended from the enslaved soldier force Ymisen created in each country they overtook. Mirmeki soldiers were always at the front line, the first to die. And Ymisen sent Mirmeki forces in when it didn't want to risk Ymisen lives.

Piche it hard. What substance would be hard, but liquefy if people stepped on it? How long did it take rubber tree sap to harden? Could you keep it liquid until you were ready for it to gel? Could you dye it black?

The driver spoke over her shoulder. "To the docks, tha said?"

"Yes."

"Ah. Thought tha might be going to the piche works, like everyone else this morning."

"The piche works? Why?"

She glanced back at him with a wry smile. "Woke late, is't? A little too much in your cups last night? They've dug Ymisen people out of the piche."

"The ones from the ship got mired, did they?" So some of their enemy had conveniently done away with themselves. Something like this happened every so often in Carenage; a beast or a person blundered in the night onto the melted heart of the lake, got stuck, sank slowly, struggling the while, and suffocated before any help came.

"No, mestre," said the driver. "Is the ones from before. The ones the witches sank into the lake so long ago. The Mother Lake spit them back out."

The little hairs on Veycosi's arms rose up. "You lie!"

"I do no such thing," she said calmly.

"Take me there!"

"Yes, mestre."

She turned the carriage and tapped the horse with the whip. But she was going in the direction of the Lower Piche, down in the valley. The tale Yaaya had told him placed the miring of the Ymisen soldiers in the smaller Upper Piche higher up, on the plain at the head of the cliff; the one that appeared to drain downwards via some kind of underground channel, to then exit down below to form the Lower Piche. "Driver!" Veycosi called. "You going the wrong way!"

"No, mestre. Is in the Lower Piche works they find them."

"But the stories say they got buried in the Upper Piche."

"Mayhap that's where they went in! But is not where they coming out. Trust me, mestre. I take three loads of people there already this day."

So Veycosi let her go where she would. As they went, he scribbled down what he remembered of Yaaya's tale, closing his eyes betimes against the dizziness brought on by the rocking of the carriage. "Maidell," he said to the driver, "you know any stories about the three witching women?"

"Certes, mestre."

"Tell me one then, nuh?"

"Yes, mestre. This one have a picken like me in it. . . ."

THE GOOD SOLDIER JOSEPHINE

A TALE OF THE FOUNDING OF CHYNCHIN,
AS TOLD BY MAIDELL LEONI, A CABDRIVER,
TO VEYCOSI, STUDENT OF THE COLLOQUIUM

Plaisance handed Kima a gourd cup from a net bag of them slung over his shoulder. He poured palm wine into the cup from the bigger calabash he was carrying. Kima nodded her thanks, and Plaisance moved on to give the other compong people drink.

Kima stared into the milky liquid. She saw her own face reflected there. Her lips like two bows fashioned of supple wood. Her bark-brown skin. The short, mossy scrub of black and grey hair peeking out from the sweat-stained brown bandana she'd covered it with. Her hair used to be all black, before she'd been carted halfway across a world to spend her days bent over tubs of lye for making soap, blinking back the stinging fumes from her—

". . . eyes big enough to search out the deepest secrets," said the face reflected behind hers on the surface of the palm wine. Kima started, hand already reaching for her hoe lying on the ground at

her feet. The witch Maridowa laughed her laugh like kumaka tree pods clinking together in a soft breeze. She put a hand on Kima's shoulder. "You're cocked like a trigger. Set to go off at any little thing. Take some ease, nuh? Battle done."

Kima relaxed and quaffed some of the sour, milky wine. "You're certain it's over?" she asked Maridowa. "Suppose they send a bigger posse after us now?" She and Maridowa got along, but Kima still found her unnerving at times. Maridowa had a way to say not what Kima was thinking, but the thing she had just been about to think.

Maridowa smirked down at the pitch under her bare feet. "If more soldiers come, we put them to bed, too, just like these ones under here."

"That trick won't work on them twice."

Maridowa didn't look up. "A wonder it worked even the once," she muttered.

A thin, hoarse keening slipped its way through the sound of the revelry going on all around them. On the other side of the hardened pitch, the one remaining soldier still mourned. Her camel had wandered back to her. It had folded itself down to the ground. The soldier was curled into the lee of the beast's body.

Maridowa looked where Kima's attention had been drawn. "You right," she said. "It's not a trick will happen twice. But this one time will work for more years than you or me will live to see. You going to go and get her?"

Kima grinned and handed Maridowa her cup. "Don't you already know what I'm going to do? I think it's your eyes big enough to see everywhere, not mine."

The merriment went from Maridowa's face. "Not quite big enough," she said. She sipped from Kima's cup. "I will get some wine for her. She will need it."

She turned abruptly away. Kima shrugged. Maridowa was choppy like that. She knew how to be here, and how to be gone. Not the hellos and goodbyes in between. Good there was something she didn't know. Made her a little less uncanny.

Everything felt uncanny at the moment. Kima put her hoe on the ground, marking how the fresh piche glistened in the sun. The sky seemed a different shade of blue than she'd ever seen it. There were spiky, odd-angled plants growing in clumps here and there on the hill. For an instant, she wondered what they were. Oh, yes; snakeroot. Everyone knew that.

Unarmed, Kima walked down the pitch road to the bereaved soldier at its end.

The woman's camel lifted its head and looked at her. Looked like a horse's head—a powerfully ugly horse—but with the reach of a serpent's long neck. Kima clicked her tongue softly at the camel. It reared its head and opened its mouth at her. Kima stepped back.

"Don't cluck at her so," rasped a raw voice from the curve formed by the camel's belly. "She's not a bloody hen."

Kima stopped where she was. "Not coming to hurt anyone," she said.

A hand slid up the camel's neck, patted it, gave a single firm tug on its halter. "Set, girl," said the hoarse voice. "Stay." The beast lowered its head and rubbed it against the woman's hand. That was a good sign. Neither it nor the woman were going to attack. Kima sat on the ground beside the soldier and her camel.

The other woman sat up. She was a mexite, her nose Ymisen-thin, her lips Ilife-plump, her skin a red-brown blend of both, and of some other blood too besides. Her hair braided into cane rows against her scalp. The texture of it looked to be curly as vines, *rather than the bunched moss of Kima's. Her strong face was pretty, though presently puffy with weeping. She swiped her snotty nose with the back of one hand. "You've won, then," she said.*

"Yes. We're free," replied Kima. "For now."

"I suppose I am, too. No longer a soldier-slave woman."

"Yes, but weren't you all men? Before—"

"Before you drowned the most of us in tar, you mean?" The woman gave a confused look around at the near-empty plain of battle. Then she looked down at her own body; her full bosom and wide hips. "I . . . I don't know," she said. "From here on, the world has turned inside out."

Kima frowned. "But, too, it feels as though it has always been thus."

The woman nodded, seeming equally perplexed. "And now your people have a home of your own. That's more'n I do. Always been a bloody bond servant to Ymisen. My whole family, for three generations back."

Kima thought some about that. "You would like some wine?" she asked finally. When the woman gave her a nonplussed look, Kima jerked her chin in the direction of the celebration. "Palm wine. And we have wild pig, and bammie—manioc bread, I mean to say." Kima regarded the woman's strong, solid beauty, her large hands and the curve of her bosom, and longed to learn more about her. But she didn't blurt out, Would you desert the life you had and bide with us? Mayhap with me? *One thing at a time. The woman must be tired, and hungry. Food and drink first.*

The woman sighed and stood. She tapped the camel on its neck. It rocked to its feet and rose up, tall enough to throw shade over Kima and the other woman both, like some poui tree. Kima stood, too.

"*Am I your prisoner, then?*" the woman asked.

"*No!*" said Kima. Then reflected. "*I don't think so. We didn't expect to live out this day. Didn't make a plan for what to do if we won.*"

"*May I bring my camel?*"

"*I figure so, yes.*" Kima was no more sure of this road she'd started them on than the woman was. One step at a time.

"*Richard is under there,*" said the woman, nodding to the piche road.

"*I'm sorry.*" Kima found she really was.

"*He was seven,*" the woman said, her voice breaking. "*One of the musket boys.*" Her face crumpled. "*He was my son.*" The tears came again, but silently this time, with no sobbing.

Kima watched at her and tried to figure what to say to a loss so terrible. Could only think of one thing. "*Come,*" she said to the woman, reaching her hand out. The woman's camel bent its head down and snuffled at Kima's palm. It gave a strange moan, like a wail of despair mingled with a disdaining huff. It straightened its head and sighed.

The woman said, "*She likes your smell.*"

That bloodcurdling whinny had been an expression of approval? What would the camel have done, then, if it hadn't liked her? "*My name is Kima.*"

"*Hight Josephine. And the answer is, she'd have bitten you.*"

Seemed like Maridowa wasn't the only one who could hear questions that hadn't been asked. Josephine continued, "*Take us where you mean to take us.*"

Kima led Josephine and her camel back to the village.

Mama-ji. A mere picken, an enslaved mother's child, drowned in
the piche. The stories of the witches weren't so much sport when
you imagined the fairy story as real. "Thank you," Veycosi said to
the girl. He returned his table-book to his robe and pulled out the
two wrapped paan leaves he had in there, filled with toasted coconut and folded into triangles. He took one for himself and offered
one to the driver.

"Thank you, mestre."

"Warm day today."

"But not too warm."

"You think it might rain?"

"No, mestre. Too early in the season."

"Ah-hah."

It was the prattling of two people who didn't know each other
but were forced into each other's company for a bit. They spent
the rest of the trip chewing their paan and chatting awkwardly of
nothing. The driver dropped Veycosi off by the Lower Piche Lake,
at the foot of the Dead Men's Teeth Cliffs. Veycosi still doubted this
was the right place. The other piche, the Upper Piche Lake, was on
the flat atop the cliffs, was where the escaped slaves were supposed
to have made the road that became the Upper Piche Lake in a trice
and drowned a small army. Yet, by the press of people at the gates
of the Lower Piche, there was something going on. Veycosi nudged
his way through them to one of the gates. The guards, seeing the
Colloquium braid in his hair, waved him through.

The place where Chynchin produced its major export was like
a phantasm of the Crucians' Hell: the asphalt reek of it was vile,
and worse in the day, when the sun softened the top layer of piche
slightly. There were even two hell-like furnaces: big stone tanks
full of burning coal, stoked the while by two teams of blackhearts,

Deserters as they were wont to be, their heavy leather vests smeared over the chest from them scraping piche off their hands against them.

Iron bins were suspended above the furnaces. Slabs of piche hacked from the lake were being melted in those. The "lake" was solid in most places, except for the warm, syrupy "Mother Lake" at its centre. Blackhearts were mining hardened piche from the lake with pickaxes and shovels. Putting it into hoppers pulled by donkeys and cud-chewing camels, and guiding the animals over to the furnaces. Fetching the chunks of piche out from the hoppers and loading it into the cauldrons that sat above the furnaces. Others were turning the big iron cranks that stirred the melted piche. They held long hooks for fetching out the bigger detritus from the piche; branches, the mummified bodies of small beasts that had become mired and so had met their deaths. Maybe it was one of the workers who had found the first bodies of the soldiers. More blackhearts minded the big strainers through which the pitch filtered into the large molds that would form cords of solid piche the size of three men standing together. Others were setting the molds to cool in stone huts all along the shore of the piche lake. And breaking the cooled piche out of the molds. And packing the cords of piche into crates lined with waxed reed paper, sealing the crates, packing the crates into hoppers, riding the camels and donkeys pulling the hoppers down to the docks for use in Chynchin or to export to foreign for caulking ships and building roads. Shouting and movement. And the stinking smoke from the melted piche drifting over the whole scene. It was a thick smell, like the one at the very back inside of your nose when you have a catarrh, but magnified manyfold, especially to the senses of one who had been far into his cups the night previous. Veycosi's mouth made hot spit. But he refused to puke. He pulled a corner of his sleeve over his mouth and nose. It helped little bit.

Two of the blackhearts were carrying something long and heavy from out of the piche to a stack of other big, tarred objects over to the side.

Veycosi picked his way over to them. Couple times, he stepped in lumps of piche whose surfaces had begun to melt in the sun. They stuck to the bottoms of his new alpagats, bringing dirt and mud with them. Made his feet feel heavy and slowed him down. He was going to have to replace those sandals, too, for they would never get clean again. When he was a smallboy, he and his bannas snuck down here one night. No plan, just boys making mischief. They had made their way over the hardened piche in the dark to the Mother of the Lake, that one spot in the middle that was always soft. He had dared Gombey to throw his lamp into it. Veycosi still thanked his stars their mothers never found out it was them who had set the mother of the piche ablaze that night. Gombey'd lost his eyebrows when the flame sprang from Her centre, and for a fortnight, his hair smelt like farts. His eyebrows had taken a month to grow back again. Luckily, they'd been sparse to begin with, a mere sketching of black hairs on his forehead. Against his swart skin, his parents had never noticed the difference.

When Veycosi reached the gang of workers, they touched their caps to him and murmured shy greetings. Hard by was the stack of big, tarred lumpish logs, most of them the length of someone grown. Veycosi's heart started a *rat-a-tat* inside his rib cage.

A woman from the gang was on her knees by the pile. She was using an edge of an old rag on one of the logs to gently wipe away the excess piche. As Veycosi watched, she rubbed the rag as clean as she might on the leather vest she wore, where she already had a patch of old, crusted pitch on the left breast. Right-handed, then.

Many who worked the piche wore heavy leathers the while; piche burns were nasty. And when they got piche on their hands, they wiped it off against their vests. That black crust over their hearts was where they got the name "blackhearts." It was a Chynchin type of jest, to call them after the man in the tale parents used to fright their pickens into behaving. *Eat all your dukunu, or the Blackheart Man going to come at night and steal your heart from out your chest while you sleeping.*

The woman looked up when she saw Veycosi. She shaded her eyes against the sun.

A worker nearby said to her, "Sally, here's a mestre come to learn aught about these folk."

Veycosi said, "I'm not a mestre yet, goodman."

Sally pulled away her hand with the rag in it. She cocked her head and gave a considering look at the thing to which she'd been tending. "This'n has a look to him like my da," she mused.

Veycosi knew what the object was that Sally was cleaning, but knowledge was one thing; truly seeing was another. That latter one came on as though Veycosi were waking up slowly, his eyes unblearing bit by bit till he could see clear. The thing between Sally's hands resolved into wizened features, and he understood for the first time that he was looking 'pon one of the smothered from ancient times: a Mirmeki soldier man, piche-darkened face still grimacing in the agony of his death throes. If he resembled Sally's father, then her da must have a fierce gaze for true. Even with his face wrinkled like a jamun berry in the sun, the dead soldier's grim aspect held Veycosi's attention.

On that rock over there was another, bent right in half sideways, and another, or a piece of one. Over there was a little musket girl, one arm stretched above her head, probably to the living air that had forsaken her two centaines ago. Her other arm was broken raggedly off. The piche had turned every last member of the army into statues with cobbled skin, black and dull. There was even a camel, frozen wide-eyed in panic. Its rider was glued to its side in the act of trying to dismount his camel to perhaps save himself. Veycosi gazed upon the pruneate face of the camel rider, and his blood congealed in his living veins.

He knew that face. Had encountered it before, though he had believed it unreal. And now, after all these years, it had finally come for him, as he'd always feared it would.

Veycosi hadn't broken fast this morning. Not much in his stomach save the small johnnycake and paan. Now he gave even that up to the oily ground beneath his feet.

"Is guilt making you take so poorly, Maas' Cosi?"

He looked up. Yaaya stood over him, leaning on her cane. Beside her was the pretty maidell he'd met some minutes ago. She couldn't possibly be impressed by him now, with vomit smearing his lips. He hurriedly wiped his mouth and stood up. "Siani Yaaya, maidell; I was coming right to meet you. Right after I saw—"

Yaaya's companion interrupted him by walking over to the growing pile of preserved soldiers. She bent to one of the lumps of piche, then to another. Reached out to touch a stone face, a petrified hand. She knelt right down on the ground, without a care for her clothing. He wanted to call out to her that she would bruise her knees on the hard, rough piche, but for once, he held his tongue. That pretty fabric would be ruined, though.

"Samra?" called Yaaya softly. The maidell glanced briefly at her but didn't seem to see her.

Samra stroked a pitchy arm. The girl Sally, who'd left off her cleaning when Samra went over, said again, "He looks like my da. I was just telling the mestre."

Yaaya snapped, "He not a mestre."

Samra gazed into the face of the piche-drowned one closest to her. Then she murmured something to Sally. Veycosi couldn't hear the words, but Sally hesitantly reached out her hand. Samra clasped it. They bided so some few moments. Then Samra stood, patted Sally's shoulder, and came back to them. Sure enough, there were two patches of piche fouling her skirt at the knees. She resumed her place beside Siani Yaaya, standing straight as bamboo. "He could be my Lev," she said. A quiet tear climbed down her cheek.

"His Malaika should have calved by now, nah true?" asked Yaaya.

Samra regarded her like a woman being pulled half drowning from the water. She blinked. "Lev's lead camel?" she replied slowly. "Twins, she had." Her voice still sounded far away.

Yaaya put her arm through Samra's, resting on her cane as though she needed the assistance. Veycosi surmised she didn't. "Come," said Yaaya. "Let we find a carriage."

Samra seemed to come back into herself. She looked down at Yaaya, who only reached to her shoulder. "Yes, siani." She dashed a tear off her cheek and began to lead Yaaya away. The maidell had let herself have a moment of emotion, but was recovering quickly. Bamboo bends in the hurricane, the better not to break. Oh, that was good. Proverbs were a kissing cousin to old people's tales, nah true? Veycosi jotted the saying down in his book.

The siani turned to Veycosi. "Come along, Cosi."

"Me? Why?"

Yaaya's scolding gaze made him feel like a puppy that had widdled indoors. "We going to the ship. Don't tell me you forget."

"But I thought you already went," he replied. He'd hoped, any road.

Merriment deepened the lines on Siani Yaaya's face. "We were on our way there," she said. "Then we heard tell of the old-time soldiers being pulled from the piche. Had to come and see that, nah true?"

So it was well for the two women to be diverted a moment from their task, but when Veycosi did the same, it was down to a flaw in his character? It was all Veycosi could do to keep from kissing his teeth in vexation.

Yaaya and Samra headed for a break in the clamouring crowd. Veycosi followed. They had to elbow their way through. Veycosi saw a woman, standing with feet stoutly apart, fanning herself. "Mercy," she said. "I don't know which smell worse; Maas' Veycosi's flood, or the piche lake."

Veycosi sighed. Would they never forget? He put his head down and bulled through.

Trapped in the hardened rock that his body had become, Datiao lay near the kneeling girl—Sally—and seethed. The people milling all around them; their speech was little bit strange to him, but not so very changed in two hundred years. He could scarce believe it, but from what he could hear them saying, he had lain mired in that hell for two centaines! All this time he'd been fighting to get free, to return to his home and his bannas in the compong. He'd been hoping they would win the day. He'd felt proud of doing his part. He'd been ready to do more, to throw himself into the fray for their freedom, whatever might come.

Yet he'd surfaced to find this horror. The battle won, but *two hundred years ago*. He should have heeded Acotiren when she signalled him to get off the piche road. And he should have kept saying the spell they'd given him to protect him from harm. The three witches were dead and dust by now. His time, his world, his friends all fled from him. And he, what was he? Not entirely dead, not alive.

Datiao mentally swatted aside the common sense that was trying to remind him that he'd chosen this path against Acotiren's advice. That none from his compong could have known his plight below the piche, that in the melee of battle, they almost certainly wouldn't have been able to fetch him out before he suffocated. That in fact he had suffocated, and died, and the world had changed, and he was now an unnatural creature.

He could grieve his loss, or he could rage.

He chose the enlivening heat of fury. He'd done what had been asked of him. And for his troubles, he told himself, the ones he'd trusted had left him for dead.

He let anger enflame him, lend him a semblance of the fire of life. And he bethought him: dead he might in some wise be, but he wasn't yet dust. Not so long as he gripped his prize, at which he'd not yet been able to gaze, sith he couldn't bend his head.

He could, however, tell that he was not the only nonliving being that had been dug out of the piche. The Mirmeki soldiers who'd died with him; he was still among them now. The object in his hand that was preserving him; it must be preserving them all. Wherever he went, so long as he was holding the thing, those others went, too. He had risen up from the piche, and with an army bound to follow him!

The sun had softened a little the piche covering him. He could feel the slightest suppleness returning to his limbs. There was so much commotion going on that no one noticed his small twitches; a finger unkinking, a shoulder joint slipping back into place with little jerks and cracks. He was even able to draw small sips of breath. Sunlight was truly his friend. A woman of the piche army rolled an eye his way, the wetness of its white a sharp contrast to the dull wrinkles of her dry flesh. She closed the eye again.

A woman? A woman soldier? He hadn't marked any such on the day they attacked. Who sent women into battle? Except for the compong, of course; they'd needed all the fighters they could muster.

And what would happen as the day cooled towards evening again? Datiao needed a way to keep the piche from hardening on him. He needed protection.

He needed the witches' chantson.

With the earnestness of a prayer, Datiao began to mutter, very softly, the words of the protection spell the three women had devised for him. His lips scarcely moved. He kept saying the chantson over and over again, even as he and his fellows, plus the piche-imbued camels and horses, were loaded onto donkey carts and trucked away from the Lower Piche Lake.

The Ymisen trade ship, a galleon, bobbed on the water by the docks. She was, as Chynchin trading vessels were, roundish with high sides. Her hull had been painted with yellow and black stripes. She was a three-master; give her a good wind, and she would skip gaily over the seas to her destination. Her gangway had been let down onto the dock. Ten Chynchin guards stood there, at the foot of the gangway. At its head, on the ship, the same number of Ymisen guards.

Yaaya muttered, "Is time to begin this pantomime." She leaned on Samra's arm, feigning feeble. Together, the two women toddled up to the guards, Veycosi trailing along.

Yaaya peered up at the galleon. "Lawdamassy!" she said in a wittering voice. "Such a big ship! I hope it won't pitch too much. I might get sick!" She winked at Veycosi. One of the Chynchin guards shot her an astonished look. Siani Yaaya came from a long line of fisherfolk, and everyone knew it. She could probably have steered this bark single-handed. Samra approached the guards and showed one of them the cacique's official seal, which deputised Yaaya to seek entry onto the ship. Four guards escorted the party up the gangway, Yaaya going on the while about how much she hated to be on the water. They showed Yaaya's pass to the Ymisen soldiers. Two of the Ymisen guard left to fetch somebody or other. And during the wait, didn't Yaaya go on about how overwarm their soldiers looked in those wool suits, poor dears, and she wondered didn't they miss their families something dreadful? She feigned alarm at the ship's rocking, and bade Veycosi and Samra bear her up, and generally played the biddy.

Veycosi's stomach had settled. He closed his eyes, the better to feel the movement of the ship in the water. Where had she wandered? What shores had she touched? Had she been to Ifanmwe? Would he ever get to go there now?

Little more time, a couple sailors came above decks, bearing wooden benches and a table. Behind them came the functionary. He hemmed and hawed and directed the sailors to place the furniture now this way, now that. Finally satisfied, he reached for Veycosi's hand. "Gunderson," he boomed.

Was that word a greeting? Oh, he remembered now; it was the man's name. But why he didn't make himself known to Yaaya first, and she obviously the elder amongst the three Chynchin visitors to the ship? "Siani Yaaya is on the council," Veycosi told him, gesturing towards her.

Gunderson furrowed his brow. "What say you? Can't make out you people's rough speech."

Yaaya tilted her head towards him. "Maas' Veycosi, what he saying? Man a-chat like somebody sew him lips together with twine."

Samra stepped forwards. "You needs must greet the siani," she told Gunderson, indicating Yaaya. "She is an elder on our council. She is here to welcome your'n, and we have with us aught to refresh the crew."

Gunderson raised a brow at her Mirmeki speech, which had its origins in his language, but only the form of it spoken by the people they conscripted from the nations they'd conquered to form a disposable army as a bulwark to protect Ymisen soldiers. He stared pointedly at her tattooed knuckles. Ymisen Mirmeki were forced to be tattooed thus. Their Chynchin descendants did so as a matter of pride. But to give him credit, he immediately bowed deeply towards Yaaya. "Dama," he said, "please excuse my manners. I am not schooled in your ways, nor my ear to your speech. Do sit."

Samra translated for Yaaya and Veycosi, and somehow the four of them managed to get through the simple formalities of introducing themselves without causing enough offense amongst them to bring their two nations to war then and there.

The grey man came up from belowdecks; the Chynchin turncoat who acted as advisor. Gunderson looked relieved. "Hie thyself here, Androu," he said. Veycosi was beginning to understand him little better. "Come tell me what these people want."

Samra pursed her lips. Veycosi could understand her irritation. She'd been translating well enough. This Androu person wasn't needed.

But Androu came and stood by Gunderson's right hand. "Give you good walk," he said, looking good at each of the three visitors in turn.

Yaaya exclaimed, "And to you, young man! Samra, you have them?"

"Yes, siani." Samra motioned to Veycosi to give her the parcel he had been lugging for her. She put it on the table, then untied the string and unwrapped the brown paper to reveal a fancy silver dish, big enough to comfortably hold a goose, covered with an equally fancy silver lid. No wonder it had been so heavy!

Samra took the lid off. The dish was piled high with—

"Sweetmeats," Yaaya said to Gunderson with a self-satisfied smile. "Of tamarind and sugar. For your men."

The grey man narrowed his eyes. Gunderson glanced his way, then said, "Oh, that's very lovely, I'm sure, but you must understand, dear lady, we cannot—we dare not . . ."

They feared poison, then. "They not going to harm you," Veycosi told them. "Regard." He leaned forwards, snatched up one of the tamarind balls, and put it to his lips.

Suppose it actually was poison? Before he bit down, Veycosi glanced at Yaaya. She looked a mite surprised at his action, but not alarmed. Samra looked amused. So Veycosi sucked on the tamarind ball. Tart tamarind paste, not too much sugar, a little hot pepper; just the right blend of flavours. And someone had put fresh mint into them, too. The tamarind ball began to melt pleasingly from the warmth of his mouth.

Yaaya also helped herself to one of the tamarind balls. The grey man relaxed somewhat. Yaaya gestured to Gunderson that he should try one. He picked up a tamarind ball and sniffed at it. He took a small bite. Made a startled face at the taste. Worked it around in his mouth. He took another bite, then popped the whole thing into his mouth. He reached for another.

Grey Androu said, "Thank you, siani."

"Oh. Yes," mumbled Gunderson with a full mouth. "Very nice."

Yaaya preened as Samra translated. "Of course, nice," she replied. "After I made them myself, just like one of my das used to."

The grey man leaned in and took one. He ate it slowly, his eyes closed. He even smiled a little. Gunderson called another man over to try the confection. Tall and lean, this one, with a peaked hat.

Gunderson called him captain, as though men could be such. Perhaps he could; these people did everything strangely. Before long, everyone above decks was eating tamarind balls, even the soldiers. Yaaya said, directly to Androu, "You know to tell them not to eat too much, yes? Lest they get the belly-runnings."

He grinned, as though the thought sweeted him. "I know, siani." Yet he didn't warn them.

With Samra and Androu's help, Yaaya and Gunderson commenced to jawing about this and that: he kept running his mouth about how fine the weather was here (as though that were unusual); how strange it was that the cullybrees never alighted anywhere; and whether people in Chynchin ever wished for cooler weather.

Veycosi had no direct part to play here. Bored, he wandered away from them. Presently, he came to the side of the ship. He leaned out to see what he might see. Nothing. Sea lapping at the ship's flank, cullybrees overhead. Same old Chynchin.

He turned his back on the sea, and, still leaning, took out his crooking. The piece was now large enough to be unwieldy, so he tailor-sat on the boards, laid it across his knees, and began working more loops into it. It was still cloud-shaped, which was to say, no shape at all. But it had developed a lacy overlay; a tracery of hollow tubes clambering and branching this way and that. Veycosi had used the thinnest yarns for the tubes that he could find; some darning thread from Da Woorari's mending box, a kind of bark colour.

"Ah!" came a voice from close by. Veycosi looked up. Walking towards him was the oddly convivial person who'd been among the party being marched from the ship the day prior; the one of whom the sailors were wary. Ee was watching at Veycosi's crooking and clapping ir hands in glee. Ee grinned and pointed at it. In ir ungendered voice, ee burbled forth a spate of Ymisen speech, too quickly for Veycosi to follow.

Veycosi held the piece up. "You like this?" he asked ir.

Ee nodded. With the eagerness of a child, ee came and squat-ted at Veycosi's side. Ee pulled something out of the side hip of ir britches. It was a piece of string. Ee held it up to show Veycosi, as though it were a treasure. Was ee addled, then?

Then ee proceeded to knot and pull swiftly at the string. In a trice ee held it up again, only this time, there was a shape loosely woven into it. The person said a word that sounded familiar, and suddenly, the picture dangling in the net between ir fingers became obvious.

"Is a ship!" Veycosi exclaimed.

Ee nodded. "Ship," ee repeated, a little more closely to the Chyn-chin way of saying it.

Ee moved ir fingers in a kind of way, and the ship seemed to dance along its strings. What a marvel. Veycosi laughed out loud.

Ee shook the string out and gabbled a phrase. Ee worked ir fin-gers through the string and held it up again. Ee said a word.

"Cup?" responded Veycosi.

Ee gave a quick, satisfied nod. "Yes, cup!"

Ir skin was so pale, like steamed bao bread. Ee made yet another design, then held up the new pattern. It was beautiful. Lines and struts and joists supporting the whole. Veycosi smiled. "Bridge."

A voice spoke softly into his ear. "Some of the sailors call that one 'Hell's Ladder.'"

Veycosi whipped his head around. It was Androu, the grey man. Over by where Yaaya was, she sat chatting with the Gunderson man, who'd apparently decided Samra would serve well enough as inter-preter.

With Androu bending this close, Veycosi could see how beau-tiful he was, despite how hard he worked to make himself unre-markable. Veycosi's breath caught a little in his throat at the strong lineaments of Androu's face.

Androu indicated the other person's string sculpture. "Ser," he said, "may I?"

The person nodded and let go one end of the string. Ir beautiful bridge unknotted into just a simple loop of dirty twine. Ee held it out to Androu, who commenced to looping it.

Veycosi asked, "Ir name is Ser?"

Androu smiled. "No, mestre." Androu held the string up. It was now in the shape of a skull.

"I'm not—"

"Is an honorific reserved for the highest in the land. You been playing cat's cradle with the late heir to the throne of Ymisen." With a dip of his chin, he passed the thread back to the other person.

"Late?" squeaked Veycosi.

Androu's smile grew more merry, even a mite spiteful. "'Late' meaning 'no longer,' not 'passed on.' The affairs of Ymisen are in a mickle of a set-to of late. Some of we who are loyal to the throne have spirited Ser away to safety until things in Ymisen be settled down."

The late heir to the throne of Ymisen looked from Veycosi to Androu, pink-cheeked, smiling faintly, and waiting for Androu to translate what he'd just said.

Oho. Here was the heart of the onion, squatting beside Veycosi on a ship's deck, playing pickens' games. Behind the layers of threat and pomp was the spider at the centre of the web. The thing now would be to make friendly with the heir. Veycosi smiled at ir. "Ser," he said in his best Mirmeki, "wouldst take a tour of the city with me?"

Ee grinned back. "One would rather visit the Colloquium," ee replied.

Veycosi was beginning to comprehend Ymisen speech. But one what? He looked to Androu to clarify. Androu said, "Ee means

irself. Sith once the throne passes to ir, ee is to be the heart of the
whole of Ymisen, you understand."

Veycosi didn't understand a rass, but they could at least discuss
the Colloquium. The heir clearly knew what the gold ribbon woven
into Veycosi's hair meant. Perhaps ee was a fellow seeker of knowledge? Veycosi said, "I can take you there. What subject interests
you, ser?"

"One has heard that the Colloquium possesses Ad-Din's *Zij*?"

"Certes." The book was definitely in the Colloquium's archives.

"The translation, surely?"

The heir was approaching the limit of Veycosi's ability to understand ir. "No, ser. The original."

Ee literally began to tremble. "But it was lost!"

"And we found it, and so many more. You are an astronomer,
then?"

The word "astronomer" the heir apparently understood. Ee nodded, ir eyes wide and pleading. "Yes. More so than an heir to any
throne. It was why one came here."

This was the person really in charge. And ee was fascinated
by the Colloquium. If Veycosi could use that fascination to sway
this one to sympathy for Chynchin, they might manage without
any bloodshed. Veycosi could save his standing yet! He clasped the
heir's over-warm hand in both of his and treated ir to his most winning gaze. "Ser, we don't have kings nor heirs at the Colloquium.
All are equal in the search for truth. So what name I should call
you by, then?"

Androu made an offended sound, but Veycosi didn't business
with him. For ir part, the heir looked delighted. "Hight Tierce,"
ee said.

If Androu went any more pop-eyed, his eyeballs would just

drop out right here so. He touched Tierce gently on the shoulder. "Ser," he murmured, "I know these people. They're crafty."

The wretch! "You should know," Veycosi said. "Since you're one of us."

Tierce looked uncomprehendingly from one of them to the other.

"Ser Tierce," Veycosi continued, "I would be honoured to take you to the Colloquium of Fellows of Chynchin."

Androu said to Tierce, "You can't just go with one of them into their midst! You can't risk it!"

Tierce shook Androu's hand off ir shoulder. "Yes, one can," ee said to Veycosi. "Right this instant."

Oh, this was fine sport. "Maas' Androu," Veycosi said, preparing himself to trot out the dwindling remainder of his Mirmeki, "shall't accompany us? Certain sure the heir would be safe with your doughty self along to protect ir?" Veycosi found himself hoping that Androu would say yes. There could be something so pretty about a sullen face.

Tierce all but did a jig. "Yes! There's the solution! Come with us, Androu! And two of my guards, if such seems goodly to you."

Veycosi thought about how things stood at the moment between him and the Colloquium. He'd best ask them permission first before bringing the Ymisen heir to visit. "Not today, begging your pardon. I have to arrange your passage first."

Tierce pouted and Androu looked relieved. Right then, Yaaya called for Veycosi to depart with herself and Samra, so Veycosi took his leave of Tierce, promising to return right soon to escort ir to the Colloquium. He would tell Gombey what he had discovered, so that Gombey could inform the council. In the meantime, Veycosi needs must continue his dreary assigned task of collecting stories. Perhaps that Samra could help him. She seemed to have a quick mind. And Kaïra, eager as she always was to be tripping on the hems of Veycosi's robes.

As the carriage took Veycosi, Yaaya, and Samra back to their homes, it occurred to Veycosi: Suppose he found out how the three witches had achieved their trick of vanquishing the Ymisen squadron two centaines before? Then, even if the Colloquium denied Tierce's request to be allowed to visit, Veycosi would know the means to protect Chynchin. Surely that would regain him enough status to be allowed back into the ranks of postulant? Heart churning with excitement, he turned to Samra. "Maidell, will't aid me in assembling the stories of Chynchin the council has bade me collect? When you not busy with Siani Yaaya, of course."

Samra looked to Yaaya for permission. At Yaaya's nod, she said, "What would you have me do, sirrah?"

Yaaya answered before he could. "He want you to be his scribe while he go around collecting tales, as Macu charged him to do."

Veycosi didn't trouble himself to contradict her. Samra could do that for him as well as aid him with conducting experiments based on the information he gleaned from oft-retold, poorly remembered, oft-embellished fragments of Chynchin history. He was silent the rest of the trip home, plotting non-magical ways to drown a troop of soldiers in a river of piche.

Chapter 3

KAÏRA AND VEYCOSI CALLED out, "Samra!" same time. The make-shift winch wasn't too steady, and Veycosi's hands had slipped on the rope holding the iron bucket full of boiling rubber tree sap.

Samra leapt out of the way as the bucket above them clanged down where she had just been. It rolled around in a circle on the flagstones outside Yaaya's empty apartment, spilling whitish sap as it went. Veycosi grimaced. Whether it hardened or no, he would have a rass of a time cleaning it up.

Samra snatched up a wooden rule of his that was lying on the ground. She used it to hook the bucket through its sap-fouled handle and pick it up. "What happened?" she asked Kaïra and Veycosi as they reached her. She peered into the metal bucket they'd been heating in the outdoor fireplace of Yaaya's compong.

"You all right?" Veycosi asked. "It didn't catch you anywhere?"

"Sound as a drum, sirrah. Dinna fret."

"Cosi let go the rope," chirped Kaïra.

"Your behind. It slipped from me." They had been trying to work out how much heat to apply to the rubber tree sap. Too little, and it wouldn't set at all. Too much, and it would set permanently.

They needed the exact temperature that would set it just enough that it could be liquified again. If rubber tree sap worked that way.

Samra asked, "Did you get this notion from one of the tales you've collected?"

Veycosi sighed irritably. "No. Is just conjecture." He looked inside the bucket. The gods-damned sap was still runny as a raw egg. "Even if we get the temperature right," he said, "we still would have to calculate how to dye it black, and how to make enough to pave a road long enough to hold seven rows of camels."

Samra looked doubtful. "The dye should be easy. I'm sure any dyer could manage it. But you really think that is what the witches did, poured a trench full of semi-hardened black rubber sap in order to make it look like a road?"

"I don't know! If I could travel to Calliope Island, I could find out from the rubber plantations there how to work the sap."

"So is that you going to do, then?" asked Kaïra excitedly. "I could come with you?"

Veycosi kissed his teeth irritably. "I been banned from travelling, you recall. Too besides, you know you not allowed to leave Chynchin until after Mamapiche."

Kaïra's face fell. "I know."

"Why you pestering me with the question, then?"

Samra asked him, "When they going to lift the ban on you?"

"After I create a book of collected tales of Chynchin."

"So why you not doing that? Instead of . . ." She pointed at the white ooze of rubber scattered in the dust.

"I could cobble together some book of fanciful tales as a project intended to punish me with busywork, or I could find a way that might save us from Ymisen. Which you think the council would rather see?"

"Mayhap you're right," replied Samra. "But you're casting

about in the dark. Even if it was tree sap they used, we still don't know whether they could get it to liquefy again on a sudden."

"Let me think of one thing at a time, nuh?" Veycosi rubbed the soul case at his neck.

Kaïra said, "Maybe the council would let me go to Calliope if I had you to watch over me!"

"Picken, you don't have anything better to do than bother out my soul case? We can't leave, I say!" All day Kaïra had been wearing Veycosi's patience thin; what this, what you going to do with that, how the conversion to Mamacona happened, whether it would hurt, whether she would still be herself when she came out from the piche. "You don't see is serious work we doing here?" Veycosi asked her. Couldn't she see how important this was to him? "Like you want me to send the Blackheart Man for you, or what?"

Kaïra scowled. "I'm too old to believe scare-baby tales," she muttered sullenly. "Little more time, I going to be Mamapiche, and then you won't be able to speak harsh to me."

That just riled Veycosi even more. "Why you don't go and look for your bannas, eh? Play some jacks, or plan whatever Mamapiche japes it is allyou planning. Leave big people business to big people."

"All right," she replied in a small voice. Immediately, Veycosi felt shamed for speaking harshly to her. But what was done was done.

Samra put an arm around Kaïra's shoulders. "Cosi have plenty on his mind right now, picken. Best you come back when he's not so fractious."

Veycosi kissed his teeth. Of course he was fractious! Who wouldn't be?

Kaïra looked even sadder. She nodded and pulled out of Samra's embrace. She padded away slowly at first, hand on her tummy, but before long she was running the distance to the doorway of the big, empty room. Kaïra never walked if she could run, skip, climb, or jump instead. She ran right out into the yard. Veycosi could hear her footsteps pattering away from there, getting less and less distinct.

Samra turned to him. "The child was working hard for you, Cosi."

So shyly she said "Cosi." It warmed Veycosi's heart, but he ongle replied, "Chuh. She was underfoot."

"Under*foot*? She been running to and fro all morning, following your instructions."

"Pesky younggirl." Veycosi tested the handle of the bucket with a finger. Cool enough. He took it from her.

Samra said, "Things not easy for Kaïra, you know."

Veycosi snorted. "Of course I know that. I was just a little short today. Matters weighing heavy on my mind."

She glared at him. "Mayhap my presence is weighing on you as much as Kaïra's. Perhaps I will shut my gullible Deserter trap and leave you in peace."

Veycosi caught both her hands in his. The words tumbled from his lips. "Na, sweet. Wouldst have me pine for lack of the sound of tha voice?"

She risked a small smile at him imitating her Mirmeki speech. "Tha sounds like dogs barking."

Time was, Thandy and he used to pitch woo at each other so.

She said, "Just remember that being Kaïra is not all sport."

"I promise I'll be gentler with her tomorrow. Thank you, my fair fellow, who generously scatters wisdom like corn for guinea fowl. In the meantime, bid you good walk. I must attend practise."

"I will walk with you. I'm going in the same direction."

It pleased Veycosi that they would have a few more minutes in each other's company.

Talks between Ymisen and Chynchin were not going well. Ca-cique Macu had refused outright capitulation to the demands of Ymisen. She had called a council of the rest of Chynchin's caciques from the country's other districts, who had now also entered into the negotiations with Ymisen. Veycosi told himself that if he scarce saw his friend and co-betrothed, Gombey, nowadays, it was be-cause that one was so busy with the negotiations. It had nothing to do with how much time Veycosi was spending with Samra, col-lecting tales and studying on ways to recreate the act of the three witches that had saved Chynchin.

As they approached the Colloquium's choir hall, Veycosi stopped to bid adieu to Samra. "Someone you're visiting on campus?" he asked.

"I am." That was all she said on the matter, and good manners dictated he shouldn't press further. Biting back his curiosity, he gave her good walk and continued into the hall.

Her Lev, perhaps?

Now he could hear the members of his cohort, warming up to rehearse their arrangement of the only known copy of al Alim's *De Motu Sideris*, or *On the Movement of the Stars*. When they had been assigned it three years before, in their first year of study, they had decided to render it as a progressive roundel.

A kalimba and a cuatro were trading riffs on the third move-ment of *De Motu*. Veycosi recognized each one's style. The kalimba player was surely Keïta and the cuatro player Luba, the former as taciturn in affect as the latter was effusive. The two disagreed about near everything, but when they played together, Veycosi had seen the beauty of it bring a tear to Steli's eye.

Kylet, as usual, was singing his scales a hair too quickly, relying on the apparent virtuosity of speed to cover his tendency to be a mickle off pitch. Veycosi entered the room, his nose prickling at the familiar smell of rosin. He smiled at them all and took his sheet music and stylus out from his sleeve pocket.

Steli spied him. "Son," he called out over the cacophony, "put those away. You not part of this class."

The sounds of music practise lessened as some of his cohort quieted, the better to hear the goings-on. Steli strode over to Veycosi. "I know you heard what I said in the council meeting. You are on hiatus until I deem it meet to let you rejoin your cohort."

"Mestre, you can't be serious about that!"

Steli's jaw was set, his eyes stern. "Quite serious, Maas' Veycosi. You ruined a precious text and flooded a goodly portion of downtown Carenage. That can't go unpunished. You should be getting along with your business of collecting Chynchin tales."

Veycosi spluttered, "But the heir to the Ymisen throne . . . I promised . . ." Surely Steli wouldn't prevent him from bringing Tierce to the Colloquium. Surely he wouldn't take the privilege from Veycosi and assign it to another!

Steli's forehead creased into a frown. "What you blathering about now? I have a rehearsal to direct. So you just take yourself—"

"Mestre Steli! I thought I heard your voice!"

It was Samra, entering the rehearsal hall. What, had she followed him to witness his shame?

Steli saw her, and his visage lit up. "Maas' Samra! How do, my girl?"

Maas' Samra?

Samra drew close, scarcely glancing at Veycosi. Steli took her two hands in his. He was beaming. Veycosi had never seen him look so happy. "My Samra this," he said to Veycosi. "My former student, fled to the ingenieur's hall of the Colloquium. How they treating you over there, my girl?"

Samra's face clouded so briefly, Veycosi wasn't sure he had

marked it. The smile that now stood in its stead was relaxed, congenial. Studiedly so. "Well enough, mestre. And I do know Maas' Veycosi; I recently made his acquaintance."

"Oh, so you know what a mischief he is."

Samra patted Steli's hand. She leaned in and softly said, "Certes. And I also know you're secretly fond of your rapscallion students."

Steli slid a glance at Veycosi and chuckled. "They do keep me lively." Then his expression got stern again. "But, maidell, do you know what he did this time?"

"I do. Yet he and I are aiding Siani Yaaya as she gathers information about our Ymisen visitors. In that wise, mestre, we have a favour to ask of thee."

We do? Veycosi found himself lost for words, yet before he knew it, the thing was arranged. Veycosi would bring the royal Tierce and ir escort to the Colloquium to witness the singing of a formerly lost book as it was formally ensconced in the Colloquium's archives. "Thank you," Veycosi muttered to Samra as Steli returned to the rehearsal.

The members of Veycosi's line broke into his solo from *On the Movement of the Stars* as he and Samra were leaving the hall. Veycosi's heart panged to hear his line rehearsing without him. And stumbling over his section, from the sound of it. He stood awhile, on the outside listening in, while the consequences of his rash act crashed about his life, breaking apart and dispersing the pieces of it like the winning seed in a guamajico game smashed the others into crumbs. Samra regarded him with pity. That nearly undid him.

Once outside the hall, Veycosi turned to Samra. "Why did you hang back, instead of coming in with me?"

"I suspected that Steli would have to be stern with you. Bad enough your cohort would be present. I wished to save you the shame of having me as a witness into the bargain."

He should be thanking her for her thoughtfulness. He couldn't bring himself to do it. "So you're a student of the Colloquium, like me! You never said." The words ground out between his teeth.

She only grunted a vague assent.

Veycosi sighed. "Whereas I, it seems I've gone and bunged my life up good and proper. Suppose Steli never lets me rejoin my studies?"

Samra gave him a measuring look. "What will't do then?" she asked.

"Wish to high heaven I never dropped those bombs into the reservoir?" Veycosi replied. "Not to mention that book? Or maybe start praying to Mamagua? A response from her have to be at least as likely as anything good coming of this."

Samra smiled a little. "Or as likely as you suddenly turning believer," she said. "For myself, I wish I had never quit the Hall of Records for the Hall of Ingenieurs. They treat me like a mere nothing over there."

"Why not come—go back to the Hall of Records, then?"

Her face fell. "Truth is, I am no longer a student at all."

"What?"

"I quit my studies some months ago. So you see, you and I are both failed scholars."

"You left because of some sideways glances?"

She frowned, which wrinkled her nose most fetchingly. "It was more than that, maas'. Their harassment was relentless. They made it impossible for me to do anything but depart the Colloquium." She looked at the ground. "I have no Sept."

Ah. There was the heart of the matter. She couldn't complete her prenticeship as an ingenieur until she had had a dream walk—a Reverie—to determine the direction of her specialty. Her Reverie would be witnessed by seven full ingenieurs. Six to witness, and one more trained to administer the bouffe that would enhance her sight and keep the ceremony on its rightful road. If she passed the test, that one would become her mentor and guide for seven years, as Steli was his. "You never asked for a Sept?"

In a clipped tone: "Oncet."

"And what happened?"

Softly, she said, "How many ingenieurs you know who are women?"

"Well, is rare, but I'm sure—"

"How many?"

"You."

"None, then. And how many you know who are Mirmeki?"

"Ha, got you there!" Veycosi started counting off on his fingers. "I've heard tell of Iniate on the south side of Chynchin, and Gayambee . . ." He trailed off, for he couldn't name more than that.

Samra nodded. "That is what happened the first time I tried. Couldn't find seven who would stand as my Sept."

"Why they have to be Mirmeki? Why do your kind stick to yourselves so tightly? Don't you think it would go better if you didn't hold yourselves above others?"

She glared at him so fiercely he took a step back. She snapped, "They need mun be Mirmeki, sith everyone else refused me, except Mestre Bohai."

"He is of the Sushen race, nah true?"

"He is. And he was happy to do me this service. So the ones wedded to cleaving to their own are your'n, the ones with the power. You and the Ilife."

"I—"

She cut him off with a quick, thin laugh and a dismissive wave of her hand. "Nah, man. Don't fash. I will achieve my ends. Eventually.

I just want to hang on with Siani Yaaya until her home is dug out
from the flood. She act tough, you know, but she well past her three-
score and ten years. She could use the help."

It was always so when he talked with Samra. Matters between
them would be going along well, and he would buck up against
some difference in how life worked for her kind that he had never
kenned before. It was as though he and she lived in different countries, not the selfsame one.

There was a commotion going on around them; students and
others all heading pell-mell in the direction of the batey courts.
Someone tapped Veycosi's shoulder. It was his friend Chinel, a student griot of another line. "You coming to the roda?" Chinel asked.

"Why? A roda is no great matter." The battle mestres held them
monthly, after all, as part of their students' training.

"This one is," Chinel replied, already beginning to jog that way
again. "We preparing to defend ourselves against Ymisen!" He
took off well ahead of them and blended into the rushing crowd.

Samra took Veycosi by the sleeve. "Come on, then! Let's go
and see!"

The batey court was full today; not with players, but as a make-
shift training camp for fighters. Since Ymisen had returned, seemed
everybody and their parrot wanted to train to fight. Didn't they
see how skilled the Ymisen were at swordplay? And muskets? And
cannon? Chynchin only used muskets for hunting the island's small
game, not for battle. If it came to warfare, the Ymisen force had
the greater firepower.

In one corner of the court, a capoeira mestre was drilling a band
of people in the makak style. On the other side, a white-haired woman
with strong arms was showing another set of people how to load

a musket. There was a roda going, too; people gathered around in a circle, all waiting to challenge the one in the middle. Two drums and the berimbau marking time.

Veycosi and Samra joined the handful of onlookers around the edges of the batey court. A determined-looking younggirl, maybe eleven years old, entered the capoeira roda to challenge the winner of the last bout. And who was the younggirl challenging? A thick, centred Ilife man wearing the pink-and-green bandana of a master fighter tied around one upper arm. The arm so brae that the bandana had had barely enough length left to tie a knot. The mestre was shaking looseness back into his muscles after defeating his last challenger, a dazed-looking man sitting on a stool outside the batey court, shaking his head like a donkey chasing flies, as one of his bannas poured water on the big, gravel-burned bruise he was now sporting on his shin.

A small old woman standing beside them said, "But what that little picken-girl think she doing any at all, eh?"

A voice from behind them said, "Is my sister that."

Veycosi turned. It was a youth man, Ilife himself too, maybe three years older than the girl. His chin sprouted a few lonely hairs. "She wouldn't listen to me," he said. "Going up against a mestre." His voice was still breaking into manhood. He looked to where his sister was doing the steps of a tentative ginga. "She hard-ears," he said proudly, "but she good. Better than me."

"Hush, nuh?" said a woman with a baby at her breast. "They starting."

The younggirl spun into a kicking handstand, landed a glancing blow on the mestre's arm. He brushed it off and slid so quickly into a grapple with her that Veycosi didn't see him move. Immobilized by his size and strength, she tried in vain to push him away.

"Maitefa," groaned her brother, "you know not to let him inside your guard! This isn't play, girl!"

The mestre threw Maitefa into a fall. The crowd gasped. Maitefa twisted like a cat mid-fall, and just managed—just—to land on her hands and feet instead of on her back. Before she quite had time to stand, the mestre was on her again. He picked her up, but she slipped out of his grasp and cartwheeled—an aú—the moment she landed. She stood, dancing ginga for the moment out of his reach.

"That's right," muttered the woman beside them. "Use your small size."

"Why they let a slip of a girl like that into the roda?" asked Samra. She was gripping Veycosi's forearm so tightly that she was cutting off blood flow to his fingers.

The mestre lunged forwards into a low, sweeping kick. Maitefa leapt over it, but the mestre had already stood, positioning himself right in her path while she was still in midair. He clutched her. She jabbed her elbow into the crook of his neck and shoulder. He twitched and let her go. Abandoning form, she ran out of his reach and stopped, panting, to watch him. Her face was dusted with Chynchin red dirt, her look wary.

"That's right!" said her brother. "Dogson didn't expect you to fight tough, eh?"

"You want pax?" the mestre asked her, his voice pitched to carry so that all nearby could hear his offer. She gave a quick shake of her head; no. Her eyes remained fixed on the mestre's movements.

"She should take the pax," said a man nearby. "Best she can hope for is a technicality."

"Yer rass," said Maitefa's brother. "Bruise him up, Maitefa!" he shouted.

"Shh," the man said. "You going to distract her."

"Thought you wanted her to beg pax?" asked Samra.

The mestre moved on Maitefa. The picken scrabbled backwards, then to one side. The mestre threw a forearm block her way. She crouched down underneath it, rolled between his legs. She was behind him now. He started to whip round. But that put one of his feet on toe-tip. Maitefa, still squatting on the ground, grabbed that ankle and pulled with all her strength. The mestre overbalanced. Voices in the crowd cried out in appreciation. Maitefa didn't rely on that one trick, though. Before the mestre could recover, she leapt lightly into the air, wrapped both small fists around his queue, and pulled him down by the hair with her body weight. The mestre crashed to his back in the dirt. Maitefa backed away from him with a cautious ginga step. The win was Maitefa's!

"Yes!" shouted her brother and the man who'd wanted her to call pax.

Maitefa turned towards the sound of her brother's voice. She grinned. Behind her, the mestre flipped himself back onto his feet. "Good, Maitefa!" he said. Maitefa whipped round to face him. He took a little hop and sent the child flying with a roundhouse. He didn't much pull his blow, either; Maitefa rolled three times before she managed to twist and crouch into a creditable esquiva baixa, one knee down, defensive arm across her face, facing the mestre.

"Shame!" Samra cried out.

"Cheat!" Veycosi shouted, along with others in the crowd. The mestre had landed on his back; the fight had been over. "Censure!" Veycosi yelled. A capoeira mestre making free with the rules like that!

Maitefa's brother yelled, "Sister, you all right?"

Despite the stunned look on her face, the picken-girl nodded. She kept her eyes on the mestre. Her brother gave a howl of rage and jumped over the barrier to run towards the mestre. The monitor stepped in front of him, held her stout staff sideways to bar him. "He's a coward!" shouted Maitefa's brother. He went to rush past the monitor, but she pulled him down with the hooked end of her staff, and held him there on the ground.

Maitefa stood. There was a scraped track of red down her forearm to her elbow. Tears ran down her cheeks. The mestre asked her something. Veycosi couldn't tell over the shouting what he was saying. *Now* the man looked concerned, after he'd thrown an adult's blow at a picken. But Maitefa stuck her stubborn chin out and shook her head. Her face set in misery and her small body visibly shaking, she faced down the mestre once more and moved into a swaying ginga.

"Why they don't stop this?" asked the woman feeding her baby.

"You think an Ymisen soldier would fight fair?" the old woman asked her. "This is serious training, not a joke."

"But still," said a nearby man in a chantwell's uniform. "A picken."

The mestre signalled for the berimbau and the drums to cease playing. At the silence, everyone on the batey court stopped and turned to view the situation.

The mestre crouched down. Smiling, he opened his arms to the picken.

"Don't make him fox you!" shouted someone in the crowd.

A monitor went and stood behind the mestre, her hand on the mestre's shoulder. The monitor nodded at Maitefa. The picken hesitated, then ran into the mestre's arms, where she commenced to weep full tilt.

The mestre stood, cradling her still. "Koo ya, allyou!" he shouted. He turned in a slow circle to present Maitefa to the crowd. "See this picken! See how grand she rise up, black as piche, to best me? Now, *that* is a warrior! If we go to war, make we all have her cunning and determination."

People clapped, huzzah'ed, clicked their fingers. One of the drummers riffed off a couple fancy licks. Little Maitefa's tears were replaced by a proud grin that she didn't quite manage to hide by burying her face in the mestre's shoulder. He took her over to her brother, who scowled and pulled her out of his arms. But the joy on Maitefa's face!

The drums and the berimbau started back up. Two young men moved into the roda this time to take the mestre on together.

"Lunch?" asked Samra.

"Lunch." She and Veycosi resumed on their way.

"You saw that?" Veycosi asked her. "That picken. How you think she convinced herself to go fight that big man?" How did you face something more powerful than you down when you knew you had no chance?

They walked on a bit while Samra considered. Then she said, "When my Lev ground-ties his camel, the camel is certain sure the end of the rope is knotted around a hitch. He so convinced of it that he don't stray from that spot."

My Lev again. Who was this Lev of whom she was so fond? "You think Maitefa was convinced she would win, so she won?"

She shook her head. "No. You saw how frighten she was the whole time. I think the mestre couldn't believe he would lose. She used his arrogance against him."

"And caught him off guard."

"Yes."

Veycosi snatched her up around her waist. "Like this?" he asked.

She squealed and wriggled something lovely in his arms. There was a firm bottom under her modest clothing. Her tetas were crushed against his chest. And she'd scented her hair with cinnamon.

Suddenly, she pressed her feet against his thighs and broke through the circle of his arms. She leapt to the ground and faced him. "No, more like that," she said. She clicked her fingers at him, did a ginga and a quick roundhouse. The flash of thigh she showed as her leg flew past his face made his blood rise more. She faced him in a crouch, grinning. "Tha's out of practise, my lad!" She straightened up. "Tomorrow. Meet me at that batey court mid-morning, nuh? I want to drill with the rest of them!"

"Bare-hand fighting?" Veycosi asked her. Not his type of sport, but he could manage when needed.

"Yes, man. We might end up going to war, Cosi." Her face went grim.

Ymisen could break Chynchin if they wanted. All these years, they had only left the island alone because Chynchin had convinced them it was invincible.

Veycosi sighed. "All right; tomorrow. If you promise me to make your Reverie the minute Siani Yaaya's in her new compong."

"If I can find a Sept. And if Ymisen don't overturn everything by then."

One sennight left before the cacique had to give Ymisen an answer. Veycosi felt all the bright possibilities, all the lines and trails of them, emptying away into one common cesspool: Ymisen. "Yes," Veycosi said. "If we send Ymisen away."

"Done." She playfully shoved his shoulder. "So tomorrow at the drills, I'm going to test your mettle."

"Then lunch will lend us both strength for tomorrow."

She nodded. Veycosi offered her his arm. She took it warily, but Veycosi was too sombre now to make any mischief. Holding fast to good cheer, they promenaded along.

Some had it to say that Chynchin had more luck than anywhere else, for it should have lost the skirmish that set it free. "Who is Lev?" Veycosi blurted. Shame flushed his face at the naked, unmannerly question. "Never mind."

Politely, she pretended he'd never spoken. He was grateful for her grace.

Maybe Chynchin *was* more goodlucky than anywhere else. That girl picken besting a capoeira mestre; what was more unlikely than that? Seemed Chynchin people had a way of beating the odds against them. They'd made shift to break the laws of nature once to birth Chynchin. Perhaps those laws had never mended back quite the same way again. That was what some versions of the story of the Three Witches said, any road. Suppose it were truth? Veycosi cautiously tried on a bit of hope, like putting your toes into the river water before you jumped in. "Maybe this Ymisen business will all come to naught," he said.

"Mayhap."

Unlike *her Lev's* camel, she didn't seem convinced.

There was an eating hall mostly frequented by the Colloquium, not far from his apartment. The food was good enough, but Veycosi preferred the one a little farther down, near the surgeons' lecture hall. The cook there had a firm hand with the spices. And Veycosi would be less likely to run into fellow students he knew. He led Samra to that one.

Veycosi eagerly dipped a ball of fufu into the bowl of peccary stew he and Samra were about to share, to sop up some gravy inside. Samra looked at the bowl, bowed her head, and quietly began to murmur a gratitude. So he waited for her to finish, gravy from the fufu trickling down his fingers. It smelled so good! His belly grumbled at the delay. Samra must have heard it, for a little smile passed across her face.

The outside seating for this meal hall had a shade roof. All around them were students—thankfully none he recognized—and other people, seated as Samra and he were at long, solid trencher tables with heavy benches along each side. There was an old woman two tables over, wearing a much washed and mended bubu and two-yard cloth. New ones were always there for the taking at the market, but she was clearly not one to waste the gifts of the land. She waved at him. She and Veycosi saw each other often here. He waved back. Silently, she twitched her head at Samra, giving Veycosi a knowing, gap-toothed smile. He shook his finger at her, mock-scolding, and she laughed and fed something to the parrot on her shoulder.

Samra completed the gratitude. They both said "Aché," and she picked up a wedge of flat cassava bammie to dip into the bickle. Besides the meat sauce, fufu, and bammie bread, they had a big plate of greens, and boiled yellow yam. Veycosi bit into his fufu. His mouth sprang water at the taste. Cookie had worked wonders again. As he chewed, he watched Samra's face. She was preoccupied with using her bammie to lever a morsel of meat from the bickle.

She looked up from the bowl, and her eyes caught the sun and put a little catch in his throat. A layered green-brown, those eyes. Holding the light like jewels. She tasted the food, and her eyes went wide.

Veycosi recovered himself enough to smile at her, just as a man and boy sat down at the empty spaces at their table and nodded them a greeting. The man was dressed in chantwell colours, though Veycosi didn't recognize him. Likely someone who'd graduated earlier. He nodded back at them and said to Samra, "You can tell when is Mestre Cookie who supervised the making of the meal. She fashions miracles." He helped himself to some from his own bowl.

"What she put in it?" Samra asked. Her face was still open with astonishment. She took another bite, lingered over eating it.

"My cousin from away just started to prentice in the kitchen here," said the boy. "He say he misses getting *paid*, with *coin*. Imagine!"

His father swatted him lightly on the shoulder. The boy said, "But is that he says!"

"Pickens should be seen and not heard," the man replied. "Eat your food."

The boy scowled and returned to his meal. His father said, "My sister and her boy just moved here from Pettipan Island. They still getting used to our ways."

"All are welcome," muttered Veycosi automatically. It was the motto of Chynchin, from the early days when the new settlement had needed all the willing hands it could find. The full motto was "All are welcome, an' they act justly."

Veycosi rolled another ball of fufu and ate more stew with it. He thought about trying to tell Kaïra she should be seen, not heard. Now, that would be a futile endeavour.

Samra picked up one of the tightly curled greens from their shared bowl. She crunched down on the vegetable and said, "Mama-ji! This too! Taste it, Cosi! Is cinnamon that?"

"And chives," replied the man sitting with them. He'd scarcely lifted his head from his bowl to answer. The buzz of talk from the meal hall's tables was low. Everybody with their noses in their bowls, like piglets to the trough. Cookie had outdone herself today.

Veycosi tasted one of the greens. It crunched and broke apart in his mouth, releasing the most delicious set of flavours along with the crisp freshness of the vegetable. "Cinnamon and chives, yes," he said. "And something else too besides." He took a couple more pieces. This food; he had to talk to Cookie about it. When he arrived, he hadn't spied her directing the servers inside the meal hall.

She wasn't out here, either. "Camel ears, we call these," said Samra through a mouthful of the greens.

"Mmm." *Her Lev* had a camel, she'd said. As a youngboy, Veycosi used to want a camel something bad. He imagined putting a tasselled seat over her hump, Deserter style, and him racing her in those games the Deserters sometimes held out on the scrub plains. "She swims with her forearms," Veycosi sang softly, "fleet as a male ostrich."

The man and boy looked quizzically at him. Samra only lifted a single eyebrow, eloquent as a cocked crossbow. "'The Ode of Tarafah,'" she said. "Now I see you at your craft, Maas' Veycosi."

He blushed and looked to one side. The praise-song to a camel had been one of the earliest he'd had to memorize when he began his studies at the Colloquium.

"Is not right!" came a raised voice from a nearby table. "Is Mirmeki dead those are!"

It was a broad-beamed, well-favoured Mirmeki lass, dressed for some kind of dirty work in heavy brogues, with her lower legs wrapped in strips of cloth. Her older companion also bore Mirmeki tattoos. Her features were largely Sindhu. That one muttered, "Hush your mouth, Cherleen. You know the elite don't business with what the Mirmeki want or don't want."

Samra piped up, "Excuse me, sestras, if I may. What matter you discussing?"

Cherleen replied, "The soldiers from long ago, the hardened ones that came out of the piche; you know what they did with them?"

Samra shook her head no. The older woman said, "The guard stood them in two lines flanking the avenue to the Palavera! As a jest!"

Veycosi didn't hear Samra's reply, because he'd just spotted the woman he wanted to see. She was coming out of the kitchen, into the pavilion. "Cookie!" he shouted. The youngboy at their table startled. Samra looked around to see who he was calling.

Cookie didn't react. Her old ears weren't hearing him over the low rumble of people taking their bickle.

Have to take the moment when it comes, nah true? "Soon come," Veycosi told his table fellows. He leapt up, and nearly snagged his feet in the hem of his robe. He caught the hem up in one hand and ran towards Cookie, dodging around the tables, benches, rambling toddlers, and stray dogs picking up scraps. Cookie turned just as he pounced on her and embraced her. But with care. She was getting on a bit. A strong embrace might break her. "Cookie!" Veycosi said again. He caught a flash of a laugh from the siani who'd waved at him. "But you're a genius, for true! What you seasoned the peccary stew with? Catnip? Cassareep?"

Cookie extricated her mawga twig self from his arms and looked down her nose at him with a mock glare. Damned woman was as tall as the cocoanut palms. Her skin was a deep Ilife brown. With a smile threatening to break through her glower, she said, "Well now, Maas' Veycosi. Thankee plenty for the kind words. So you liked the stew?"

"Like it? Cookie, darling, I too love it. I want to make z'anmi with it!"

Cookie chuckled, probably at the thought of him pitching woo to a peccary stew.

"And the greens!" he continued.

Cookie nodded. "Fiddleheads. Me have one cousin up in the hills. He know the cool places where they grow."

"Hmm." Veycosi bounced on the balls of his feet, impatient to know. "I tasted chives, and cinnamon. But what else?"

Cookie's eyes were twinkling. "Not catnip, Maas' Veycosi. Nor cassareep, neither. An infusion of mint and ginger with burnt sugar."

"You mean similar to a reduction of sekanjabin. Yes, that was in the stew. A novel choice. But what about in the camels' ears?"

"Camels' ears, you calling them now?" said Cookie. "Mestre is making new friends, I see." She watched at Samra, who was grasping hands with the two women to whom she'd been speaking. Then she got up from the table and started walking towards him.

"You put something more in the greens, Cookie. Something that tasted smoky, almost sulphurous."

Cookie busted out in a belly-deep laugh. "Looks like I can't fool you, Maas' Cosi!" she said, throwing a measuring glance Samra's way as she drew level with them. "All right, here's the trick of the thing; I had the bannas in the kitchen steam the greens little bit, then drain the pots and stir in coconut oil, cinnamon, chives. Little bit of salt. To finish it up, you take a stick where one end was dipped in piche—"

"Piche? For why?"

Samra's eyes lit up. "You set the piche on fire, dip it into the pot, and use it to stir the food around."

"Just so," Cookie replied.

"Piche?" Veycosi squeaked. His nose wrinkled. "We were eating piche?"

"No, maas'. Just a bit of flavouring."

"We do that!" Samra said excitedly to Cookie. "But in callaloo. I never tasted it with camels' ears before! I'm going to tell my Lev how good it tastes that way!"

Blast *her Lev*. She never mentioned a second husband, so she likely wasn't married. Though some marriages started out as two, or became that way if one of the three died, or divorced the others . . .

Veycosi said, "So this . . . this thing with the piche; it's a Deserter thing?"

Those jewel eyes could practically throw sparks. "We are Mirmeki, an't please you, Maas' Veycosi."

"Yes, I know," he replied. "But everybody calls your people 'Deserter.' No harm meant."

"And none meant by displaying the bodies of Mirmeki ancestors like a pappyshow for people to laugh after us."

"What?" Veycosi asked, confused. "I not laughing at anyone."

"Well then," Samra replied, "I suppose I'm off to Siani Yaaya's now." She nodded at Cookie. "Good day, Mestre Chef." She turned and walked away almost before she'd finished speaking.

"At the batey court tomorrow?" Veycosi called out. But it seemed she didn't hear him.

"Ah, Maas' Cosi," said Cookie, laughing, "you can't call the chicken and pelt rocks at it the same time."

"What? But I didn't mean it rudely," he said. He admired Samra's retreating figure. That high, firm rump of Samra's was pure Ilife. She was dark, as Deserters went—Mirmeki, if she was going to be so sensitive about it.

Cookie replied, "Then don't say what you don't mean. Glad you liked the food, Maas' Cosi." She went back into the kitchen.

He returned to his table. The man and boy had left. They had put their empty bowls neatly under the bench, for the stray hounds to lick.

His food had gone cold. Veycosi dabbled a lump of fufu in the gelid gravy and put it to his mouth. Even cold, the food was tasty. The taste lingered on the tongue. It made you feel like a cool day by the river, with a fishing line and a good friend. Like belly-full, but not too full.

Certainly, Samra was Mirmeki, though she, as with almost everyone in Chynchin, had a measure of admixture in her blood. She had some of the Cibonn' sturdiness about her. Veycosi's own family was

Cibonn' on his mother's and Da Woorari's sides, going back from when Chynchin was settled. The Cibonn' had lived in this region of the world for millennia before other peoples arrived. They had mastered the making of boats in which to travel amongst its many islands. But they had largely ignored barren Chynchin, save as a way stop for fresh river water when they were on a long voyage. Why bother with one so-so dry dirt island, when they had all the space and verdure they needed in other lands in the region?

That had changed when the marauding Ymisen had swept down upon them, besting one Cibonn' settlement after another, and taking the hale into slavery before moving on to faraway Ilife to do the same there. The band of escaped enslaved that had successfully settled in Chynchin had toiled for near a century to make it the paradise it was now. Would Ymisen despoil this, too?

His old friend with her parrot came and sat beside him, her back to the table. She squinted and gazed up into the sky. "You think it's near time for the cullybrees to hatch?" she asked him. Her voice was squeaky, like the sound of the mice under hiding in walls.

"Air's too dry," he replied. "You see how brown the tips of the corn leaves in the fields are?"

She nodded. "I mark it, yes. But they're late this year, man. Near a month now I been keeping the big cook pots ready to carry out in the open come hatching day."

"Time will come," Veycosi said.

"Young maas', we going to war in truth? Macu just rejected the Ymisen demands."

"In truth?" He hadn't been paying attention to the bulletins posted in the streets.

"In truth."

His spirit sank at the news.

The donkey cart jounced over a rut. A pile of empty jute bags slid over the side and plopped into the dirt. "Rest," Veycosi ordered the donkey. It came to a stop. "Simon, you all right?" he asked the youngboy sitting in the cart; another of Yaaya's helpers.

"Yes, maas'. Sorry, maas'." Simon jumped out to retrieve the empty bags, but Samra had reached before him.

"Samra," Veycosi said, "Simon could do that."

Samra scowled up at him from her stooped position. "Or me and Simon could do it together," she replied.

Saucy chit. She was calling him out of his high-status ways. And he had to confess to himself that it was true; he saw Simon as a servant. But Veycosi knew himself to be someone who saw things for what they were. Status was real in Chynchin, and some citizens had or earned more of it than others. Wasn't as though he was being rude to Simon. He had even made note of Simon's dreary version of the tale of the king who ate the hummingbird, whatever a hummingbird was. Chuh. Damned things kept showing up in the tales people told him, but there was no such bird in Chynchin. Why would a bird hum? How would it?

Veycosi bent and helped Samra and Simon gather the bags into the cart. Simon scrambled back in.

"Watch them good this time," Veycosi told him, looking away from Samra's measuring glance.

"Yes, Maas' Veycosi." Simon put a bare, dusty foot on the bags to hold them.

"Mash," Veycosi told the donkey. It started up its slow amble again. He and Samra kept pace with it.

Veycosi resumed their argument about the piche mummies Carenage Town's guards had transported on some kind of necrophiliac whim to the town centre, lining the broad avenue to the Palavera with them. There the mummies stood, glistening black statues memorializing Chynchin's victorious past. Some of the Mirmeki had gone to the site to protest, and the guards had been none too gentle in suppressing them. "I just saying the Mirmeki can't have it both ways," Veycosi told Samra. "Complaining on the one hand that Chynchin won't clasp them to her bosom, but then having this destructive riot over two-three petrified piche soldiers."

Samra kissed her teeth. "Is like you think we all move with one mind. Was only a handful of Mirmeki took courage to protest the desecration of our dead—"

"*Your* dead? So allyou from Chynchin then, or you claiming Ymisen citizenship? Because Ymisen won't have you. The Mirmeki should be grateful—"

"Let me finish, please. Only a handful of Mirmeki took to the streets with their complaint over the treatment of the piche soldiers. And if it was Ilife people protesting, or Cibonn', you would be calling it a peaceful protest, not a riot."

Veycosi chose to ignore that jibe. "You saying you don't agree with the protestors?"

"Certes I agree with them! Plenty of us do! You would like your own forebears treated with such disdain?"

Her face was red with frustration, and still beautiful. This business really had her upset. Veycosi considered her argument. He nodded slowly. "I take your point."

She only sighed. It seemed half their time together was spent arguing this kind of thing. And yet they kept seeking out each other's company.

A group of Ymisen soldiers strode by, sweating in their wool uniforms, their skins pink as boiled shrimp from the unaccustomed sun. They touched up people's wares, snatched up unfamiliar foods and bit into them, and if they didn't like the taste, dropped them wastefully right there-so on the ground. They were like babes in arms, with no care for mannerly ways. Worse, they openly wore swords belted around their waists. Weapons were for hunting game for bickle. Displaying them like that said only one thing: you were ready to hunt *people*. As far as Ymisen was concerned, all Chynchin citizens were game to them. Veycosi and Samra both looked away from the soldiers.

Midmorning, and the heat-buzz of the cicadas was beginning to compete with the humming of the cullybree birds as they flitted amongst the yellow butterpot flowers that lined the roadside. Market day. Veycosi had volunteered to help Samra to fetch provisions for Yaaya's compong's kitchen. The cart was loaded with sweet yams, ground nuts, chataigne, and skellion.

"What else we have to get?" he asked Samra.

"Mangoes," she replied shortly. "And mamapom."

Veycosi's ma and das had refused to flee to the safety of Que' micaon, an Ymisen-run island three days' sail south of Chynchin. Said they had no coin with which to start over in a country that measured status with gold. Thandy was steady fretting about whether she should close down her fishery; empty out the ponds, tell her workers to find new employment—though if it came to war, so much employ would consist of soldiering—and wait to see what this new Chynchin would be like. Suppose Ymisen forced money and usury upon them? Chynchin ways would collapse. And even should Macu want to give in, would the other Chynchin caciques agree? Two weeks ago, the biggest obstacle to the wedding of Veycosi, Thandiwe, and Gombey had been how long it would take Veycosi to return from Ifanmwe with his prized book and be uplifted to a full Fellow of the Colloquium.

More people were on the road now that they were nearing the

market; camels, donkeys, and tricycles pulling carts, some empty, some piled high with shoes, cloths, woven mats, lines of crabs tied to sticks with long green strips of cocoanut leaves. Samra lifted her skirts to step over a pile of camel dung.

There came a yell from a nearby stall. Its owner, a tall piment of a man, had let fall the fat, round watermillion he'd been about to slide into a customer's string bag. A younggirl was accompanying the customer. She made shift to wrap her arms around the fruit before it hit the ground, but she slipped in a mud slick at her feet. The watermillion flew from her hands as she went down. It made an arc in the air. Over at the next stall, a higgler woman had unrolled a bolt of indigo cloth to show it off. Her intended customer was holding the bolt end. The length of cloth was draped like a hamaca between the two. The airborne watermillion fell into the cloth. The higgler woman shouted. Startled, the other woman pulled taut the end she was holding, only an instant before a stray goat being chased by two pickens ran in panic underneath the fabric. Its head butted the watermillion, which took the air once more, to be caught by the surprised matron, who dropped her end of the higgler woman's cloth in order to do so.

The goat ran off again. It leapt onto, then over, a stall of baigan to freedom. The long purple baigan had been stacked in a pyramid, but when the goat's hooves touched the table, they slid and rolled downwards to the ground. The two pickens chasing the goat skidded to a halt, squashing some of the vegetables as they did.

The watermillion man's customer checked that the younggirl was okay. He picked her up out of the mud and helped her to brush some of the mud off. Then he strode up to the matron, thanked her, and claimed his produce. Laughing, he turned to Samra and Veycosi and called out, "Is so I know I'm back in Chynchin! Only place in the world where a watermillion could bounce."

It was Androu, the Chynchin Mirmeki man from the Ymisen delegation. The quiet one who was the real advisor. Veycosi muttered, "Ymisen dogsbody." Samra grunted an agreement.

Androu handed the watermillion to the picken with him and began helping the two other pickens to collect up the baigan and return them to the scowling youth who was minding the stall. Veycosi would have urged the donkey on, but Simon jumped down from the cart to help as well.

The matron had moved on. The higgler, tutting, rolled her bolt of indigo back up. She shook the dust out of the end of it as she did. The youth who ran the baigan stall began to harangue Simon and the two pickens for damaging his wares, but Androu took the smashed ones and added them to the basket the younggirl with him was carrying.

"Simon!" Veycosi called. "Come, nuh? We have to deliver these goods to your compong."

Simon came, but along with him came the Androu man. The younggirl struggled behind him with the weight of their basket. What, like he was too high-and-mighty to help his own servant? The man gave Samra and Veycosi a cheerful smile. "Is only three baigan the pickens-them break," he called out as he was drawing near. "I going to make a choka with them. Years since I taste baigan choka."

"Too bad for you," Veycosi muttered.

Simon was back in the cart, so Veycosi clicked his tongue for the donkey to continue, but Samra reached for its halter and stopped it. "Lass," she said to the little girl, "do thou ride in the cart as well."

The Androu man gave her a quick, measuring glance.

"I can carry it," protested the younggirl.

The man said, "She is my cousin's daughter. She willna hear of me taking the basket from her even though it be full right up."

Samra smiled, her expression thawing a little. "So I see." To the picken she said, "But even the strong must rest sometimes, nah true? Come; into the cart wi' thee. Simon, boost her up."

So Simon did, and then there was nothing for it but to have the man walk along with them. What the blast Samra had to go and do that for? Veycosi snatched the halter from her hand and got the donkey going again. The man fell in beside him. "We met before you came on the ship t'other day, yes? You were in the first meeting with Cacique Macu?" he asked.

"Yes."

"Thought that was you! Nice to see a friendly face."

Presumptuous bastard. Androu touched his forehead in greeting to Simon. "Young maas'," he said. Simon grinned at being addressed like he was of high status. Why he had to go and mock the boy like that? Then he bowed to Samra. "Good to see a beautiful face as well. I didn't mark your name from the last time we met, on the ship."

"Hight Samra," she said. "And you?" From the measuring regard she gave the man, she was having none of the flattery. Veycosi smiled a sharkish smile.

"Hight Androu Joinerson. Be you Mirmeki, then, maidell?" the man asked.

"That I am. Canst not hear it in my speech, see it plain from my marks?" She held out the backs of her hands to show him her Mirmeki tattoos.

Chuh. So many folderols and curlicues to their words, Veycosi could scarce understand them. He clucked at the donkey and pulled its halter to move it along faster.

"Seen those who take on the marks as an expression of art, not affiliation."

She nodded. "True that. Know, then: Mirmeki on my dam's side,

Mirmeki on my sire's. My family is mostly Pelest, with some Ilife blood far back in my dam's line."

Veycosi chuckled. "I know something had to explain that caboose."

Samra glared at Veycosi. "Hush, you." To the man, she said, "And you? An Ymisen man, from the look of you?" Veycosi had come to recognize that teasing tone in the handful of days he'd known Samra. She was staring pointedly at the man's scarred, uninked knuckles.

The man stopped dead in the road and clutched at his heart. "Ymisen? I? Ah, such a blow she strikes me, and we barely acquainted!"

He staggered about the road. His niece chortled. "Uncle Androu," she cried out, "you're not hurt!"

"But I am, most gravely; the maidell has dealt me a shot to the very heart!" He threw himself to the ground and stretched his measure out on his back in the market dirt. His niece and Simon laughed to see him make sport. Even Samra chuckled. A few people stepped around him, giving him curious stares. Joinerson was a fool, but for all that Veycosi found himself smiling at his antics as well. He stopped the cart and regarded this Androu. A handsome fool, though. He was dressed in a Chynchin style this day. The hem of his robe had turned up as he fell, showing off strong, muscled calves. His eyes were closed, but his lips twitched in a smile. Relaxed, his face didn't look so watchful and plotting.

Veycosi leaned forwards and held a hand out to the man. "Come then, Maas' Androu; up out of the dirt wi' ye."

Androu opened his eyes. The watchful look was back. But he took Veycosi's hand and stood. Samra helped him dust off his robe. "Ah, my friends," said Androu, "beg pardon for my tomfoolery. Being back in Chynchin air making me exuberant, is all."

"Never mind," Veycosi replied. Again the man presumed to call them friends. He was setting Veycosi's teeth on edge.

"But I mind, yes," Androu told them. "I making you uncomfortable, is clear. So I going to make it up to you. I'm about to cook a midday meal for my young companion. Would allyou visit and partake with us?"

Veycosi squatted down beside Androu, in front of the iron pan set onto hot coals in Androu's backyard, to watch him prepare the choka for their meal. Samra sat with Androu's niece, Mireille, on stools to one end of the low table, grating manioc and forming it into flat bammie breads to cook on the bure'n. Androu had offered Simon to eat with them, but the youth said he had to take the provisions back to Siani Yaaya and prepare her midday meal. So he had gone off with the donkey cart.

Androu had already cut slits in the shiny purple skins of the three baigan and inserted garlic wedges. Now he slid fragrant red slices of love apple into the baigan as well.

"Why love apple?" Veycosi asked him. "I never see anybody do that before."

"Tart to balance the must of the garlic," Androu replied. "Both have bite, but in different ways. The unctuousness of the roasted baigan will bring all the flavours together something wonderful."

Rather than stay on the ship, Androu had taken a private flat in Carenage Town for his sojourn in Chynchin. His temporary residence was surrounded by a chest-high wall of pierced brick, newly whitewashed. And it was solitary. That is, plenty of similar apartments on this street, intended for visitors to Carenage. But they were all in a line on both sides of the street, separated by walls and fences. There was no compong, no place to meet your neighbours if you wanted someone to share your chocol'ha with, or to argue with about politics. No place to show your face so your neighbours could know you.

Androu put the baigan to soak in a bowl of the same hill beer they were all drinking. Sojourner brand; highest rated in Carenage Town since two years now. He'd refused to let Simon make the journey back to Yaaya's without a watered flask of it and two fat pickled onions "to mind you along the way." So clearly he hadn't forgotten all his Chynchin manners.

Androu handed Veycosi a big scarlet love apple, along with a knife. "Here. Chop up the rest of this one for me, nuh? We going to have it fresh with the poor man poke as salad." A big bunch of aromatic poor man poke leaves was on the table, next to green lengths of shallot, white-bulbed and root-bearded at their ends, and a few tiny red-and-yellow balls of wiri-wiri peppers.

Veycosi sighed. "This is the kind of thing I usually set Kaïra to do if she seem to be lacking employment."

Samra grimaced. "So perhaps you could use the practise."

Veycosi swallowed his pique and set to chopping, wondering whether poor man poke might have any of the salutary effects of chewed nutmeg. Maybe boiled down to a decoction . . .

Androu said, "Kaïra is daughter to you both?"

Samra looked at the ground, and Veycosi could feel his face flushing. "She's the daughter of my betrothed," he replied. "She's Chynchin's next Mamacona."

Androu shook his head. "Poor wight. Her life will become nothing but blessing new compongs and opening the batey season every year, until another twinning child is born to take her place."

Veycosi grunted in agreement. "Not to mention prancing about the market, hiding people's bicycles."

Around the stem of the cheroot she was smoking to keep mosquitos at bay, little Mireille asked Samra, "Which part you live?"

Samra accepted a pull of the cheroot from the picken-girl. "My family come from Bittern Flats, close by the Lower Piche. But right now I living with Elder Yaaya, till I go back to school to finish my studies."

Veycosi said, "You don't need to resume them. You already finish. You just need to sweet-talk your way into a Sept so you can be declared a Fellow. You give up too soon." He smiled encouragingly at her, and was mystified and not a little vexed when she repaid it with a glare. Were they to have more of her sulks, then?

Androu stood sudden from the table and went over to the fire. He slapped the three baigan down on the glowing coals to char. They landed with a sizzle. "Fortunate maidell," he muttered, "to be allowed to get so far along in your schooling. I had no such fortune; so I fled and made the sea my tutor, to wash the stench of Chynchin from me. Have things changed so much here, then, that they let you into their precious Colloquium?"

Samra's bark of laughter was bitter. "Not changed enow, as I've just recounted."

Veycosi sucked his teeth. Now he had two grudgeful Deserters on his hands. Why did they hate Chynchin so? "Ymisen soap must smell sweet, then," he said to Androu, "for you to run to them."

Androu smiled thinly. "I thought it would. But when I got there, I learned that one must needs perfume oneself well when one leaves one's dwellings, to smother the stench of the city of Ringloith. Filth running in open drains in the streets. Dung, human and animal. If a horse is worked to death, it stays where it drops, and rots as it may. You can buy posies and pomanders in the streets to hold to your nose, so your retching don't add more offal to the decaying stew beneath your feet. If you have the coin, that is. Everything there is about coin. And the spring rains are the worst time. Water thaws the scat that the cold had mercifully frozen, then swells the drains until the very streets run with ordure." He smiled wryly, shook his head as he looked at the raised, bark-like scars on his knuckles. "I had my marks burned away with acid, sith in Ymisen, having them marks you as chattel. I learned to traipse about in wooden clogs a handspan high, to keep my hems out of the muck. In Ymisen, maidell, you would not even have been permitted to attend university, sith they believe women's minds too feeble." The smile went sour. "And for all that, the whole place in the wettest day of the wettest sennight of the year smell sweeter to me than the reek of pretense hanging over Chynchin, calling itself a fair nation, but obliging such as me and maidell here to bow and scrape for any least crumb of status."

Samra made an irritated noise. "Belike my untravelled ears lack understanding, but wasn't it you that in the carriage on the way here just now, telling us how the smell of Chynchin's shores did sweet you when your ship was making land?"

Androu scowled. He stared sullenly at the roasting baigan for a brief time, then squared his shoulders and looked at her. "Maidell parries well," he said. "Beg pardon. I shouldn't be treating my guests so."

Veycosi stood. "No trouble to relieve you of the task of hosting us." Samra nodded agreement and made to join him. They could find a carriage to fetch them thence.

"I want them to stay, Uncle," said the child.

Samra smiled at Mireille. "You think you can make your uncle mind his manners, then?"

Mireille nodded. "Uncle, tha' mun be nice," she instructed Androu, so gravely that Veycosi couldn't help but chuckle.

Androu joined him. "Ah, so then I shall. The picken orders it, and she is a picken knows her mind." He knelt, and she ran to him. He picked her up, cotched her on one hip. He gave her a big buss on the forehead. "Ah, my companions," he said, "you see I'm a bitter man." His voice carried the same lightness he was wont to affect, but his face remained serious.

"No cause for astonishment," replied Samra. "Th'art Mirmeki, with or without the tattoos. Were't cheery as the morning sun, I would fear for thy senses."

Oh, so they were thee-thouing now, were they? Like old friends? All slight forgiven?

Androu chuckled. "Well spoken. And I see thou understands what it is to make troublesome bargains."

"I do at that." Samra glanced at Veycosi, then sat again to table. Her face as she formed another bammie bread was expressionless. What a way she could make him feel rueful for the chance that had made him have been born into a high-status family!

Androu continued, "But I didna set out to run to Ymisen, look you. I ran to sea."

Veycosi nodded. This frustration he understood. In Chynchin, captaining ships was the domain of women and third-sexed eierí-i'naru'. Men were denied.

Androu continued, "I fancied myself on the deck of a ship, my own trading ship. Me giving the orders. So I found hire, worked some years as a cook on a pettitauger running goods between Pry-thee and these parts. Saved enough to get me a fine little bark and some commissions ferrying traders and their goods. Hired a small crew, almost all of them Chynchin people."

Startled, Veycosi asked, "You found that many who had left Chynchin for foreign soil?"

Androu and Samra exchanged an amused look.

"So how you get to be where you are now?" asked Samra. "Instead of captaining your own ship?"

"As a tattletale for Ymisen, you mean?" The trickster grin was back. "Ah, don't look 'pon me like that, maidell! Sith I mun be a rogue, I'd fain be an honest one." He turned the softening baigan with his fingers, not seeming to mind the heat of them. "Let me get the rest of our meal cooking. I will tell you both my sorry tale while we eating. Bring me the bammie there, Mireille." The child went and fetched the platter of flat, round, white cakes to him. He inspected them and smiled. "You do good, little one. They firm, but not too fat. Oh; and thee of course, too, maidell." He sketched a bow in Samra's direction. She twinkled at his wordplay. Veycosi wanted to reach over and slap him.

Androu commenced to laying the raw bammie breads on the bure'n. "Veycosi, how the greens doing?"

"So, Samra is 'maidell,' but with me you making fast to call me by my name?"

Again that grin from Androu, and again he didn't look up from his cooking. "You make me feel less shy than does she," he said. "Though you both be well pleasant to look 'pon."

Samra gave a snort of laughter. Veycosi took a swig of beer to cool the sudden flaming of his face, and set about his chopping again. Samra slid the big empty bowl on the table over to him. She began tearing the poor man poke leaves into it. Their sweet, spicy smell fragranced the air, mingling with the scent of the roasting choka. Mireille took to plaiting the long strips of manioc skin that were lying on the table. She hummed the red rubber ball song to herself. Samra sang along, the while sharing the task of assembling the greens with Veycosi, and Androu switched kept turning the bammies and the baigan for the choka with the efficient grace of one used to the kitchen. The cullybrees wheeled far overhead and the cicadas screeched their greeting to the late afternoon sun. The beer was good.

Androu said, "What is this Sept you'uns just mentioned? What is standing in the way of maidell's ascension in the ranks of the Colloquium? I'm unfamiliar with Colloquium ways."

Samra and Veycosi described the dreaming ritual to him, and the bouffe that prompted the dream.

"And simple nutmeg is a key ingredient?" Androu laughed. "Such a waste. I'd rather use the stuff as a carminative to ease my belly, or sprinkle it to flavour an egg cream."

Samra nodded. "Many do use it the usual way, in Chynchin and abroad. It is our second biggest export, next to processed piche."

Androu commenced to stripping the skins off the grilled baigan. "The things I'm learning about the place of my birth."

"Androu," said Samra, "who your people are?"

"Joinersons from over by False Brook. And your'n?"

"Cintiabre. Descended from Josephine."

"Josephine the Mirmeki soldier? The first one the Ilife and Cibonn' runaways took in?"

"She same one."

Was a jolt to Veycosi to hear his ancestors called "runaways." That was the kind of talk Deserters probably used among themselves, but you didn't say that word aloud in the hearing of anyone with Cibonn', Ilife, or Garfun blood lest you were spoiling for a fight. Veycosi sniffed. He was descended from freedom fighters, not runaways.

Androu began pulping the baigan flesh with a new mash stick that had come out of his bag of market procurances. "I come to find out a strange thing in my sojourn in Ymisen."

"Ah-hah?" said Samra.

"Ymisen," Androu said, "don't have any female soldiers."

"Why?" asked Samra. "What they did with them?"

"They never had any."

"But that can't be right," Samra replied.

"Chuh," Veycosi said. "Like they can't even get their own records straight?"

"More than that," Androu continued, "the Ymisen military don't use camels; never did."

Veycosi remembered the mannerless Ymisen sailor who'd visited the fish hatcheries in the market that first day. He hadn't self known what a camel was called.

Androu told them, "The poor sods languishing in the ship over by Pettipan Island wouldn't know the arse end of a camel from the front of it."

"Not so easy to tell the difference sometimes," said Samra. "Both ends spit."

Mireille giggled at that. "Samra's funny," she said. "I like her."

"I see th'art a picken with discernment," replied Androu.

"But it didn't go so," Veycosi informed him.

Androu raised an eyebrow. "How not?"

"We know there were women soldiers. Josephine—"

"I know a story," said Mireille. "Perhaps Josephine was no soldier, but a doxy brought there to entertain the men."

"That can't be right!" The argument swirled amongst the three, each talking over the others.

"The Tale of the Three Witches is clearly not true history, so it must be a simple folk story."

"I know a story, I said."

"The Chynchin histories say—"

"And the victor's histories always speak true, I suppose."

"I know a story!"

Samra stroked Mireille's pale hair. "Lass, tell us thy story."

The child puffed herself up proud and said, "I fly and fly but am never free. What am I?"

In a kindly tone, Veycosi told her, "That not a story, Mireille. Is a riddle."

Mireille pouted. "What am I?" she insisted.

Everybody knew that one. Veycosi sighed and answered, "The wind," same time Androu replied, "A cullybree."

Mireille smiled and pointed at Androu. "Uncle has the right of it!"

Veycosi said, "But when I learned it as a picken, the answer was 'the wind.'"

Androu said, "Mirmeki tell it differently."

Samra said, "Write it down, Cosi."

"Why? Is not a story."

The picken piped up, "A riddle is a story with an answer."

Androu burst out laughing. "Th'art a man of wit, Cosi, but few can best my niece for chopping logic."

How dare the man make so familiar with his name? His blasted niece smiled a fulsome smile, well satisfied with herself.

And after all, it was a fair point. Veycosi got out his table-book and scribbled down the riddle, "As Told by Young Mireille, a Wise Maidell of the Chynchin Mirmeki." "Which answer to put in?" he asked them all.

Samra replied, "Both of them, of course."

"You realise this have nothing to do with the story of making Chynchin. And the cullybree answer don't make sense. How is a cullybree unfree?"

Androu's devilish blue eyes glittered. "Who can say? Write it down anyway." He finished stirring the spices into the paste of the baigan choka and put the bowl on the table with a plate of bammie, now cooked so that the outsides were crunchy and the insides chewy and absorbent. "The greens ready? Then come, allyou. Eat."

He regarded the table. "Wait one little minute. We need more beer. Mireille, come and help me bring out the beer, sweet."

He tore off a piece of bammie and scooped up a decent serving of choka with it. "For the littles," he said.

"You're a man of superstition, then?" Veycosi asked him.

"Perhaps I am indeed superstitious," Androu replied. "Or maybe I just have respect."

Bastard. Before Veycosi could fix his mind on a retort, Androu had taken the offering and the flagon over to the stoop outside his room. He put the bickle on a small plate there and poured the dregs of the beer into a cup that stood beside the plate. "Soon come," he called. He and Mireille disappeared inside.

Veycosi kissed his teeth and reached for a piece of bammie. Samra stopped his hand. "When he come back, all right?"

"All right." Chastened for his lack of manners, he pulled his hands into his lap. They waited. Cicadas screeched in the heat, and nearby was the sound of a carriage in a hurry, the horses' hooves clopping quick time, the jangling of their reins, the grinding of the wheels on gravel. Flies began to express their interest in the food. Veycosi waved some away. "Bammie going to get cold," he grumbled. "Like he fall into the privy, or what?"

"Privy over there-so," said Samra. "In among the banana trees. I didn't see him come out and go that way."

Veycosi frowned. "Me neither." He stood and went over to the back window. He tried to peer in, but the jalousies were near-closed, and their angle only showed the ceiling inside. "Can't see nothing," he said.

"Good thing, too," replied Samra. "You shouldn't be fasting up yourself to spy inside the man's house."

So she thee-thoued Androu, but for some reason, Veycosi was once more the formal "you"?

"Inside!" Veycosi called out. No answer. Samra joined him. They both shouted for Androu and Mireille, then Samra banged on the door. Still no answer.

"We have to go in," she said.

"You stay out here. In case he come back." He pushed the door open. "Androu? Mireille?"

Nothing. He opened the door wide and went inside. He found himself in a small, neat sleeping room.

The other room was probably the pantry. Is there Androu would have gone to fetch the beer. "Androu?" Veycosi called. He pushed through the curtain of clay beads in the doorway, and nearly tripped over the pieces of the broken flagon. The front door was flung open. "Androu!" Veycosi ran to the door and looked out. Long wheel scores in the gravelled front path leading to the road, and horses' hoofprints.

"Samra!" Veycosi bellowed. "Come, quick! Androu and Mireille gone!"

"Cosi?" came Samra's voice on a sudden, startlingly close to him. "Look at this!" She had found a note on the writing table, written in a neat hand:

My friends,

Thank you for gifting me with another nail in Chynchin's coffin. And such a flavourful one, at that! I'm off to tell my masters. Maas' Veycosi, do hasten to take the heir on ir tour of the Colloquium. I feel sure that will make ir soften to Chynchin.

My regrets for this, but at least I betray you openly. Honesty is really the only coin I have to spend.

—A

Veycosi kissed his teeth. "What the bastard mean, a 'flavourful' nail?"

Samra shook her head. "I can't tell."

But by the following day, they knew. Ymisen let fly its next volley in the negotiations. It claimed the right to all the nutmeg groves in the island—sith, said Gunderson, they were "Ymisen's, descended from seed our slaves from these islands stole from us when they escaped two hundred years ago."

"In other words," said Yaaya from the hamaca on her porch as she watched Veycosi and Samra replant her garden with hibiscus cuttings, "you gave our would-be besieger ammunition to use against us. What the rassa would make the two of you break bread with that man?"

Veycosi blurted, "We were gathering useful information about Ymisen!"

"Is so it go?" Yaaya replied. "So tell me then, nuh: What you learn that could help Chynchin?" She took a long pull from her pipe as she awaited their response.

And really; what had they discovered, anything at all? That the streets of Ymisen's cities were foul? That Ymisen had disremembered the existence of its female soldiers of two centaines previous? Veycosi risked a glance at Samra. She looked as shamefaced as he felt. Yaaya cut her eyes at them. "Nothing? I thought as much."

Veycosi grasped at the one thing that might redeem them both a little. No need to mention that Androu Joinerson had advised them to get about it quickly: "The Colloquium. Heir Tierce wishes to be shown its secrets. Ee may look more favourably upon us if we do this."

"Yes," said Samra eagerly. "We already asked permission of Mestre Steli, but it turns out his fellows are none too keen at the idea." The Colloquium's reticence had been quite the blow to Veycosi's plans.

Yaaya raised a brow. With her cane, she motioned at Veycosi and Samra to come onto the porch. "Tell me more about this," she said.

Couple days later, Gombey had Veycosi summoned to his office. "Banna," his friend said, "things grim. So Yaaya spoke to the council and to the Colloquium. You have been empowered to take Royal Heir Apparent Tierce to visit the Colloquium of Fellows of Chynchin."

Veycosi felt as though he could breathe freer than he had in the past two days. Ymisen soldiers had laid claim to a warehouse on the docks that was full of nutmeg packed into jute sacks and waiting to be shipped a-foreign. While the harbourmistress betook herself to the Palavera to protest to the council, Ymisen soldiers carted sack after sack on their backs into the hold of the trade ship. Things had nearly come to blows right there and then.

Gombey said, "Ee can see the archive, and ee can be present at this sennight's upcoming book consecration."

"That is well. Thank you." Veycosi would call on the Ymisen ship this very day, to make plans with the heir.

"And you are to be under the watch during the whole visit of a guard detail of five, plus Chantwell Mestre Steli."

"Why he?"

Gombey pursed his lips. "To prevent you from doing or saying anything to worsen the situation."

Veycosi fumed, but had to admit to himself that he'd done nothing yet to help Chynchin send Ymisen packing.

"One more thing, banna."

"Yes?"

"Is about that woman, Samra. You really think now is the best time to be taking a lover?"

"She's not. Too besides, we three not wedded yet." Chynchin placed no social constraints on dalliances undertaken before marriage.

"Yes, you right, but—"

"This is no different than Thandy and that zemi carver she spends time with, or you and that councilwoman."

"I know," Gombey said. "Is not that I'm talking about."

"Then what?"

"Cosi, we are at war!"

Veycosi startled. "How you mean? Nobody attack us yet."

Gombey sighed. "Brother, I love you for your innocence. But sometimes you could stand to bethink yourself more. This is at the very least a trade war, make no mistake. Those begin well before any blows get struck. Sanctions here, stockpiling there."

"I not wooing Samra," Veycosi said. He wasn't, though his blush betrayed his true desires. "She helping Yaaya and me to learn more about Ymisen."

Gombey stared searchingly at him. Then he shook his head. "Is just advice I'm giving you, banna. You will do what seems best to you."

Oh, but he was irking Veycosi now! "So I will," he snapped. "Give you good walk, Gombey. I have to be about the council's business." He turned on his heel and stalked out of the building. He was still fuming as he hailed a carriage to take him to the docks. If he were honest with himself, he well knew the flavour of that pique; is just so he used to stomp and surl as a picken when an adult caught him making mischief.

Veycosi had been on edge since they'd collected Tierce from the Ymisen ship to take ir to the Colloquium. In all, their party comprised five guards of the Carenage Town constabulary; four uniformed Ymisen soldiers, weapons ostentatiously on display; Veycosi, Mestre Steli, Androu; and at the centre of it all, the focus of everyone's attention, the royal heir to all of Ymisen. Ir beaten felt sandals were dyed a deep carmine and embroidered with gold thread in an ornate pattern of some kind of leaf. The chains that attached at the ankles to hold the sandals' curled, pointed toes upright looked to be pure gold. Red pantalons billowed above the sandals, caught up about the waist with a gold cummerbund. A simple white linen tunic provided relief to the eyes.

All the way to the Colloquium, the heir fairly jittered with excitement. Ee peppered Veycosi and Steli with all manner of questions about the archives: how many volumes had they; what systems of classification they used; how were the books preserved; were there translators assigned to the material. Androu translated back and forth, but to Veycosi's surprise, the heir said not a few phrases in a creditable attempt at Chynchin speech. The wretch knew how to ingratiate irself, that much was true.

There was so much riding on this. Veycosi craved a cooler head with which to manage the next few hours, and he knew how to obtain it. First chance he got.

The carriages and horses pulled up to the entrance to the Colloquium's archive. It was a solid, blocky building. Dark inside. Stultifyingly quiet. One might think the rescued wisdom of antiquity would be exciting, but it was rarely so. Ancient account books detailing every measure of hops delivered annually to some pitiable long-gone brewery in a faraway land. So many records of births and deaths in small villages forgotten to time. Veycosi had spent many hours in there, reassembling half-burned, mildewed, or torn pages onto clean pieces of paper with tweezers and paste, trying not to fall asleep with his nose in the paste pot. He missed it terribly.

The establishment had been closed to other visitors while the heir was on the premises. As ee stepped out of the carriage and clapped ir eyes on the archive building for the first time, Tierce's face fell. In the Chynchin way, ee said, "Is so small."

Veycosi replied, gently, "Books don't make library." Tierce looked confused, and with good reason; that hadn't exactly been a reply. But at the boulay ceremony later, the heir would come to understand the meaning behind Veycosi's words.

The Carenage guards stationed themselves outside the entrance. The rest of the party made their way in, flanked by the Ymisen soldiers.

Mestre Steli bowed to Tierce. "Ser," he said, "permit me the honour of showing you around Carenage Town's pride and joy." Steli's expression made it clear he didn't feel honoured in the slightest, but if ee noticed, Tierce was either too eager or too polite to pay it mind. Ee signalled to Steli that he should proceed. Steli inclined his head grimly in acquiescence, and off they went.

Books and books and fragments of books. Vellum. Parchment. Ink, some of it runny and faded. Tierce's eyes glowed. Ee touched the volumes gently, with reverence.

Steli led them pointedly past an empty place on one of the shelves, a space Mauretaine's book would no longer fill. Veycosi's heart stuttered at the loss of it, and the enormity of what he had done. Steli was generous enough or perhaps politic enough not to point out Veycosi's folly to the Ymisen heir. Veycosi stopped for a few seconds to touch the wood of the shelf where the book had been. He was still dashing water from his eyes when he returned to the group. Steli was droning on to a rapt Tierce about the Colloquium's acquisition a few years ago of a scrap of a scribbled note which appeared to be a shopping list for most of the ingredients of mafeisan, an ancient soporific formulation once of great value to surgeons.

The tour went on until the Colloquium's bells had marked two hours gone by. Then there was nothing for it but to stand politely by while Tierce solemnly presented to Steli the book ee had brought all this way. It appeared to be a very old child's exercise book, with letters and quotes from what were probably Crucian scriptures. In some places, a child had copied the text with a wavering hand. Veycosi's fingers itched to lay hands on it so he could study the words and images. Steli accepted the book with thanks and placed it on a shelf near the front desk to be processed. Then he indicated that it was time to move on to the next programme of the evening.

When the party exited the building—an excited Tierce still jabbering on about the books in ir Ymisen tongue, and about the book ee had brought to give to the Colloquium—a small crowd was gathered outside to see the personage who was bidding fair to reinvade Chynchin.

The eyes of the man sitting in the booth at the entrance to the main performance hall of the Colloquium of Fellows were big as he took in their party. He was doing his best not to act overawed at all this pomp and splendour, but his eyes gave the lie to his nonchalance. He couldn't stop staring at the heir. "You and your friends attending the boulay, Mestre Steli?" he squeaked. But of course he knew who they were, and why they were there.

Steli pursed his lips disapprovingly and quirked his head in Veycosi's direction. "This is Maas' Veycosi's undertaking. He will tell you the details."

Tierce frowned as ee looked from Steli to the attendant, trying to follow what they were talking about. "Boulay?" ee said. "That is the name of the ceremony, yes?"

Androu replied, "Yes, Excellency. When a team of griots have committed another ancient book to song, they celebrate each time."

"One realises this. One simply never dared hope to be fortunate enough to witness it. Which book?"

The attendant checked his records. "*On Sphere-Making.*"

Tierce gaped. "Great god. Where did you find it?"

Veycosi smirked. "We never say."

The longing on Tierce's face would have melted a rockstone's heart. "Will . . . will they read from it? At this boulay?"

Veycosi shook his head. "No, friend. Better than that. They will chant it."

"I will see this. Please. Yes." Tierce pulled a startled Veycosi into ir long arms and bussed him soundly on each cheek. "Thank you. Thank you. I have longed for this." The Ymisen heir was wearing a smile broader than the oceans.

Veycosi pulled out of the embrace and airily said, "Let's just hope is entertaining this time. I near perished from boredom when Olifa's lineage of singers chanted the *Journal of Axel the Bold.* Plainsong for a diary. So unremarkable a choice."

Grey Androu smiled, an uncomfortable look on that dour face. "I was here as a youngboy," he said absently, "when the same lineage sang the Gospel of Eve."

Veycosi said, "I read that one. Would like to have any chantwell sing it to me around my hamaca every night before I fall asleep."

That caught Androu's attention. He looked almost merry as he said, "You scoundrel! That book was perverse. Swallowing semen as an act of worship?"

Mock-solemn, hands in prayer, Veycosi replied, "I feel worshipful every time I do it." Let Yaaya play the simpleton with this lot. He would play the bawd.

"Ah," said Androu teasingly, though his gaze shifted from side to side, peering into the shadows, "I do comprehend."

Veycosi couldn't help it; he busted out in a belly laugh. He reminded himself that he couldn't trust Androu and Tierce, likeable as they were.

Steli looked shocked. "Maas' Veycosi," he muttered, pitching his voice so only Veycosi would catch his words. "Not in front of the heir."

Veycosi bowed his head in mock acquiescence. He made his visage stern again and checked his timepiece. "Come. Ceremony starting soon."

He led his enemies in through the gates of the Colloquium, down Fellows' Walk, lined with glossy-leaved ackee trees. They were in season; the branches laboured under the weight of numerous ackee fruit, their pinkish-red pods open to reveal their pale yellow triple lobes, each with a shiny black seed at its tip. Chynchin had it to say that the triple lobes of an ackee were a reminder of the Act of the Three Witches that had freed the country. Cookie would soon be serving ackee and salt cod at meals, its scrambled egg texture the perfect creamy carrier for fragrant flakes of dried fish, pungent garlic, aromatic chardon beni, the spicy snap of ginger, and the bright red bite of snips of hot pepper. And of course nutmeg; the ever-present nutmeg.

As their little procession went along, they passed others of the Colloquium: Mestre Adafis, leading a class in throat-singing beneath the shade of a poui tree; divers students scurrying to and from classes; Mestre Penelo, striding absent-mindedly to somewhere or other with her mind in the clouds and the hem of her ink-stained robe trailing in the dust. When Veycosi came upon other postulants of his line, he shamefacedly avoided their gaze, pretended not to hear their curiosity-laden greetings. He didn't know who he was if he could no longer be one of their number.

They came to the fountain. The stone effigy of Mamagua in the middle was once more letting water fall from her caiman jaws to lave her breasts and belly. Not that anyone would thank him for wetting Mamagua's dry throat by getting the water flowing again. Veycosi swallowed down his bitterness. He bent to the fountain's pool and flicked some of its blessed waters across his neck and breast. Androu, after a moment's hesitation, did the same. Tierce asked, "What are you doing?"

Veycosi explained, "Begging a little blessing from Mamagua. Leastways, I was. Not sure what Androu was doing."

Androu looked bashful but said nothing.

Steli excused himself. He was a key part of the boulay. He had to go and prepare.

All along the route, glances of fear, of anger, of interest told Veycosi that people marked who he had with him.

This game of wearing two faces, Mamacona-like, was tiring. He needed to be more composed if he were going to keep playing it.

He approached the Chynchin guards flanking them, and told them he had to answer a call of nature. He told Tierce he would be back in mere instants. Then he dashed to his quarters. He had just enough time to grab his Reverie cache, first tucking a wafer of it into his cheek. It was supposed to be only for inducing trances in postulants during their Reverie ceremonies, but any Colloquium student knew how to obtain small amounts of it.

He sucked on the bitter, blessed lozenge as he hurried to rejoin his charge.

The audience sat respectfully around the stage in the vaulted shell shape of the Abeng, the Colloquium's performance hall. The music from the choir echoed from the high ceiling to every part of the Abeng. No matter where you were in the hall, you would hear the least whisper coming from the stage. Veycosi's head was spinning pleasantly with the onrush of Reverie. Kaïra was in the audience with some of her bannas. She spied Veycosi, waved, and smiled at him. He waved back, grateful the picken had recovered her light heart after he'd been so snappish with her. She lifted one foot to show him; she was wearing Gombey's old alpagats! She loved those sandals, even though they were too big for her. Plus, wearing them to a performance would count as a Mamapiche jape. Clever picken. He would go visit her tomorrow evening with some gulab jamun. It was a favourite of hers. Maybe he would go walking with her by the river. They could play at searching for Mamagua in the water.

Kaïra's friends were pestering nearby mestres of the Colloquium with questions. But Kaïra's eyes were all for the figure standing on the stage, in the shadows behind the choir. The apparition's head was hidden inside a lightweight balsa-and-paper caiman mask. Her garments were Mamagua blue, to match the navy tanned caiman tail belted around her waist. She was holding a blue straw fan. This was Li Jing, the outgoing Mamacona, dedicated to Mamagua due to the luck of her birth. She had some thirty years, Veycosi recalled. After twenty-odd years representing the goddess, she was probably more than ready to have Kaïra replace her.

Kaïra waggled her fingers at Li Jing, who gave a small wave back. She had been responsible for Kaïra's Mamacona lessons since the picken was big enough to start them.

Steli was sitting in state in a deeply carved armchair at the edge of the stage, beside the matching one in which the Colloquium's chancellor was already sitting. Steli was keeping watchful, disapproving eyes on Veycosi and his companions, the interlopers in their midst. Chuh. Steli had to realise Veycosi was just playing the part their cacique had ordered him to play.

What was the blasted book name that they were honouring, again? *The Book of Circles, The Roundabout,* something so? Oh: *On Sphere-Making,* by some long-ago mathematician.

The chancellor nodded, and the music began. The praise-singers assigned to it had made it a pretty little ditty with an audacious minor A contrapuntal. The kora player plucked out precise notes in a spiralling procession, underpinned by the soft ringing tones of the balafon. As the choir chanted, two of their number traced out the diagrams in chalk on large blackboards up on the dais. Li Jing wove gracefully around the stage, mimicking Mamagua's waters, the life that buoyed up Chynchin. When it was Kaïra's turn to attend ceremonies such as this one, she would need to play this game in Mamapiche's tricksy ways; cutting a rug, bobbing about the stage, and trying to distract the performers. Doing at all times her best to demonstrate a prankster nature that didn't come naturally to her.

Listening to the book, Tierce was near beside irself. Couple-three times, ee leaned over to ask Veycosi what a word meant, only to realise that while ee was doing that, ee'd missed the next few lines. Ir dismay was most amusing to watch.

Chanting the while, one of the chantwells stepped forwards. She reverently placed *On Sphere-Making* on the three-cornered stack of bound snake canes in the small stone pit at centre stage. Tierce sighed. "Such a beautiful ritual," ee said.

The chanting swelled. The chantwell woman bowed to the chancellor of the Colloquium, who gave an impatient nod back. Poor man; he had to attend each and every single one of these boulays. The woman pulled a tinderbox from her sleeve and struck it.

As she bent to touch flame to the bottommost layer of wood shavings beneath the snake canes, Tierce gasped.

The fire caught right away, sending curious fingers of flame stretching out to caress the book. The singing swelled to match the growing flames.

Tierce cried out, "No!" Ir voice was drowned out by the triumphant, blossoming music of the final movement. Only those close to Tierce heard ir. Before Veycosi could stop ir, ee began elbowing ir way through the crowd, ir guards crashing after. Affronted people made small indignant exclamations. The fire clasped eager hands around the book. Those too far away to realise the commotion said as one the final benediction for a book made permanent: "Committed to memory, rendered to ash." Tierce had pushed irself to the front of the crowd. The woman chantwell noticed ir, turned in ir direction, but ee was moving at speed; ee launched irself into the air, avid hands stretched out towards the fire.

Tierce landed with a crash on top of the burning book and withies. The music came to an uncertain halt, choir and musicians too taken aback to know what to do next.

Tierce pulled the book from the flame and slapped out the flames with the hem of ir heavy stole. "Are you barbarians?!" ee screamed at those gathered. Some of the choir made to rush Tierce. They couldn't attack the heir! That would be war for certain!

But Steli shouted for calm in his bright, brassy tenor. His voice rang out, and everyone held their ground, heeding a chantwell's commands, as they were used to doing.

Tierce stood, the book pressed to ir bosom. Its charred corners smeared a streak of black on ir stole and tunic. Ir hands were blackened with it. The guards circled ir protectively, facing the gathering and the choir, bayonets at the ready to defend the heir.

"Savages!" Tierce shouted. "What are you doing? I'm never

giving this precious volume up to you. I will burn this island to the ground before I do!" Ee blew a lock of that lanky pale hair out of ir face and glared defiantly at the chancellor. Kaïra, open-mouthed, kept looking from Tierce to Veycosi and back again. The outgoing Mamacona had situated herself sensibly as close to Steli as she could. The audience was frozen. Had they just heard a declaration of war?

The chancellor's brows knitted. "What is the matter, Ser Tierce? Like oonuh just looking for any reason to make war on us."

"Oonuh?" replied Tierce, confused.

Veycosi felt his plans driving to calamity, even worse this time. Quickly, he said, "You. 'Oonuh' means you, plural. All of you Ymisen who land up on Chynchin soil to threaten us. Please, ser. The book is not harmed."

Androu had found his way out of the crowd. He held his hand out to Tierce. "Ser, come down from there. This not necessary—I mean, isn't necessary."

Tierce pressed ir lips together and shook ir head.

The chancellor waved a dismissive hand. "Look, you want the book?" he asked Tierce.

Tierce looked confused. "I may have it?"

The chancellor nodded. "Surely, if you want it so bad that you invade us just to have your way. We don't need it anymore."

"Don't need it?"

"Maas' Veycosi," said the chancellor, "like your charge don't have all ir senses, or what? All ee doing is repeating what I say, like ee is part parrot." He chuckled at his own joke.

"Yes, mestre. We going, mestre."

At an urgent whisper from Androu, Tierce signalled ir guards to stand down. With Steli and the chancellor glaring at them, the party moved towards the exit.

"And Veycosi?" called the chancellor.

"Yes, mestre?"

"That person can't come back inside here."

"Mestre, we can't prevent ir. Ee asked nicely this time. Ee might not again."

Tierce nodded, ir eyes narrowed. Voice raised to carry, ee announced, "I' faith, we will not. We are of royal blood, and you are all the descendants of runaways. This nation, this island exists because *we* suffer it to. An' it please us, we will make it Ymisen's."

The chancellor scowled. "Beg pardon, Royal, but you must know that Ymisen people are forbidden to enter the Colloquium. We showing you a courtesy by letting you in."

Tierce's nostrils flared. Haughtily, and in mostly accurate Chynchin speech, ee said, "Is not like no one from Ymisen has set foot in Chynchin before this. There have been many Ymisen spies already in Chynchin, even in this great Colloquium, claiming nationality from Sverige, from Holtland; from anywhere but Ymisen." While the chancellor's mouth was still working as he tried to figure out how to respond, Tierce continued, "But we see that we have somehow given offense, so we will take our leave to place this precious tome safely somewhere away from Chynchin's depredations. We give you good walk."

With Androu beside them and the pickens flitting like nectar-stunned butterflies around them, Veycosi led a huffy Tierce and ir guards away. The titters of the audience provided accompaniment. Tierce was staring down at the book in ir hand like ee'd never seen a book before. "They don't need it," ee said wonderingly.

Veycosi said, "We don't. Books get stolen. Get lost. Get burned. When Ymisen came to the lands of Ilife forebears to wage war 'pon them and take them into slavery, they first burned the books. So much knowledge lost! But the song of this book going to live down the generations of the chantwell line that have it memorized. Each person in the line have a different piece of it; melody, harmony, diagrams. Each will pass it down to their generations. It will last forever."

Tierce eyed Veycosi doubtfully. "People die," ee said. "Families . . . get killed. Or locked away. Sometimes people don't want to take up the family mantle."

"Yes, people die. So each part of a book is memorized by five people in a chantwell line."

Tierce looked no more comforted. Veycosi found himself wanting to reassure ir. He would have to watch that impulse. Tierce had just demonstrated publicly that ee was no friend to Chynchin. Still, the best way to manage someone was to open your heart to them, even a little bit. "I going tell you a secret," he said. "The Colloquium make five copies of each book for the archives. What you holding is one of the copies, not the original."

Androu shrugged. He didn't look surprised. It was an open secret in Chynchin. Down the tunnel of mild vertigo created by the Reverie taking effect, Veycosi chided Androu, "You might have informed your charge that ee was about to witness a mummery. Is clear you knew that."

"So might you," retorted Androu. "Or your master."

As to Tierce, ee blinked stupidly at Veycosi, like ee hadn't taken in what he'd said. Veycosi continued, "Making the copies takes a rassclaat long time, too. Five chantwells doing the copying, supervised by a mestre skilled in the Matter of the Book . . . hmm." Time to play the bawd again, lighten the mood. Twinkling at Androu, Veycosi said, "I wonder who the mestre was for the Book of Eve? That book had some styles of swiving in it that I had never heard tell of, and believe me true, I know plenty of them."

Androu paid him no mind, leaving Veycosi feeling foolish. Tierce was still regarding the book in ir hands like it was a baby ee'd saved from the flames. "This is a complete copy of *On Sphere-Making*? And the original is unharmed?"

Veycosi nodded. "Safe in the archives."

Tierce suddenly crushed Veycosi in an embrace, accompanied by a hearty buss on the cheek. Veycosi pried himself free, brushing away the burned bits of book that Tierce had smeared on him. What a way Tierce was quick to clasp people to ir bosom! Ee was stronger than ee looked, too. Veycosi said, "Just promise me you won't let this secret escape, or it going to ruin me completely."

"We swear to you on Our word as the eldest offspring of a king," ee replied, grinning broadly. "We are so happy to hear this."

Veycosi didn't bother to tell ir that only one of the copies was in the library of the Colloquium. The Colloquium had learned its lessons from book burnings the world over. The remaining copies were scattered to the four winds. The record of where they had been sent was rendered in some kind of cypher that few knew how to translate. Ymisen could burn Chynchin down to the ground, but the library would be safe, if distributed and secret.

"Come," he said to Tierce and Androu. "Plenty more sport to be had in Chynchin."

"Ser," said Androu, "an't please you, we should get back to the ship. You have business you must see to."

"In time," Tierce replied, waving Androu away. "Do thou return thence, though. Take the soldiers with you, and the local guards. Our friend will get us back to the ship."

Androu regarded Veycosi with suspicion. "He is only one man, ser. He cannot guarantee your safety."

With all hauteur, Tierce responded, "Nevertheless, it is what we wish."

"I will escort the heir back myself," Veycosi said. "If needed, I can commandeer some more of our own guards for protection."

So there was nothing for Androu to do but reluctantly leave with the Ymisen soldiers. To their departing backs, Veycosi cheekily called out, "Give you good walk!"

Once they were out of sight, Veycosi said to Kaïra and her friends, "Look smart, now. We need your help!"

The pickens jigged about in excitement as Veycosi explained to Tierce what he wanted to do. The heir thought that would be a fine ploy indeed. So Veycosi told the pickens, "We need to disguise the heir so ee could walk about freely tonight without being so conspicuous. Wu, that long vest you wearing should fit Ir Highness. Please to lend it to ir for the night. Gilead, it look like you and Ir Highness wear about the same size shoes. I think you might like to trade for one evening, yes? See how pretty ser's fancy shoes are!"

Wu and Gilead were eager to help. The change was accomplished with much tittering, while Kaïra reminded them to keep their voices low. Tierce now looked more or less like a Carenage citizen, if one didn't examine too closely. Ee gave Veycosi a conspiratorial grin. "One seldom gets to do as one wishes with one's time. Where shall we go first?"

For days, Veycosi had been asking himself this very thing. He had a plan. "Ser, your soldiers are bidding fair to take our nutmeg from us. If you do this, you will strike at the living heart of the Colloquium. You would destroy it as a place to preserve knowledge."

Tierce's face fell. "We would?"

"Is that what you desire, ser?" Despite the calming drug, Veycosi broke into a cold sweat. Was he about to put the Colloquium itself at risk?

Earnestly, Tierce replied, "Of course we don't! We want to study there, not harm it!"

"Well." Veycosi might triumph for Chynchin yet, and spare his nation any bloodshed. He smiled at Tierce. "Then come with me, ser, and I will show you how Colloquium scholars choose their specialties."

"Are we to go back to the Colloquium, then?"

"No, ser." In fact, they would need to be as far from scrutiny as possible.

"Cosi," said Kaïra, "we coming with oonuh, yes. Since we helped?"

This hadn't been part of his plan, but he was feeling expansive. Elated to be in his future daughter's good graces again, Veycosi put an arm around her shoulders. "Of course you may, picken! You all may!" Having them there would probably even help Tierce stand out less.

The effect of the wafer he'd swallowed was already fading. As Veycosi led the jolly party away, his mouth was nearly watering as he thought on the pungent distillate of nutmeg that was Reverie he had stashed in his pocket. There was plenty more than enough there for himself and Tierce.

MORE ON THE MIRMEKI WOMAN JOSEPHINE, MOTHER TO CHYNCHIN'S FIRST MAMACONA

FROM A TALE RECOUNTED TO COLLOQUIUM
POSTULANT VEYCOSI BY POSTULANT SAMRA,
TO WHOM JOSEPHINE WAS ANCESTOR

When Josephine's belly began to swell, Kima was above all glad. Maybe with a child, Josie wouldn't want to leave.

"Thee doesn't mind?" asked Mother Letty one day as they were toiling beside one another with their machetes, part of the group chopping cocoanuts in half. They would prise out the meat and set it to dry for oil.

"Mind what?" asked Kima. She straightened up from the rows of open cocoanuts laid out on coir mats, and wiped her brow with her bandana. She glanced over to where Josephine, her plumpening belly barely showing through the folds of her robe, was catching the cocoanuts that Goat threw down from the top of one of the cocoanut palms. Sweaty as she was, Josephine's mexite skin shone like burnished brass.

"Mind that Josephine making a baby with somebody else." Mother Letty slung two cocoanut halves onto the pile from which the pickens were taking them to arrange them on the coir mats. "Mind that she ain't even self tell you. You had to find out from the evidence of your eyes."

This again. "She didn't know," replied Kima. She bent for a co- coanut, sliced only the top off with her machete. She put her lips to it and gulped down the refreshing cocoanut water. Waited for the usual words, the ones she'd exchanged with far too many people since it became obvious that Josephine was making baby.

"How you mean, she didn't know?" said Letty. "A woman swives a man, she's like to get a belly, unless she use chenette."

Kima sighed, chopped the cocoanut near in two, and tossed it on the pile. "A-true. But she ain't been with no man since she come to us. To me."

Mother Letty dispatched three cocoanuts, one after the other. She let the water spray out and disappear into the soil. No mat- ter. Plenty of green cocoanuts dey-bout. She straightened up and stretched her back out, looking up into the sun-bleached sky. "Ah. And tha kens thy woman well. So if thou believe she speaks truth, then like as not, she does."

Huh. Those were not the usual disbelieving words. Nor the usual manner; no eye roll, no kiss-teeth of derision or pity. Mother Letty spoke as though what Kima believed of Josephine held weight. And,

Kima now realised, Letty'd well known what Josephine had been saying about her pregnancy. Sly one, Letty. Through the small burst of vexation at Letty's attempt to handle her, Kima replied, "Is truth Josie's telling." Josie might throw Kima's gifts back in her face; she might rage at her all night, giving her the full weight to bear of the compong people having killed her child and her fellows; she might be languid and joyful one moment, and then morose for the next sennight, as though she purchased the one emotion with the other. But she had never lied; not to Kima, not to anybody. Kima set about her chopping with a will, using her ire for fuel. "Allyou don't know Josie by now?" she muttered, not caring whether Letty could hear her or not. "She do the same work everybody else do, she don't complain—except to me—she don't bother nobody, she speak her mind plain. And she speak the truth. Every." Kima chopped. "Blasted." Another chop. "Time." This time, the force of her strike took her machete blade right through the cocoanut. The chopped-away half thumped onto the sandy soil below it. Kima stared at it and muttered, "Even though sometimes I don't want her to."

Josephine looked their way. Even though she couldn't hear them over the surf and the shouting, Kima's movement had caught her eye, and she knew how to read Kima's mood from every twitch she made. She lifted her chin at Kima; a question. Kima shook her head no. No need to bring down Josie's wrath on Mother Letty's head.

"A twinning child, then," said Letty, wonderingly. "I hear about this, but all my years witching, I never see it before."

"A twinning child," repeated Kima. Speaking the words made them real. "In another few months, I going to be living with two Josephines."

Mother Letty's bray of laughter frightened two perrokets from the nearby mamapom tree. "And may heaven help you then!" she said.

Chapter 4

THE STORY GOES THAT *a long-ago cacique thought himself too grand to be bound to the laws of tapu. He caught, killed, and ate a sacred cullybree. Mamagua rose up from the river in her caiman form, swallowed him whole, and shat him out many years later. When he came out, his whole world had changed. No one remembered him and all his kin were dead.*

Veycosi had slept the whole day away while his body shook off the last effects of a powerful dose of Reverie. Night was borning and the fireflies were lighting his way. He and Tierce must have had quite the dream-up last night, out on the outskirts of town where no one could see them. He was grateful for the freshening breeze, for his head was muzzy, the remembrances foggy and haloed. He hazily recollected delicious details of the false ceremony. Afterwards, he must have sent the pickens home and arranged for the heir to return to ir ship.

Twelve pairs of inscrutable eyes turned his way. "Listen to
me!" he shouted.

––––––––––

Veycosi shook his head to clear away the Reverie phantasms. They
had turned bad for a moment while he and Tierce were in trance.
The memory was trying to haunt him now. But in the end, it had
all been for the best, hadn't it? He felt sure he'd convinced Tierce to
at least cease the hostilities against Chynchin's nutmeg production.

Basking in his sense of triumph, he quickened his pace. He had
a game of Trade Winds to win.

He stepped to one side to let a camel and its rider go by. The
driver called out her thanks through the flapping indigo of the veil
she wore against the dust. The camel trotted away with its long,
knobby-kneed legs.

Most youngboys craved to own a camel. Unless they were Mirmeki, which case they were likely already familiar with camels, so
there was little novelty in the having of one. When Veycosi was a
picken, he and his bannas would play at being old-time freedom
fighters and Deserters. They would gallop on imaginary camels,
shooting each other with imaginary muskets and drowning their
enemies in imaginary piche. For all that, camels scarcely came into
Veycosi's ken these days, unless he was dodging the back end of
one that was doing its business in the middle of the street.

There was an old man sitting on a stool at the roadside, near
the wall of Salim's Cobblers. He was singing a tuneless ditty in between sips from a small calabash. There were things piled around
him on the ground. Veycosi spied a stack of calabash bowls of different sizes. A heavy piche-worker's vest of leather, with the characteristic smear of hardened piche down the left side. The old man

was right-handed, then. There was a coil of stout rope. A large leather cameler's saddle, much worn.

The man spied Veycosi approaching. "See owt you like, sirrah?" he croaked. "Take it. Take anything." He waved his free hand at the goods piled around him and drank from his calabash again.

"You're holding a generosity?" Veycosi asked him.

"Surely am. I'm getting on, lad. I don't ken how much longer I'll be around. That's good rope. Don't see its like nowadays."

He *was* getting on. His age was impossible to guess, save for "old." His skin had been tanned near to leather from a lifetime of working outdoors. The leather vest, the speech—a blend of antique Ymisen and modern Chynchin—and the marks on his knuckles (all but invisible, so weathered and dark was his skin) all proclaimed him Mirmeki. Many Mirmeki worked the piche lake, trudging out onto the solid black mass of it to chop blocks of it free. Chynchin sold piche to foreign, for caulking ships. Dirty work, but with its rewards; a small stipend of geld for buying goods from foreign, for instance. And they didn't have to petition for land. They were given a decent enough plot of it so long as they lived in the piche workers' compongs.

A generosity could be an entertaining event. In a lifetime of accumulating belongings, some people were natural curators, keeping only those things that possessed the value of sentiment, beauty, or quality. You could sense they had been cherished, and in taking them to yourself, you felt moved to cherish them in turn.

But sometimes people held generosities because they had despaired of the world. Veycosi asked the man, "You not going to make away with yourself, are you?"

He grinned. "Nay, lad. Chynchin will not be shut of me so easy. Neither will my son. Going to bide with him from now on. Need fewer things."

Veycosi had to pay mind well to his words to catch them all. His Deserter burr was strong as Samra's had been when the emotion of finding the piche-drowned Mirmeki had lowered her guard.

The man said, "Been here all day, bidding farewell to my surplus goods. These few things are all's left. Dost wish any of it?"

"No, thank you, goodman." Then, shyly trying out his tongue, Veycosi continued, "There's naught here I need, stout though your goods surely are, and tested by age and use. Will't share some tabac with me, though? I've the makings with me."

"Tha's kind to an old man. I will, at that. Share my maize beer with me?" He reached down beside his stool and picked up a clay jug.

"Thankee, goodman."

Smiling, the man refilled his calabash cup. "Tha must open thy throat on the word 'naught,'" he said in an amused tone. "Tha croaks it like any bullfrog." He wedged the jug between his thighs and held the cup out for Veycosi to take.

Veycosi had three good swallows of the spirit, till he couldn't tell any longer whether the warmth in his face was from strong drink or embarrassment. He handed the man back the cup, but he didn't take it. He remained squinting in Veycosi's approximate direction, an alert smile on his face. Veycosi said, "Brother? Thy calabash." His heart jumped a little as he said the intimate "thy," even though the man had been familiarly thee-thouing him from the start, as was to be expected from an elder.

The man started a little and adjusted the direction of his gaze. He reached his hand out. Veycosi put the cup into it.

"Eyes not so keen as they oncet was," the man said.

Veycosi nodded, then realised the man might not be able to see that. So he said, "Ah. A little moment, brother, while I fill my pipe."

He squatted on the ground beside the old man, took the makings out of the pouch in his sleeve, and set about filling and drawing the pipe. The two men shared the pipe and the cup of maize beer back and forth in comfortable silence until they were both done.

Then the old man corked the jug, put it on the ground, and overturned the calabash on top. He stood up off his stool and stretched. "Well, no need to bide here. Tha sounds like a strong young lad. Help me stack the remains up against this wall here."

"Let me do it, goodman."

"As tha will't. The stool as well, mind. Stand the jug on it."

Veycosi picked up the jug. It was still mostly full. He stacked it and the few remaining goods against Salim's wall. Passing souls would recognize a generosity and know to help themselves.

"All done?" the man asked. "Good lad. It's me for Kweku's now."

"I could walk with you? Was headed there myself." He remembered that now. His regular game at the rum shop with his bannas. There would be old-talking and distraction. He felt the need of distraction this evening. Reverie dream voices broke into his thoughts again:

"Not me! Don't take me!"

"Who, then? The pact must be honoured."

Veycosi shook his mind free of the distraction. His new companion was speaking. "Certes, we can walk together," the man replied. Then he clicked his teeth and gave a low whistle. "Come along, Goat. Nay, I don't mean thee, lad! Ah, here she is, the stubborn old biddy."

An ancient, swaybacked camel lumbered out from between the shops. Her hide consisted of knots, tufts, and mangy bald patches. She was splay-footed, knock-kneed, and a good eighteen hands high. Veycosi couldn't be sure in the gathering dark, but she seemed walleyed.

"Your camel's name is Goat? You named her after the witch's son, then?"

"Aye, so I did. And I hight Jacob."

"I name Veycosi."

"Maas' Veycosi, hope you don't mind walking alongside me and Goat."

"An honour," Veycosi replied, feeling anything but certain. The camel looked mean.

"She purely loves a dram of beer now and then, never mind it gives her gas. Even though I can scarce see, she'll lead me right to the rum shop."

"No fear, brother. I will make sure you get there."

Goat dipped her head, regarded Veycosi, and belched fragrantly in his face. Veycosi skinned up his nose and waved away the smell of fermenting straw. They set off, all three.

Jacob looked up at the darkening sky. "It'll be good to be inside, for the outside will be damp soon enow."

Veycosi felt a chill of dismay. "How you know?"

"It's like to rain ere the first evening bell."

"That would be rare. Is still dry season." Had he cleared the reservoir's pipe to Carenage South? Suppose he'd broken it instead, destroying the safe channel for the water supply to flow through? He didn't want to countenance a second flood so soon after the one he'd just caused.

"True," said Jacob, "the tips of the corn in the fields are dry and wilting, but the air freshens. Rare or no, I can feel it on my skin, coming on two days now. And last night I felt a dew underneath some jasmine leaves as my hand brushed past them. It is only four chances in ten, but the rainflies will come out to dance their wings off ere morning, I warrant."

Probably the Works Department had already investigated the reservoir, healed any damage. Veycosi laughed, trying to make light of his worries. "Oh, a betting man, is it?"

Jacob inclined his head. "I'm afraid it is, lad. Bad habit. Nothing else to do with the geld they gave me when I worked the piche. Is useless in Chynchin, and I never went elsewhere."

Was the air freshening? For true? He was afraid to find out whether he'd wrought more damage than he thought. Mama-ji, please, no. Please hold off your tears a little longer.

Though he knew the half memories of last night's Reverie to be false, the dream tide crashed over him briefly again: *Heart swelling with love, he opened his arms to embrace the giant caiman standing on its hinders.*

He opened his eyes again. They were only a few doors from Kweku's.

———

Kweku's rum shop was beginning to fill up for the evening. Most of the tables already had people sitting on the benches around them, laughing and old-talking. Kweku's servers were being kept hopping, their trays heavy with calabashes of beer and palm wine and mugs of maize beer and rumbullion. Man with his bannas over to the right was giving them a blow-by-blow of the last batey match, where Heaven's Best had trounced the Makaks. At the bar, a woman and a man were alternately laughing at and comforting a man who swore he'd just seen the Blackheart Man peering through his jalousies. A big, noisy table in the corner looked to be from the Ymisen ship that had recently made port. They were tossing about geld like watermillion seeds, getting fractious because few of the servers jumped smart at the sight of it. Too right they weren't; offering a soul mere coin for their labour was the same as saying *I assume you are a layabout who must be bribed to do an honest day's work.*

Veycosi spotted Toimu and Chorito. They still had some space at their table, if everyone smalled up little bit. He waved to them.

Chorito waved back. "Koo my bannas over there," Veycosi told Jacob. The man nodded, and Veycosi led him over to where they were.

As they got close, Toimu opened up a Trade Winds board with a snap, set it down hard on the table. Ee glared at Veycosi. For why? Veycosi tried on a smile. Toimu's face remained hard. Veycosi shrugged. Wha' feh do?

"This is Jacob," he told his bannas. "Met him on the way over."

"Good," said Chorito. "We have room for a fourth. Goodman, you will play Trade Winds with us?"

Jacob tipped his cap in the direction of the voice. "Mestres," he said. Chorito nodded back. Jacob and Veycosi took their seats.

Toimu was still pouting. "So you finally decide to grace us with your presence," ee said.

"Is what do you?" Veycosi asked. "Your wife draw the curtain across her door on you, or something?"

"Nah, nah. Allyou stop it," interrupted Chorito. "He here now. Bad luck to start a game with harsh words."

Toimu grunted. Ee took the chamois pouch full of game pieces from the middle of the board, shook it like ee was wringing a fowl's neck. Ee dropped the pouch back onto the centre of the board. It fell with a gentle clacking of the bones inside.

A small brown moth landed on the wall above them, near the beams of the ceiling. A little lizard darted out from the shadows and took it whole. The moth's two wings stuck out either side of the lizard's muzzle, then started crumpling into the lizard's mouth as it chewed.

"Kweku," Veycosi called to the rum shop owner, who was over behind the bar, "beg you a calabash over here. Rumbullion."

Kweku nodded that he had heard. Toimu loosened the tie at the throat of the pouch. Ee was still giving Veycosi the cut-eye.

"One-a-quattie, two-a-quattie," Veycosi warbled under his breath.

"Four more pickens missing this morning from Carenage Town," said Chorito, reaching for the pouch. Veycosi's heart jumped in his chest.

Kweku came over to their table, carrying a tray with four red clay mugs and a knotted circle of madras cotton on it. A decent-sized calabash sat in the centre of the madras scarf. The shell of the calabash was carved with the words DRINK AT KWEKU'S in Djuka script, and with the stamps of approval of the three highest houses in Carenage. Kweku put the mugs down at their places. From the calabash, he began to pour rumbullion into them. "Two of those pickens come from my compong," he told them. "All of us been frantic, looking everywhere for them."

What the rassa they were on about? Veycosi would have heard news that big. The papers would have been full with it. He put a mug into Jacob's hands. "Who?" he asked his friends. "Missing how?"

Chorito raised his eyebrows. "Like you really been in the caiman's belly these past two days, man."

Hand trembling, Veycosi reached down and rubbed the side of his ankle. The old injury was paining him today. But wait—"Allyou said there were more missing pickens than that?" he asked.

Toimu replied, "Yes. I think last night make it nine in total. Me and Summer and Geraint keeping our two pickens home safe."

Chorito said, "People saying is the Blackheart Man take them."

Veycosi had a taste in his throat like burned piche. He snatched up one of the mugs and knocked back half of it. The killdevil warmed his tongue and throat going down. It was good rumbullion, tasting of mellow cedar, and tapped neither too high nor too low from the barrel. Veycosi lowered his mug and marked that Jacob, never mind he looked so desirous of the drink, hadn't tasted it yet. Neither Toimu, nor Chorito. They were regarding him as though he'd spat a gobbet on the rum shop floor.

His manners. Of course. He was the one who'd ordered the drink. He tipped a drop from the mug to the floor, an offering to the zemis of this establishment. The others followed suit. The old scar on the side of his foot started a sudden burning.

Jacob said, "This morning's broadsheet made it ten pickens. My grandson read it me."

Toimu made a tutting sound.

Chorito chimed in, "Younggirl named Maitefa. She the last one who didn't come home."

Maitefa. He knew that name from somewhere. Suddenly, Veycosi couldn't bear all this palaver. He hummed the quattie song, tapped his fingers in time on the Xaymaca mahogany table. "Cully-bree hatching soon, oonuh think?" he asked. They all stopped their nattering and looked at him, their expressions odd. Not a one of them answered his question. "Jacob here thinks it might be tomorrow, but that can't be so, you know." Veycosi half noticed Kweku taking his leave. "The eggs don't hatch till we've had at least four damp nights in a row."

"Nah, man," said Toimu, finally. "Last year the weather was still dry when the eggs started falling."

Jacob was quiet. Sitting and peering around him with his dim eyes.

"I remember it good," said Toimu. "Dry like bone for days, and the piche works smelling rank to high heaven for lack of a breeze to blow the stench away."

Jacob chuckled. "Aye. I remember that hatching well. All of we working in the piche boiling house had to wear rags tied over our faces, never mind we so accustomed to the smell. One young lad was overcome the day before the eggs fell. Had to wave bitter salts beneath his nose to revive him. And there was no rain."

Toimu looked smug. "You see?"

"The sennight before, though," said Jacob, "it was damp near every night. Not rain, but mist come four-day morning when it finally got cool. Doubt you young lads would have marked it, but it made my old bones ache for days. Goat's, too. All that week, she was fractious as a babe getting its first tooth."

"So it might be like that tonight, then?" Veycosi asked him. "Not rain, but only a damp mist?"

"It might."

That was something. Veycosi vowed to himself that tomorrow he would ask at the Palavera whether anyone had been dispatched to the reservoir to check the soundness of the pipe. They needed to go up there before the eggs hatched. The place was tapu, forbidden, for a sennight after.

Toimu said, "Cosi, what colour you going to play?"

"Green."

Chorito said, "Give me the red there." He always played red.

Toimu gave Chorito his pieces. Glanced at Veycosi. Looked to Jacob. "Your pleasure, Jacob?" ee asked, a little too stiffly for Veycosi's liking. He well knew Toimu's distaste for Mirmeki, but surely his friend would mind ir manners with Jacob sitting right there?

Jacob only smiled. "White, an't please you," he replied. "Dark in here. The old eyes too blind for me to mark any other colour clearly." He squinted down into his mug and took a long swallow of the rumbullion.

One by one, Toimu flicked the seven white pieces to make them slide across the table towards Jacob. Jacob trapped every piece beneath one large hand. He didn't miss a one, and he didn't take his face from out his mug the whole time. Chorito raised a brow.

Jacob put his mug down. He wasn't smiling. "Eyesight not too good, young 'un," he said to Toimu. "But the ears plenty keen."

Chorito went from stern to merry. He snickered. "I have a feeling this going to be a good game tonight."

Toimu kissed ir teeth. With an ill grace, ee dealt irself the blue pieces. "Throw in," ee said.

Jacob ran a heavy thumb over his pieces, selected one, and placed it onto the board. It was etched with the image of an ear of corn.

Chorito pitched in a red, also a corn-ear; Toimu a blue, a machete. Machete cut the play and forced it to switch to a new one. Toimu was starting out aggressive.

Veycosi fanned his markers out in his hands and looked them over. One was river, with the three wavy lines etched into it. Could go any of three ways. Always a good marker to start a play with. One was cowrie, with its rude, fig-shaped cunnie. He would hold that one back for when he really needed it.

"Cosi, you playing, or what?" Chorito asked.

"Hold your horses. Soon come." Veycosi was pondering whether to lead with the thrice seven. Would take a cowrie and two rivers to beat that one. He looked to Kweku's house zemis, their little clay bodies all in a line on the low outside wall. In the flickering lamplight, one of them, shape of a woman squatting to give birth, seemed to whisper to him. He strained to read her lips. *How many pickens?* she seemed to say. He ignored her. Reverie phantasms.

Oh. He marked he had a cullybree, too, with its tiny flit-wings and needle beak. A canny, trickster choice. He slid it out from amongst the others and made ready to play it.

"The missing picken that came back this morning," Toimu told them, "went to her father's house, picked up a musket, and tried to shoot her auntie dead."

Veycosi dropped the cullybree. It landed edge-on on a bony part of his foot. He swore at the pinpoint sharpness of the pain. He fumbled around under the table, picked up the marker, and positioned it on the board. "We playing this game, or not?" he said.

Toimu placed a river bone edge-on to Veycosi's. "Wasn't we who delayed the game by two days," ee said.

The sulphur taste of piche rose in the back of Veycosi's throat. "Stop talking horseshit and play," he told Toimu. He knocked back more of the killdevil.

It was Jacob's turn, but he had his nose buried in his mug, his throat working with each swallow.

And so the game went: Jacob in his cups and having to be reminded all the while to take his turn, Toimu irritable, and Chorito trying to keep them all merry. Then Veycosi had one more bone to throw. He went to make his move, studied the board. All routes blocked. "Chuh, man."

Slowly, it came to Veycosi that Jacob had won the game. Toimu and Chorito looked at Jacob, splay-mouthed. And, Mama-ji forgive him, Veycosi regarded the board to follow Jacob's plays again, lest the man had cheated.

No, he really had won.

Jacob looked down into his mug. Sighed. Looked sadly at Veycosi. "Ah, now, lad," he said. "For my prize, I have a boon to ask of thee."

Veycosi was still staring at the board, replaying the last few moves of the game in his mind. How the rassa had he done that? He looked at Jacob. There were tears glistening in those milky, tricksy eyes.

Veycosi set his shoulders square. "Ask me your boon then, nuh?"

Jacob sat up straight. "I can tell you have a caring heart," he

said. The drunken slur was gone. "And a spitfire soul. She needs
that. She needs both. You'll take care of her for me? I beg you,
sirrah."

"And is who you want this gadabout to look after, Jacob?"
asked Toimu merrily. Ir irritation at being made to sit to table with
a Deserter had apparently drowned in ir glee over seeing Veycosi
put in an uncomfortable position. "Whoever it is better be comely,
you know."

"I can't lie and say that, maas'." The old man really was weeping! "It's Goat. I can keep her no longer. It's not her at fault, sirrahs,
but me. The eyes getting worse. I can brush her coat by feel, but I
can't always find ticks when she has them, or rockstones between
her toes."

Ticks?

"I leaving my compong to go and live with my son. He's a good
boy, but there's no room for her there. I cannot give her roof, and
her old bones ache so when it rains." He fumbled for Veycosi's
arm. "Beg you, lad."

There came a crashing sound just outside the rum shop, as
of earthenware breaking. The four of them dashed outside, with
Kweku hard on their heels.

The sound had been the breaking of crockery. Goat the camel,
not content to suck down the stale beer Jacob had asked for her,
had stepped on the clay jar it was in and crushed it. "What is
it?" asked Jacob. Veycosi told him. Jacob gasped and rushed to
Goat, began feeling carefully along her toe pads to be sure that
she hadn't harmed her feet. As he did, the pesky beast nibbled
lovingly at his ear.

The rum shop owner kissed his teeth and glared at the old man.
"You see why I don't like having you people in my shop?" he said.

"Lef' it alone," Veycosi growled. Two days late, Toimu had said. But hadn't they set the game for today?

Kweku grabbed the old man by the collar. "You listening to me?"

Veycosi stepped in, put a hand on Kweku's arm. But before he could intervene proper, Kweku staggered backwards and yipped in pain, clutching at his breast. Goat had butted him in the chest. The others burst into laughter. "Woi!" said Chorito. "Like the old banna have he own bodyguard, yes!"

Kweku's face was clotted with fury, but he stayed his distance from Jacob and the camel. "You going to leave right now!" he said.

Jacob straightened his back and looked calmly in the direction of Kweku's voice. "Apologies, mestre," he said. He jooked his chin in Goat's direction. "She don't like to see the strong set upon the weaker. I will go, soon as Maas' Veycosi and me finish our matter."

Veycosi said, "Maas' Jacob, you sat to table as my guest. Kweku, lef' it alone. You can get another jar."

"And what about the way the camel attack me?" spluttered Kweku. He shook his finger at Jacob. "I calling the guards to arrest you this instant."

Veycosi would not have that, not a bit of it. "Then you going to have to tell them to also arrest a Nitayno postulant of the Colloquium of Fellows, working under orders from the cacique of Carenage Town." While Kweku was still looking nonplussed at that, Veycosi told him, "Is my camel. I just, ah, won her fair from this goodman."

Jacob's face brightened with joy. "You'll take her, then? Blessings, lad!"

Veycosi nodded. He would follow where this road led. He made up his mind to get a tale from Jacob, so that his bombastic claim to Kweku just now might be more than just grandcharge.

"I'll walk her home with you," said Jacob, "so she knows to stay where I leave her."

True, with Goat along, they would have to walk back to his apartment, rather than take a carriage. No matter. Walking would be easier on his throbbing head than being jounced around in a carriage. Veycosi realised he'd been nursing the headache for some time. And a certain queasiness of the belly, from too much Reverie. What had he done last night, in truth?

Jacob untied Goat.

"Let me walk a little way with you," said Toimu. They took their leave of Chorito and set off down Camara Street. That was the quickest way back to the student apartments of the Colloquium.

The night air was damp, making the flames in the street lamps gutter. Fretting about whether it would rain, Veycosi wrapped his stole around his shoulders. He glanced at Goat. "She fight like that all the time?" he asked Jacob.

"Just don't vex her."

Toimu chuckled.

What would vex a camel? And where the rass would Veycosi keep her penned? "What to feed her, Jacob?"

"Oh, she can eat most any green, sirrah, even should it have prickles. She needs about five bushels a day."

Toimu laughed outright. "I think you better add a lot of fast-growing maize to that garden plot of yours, banna."

Jacob brightened. "She will give you plenty of manure for fertilizer, sirrah."

Damnation. "And how much water a day?"

"If you're feeding her fresh greens, she will scarcely need any. And give her coat a good brushing every couple sennights or so. I have her brush right here." He patted the satchel slung over his shoulder. "And please, if you can give her somewhere to shelter from the rains when they come. Her old bones ache if she stays too damp."

Veycosi tried not to think about rain. "How you know when her bones are aching?"

"She will get little bit cantankerous."

"She can get more cantankerous than she was just now?"

Goat released a loud, long fart. Veycosi tried to wave away the warm manure scent.

"Good girl," said Jacob, patting her side. "Oh, lad; don't let her have too much beer. It gives her the bloat, as you can see."

Toimu roared with laughter. Then the gods-cursed animal belched, at which Toimu doubled over, laughing so hard ee was having trouble keeping up with them. Veycosi silently cursed his own sense of fair dealing. This time it had made him the owner of an own-way old camel so far past her better years that she couldn't bear burden anymore. Not to mention her having a taste for beer, a mean bite, and a chronically colicky gut.

Toimu had recovered little bit. Wiping tears from ir eyes with a corner of ir robe, ee said, "Like you find yourself a wife, banna." Ee seemed to have gotten past ir dislike of Mirmeki. Of this one, any road. Toimu continued, "Jacob, is that you really doing, ain't? Making you and Cosi into husbands for your camel?"

Veycosi responded with an irritated cheups. Jacob chuckled. "Belike, my friend, belike. First I'll have to see if she will gang wi' him, though, before the three of us set up house together."

Which sent Toimu off into more howls of laughter. "You won't be able to disappear for a day and a night with that there wife," ee said. "Wouldn't want to get her vex, eh, Jacob?"

Enough of this chivvying. Veycosi stopped dead in the road, leaving Toimu, Jacob, and Goat to walk on couple-three paces. Toimu slowed and looked back to see why Veycosi wasn't beside them.

"What it is you going on with any at all?" Veycosi asked him. "I didn't go away anywhere!"

What had he done last night, though? He remembered laughter and others present to share the joke. But not what, or who, or where.

The pickens, holding their bellies, grimacing in pain . . .

Jacob whistled at Goat to halt her. Toimu stepped towards Veycosi, the vexed look back on ir face. "You were supposed to meet us at the rum shop two evenings ago. We waited, but you never came. Never even sent word."

"But I never—!"

"Then tonight you just waltz in, merry as you please, carrying on like nothing happened. What kind of way is that to treat your friends, Cosi?"

Veycosi's leg was burning again, and his head all a-hammer. His mouth tasted like he'd licked a camel's bunghole. He didn't have patience for Toimu's chivvying. "You better find yourself home," he told Toimu coldly, "before your wife come walking the streets to find out did the Blackheart Man thief away her precious spouse."

Toimu kissed his teeth. "You go 'long, then. You just keep going the way you going. Maas' Jacob, good walk to you."

"Good walk, friend."

Toimu turned and strode away. Veycosi sighed and resumed walking with Jacob and his camel.

"Chuh. Probably ee just had the date wrong."

"Belike, lad."

"Last month ee kept me and Chorito waiting at the rum shop for a good two hours. Forgot it was our usual evening to lime."

"Hmm," murmured Jacob.

"Not to mention the time ee missed ir own soul day feast. All of us waiting at ir house and the lobster soup getting cold, and Toimu was down at the knife-maker's shop, looking to get a new handle for ir machete."

Jacob tut-tutted. "Ir mind is a little careless, then, say'st thou?"

"Too right."

They plodded along the street. "Jacob, what day it is today?"

"Firth."

"To rass." Two days later than Veycosi had reckoned. He and Jacob passed the rest of the walk in silence, except for occasional eruptions from Goat. Veycosi's mind was in a turmoil as he tried to conjecture what had happened. Something . . . something his mind skittered away from as soon as it got close to the memory.

The camel ambled along easily enough while Jacob led her. Other students liming with their bannas on their porches, or playing kickball in the courtyard, stared curiously at the strange procession walking the Colloquium grounds. Few showed any surprise, though. They were accustomed to Veycosi's antics. Goat cast a curious, evil eye around her at everything and everyone.

When they reached Veycosi's apartment block, he walked them through the alleyway to the back of the building. Goat was meek— if gaseous—as Veycosi opened the back gate so that Jacob could lead her onto his garden plot; five strides by ten where he haplessly grew callaloo, eddoes, and bitter gourd. He was a poor gardener. He often let his crop die, and he was none too quick to clean up the dead and dried-out straw, vines, and leaves. But from what Jacob had said, Goat would nyam all that up for him. This arrangement could be a good one.

If Chynchin avoided war with Ymisen and life could continue as usual.

If the Colloquium allowed Veycosi to continue his studies so he could receive his appointment as a Colloquium Fellow and finally plan his marriage with Gombey and Thandiwe.

If the rains didn't come and the reservoir outlet wasn't cracked.

Jacob pulled on the halter until Goat's head dipped level with his. He grabbed her by the ears and spoke into one of them. "Old gal, tha must bide with this man here. You mark me? Get a sniff of him. Come, Maas' Veycosi. Turn thy neck to her. No, she won't bite. Goat, dost mind me? Bide. Here."

Goat snuffled along Veycosi's neck. Her nose was surprisingly soft, like the sensitive skin of one's lips. He dared to reach a hand up to pet her head. She flinched, but let him touch her. She turned her head so that a spot behind her ears fell under his hand. He scratched right there. She spraddled her legs a little and pushed her head back against his hand, making a soft groaning sound of pleasure. Jacob smiled. "Yes, just so," he said. "She too love that."

Veycosi knew Ma was going to laugh after him with this new escapade. She was forever telling him that his heart was too soft.

Ma! Had he even visited her and his das to urge them to flee Chynchin? His belly churned with the knowledge of what a bad son he was. He tried to cast his mind back to the past two days, but there were only foggy impressions. *A picken's giggle. A brown liquid bubbling in a pot on a fire.*

Jacob said, "Make sure she always has salt." He was still blathering on about the blasted camel. "And keep her away from beans if tha canst. Tha marks how her stomach is delicate." "Delicate" wouldn't have been the word that Veycosi would have put on it.

"Yes," he said. "I mark." He felt too unwell to travel tonight. He would visit his parents tomorrow, after he found out what had befallen him to lose him two days.

"If tha canst find it in thy heart to give her some beer betimes, it'll help keep her temper sweet." Jacob gave a sad chuckle. "Sweeter, any road, than it be *without* a dram from time to time. Only a little, look you. Not even half that jar I fetched her tonight, and only oncet every sennight or three." He drew Goat by the neck closer to him, and nuzzled his face in her ratty pelt. "Oh, and she willna take well to being tied." He ruffled the knotted pile on the beast's neck. "Eh, Grandame? Birthed too many young 'uns and seen too many years to be treated thus, nah true?"

"Ah," Veycosi replied absent-mindedly. He would have to remember to close the garden gate.

"Never too much fresh greens. Not the soft kind, any road. Not your eating greens. Gives camels the belly-runnings."

"What, then?"

"Better she feed on scrub and weeds. Or hay."

As though she'd heard them, Goat went straight for the dried stuff in one corner of Veycosi's plot and started munching.

"Keep the flies from her, else they'll lay eggs in her nose."

Mama's tits.

Jacob and Veycosi stayed silent some little while; that clumsy pause between fellows who don't yet know each other well enough to take ease in the other's silence. Then Veycosi had a thought. "Jacob, you could come and visit with her some days?"

"Th'art kind to an old man," said Jacob. "I willna say nay."

"Thank you."

"Shall I bring some hay with me when I do?" He sounded amused.

Veycosi yawned. "Beg you, please."

Jacob laughed. "Then so I shall, lad."

Veycosi's eyes were smarting from lack of sleep, and the beer was threatening to turn sour in his belly. The air was damp and chilly. He wanted his bed. All would come clear tomorrow. Probably.

"Well, lad, the night's getting old. I will leave thee both, then."

"How will you find your way home?" Veycosi asked.

"I'll hail a carriage. Dinna fret."

"Walk good, then," Veycosi replied guiltily. He wasn't feeling guilty enough to draw out the goodbye, though. Jacob patted Goat once more, his worn face crumpled in sorrow. Then he let himself out by the gate and headed down the alleyway.

Veycosi pulled up a handful of half-dead mint and offered it to Goat. She followed the scent of it as far as his little back porch. He could tie her to the banister post there, just for the night. To make sure she didn't bolt.

Bleary-eyed, he was just making the first loop of the knot when Goat threw her head up, yanking the rope out of his hands. She looked around her wildly. "Don't fret, girl," he told her. He reached for the knot again, but Goat sidled beyond his reach. She butted the gate open, then, legs kicking every which way, she took off at a run down the alley. Damned flea-bitten brute could move quickly when she wanted. Veycosi sighed, snatched up his hem, and ran queasily after her. Some students sitting and drinking on a porch set up a cheer and urged the camel to run faster. Not one of the ratsons offered to help.

A little way off, Goat halted to crop at a sweet-lime bush bordering someone's plot. Quietly as he might, Veycosi made his way over to her and pounced on the lead trailing from her neck. "Got you!" The action of bending so quickly made his head spin so till he feared he would toss up his night's imbibing then and there.

Came the thumping of running feet. It was Gombey, shouting, "Cosi, you have to come! Now! Is Kaïra! The Blackheart Man come and take Kaïra!"

A lump of fear swelled Veycosi's throat. "But I just saw her—" He realised that he couldn't say when last that was; after he hadn't even known what rasscloth day of the week this was. Goat dragged him another few feet. He shouted for her to stop. Suddenly, there was Jacob. He got hold of the camel's halter and jerked it hard. "Goat!" he barked. "Hold!" Goat stopped and stood, perfectly still.

Veycosi asked Gombey again, just to be certain, "Kaïra went missing?"

"Yes!"

"You sure she not at some other house in the compong?"

Gombey shook his head. "We asked everybody. Nobody can find her."

"I will take Goat back to thy yard, lad," Jacob said. "She will mind me."

"Thank you. Lock the gate good this time!"

Gombey and Veycosi rushed to the carriage Gombey had waiting.

———

The carriage jolted them through the streets to Thandiwe's compong. It made too much noise for Gombey and Veycosi to talk with ease, so they mostly kept silent. Gombey stared intently out at the road ahead, as though watching at it would make it roll by faster.

Veycosi still couldn't quite believe that Kaïra was one of the missing, but Gombey swore this was the second night now she hadn't returned to her home or sent word to her mam.

What the backside Kaïra was up to now? Some Mamapiche trick, probably. If Thandiwe didn't tan her hide for him when she came back, Veycosi might be tempted to raise a hand to his intended's picken his own self.

Gombey said something. The wind took the words away. "What?" Veycosi asked him.

"We didn't worry at first!" he shouted back. "Mamapiche, you know?"

"I know!" Mamapiche Festival. The cullybree chicks would be

hatching soon, and then it would be time for the parade, led by crewes of Carenage Town's pickens. Every year the crewes tried to come up with something more spectacular than the year before. Pickens always got secretive and scarce around this time of year. Huddling in groups. Whispering and laughing quietly with each other. Looking over their shoulders and scowling at any not of their number who came within earshot of their plotting. Disappearing for hours and returning with mysterious things caught in their hair and their garments: powdered chalk, melted glass, chicken feathers. And objects would go missing from people's houses. Thandy hadn't been able to find five of her six precious silver spoons for days now. Coming up to Mamapiche, wasn't rare for a picken to be gone for a night or two, and to return home back looking tired and preoccupied. They started asking strange questions, too. What was that Kaïra had asked Veycosi the other day—something about throwing burning oil into water?

His heart clenched in his breast. Mama-ji, please say the picken hadn't hurt herself by trying it, wasn't lying somewhere secluded, too injured to help herself. But alive, yes? Alive. Kaïra was hasty, but she mostly had sense. And she heeded Veycosi. "We will find her," he said to Gombey.

At the sound of Veycosi's voice, Gombey snapped his head around to look at him, as though startled to find someone there beside him. Apparently, his preoccupied thoughts were only on Kaïra. Gombey cupped one ear. "Say again?" he shouted over the noise of the carriage.

Veycosi raised his voice. "We going to find Kaïra!"

Gombey nodded a vague yes and turned his eyes immediately to the road again.

Mamapiche was an overturned time.

The carriage clattered past a group of people, laughing and

talking as they walked the street. Veycosi only glimpsed them in the dark, but he had come to recognize that swaying form. He rapped on the ceiling for the carriage to stop.

"Stand!" yelled the driver to the horse. It came to a halt.

"What you do that for?" said Gombey. "We have to get to Thandy!"

"Just one moment," Veycosi replied. He leaned out the carriage and shouted, "Samra!"

The carriage had stopped some little way past the group. They took their sweet carousing time making their way to it. Veycosi yelled, "Make haste, nuh? Kaïra went missing!"

They paid heed to that. Plenty knew Kaïra's name in Carenage Town. They hurried up, a band of five Deserter folk, men and women both. Veycosi nodded briefly at them.

"What happen to Kaïra?" asked Samra. Why did she look 'pon him so sourly?

"We don't know," Veycosi answered. "Get in, nuh?"

She raised a wry eyebrow but gave her fellows a hasty good walk. Veycosi reached a hand out to her, palm and fingers tingling at the imminent touch between them.

"Sammie," said one of the men, "you going to be all right?"

"Surely, Lev. Don't fret." She didn't take Veycosi's hand, but clambered in unassisted to sit beside him. Veycosi rapped for the driver, and they were on their way again.

Samra was decked out in evening finery of woven skirt and gold soutien-seins, Cibonn' style. She carried a camel-hair serape against the night chill, but she'd only draped it over her shoulders, not wrapped it around her form. Her bare tetas bobbed saucily with the rocking of the carriage, even though the chain that secured the golden rod of the soutien-seins beneath them was drawn up tightly around the back of her neck.

"Been having a fete, then?" Veycosi asked.

"From the smell of your breath, you've been doing the same." She nodded at Gombey, who'd been watching at her curiously. "Give you good walk, mestre."

"You are Samra? Who works for Yaaya?"

"The same. What happening with your daughter-to-be?"

"Two days now Kaïra hasn't come home," Gombey replied, "and no word from her."

"So that was *your Lev*, then?" Veycosi asked Samra casually. "A comely soul, he." He lied. He hadn't gotten a good look at the man.

Samra gave Veycosi an irritated look. "Hush little bit," she said, "so I can hear the mestre."

"Some of Kaïra's young bannas are missing, too," Gombey told her.

"Some kind of picken Mamapiche game, then?" asked Samra.

"That's what I was telling Thandy," replied Gombey, "but one of Kaïra's bannas come back yesterday; one little girl picken."

Veycosi's skin started crawling, as though in prescient fear of what Gombey was going to tell them.

"Her elder brother saw her first. Domingus, that's his name."

"And?" said Samra.

"She bit half his little finger off before anybody could stop her."

"Swive me," Veycosi whispered. Samra gasped.

"Domingus say she just set upon him. That she was fighting wild. 'Like a thing that don't know it could die,' he said. We have to find Kaïra now-now!"

"Shite," Veycosi muttered. Then, more loudly: "And what happen to the little girl picken? Where she now?"

"Home," Gombey answered. "Under lock and key. But she not violent no more. She not anything."

"How you mean?" asked Samra.

"She won't mind anyone. She won't speak, she won't move from one spot. If you don't feed her, she won't eat. She heedless as any rockstone." Gombey closed his eyes. Opened them again. "Cricket, what if the same thing is happening to Kaïra?"

Veycosi reached for the comfort of his obi bag at his neck, but it wasn't there. He must have left it home. "We will find her" was all he could say. "Soon."

They rumbled on in the dark. Why Samra was being so cool with him? She gave him a look he couldn't read, then edged closer to him, put her lips near his ear. She smelled of sweet passiflore. "Two days," she said. "You never met me to train, and for two days I couldn't hear from you."

"So I come to find out," he replied. "Samra, I tell you true, I don't know where those two days went. I don't know where *I* went."

"Drunken? Too much Reverie?"

"I don't know," he said glumly. "Let we talk on it once we find Kaïra, nuh?"

She frowned, then nodded. She said, "So I finally going to meet your Thandiwe?"

"Yes. I wish at a happier time."

Samra said, "Siani Yaaya plenty vexed with you."

Mama's tits, what now? "Why?"

She drew back, puzzled. "You and I were supposed to visit her compong yesterday, to continue helping with rebuilding her home."

Oh, yes. The privies needed re-digging. Veycosi wrinkled his nose and closed his eyes. "Not tomorrow?"

She leaned towards him again. He tried not to contemplate how close that brought her bare and bouncing tetas to his arm. "We waited for you there. In that stench and rankness. Then the siani sent me to fetch you, but you didn't answer to your door. That was the second time you let me down in two days."

"Oh, Mama." Wrong building upon wrong. Piche flowing over his head like cold molasses. "You're sure this isn't Zemi night?" he asked, hoping beyond hope.

Too loud, again. Gombey raised up his head at the sound of Veycosi's voice. He looked curiously from Veycosi to Samra.

"This is Firth night," he said. "Morning of Penth, to be exact." Then he rapped on the ceiling of the carriage to get the driver's attention. "Turn left here!" he yelled. The driver slowed the horses and turned them down the lane that led to the compong where Thandy's house was. Veycosi hadn't even marked that they were close to it. He stared through the window of the carriage at the flickering lights of fireflies. He wrapped his arms around his chilled self and tried to think on why time had run amuck on him.

Samra reached over him to give Gombey's hand a comforting pat. "Try not to fret," she said to him. "You need your head clear now." As she settled back beside Veycosi, she murmured in his ear, "Lev is my brother. Can we have done with your sulks about him?"

Sheepishly, he nodded. That netted him a small smile, for which he was grateful.

―――――

This fore-day morning, Thandiwe's house was still as the river at dawn. No lamplight dancing in the windows, no smell of cooling ash from the barabicu out back. Gombey clanged the latch of the metal gate. "Inside!" he called. "Thandy, you deh-deh?"

No response. Gombey crossed his arms, his shoulders hunched as if to ward off blows. "I know she's in there," he told Veycosi and Samra. "Tonight, she would usually take"—his voice hitched slightly—"Kaïra to help with the lamplighting."

If Kaïra's future hadn't been already laid out for her, she would likely have become a lamplighter. She'd taken to it last year, and hadn't lost interest since. She was on the roster in her parish to help once a week with lighting the lamps in her block of streets. She was apprenticing to learn how to build and maintain streetlamps.

Gombey said, "Thandy had been working at the saltwater fish pens. She told me she went home like usual, made Kaïra's supper, and waited for her. Sun went down, and she never came home."

"Maybe nobody took her?" asked Samra. "Maybe she's liming by someone else's house in the compong?"

Veycosi shook his head. "Nah. Kaïra love the lamplighting can't done. She never miss her turn on the roster." Kaïra had even made Thandy go with her on Veycosi's naming day fandango the year previous. The work had finished too late that night for them to come and celebrate with Veycosi and Gombey.

"Besides," said Gombey, "we asked through the whole compong. Nobody seen her. And her alpagats gone. If she was still in the compong, she wouldn't be troubling herself to wear shoes."

Kaïra's favourite leather sandals; actually, Gombey's. Kaïra had her own, but she wore an old pair of Gombey's as often as Thandy would allow. Veycosi's skin prickled. Caiman eyes, rising up through murk. You threw the bones and worked the odds, but you never knew when fate would take you in its jaws and pull you down.

More time, Veycosi could see a candlelight through the wooden jalousie windows, progressing from the bedroom to the drawing room, flickering from one window to the next like a jumby. The front door opened and a candle flame floated forth from it. Behind it, a dark form was outlined against the black of night, holding the candle aloft. Veycosi hesitated, but Gombey ran in ahead of Veycosi, calling out, "Thandy!" The candle flame dropped to the ground and went out. When Samra and Veycosi followed, they found Thandiwe and Gombey, forehead to forehead, holding each other's hands. Thandy spied Samra. She looked startled and broke the embrace.

"This is Samra," Veycosi said. "Councillor Yaaya's chatelaine. She and Kaïra been helping me collect tales of Chynchin."

Smiling a thin welcome, Thandy said, "Well met, Samra. Veycosi has told me wonderful things about you."

Samra took Thandiwe's hand. "You have a fine child, sestra. And we will find Kaïra. Belike she's off playing jackanapes with some of her fellows. Anywhere she's biding, we will find her."

"Gods willing," Thandy replied. She held tight to Samra's hand.

Part of Veycosi's mind noted how Samra switched into Mirmeki tongue when she wasn't minding her words. The other part ached at Thandiwe's misery. Her one picken, gone. Mama-ji. Beg you they find Kaïra soon.

The dark of night was blueing into morning light. Harder to see the fireflies, easier to see the leaves on the tamarind tree in Thandy's yard. Veycosi squeezed his eyes shut tight, then opened them again, trying to blink away sleep. Taste of drink sour in his mouth. Fatigue making grit in his eyes. *One-a-quattie, two-a-quattie*, round and round in his head. What a night, ee?

This was Kaïra's favourite time of morning. Plenty times she would be up before the sun, make her way down to the river to watch for Mamagua. Two-three times when Veycosi had stayed the night, Kaïra had woken him up with scuffing around the house in those blasted over-big alpagats, getting dressed to dash down to the river. Thandy never scolded the child. Spoiled her instead. Let her pretend she really did see Mamagua sitting on a big rock in the river in the early morning, combing her hair and slapping the surface of the water with a caiman tail a mile long.

"Maybe she went down by the river?" Veycosi asked.

Thandy lifted her head and stared at him, hope making her eyes wild. "The river . . . ," she whispered.

"No," said Gombey. "Down by the river for two nights now? That don't make sense. Even Kaïra wouldn't want to spend two nights wandering around down there with the mud and the caimans and the mosquitos."

Thandiwe took a shuddering breath. "You never know. She's own-way enough to do something like that. We should check. Just in case."

Thandy's front door opened and her mother, Filiang, came out of the house. She called, "What allyou doing out here, propping sorrow in the front yard? Thandy, bring them inside and make them break fast!"

"Not yet, Ma. We going down by the river to look Kaïra."

Filiang frowned. "The river? No, let someone else go." She shouted past them, "Cuffee! Come over here, nuh?"

A man who had been walking past the yard, hoe over his shoulder, stopped. He opened the gate and let himself in. Thandy looked irritated. "We can go, Ma. We can break fast later."

Filiang shook her head, then reached to take the hand of the man who had joined them. Cuffee was tall, dark brown with Ilife features, like Veycosi's ma and his da Kola. Cuffee clearly ate well. He had springy salt-and-pepper hair and a jolly face, though it was serious this morning. Veycosi had seen this Cuffee around the compong one or two times when he was visiting Thandiwe.

Cuffee nodded to Thandy, Filiang, and Gombey. "Morning," he said. "Morning, everybody. Kaïra home yet?"

"No," replied Gombey. "I took the day off work to help with the search."

"They want to go and look by the river for her," said Filiang. "But Thandy need to eat, and to rest. She didn't sleep all night. You and some of your bannas could go and check the river? See if you find her?" *Check the river*, she was saying. Not *check* by *the river*. Now Veycosi understood why Filiang didn't want her daughter to go down to the river. "Thandy," Veycosi said, "your ma's right. You have to eat. I will go with Cuffee. Me and Gombey."

By now, more of the neighbours were waking up, wandering by to see if there had been word of Kaïra. The child was popular even though she could be so pesky, Veycosi thought, then felt shamed of himself. Cuffee and Gombey were organizing two groups to search. Thandy stood and watched them, her eyes brimming. Veycosi made to join the searchers, but Thandy grabbed his hand. "I'm going with oonuh," she said.

Filiang began to protest. Thandy replied, "No, Ma; I'm going."

The search party went round the back of the compongs on Coral Lane and along the backdam strip of land between the river and the garden plots. The Iguaca flowed not far from Thandy's compong. The back garden plots of all the compongs on her street had been marshland, drained from the Iguaca while Veycosi's da Woorari was a boy. Da still talked about the fine spectacle of the twelve windmills and the water screws, pumping for ten years to make fertile land.

The sun was up. A few early risers were already out minding their plots. The back gardens were laid out in rough squares, marked by lines of raised earth between them, tamped down into narrow walkways kept in place with scrub grown over fishnet. The party picked its way along the walkways. Thandy held fast to Veycosi's hand, like she hadn't done in weeks. Couple months now she'd been drawing away from him. She'd told him she was just setting her mind to the knowledge that he would be gone for months.

But it still had been making his heart sad. Even sadder now, since it had taken Kaïra's disappearance for her to seek to lean on him again. Veycosi didn't understand what had been making her chill towards him. It felt as though there was more than she was saying.

Tears were glistening in her eyes. As they walked, she sadly hummed a little ditty, wordless. She reached the refrain:

"*One-a-quattie, two-a-quattie . . .*"

Veycosi shivered and fought the urge to drop her hand and move away from her.

She murmured to him, "I know we not wed yet, so you can dally as you like. But you had to go and thin your molasses with raw honey?" She jerked her chin in Samra's direction.

"I—"

"Maybe is for the best," she said.

"Samra and I didn't—we not—"

"Is my fault. I made you and Gombey wait too long. And I pushed Kaïra into this Mamacona thing. All this is at my door."

"Don't say that!" Never mind Veycosi'd been thinking the same things all this while, it tore at him to see how much pain they caused her. "Neither me nor Gombey mind waiting. Kaïra don't mind becoming Mamacona. Look how much she love Mamagua." The bit about Kaïra was a half-truth. The picken did mind, and he knew it, but he wanted to give his woman comfort.

Thandiwe dashed Veycosi a look so full up of hurt and regret it was like a knife through his breast. "I think I like Samra," she said. "She seem to have a solid heart. Not flighty, you know? Like those people can be."

"What people?"

"How you mean? Nah Deserters? You know how they stay."

Veycosi blinked at that, not sure what to say. They had reached to the river. The others were spreading out to search for Kaïra.

Gombey started picking his way through the tall reeds to get right to the edge of the river. Samra, who was farther off with Cuffee, waved at Veycosi and Thandy, then followed Cuffee. Thandiwe watched her go. "She's good to you?" she asked.

"Thandy, stop talking like that. Is you I'm betrothed to."

She gave a shuddery sigh. "Cosi, please just help me find Kaïra."

Veycosi started forwards to go with her. She shook her head. "You and Gombey search together, all right? I need to have some time alone to clear my head."

Veycosi nodded. He removed the hand he'd put on her shoulder. "Gods willing," he said, "we going to find her."

She twitched. The look on her face: Hope of finding her daughter? Fear of what state she might find her in? "Gods willing," she muttered in answer, her teeth locked. Anger, then? Nowadays, Veycosi could scarcely reckon her.

She took her hand back from him, dashed her tears away with it. She headed through the mangroves, away from the sounds of the others' voices who were searching.

Gombey's voice over Veycosi's shoulder said, "You don't fool her with your 'gods willing,' banna."

Veycosi whipped around. Gombey was right behind him. He continued, "She know you not a gods-fearing man."

Veycosi sat on a nearby rockstone. "A-true, I'm not. But *she* fears the gods."

"Only one: Mamacona."

"I just wanted to give her some little comfort. Is the kind of thing everybody says."

"You ever know Thandy to take easy comfort yet?"

Veycosi shook his head. "Seems I can't please her at all nowadays."

"You can't study that right now, Cosi," Gombey said. "Neither that, nor some pretty little Deserter bit." He pointed towards the river. His hand trembled. "Come," he said, his voice breaking. "Let we look for our daughter-to-be."

Gombey loved Kaïra, too. "Of course," Veycosi stammered. "I sorry, man. I didn't mean—"

Gombey grasped his hand and pulled him up onto his feet. "Is all right, banna. I know your heart." He tried on a smile. "We going to get Kaïra back safe, and she will become Mamacona come Mamapiche time, and Thandiwe going to wed us both. Just like the three of us been planning from since."

Veycosi swallowed. He nodded. Unlike his own das, he and Gombey felt no pull to bed each other, beyond boyhood investigations many years ago. Gombey's tastes really only ran to women. As Gombey said, he and Veycosi were the beads on the thread, Thandiwe the needle. That was well by all three of them.

Gombey and he began their search. As they came near one reed patch, the spring chickens hiding inside it stopped croaking. Gombey said, "Remember hunting for frogs?"

Veycosi smiled. "Yes." Plenty nights when they were youngboys, they and their other bannas would come down to the river with lanterns. They would cut sticks from the nearby trees, sharpen them with their knives. They would run barefoot through the swampy ground, laughing and shouting, vying for who could spear the fattest frogs on his stick. Then they would make a fire, gut the frogs, and stuff them with wild garlic and mint growing right there-so in the marsh. Little bit of salt, if anyone had remembered to bring some screwed up in a piece of paper. They would have a spring chicken roast by the riverside; gorge themselves till their bellies were round like gourds, telling each other scary jumby stories the while.

That brought to Veycosi's mind the one about the headless witch in the tree, how she was supposed to look for people out alone in the bush at night, and steal their heads to replace her own. He hadn't heard that one in years. He made a mental note to scribe it down, add it to his growing compendium of tales. Any story at all would add pages to his work, make it look like he was really trying.

Gombey parted some of the reeds. "Kaïra!" he called. "Kaïra-girl? You deh-deh?"

Silence, pressing down like the heat. Clinging to a reed, a little brown grass lizard puffed up the orange half-disk of its throat, bucking its head as it did so.

"Hey," said Veycosi, "you heard from Gunderson? How the negotiations going?"

Gombey shook his head. "Not so good. Now the Ymisen heir is demanding regular visits to Chynchin, with admission to the Colloquium's archives. At least it's better than war. But the Colloquium is not pleased to be forced to let the heir in."

Veycosi smiled to himself. His ploy had made an impression on Tierce after all.

Gombey looked at the swampy water beneath his feet. He slipped off his alpagats. He picked up the hem of his robe and lowered a bare foot into the water. *Caiman eyes.* "Mind yourself," Veycosi told him. "You don't know what in there."

Gombey just grunted and nodded. His foot sank down in the river to his ankle. The rest of his leg followed, slipping into the water deep so till he had to squat one-footed on the bank. He put his hands down on the bank to steady himself, letting go his hem. An end of it dipped into the river and started drawing water up into itself. Veycosi said, "Banna, your robe getting wet. Draw it off and toss it onto the bank." Gombey nodded and did as he suggested.

Nice beige linen, that robe. With images of Mamagua in jamun-purple broderie right the way around the hem. The purple of the

thread bled a little more every time Gombey washed it, but it was
his favourite. Kaïra had made that robe for him. Chosen the cloth,
stitched it together, then embroidered her design in wavery lizard
tracks of stitches, using yarn she'd dyed herself.

Not a child born of Gombey's seed, but the child of his heart.
His and Gombey's stepchild-to-be.

"Kaïra!" Veycosi yelled, making Gombey jump. "If you hearing us, don't play fool-fool any longer! Your ma pining for you."

Silence.

Veycosi had a matching robe like that one, with its clumsy,
bleeding decorative hem. The embroidery Kaïra had done on his
was intertwined nutmeg leaves and pods. Kaïra knew how much
Veycosi loved Reverie. Veycosi had worn the robe twice to show
willing; on a feast day of Kaïra's, and on one of Thandy's. He
wished he were wearing it now.

Gombey grimaced and made a noise of discomfort.

"What's wrong?" Veycosi said, starting forwards, ready to
jump in if he must, to drag his friend from the reptilian water.

"Mud," he replied. "Oozing up between my toes. Like standing
in worms."

"Oh." Veycosi halted. "I used to like that feeling when I was a
picken." Not anymore. Not since that time a caiman had attacked
him as a boy. To occupy himself, he picked up Gombey's robe and
folded it.

Gombey continued wading through the water, peering down
into it as he went. Keeping his eyes on his friend the while, Veycosi
held the wet part of the folded robe in a patch of sun to dry it.
Gombey tacked forwards and back, the better to cover the whole
area. This swampy inlet of the river was Kaïra's favourite place
for her fore-day morning jaunts. Maybe he would include her Mamagua story in his writings, even though it was pure fancy. *In the*

218th year since the founding of the nation of Chynchin, our twin-
ning child Kaïra recites that if she bides still enough down by the
river, some mornings she spies Mamagua in the play of the sun's
first light as the nighttime mist burns off the river and the day be-
comes morning.

"You see anything?" Veycosi called to Gombey, just for something to say.

"No."

Thandy too loved to hear Kaïra talk her nonsense. She would
get the picken to describe over and over how Mamagua looked.
With every telling, it got more elaborate. He could include that description in his book. "Look by the rocks over there," Veycosi said
to Gombey, who went and pawed through the tall patch of swamp
reed. Sometimes those patches were deeper than they looked.

Mamagua, Kaïra had it to say, was nearly as big as the tallest
building in the town. She shimmered brown and gold like the river
mud as it shifted in the sun.

So much faith, it convinced her she saw what others did not. If
the child had to become Mamacona, shouldn't it be at Mamagua
time, not at Mamapiche? "Anything?" Veycosi called.

"No."

Ascording to Kaïra, *Mamagua's upper body was a woman's,*
with full, hanging breasts. Her lower body was a caiman's, but fat-
ter around and longer than any caiman's; over a mile long, and with
only one tail. "Search behind the rocks, too," Veycosi told Gombey.

Fore-day mornings, Kaïra recounted, Mamagua would come
slithering through the sleeping water, leaving a caiman wake trail-
ing behind her. She would pull herself up onto the rock that jut-
ted out of the water some little distance from the bank—the rock
where Gombey was searching right now—*drawing herself up with*
her arms and flexing her tail in bunches to move her forwards.

When she reached to the highest place on the rock, most of her tail would still be trailing in the water. Then she would flex her backside—Kaïra would demonstrate this action until Thandy and Veycosi were both helpless with laughter—*to straighten out the kinks from her tail. The tail would slap against the surface of the still morning water, making an echo a half mile long. That,* Kaïra said, *was what got the still fore-day morning river started with its daytime rippling. Then Mamagua would settle in on the warm rock. She would comb through the tangles of her hair with her fingers, pulling her tail up out of the water the while, to make it coil around her. It would take her till the sun was nearly up to pull her whole tail out, and by then, the coil of it would hide her completely, and the mist rising up off the river would veil her, and when Kaïra blinked her eyes and looked again, Mamagua would be gone.*

There was a shout from over behind Kaïra's Mamagua rock. Then a splash. "Gombey!" Veycosi shouted, running for the riverbank. Veycosi couldn't see him. "Gombey!" Veycosi kicked off his alpagats, threw off his robe, jumped into the water. His heels hit the riverbed with a jarring thud. He waded to the other side of the rock.

Gombey stood up out of the water, spluttering. The water was barely thigh height on him. On both of them, Veycosi realised. Gombey said, "I stubbed my foot on one rassa of a rockstone."

"Didn't I tell you to be careful!" Mud was squeezing through Veycosi's toes. Gombey had the right of it; it was like standing in graveyard worms.

Stirred-up mud made the water chalky brown. Veycosi scanned it, twisting and turning. Was that something brushing against his leg? He jumped to one side, the density of the water compressing the action to a slow, clumsy hop.

Gombey gave him a quizzical look. "Go and search somewhere else, nuh man?" he said. "You only aggravating me. And scaring yourself," he added when he saw Veycosi's face. "Wha mek you so 'fraid of the water all of a sudden?"

"How you mean, all of a sudden? You know I been like this since that time with the caiman."

"Caiman? You must tell me about that someday."

Veycosi opened his mouth to ask him what the backside he meant by that. *(Mamapiche opened her arms wide to embrace him, her claws flexing. . . .)* "You don't remember—"

"Not now, banna," Gombey said, cutting him off. "Bigger business afoot now. You see that stand of hog plum trees upriver?"

"Yes," Veycosi replied, pouting. How Gombey could just forget what had happened that day? Gombey knew Veycosi's life story almost better than Veycosi knew it himself!

"Well, go and look round there. We have a better chance of finding her if we spread out."

Veycosi sighed and nodded. Gombey began his sweep again. Gratefully, Veycosi clambered out of the water. He unknotted his breechclout, wrung the water out of it, and knotted it back on again. The damp cloth made him shiver. Then he drew on his robe, stepped into his alpagats, and took the footpath that led in the direction of the hog plum trees.

The warm hands of the morning sun heated his shoulders. Reeds rustled around him, glowing green in places as they strained sunlight. Little brown hoptoad birds chuckled *ke-ke-ke*, following in his wake, snapping up in midair the insects stirred by his passing.

As it had since youngboy days when he first heard the story of the Three, his mind ruminated on how the trick of miring the soldiers could have happened, if in fact it had ever happened at all.

Maybe the compong had dug a long trench? Covered it in boards? Covered the boards with piche, so it looked like a road? Perhaps the boards had held just long enough for most of the soldiers to step their mounts onto the "road," whereupon they broke under the weight?

The hair on his arms began to prickle. That might do it!

But what would keep the soldiers from climbing out of the trench?

If it was filled with something that mired the army, and while soldiers and mounts were floundering, the people from the village could gather round and have at them with muskets or arrows. Like killing fish in a barrel.

How to calculate the tolerance of the boards so precisely, though? That would truly be an ingenieur's feat!

Veycosi stopped short. And how then to explain the soldiers that the blackhearts had found in the Lower Piche only a few days ago? Ascording to all the tales, the massacre had happened outside the old village entrance, which was closer to the Upper Piche.

Was there some underground connection between Upper and Lower Piche? Someone at the Colloquium might know. Whatever the answer, perhaps the villagers threw them into the Piche after killing them. It might have been an offering to Mamapiche. Veycosi shuddered. He understood why Kaïra was more drawn to Mamagua than to Mamapiche.

A tall reed dipped a sharp green tongue into Veycosi's ear. He shook his head and waved the reed blade away. He stopped on the path. Path? He looked down at his feet. Which part the path was? He was standing surrounded by green: here around him, the sunlit yellow-green of grasshoppers as they leapt from bush to bush; two steps beyond, the dank navy-green of river weeds; and beyond that, dark verdure his eyes couldn't pierce. No path beneath his feet. None before him, neither. Nor to the sides, nor behind. Shite. He must have wandered off the road without noticing. Or else the reeds had been encroaching on him as he walked, dreaming behind his eyes. Now the green tips of them tickled his chin and his ears.

A light finger scraped the crown of his head, on his mole; that soft place where the bones don't quite meet at birth. The place people said a baby's soul entered the soul case of the body sometime between its first day and its ninth. Veycosi swiped at his scalp and spun around. He was holding a green reed blade, still attached to the plant that had assaulted him. As his fist swung down, the reed bent, pavaning along with him. Veycosi cursed and yanked its fat stem, the which pulled it out of the river mud by its roots. It made a sound like a kiss as it came. He threw it to the ground. He peered out over the tops of the reeds. Surely he'd be able to see the stand of hog plums by now? He'd come some distance.

The empty blue sky went on forever, with some little fluffs of mindless clouds. Had he gone past the hog plum trees, then? But he could see no signs of them, no matter what direction he looked over the tops of the reeds.

A wetness landed on his hand, startling him. A small brown frog had jumped onto it. Veycosi shook ir off, and ee leapt away, to land on a thin reed leaf nearby. On the instant, ee tongued a fat mamzelle into ir mouth. On Veycosi's hand, the frog had not seemed so big as to be able to devour a dragonfly. Ee looked plenty big enough now. Big enough that the plant bowed slowly with ir weight, and ee slid off and disappeared into the green at Veycosi's feet.

Veycosi was enveloped in silence, as in a wave washing over him. The quiet pressed against his ears; he could feel it. And he felt the wave crest and turn as the silence became sound, and the sound made the creeping hairs on his forearms rise.

A sliding, a dragging, as of something long slithering through the reeds. Long, weighty, and large. It was coming his way. The reeds crowded him in. All Veycosi could see around him was indifferent verdure. The heat of the day steamed the air around him, made it lie heavy on his chest.

Slide. Scrape.

Veycosi turned, pushed his way through the reeds as best he might, in the opposite direction from the sound. The reed stems, fatter near the ground, scratched his ankles. He lost an alpagat in the mud, but he kept going. Reed blades whipped across his face, one so thinly that it sliced a narrow stripe over the bridge of his nose. He felt the skin part, the blood start trickling down. But he kept up the hopping run. "Gombey!" he shrieked, thinking too late that by yelling, he was only showing the thing pursuing him where to find him.

He made himself stop moving. Though he was shaking, he stilled his panting breath and listened.

The dragging sound still came behind. Clumsily, he fled, elbowing reeds from out his way.

His naked heel came down on a sharp rockstone. He cried out and fell. Whimpering, he pushed himself up, stood to run again.

"Cosi? Is what do you?" Thandiwe stood there, reedy sunlight flickering over her features.

"Hush!" Veycosi hissed. "It going to hear you!" He grabbed her upper arm and pushed her behind him, so that he was between her and the thing that crawled on its belly towards them.

"What it is?" she hissed wildly. "I don't hear anything."

Veycosi put his fingers to his lips. She hushed. The sound changed from a slithering to a crackling walk. Someone was walking through the reeds, tromping them down as they came. Thandy's expression bloomed into a desperate hope. "I hear it!" she said. Before he could stop her, she called out, "Kaïra?" Her voice wavered on the high final syllable.

"Fuck, Thandy! What in blazes you doing?" Veycosi made to drag her with him, to run from whatever was chasing them, but she pulled away and sprang through the reeds in the opposite direction, right into the monster's path. Despairing, Veycosi followed her.

Jacob stood in front of them. "I too sorry, siani," he said to Thandy. "I not your picken. Just helping to look for her." Behind him, on her tether, was Goat, absently plucking and chewing from a nearby patch of reeds.

Jacob saw Veycosi looking at Goat. "I hope is okay, maas'," he said. "I know that she's yours now, I didna mean to cross you. She saved me from drowning oncet. I thought she might be useful, if . . ." He glanced at Thandy and didn't finish his thought. Thandy put her hand over her mouth and looked away. So she did when she didn't want any soul to see her cry.

"Is all right, Jacob," Veycosi said. "That you bring Goat, I mean. She was yours first, after all. You know her best." He reached up to pat Goat's neck. She snapped at his fingers. He pulled them away.

"I going to keep searching," muttered Thandy. "Where Gombey?" Her voice softened on his name. Veycosi wondered whether is so she spoke his own name to others.

"Downriver," he told her. "Over by Kaïra's rock."

Thandy nodded. "I going over there, then." She pushed her way through the reeds, heading back the way Veycosi had come. He didn't try to stop her. His monster had been nothing but the sound of Jacob and Goat, walking together.

Goat stretched her neck up and sucked a hog plum off a branch. Veycosi had been right near the stand of hog plum trees all this time. And now he could hear the companionable shouts of Thandiwe's neighbours: "Nothing over here!"

"Over here neither! But eh-eh, Cuffee; what you doing up in that tree?"

"What you think?" came Cuffee's gruff voice.

"I think you not a picken anymore, to be climbing trees."

"Hush your mouth and help me down."

A few voices laughed.

Jacob frowned. "They shouldna make sport so," he said. "Not where thy lady might hear."

"Thandy? Laughter don't come to her too plenty. But she like to see others take their ease."

"Likely her mind's too troubled this day for laughter to give her pleasure."

"True that." Veycosi grabbed for Goat's halter, turned her neck in the way that Jacob had shown him, so she couldn't reach him to bite. And she did try, the brute. But Veycosi had her fast.

They searched till nightfall but didn't find Kaïra.

The next day, people from the Ymisen ship began to fall ill with the phthisic.

Chapter 5

SAOIRSE'S PARENTS HOLDING A nine-night for her tomorrow," said Thandiwe. She had stayed at her compong this day, as she had most days since Kaïra's disappearance. She also managed the fishing ponds of her compong, as well as the market's hatchery.

She bent and pulled a wire cage of wriggling fish out of the trough. Veycosi enjoyed watching her work: her strong arms; her confidence.

"No sense in that," he replied. "For all they know, she still alive." His caiman-bit leg twinged, but he helped her lower the cage into the big pond. She jumped down after it with nary a splash. The water came to her waist.

"Camlette told me the hope is driving her out of her senses. Waking every day, not knowing how her daughter fares. She say this way, at least it will put a stop to the waiting, even if it turn out it was a false ending."

Veycosi rubbed his leg. "Oh, so you know Saoirse's parents?"

"She's a banna of Kaïra's." Her voice was rough with unshed tears. "All of them—used to be."

"Swive me. She and Kaïra are friends? Why you never told me that before, Thandy?"

She gave Veycosi that same considering look she'd been gracing him with for some months now. He didn't like the reckoning he saw on her face. "I thought you knew. Kaïra talk about them so much. The twelve of them had formed a crewe for Mamapiche." Eleven pickens had gone missing aside Kaïra: Saoirse; Gilead, the eldest at fourteen years; Daffyd; Confound; Gza; Sem; Tubang; Sudharshan; Wu; Maitefa (the younggirl who'd so surprisingly faced down Mestre Ta'ana at the capoeira roda); and Yddyta. Yddyta, the youngest, eight years old, whose mother was Hleb, and who had as fathers Thianis and Veycosi's mentor, Steli. Now that Veycosi thought on it, the pickens' names did seem somewhat familiar. He'd likely heard Kaïra prattling on about her friends and their doings together, but he hadn't quite learned who they all were yet.

Thandy stood up straight. Shimmering water poured down her brown body and dripped off the undersides of her tetas. She bent over and squeezed more water out of the springy mass of her long black braids. Veycosi knew she was fretting about Kaïra's fate and in no mood to be flirted with. So he admired her form silently.

"Help me with the cage, nuh?" asked Thandy.

Lying on his belly on the ground, he reached under the water and held the cage steady while she crouched down under the water and opened its gate. The almond-shaped, silver-blue forms of young tilapia fish fled free. They would grow and fatten in the big pond, feeding off algae, scraps, and cornmeal until they were big enough to be harvested. Thandy lifted the empty cage out of the water and passed it to Veycosi. "Set it on the edge of the pond to dry, please."

Veycosi balanced the cage on the stone lip that surrounded the fish pond. Thandy's compong was on a terraced decline near the southwest foot of the hills above. The houses of the compong were in a spiral that stepped down the levels of the decline to the bottom. The compong's allotment was in the middle. The allotment had many of the usual smaller plants: man yam, coco, pumpkin, and watermillion mounds; garlic, gingerroot, lemongrass, onions, peppers, mint; aloe for burns and bites; gungo peas; callaloo; sorrel. Topi tambo and corn too besides. For trees, they had mamapom, calabash for making bowls and spoons, starch mango, long mango, bellyful mango, otaheite apple, ortanique, five finger, jamun, breadfruit, and cocoanut. When Thandiwe went there to live eight years before, she brought her skills at managing hatcheries. She had supervised the people from the compong as they followed her instructions, building seven fish ponds into the hillside and connecting them up with pipes that kept the ponds fed with fresh water from the rain house that stood on the highest level of the compong. Now, she and two-three of the compong people bred hassa, tilapia, river prawn, and frogs in the ponds. Guinea fowl and sensay fowl scratched among the rows and hills of plants, providing meat and eggs and keeping the snakes down. The pickens enjoyed hunting for the hidden places where the fowl laid their eggs. The compong also kept agoutis for meat, in a big run at the bottom of the incline. There were plenty people around today, working their plots. Babies rolled about on blankets on the ground. Old men and women lay in hamacas strung under the trees, old-talking. This compong was where Veycosi and Gombey would move to when Thandiwe married them. It was a pleasant place, not too far from the Colloquium, where he would continue his research, setting old books to music and learning and performing them with the griots of his line. And eventually he would be assigned his own line of students, to teach them the skills of sight-reading, scribing musical scores, and orchestral singing.

Or maybe, having proved to Thandiwe and Gombey that he

could finish what he set out to do, he would leave the Colloquium and take up a new skill; delivering mail, perhaps. Or even looking after any new pickens of Thandy's, should her womb quicken again. He realised he might enjoy that. These past few days, he'd been keenly missing Kaïra's company. Veycosi vowed to himself that when they got the girl back, he would spend more time with her. He would enjoy scribing some of her Mamagua tales "as told by Chynchin's incumbent Mamacona." He would go with her sometimes on her lamplighting duties.

Thandy sat on the lip of the pond and peered down inside it. Her face was grim, her eyes sunken. "I feel like I stopped breathing when Kaïra went missing," she said. "Like I can't get any air."

There had been no sign of Kaïra.

She stood and drew her tunic back on. "Come inside with me," she said. "Too many ears about."

Did Thandy wish to frolic, then? Despite her fretting over Kaïra? He missed Thandiwe's touch. Dalliance with others before marriage was all very well, even encouraged; how best to learn where your true heart lay? And dally they all three did, but Veycosi well loved the smell of Thandiwe's skin, her intent expression, her sucked-in breath as she was about to spend. He swallowed around a lump in his throat and followed her.

The house in which Thandy and her mother lived had thatch screens for walls. Filiang was out running errands just now. And of course, there was no Kaïra underfoot. They had the house to themselves. Veycosi eagerly followed Thandy into the room in which her hamaca was strung. She rolled one of the screens down. He sat on one of the low, polished wooden stools that she'd had decorated with carvings of Mamagua, her mile-long tail flicking like a giant whip.

Thandy turned to Veycosi. Gravely, she said, "I'm going to release you from our engagement."

The skin on his scalp tightened, as though he were cringing from a blow. Veycosi whispered, "So what; you going to throw me away just like that? Why, Thandy?"

Yet there was some relief in saying it out loud. He'd been choking on the words so long, feared to hear what she would say if he asked her plain.

She looked at him with dead eyes. Shark eyes. Then down at the little robe of Kaïra's she was wringing in her hands. "I'm carrying this heaviness all alone, Cosi. You can't help me."

"And Gombey? You releasing him, too?"

"I don't know. Without you, we are not a troie. Yet he love Kaïra like a father. He esteem me like a husband. You do neither."

"But—I do! I swear it!"

"Maybe you will find another two who want to wed you. That Samra woman seems good for you. You know whether she looking to form a troie?"

"I don't want—"

"Truth to tell, Cosi, I'm weary of your constant pranks. And how sure you always are that you know best. And how you run roughshod over people, no care for their own needs."

Her words were like blows to his diaphragm. They took his wind. He tried to choke out a reply. She spoke over him: "I know you have a good heart. But I fear that heart has had little practise. Kaïra's life will be hard. I fear you would be a better brother to her than a father. And a younger brother, at that."

"But I—"

Then they heard something out in the main space. The twin slap of a pair of leather alpagats walking towards the area they were in. They flapped like that because they were too big for the feet that wore them.

The little hairs on the back of Veycosi's neck stood up straight. Thandy gasped. Looked at Veycosi, her eyes wide and alive for the first time in days. "Kaïra," she whispered. She turned and pushed her way past the bamboo reed curtain in the doorway. Through the clacking sound of it settling back into place, Veycosi heard Thandy say, "Kaïra! Is you?"

No answer. Then a grunt, a thump, as of a body landing on the floor. And Thandy's voice again, high in terror: "Cosi!"

Veycosi was into the main room in a trice. Thandy was down on the slatted wood floor, curled into herself like a sow beetle, arms protecting her head. Her child stood over her, kicking viciously at that same head. The especial horror was Kaïra's face. There was no expression on it. No anger; nothing. Veycosi ran and snatched her up from Thandy. Still Kaïra kicked, trying to mash up the airself. One of Gombey's alpagats fell off her feet. The ball of her heel caught Veycosi in the groin. He shouted and crashed to the floor, but he held fast to Kaïra, who bit his arm right through the cloth of his robe. Veycosi tried to turn Kaïra's head away as Jacob would Goat's.

"Don't hurt her!" gasped Thandy.

She didn't see how gentle he was being? "Who you asking to have mercy?" Veycosi said through gritted teeth. "Me, or Kaïra?"

She didn't answer, but rocked to her knees and reached a hand to her child. Kaïra snapped at it, got Thandy in the flesh of her palm, and tore. Veycosi saw the blood start, heard her cry out in shock and pain, "My babbins, you don't know me?"

Looked like she didn't. She was reaching for Thandy's eyes now, her little fingers crooked into claws. And still not a word from the picken.

"Kaïra!" Veycosi said desperately. "Stop it!"

Which she did. She stood there, only stood, two arms hanging long, two eyes looking nowhere. Inside, perhaps.

Thandy wadded her robe hem into a ball and crushed it against her bleeding palm. She didn't watch at what she was doing. Her eyes were only for Kaïra. "Mama-ji," she whispered. "What wrong with her? Kaïra?"

She didn't answer. Nor Veycosi, when he groaned her name between clenched teeth. Hissing from the pain, he cupped his aching stones and rolled away from Kaïra's reach. If the girl took another fit, Veycosi wasn't ready to fight her off just yet. What the rass could make a playful little younggirl turn mad tiger like that?

Just like the other returned pickens.

Thandy touched Kaïra's shoulder with her good hand.

"Don't do that," Veycosi hissed. "You might get her started again."

But not a bit of it. Kaïra just stood there. Thandy knelt and gathered her into an embrace. "Kaïra," she said, "is what do you? You can talk any at all, daughter? You don't see me? You don't see Cosi? We been searching everywhere for you." She rocked with the girl in her arms. Kaïra's body followed along with hers, feet scraping the polished boards of the floor.

Thandy turned her weeping face to Veycosi, those big eyes looking to him for help, to make some sense of what was happening. To *him*. He missed her too bad; missed the Thandiwe who would look at him with delight, with need, with love. The first time in so long, and he had no answer for her. Veycosi struggled to his feet. "We have to get a doctor to take this fit from her." He bent and looked into Kaïra's empty eyes. Veycosi shuddered. "Tanama," he said, making shift to sound confident, like a man who could command fate. "I wager she going to know what to do. I going to get her."

Never mind that no doctor had been able to help a returned

picken yet. The last word had scarce left Veycosi's mouth when there was a shriek from outside. Thandy's neighbour Gert came running in to tell them that her daughter Gza, a girl picken who had also been missing, had stumbled back in a trance. When a neighbour boy went to greet her, she'd bitten out his throat; he'd bled out his life in the yard. "Is my cousin's boy that!" wailed Gert. "He been fostering with me. How I am to tell my cousin?"

Gert told them that Gza was now sitting alone on the floor in the room she shared with her brothers and sisters. "Fosseed's blood all over her robe and her mouth!" sobbed Gert. "And no look on her face; she didn't look neither glad nor remorseful. Cold, dead eyes." Gert burst into tears again. "Is like someone cut out her heart."

That look, that blank look from all the returned pickens as they attacked the ones who cared for them; that was how the stories started that the Blackheart Man of the scare-baby tales had claimed the returned pickens, had cut the hearts from them to feed his empty soul.

Little more, the news came that it was so all over Carenage Town. The missing pickens coming back, raggedy, drawn, and wordless, to set upon the first friend or family member they met. Twelve gone, but only eleven returned. Of the eleven, one, a picken named Confound, was killed by the best friend he attacked, as that friend fought in desperation for his life. Sem had set upon a sister ee'd been in the habit of tormenting. In fighting Sem off, ir sister beat ir so brutally that none could tell if the lassitude that came upon ir afterwards was the same one all the others were exhibiting, or some profound damage that had robbed ir of ir wits as a result of the beating. Only Tubang never attacked anyone. The first relative she'd bucked up was her aged grandda, who'd injured his legs in a fall from a horse, and who hadn't walked since. When Tubang came wandering up the path to her mother's house, her grandda had been in a hamaca strung beneath the porch roof. He had called out his granddaughter's name, and the picken had simply stopped moving. Stood there while her grandda shouted for help, and someone came to lead the picken into the house. And there Tubang had bided since, in the same helpless stupor as Kaïra and all the rest. The guards were hallooing up and down the streets, calling for the ones who had done this to the children to show themselves forth, or for any who had news to give it them.

Some bethought themselves on the Mirmeki and began bruiting it about that maybe it was the real, living blackhearts to blame, that they had poisoned the pickens as revenge for Carenage Town having put their forebears on display like so many statues. More calm heads pointed out that some of the blackhearted children were themselves Mirmeki. But suspicion fed fear and anger. One morning, a couple of young Mirmeki lads were found beaten, bruised, and unconscious in an alley outside a rum shop. They had been set upon by six masked people as they left the rum shop the previous evening. To hear the young men tell it, as they were being beaten, one of their masked assailants kept grunting, "Is so you did those pickens? Eh?"

As to the Ymisen ship, it was under quarantine. The talks had to cease while so many on the ship were ill with the flux that had come upon them. Ser Tierce was one of the first to recover. Yaaya supposed it was because, being royalty, ee had all ir life enjoyed better health than ir subjects, and thus had a more robust constitution.

———

"I don't know what more I can do for them," Thandiwe's mother, Filiang, told Veycosi. She was sitting cross-legged in a hamaca strung from the ceiling of the covered front porch of Thandy's house. She held a knife in one hand and a long manioc root in the other. "Thandiwe scarcely able to leave home in the days to go to work, and as for Kaïra . . ." She put the tip of the knife to the top of the manioc and turned the manioc round and round, scoring a spiralling cut down its length as she went. The dense white flesh beneath peered out in the line left by the knife. "Well," she said. She bobbed her chin towards the entranceway. "You go and see for yourself how she doing."

Veycosi looked at the doorway. "Thandy in there, too?" he asked Filiang.

"She there." With the flat of the blade, she started peeling a strip of skin from the manioc root.

Veycosi stepped closer to the entranceway. He couldn't see too far in; most of the blinds between rooms were rolled down. A hottish breeze from the outside blew in through the open doorway. No sound came from inside.

"Don't be frightened of Kaïra," said Filiang. "Is only one small girl."

"I not frightened," Veycosi replied. He still stood there. That small girl had dealt her mother a beating so bad, she'd been two days abed. About as long as his stones had ached from the kick Kaïra had dealt him.

"At least she not accidentally setting fire to the corn fields, or scaring me half to death in the night by pretending to be Mamapiche whispering outside my window," Filiang said. "She less harm now than when she was in her right mind. That is to say, once the killing rage passed. Thank you for calming her that day, son. If not for you, I don't know what she would have do to Thandy." She tossed a long strip of dark brown manioc skin into a calabash at her feet, put the cleaned root into a bowl on the floor, and took another of the roots from the basket cotched against her hip in the hamaca.

Veycosi set his shoulders and stepped into the house. "Thandy?" he called. "Inside?"

"Here," came Thandy's voice, from over by her sleeping room. Veycosi went in that direction. As he came closer, he could hear a soft huffing noise. He pushed aside the blind and entered the room. Thandy smiled at him and reached out her hands to him. Veycosi took them, and right away felt a peace like he hadn't for days. Since Kaïra had come back, she hadn't made any more mention of releasing Veycosi from their betrothal. Veycosi didn't mention it again either, for fear of putting the idea back in her head. And he was doing his best to show willing. He had told Samra he didn't need her help any longer. The flirtatiousness between them might be nothing more, but he wanted to keep his thoughts focused on Thandy. Samra had appeared puzzled and somewhat put off at his news. She acquiesced gruffly and had stayed away since. Veycosi missed their arguments. Though if there were any truth to the scolding Thandiwe had given him just before Kaïra came back, it appeared he missed much in his interactions with others.

"Cricket," Thandy said softly. "I been longing to see you."

Words he'd much desired to hear, but Veycosi was already looking towards Kaïra. The child's face was empty, her eyes dull. She was repeatedly sitting down and jumping up again. Her breath exploded in heavy, exhausted pants.

Sorrow clouded Thandy's face. "Kaïra, love," she said. "Stop that, please?" But it was like she hadn't said anything. Kaïra just kept sitting and standing, over and over.

"She will do that till fatigue take her. Then she will collapse and sleep for a bit." Thandy pulled her face into a smile. "Come sit with me, nuh?" She nodded towards a seating mat on the floor.

He sat. She sat beside him. Kaïra sat down hard on her own

mat, sprang back up again. "Kaïra," Veycosi said, "stop it please, picken?"

But she kept right on. How was it she'd let Veycosi command her the last time, then?

That familiar tweak of excitement plucked at Veycosi's throat-strings; the one he got just before a particularly insightful thought. Could it be? "Kaïra," Veycosi said, "sit down."

And Kaïra sat. And remained so, her breath wheezing in and out of her lungs.

Thandy put her hands to her mouth. Her eyes were big. "Kaïra," Veycosi said again, his heart hammering in his gullet, "come over here."

Still sitting, the girl started pulling herself towards Veycosi with her hands, dragging her body along the floor. Thandy made a small whimpering sound. Veycosi barked, "Kaïra, stop that!"

The picken stopped sudden, like a wall had sprung up to block her.

So she needed precise instructions, then. "Thandy, tell her to come over here to you."

"I been trying. She don't pay me any mind."

"Try again. But not a question or suggestion. Just tell her. And call her by name first, so she know you're talking to her."

Thandiwe's face was avid with hope. "Kaïra, girl," she said, "please come to me."

Kaïra did nothing, just bided where she was. Veycosi was puzzled, with a rising sense of uneasiness. "Kaïra, please stand up and walk over here to us."

And the pesky picken did exactly that. She came and stood in front of them, her gaze empty. Veycosi and Thandy experimented with a few more simple commands. Sit down. Stand up. Turn around. Jump up and down. They even called Filiang in and bade her tell

Kaïra to perform actions as well. The picken didn't respond. Filiang gave up and went back to the porch to continue peeling manioc.

Pickens' eyes in the dark, begging guidance . . . Veycosi's sense of unease increased, an unnameable anxiety buzzing behind his eye sockets.

Thandy put her arms around her insensible picken. "Mama-ji," she said, "look how the child mind you. She love you plenty bad, you know, Cricket?" Her eyes looked wet all on a sudden.

"Her?" Veycosi kissed his teeth, trying hard as he might to make a joke of it. "You mean she loved asking me unanswerable questions."

Thandy's face darkened. She clapped her hands together in his direction to silence him. "You must make fun of everything? This is my picken standing here, with not one thought in her head!"

Shame heated up Veycosi's face. He was making a mess of this. "Beg pardon." He stroked Kaïra's head. The child's hair was sopping wet with sweat. Veycosi longed for just one sensible word from her, one smile. Her energy was spent, but here they were, giving her commands. He pulled an unresisting Kaïra into his lap, cradled her there, else she'd have slid bonelessly off.

Her bones were twig-thin as a baby bird's. Every breath shook her small body. The words were out before he knew it. "Thandy, foster her with me for a little while."

Veycosi couldn't believe what he self was saying. But he kept on: "It look like she will listen to me, so maybe she won't hurt herself and you can get little bit of rest. Only until she starts to mend again." If she ever did.

"Cosi, I can't—"

"Gombey living in his ma's compong, not far from me. Between us, we won't let her come to harm. Let us do this for you, Thandy."

She was already shaking her head no when Filiang called from outside, "Cricket, come quick! Your camel sick!"

"Mama's tits!" Veycosi leapt up off the floor. "Kaïra, bring that bowl of groundnuts and come!"He stopped short. "No, I'm sorry—" He was so used to giving Kaïra little jobs to do to keep her from underfoot, he'd forgotten the state the picken was in.

Thandiwe burst into sobs. Veycosi turned. Kaïra had picked up the big calabash of groundnuts that was on the table and was coming towards him. She was hugging the bowl to her front with its wide mouth against her chest. Nuts spilling everywhere. She was doing what Veycosi'd asked. When she saw that Veycosi wasn't moving, she stopped, too. There was no denying the power he had over the girl.

Thandy looked at Kaïra. Veycosi looked at Thandy. She took Kaïra by the hand. "Sweet goddesses," said Thandy, "is what really happened to my child?"

"Cricket!" Filiang called.

Thandy shouted back, "We coming, Ma!" Veycosi told Kaïra to accompany them, and the three of them ran to find Goat.

The camel was over by the big outdoor ovens in Thandiwe's compong. She was down, lying on her side, her bamboo-pole legs flung every which way. Crouching beside her was Cuffee, the neighbour who had helped in the search for Kaïra. Goat rarely let anyone near her head. But look like she didn't have any fight in her this time. She was breathing hard, her eyes rolling. Little groans escaped from her with every breath. Near her mouth were several mounds of wet, white stuff. They reeked with the odour of vomitus. There was foam about Goat's muzzle and she was kicking weakly at her own belly with her hind legs. Veycosi knelt beside Cuffee. "What happen to her?"

Cuffee spat to one side. "Gwine kill this so-and-so leggo beast, if raw dough don't kill her first."

"Dough?"

"She eat out the dough I had rising to bake tomorrow, the bread for everybody to break fast with."

Veycosi said, "I see her eat dirt last night with no harm. How plain flour and water could make her take sick so bad?"

"It's the yeast."

Veycosi gasped. "The dough's swelled in her belly!"

Cuffee nodded. Veycosi marked how Goat's belly was enlarged, the stiff hairs that covered it standing out straight. Goat moaned again. Veycosi found a little sympathy moan escaping his lips as well.

Cuffee informed him, "She already spit out so much dough that I think it must be most of it, but her belly still swelling."

"What we going to do?" Veycosi asked.

Cuffee shrugged. "Don't know. I not no cameler."

Jacob would know what to do, but suppose Goat died before he could find him?

A little voice piped up, "Tha mun give her saleratus." It came from a dirty-faced youngboy lying along the top of the compong's cement wall.

"Akeem!" said Thandy. "How many times I have to tell you not to spy like that? Why you don't bide with your own people's camps out in the dry lands?"

"Yer camel going to dead in no time, an' ye don't pay me mind," he said. "Belly go rupture, and she dead."

"Saleratus could work, though," mused Veycosi. "If gas is what making her belly swell, saleratus could relieve it. You have any, Cuffee?"

"Yes. I use it to rise certain breads. How much to give her, Akeem?"

"I could come inside?"

Cuffee glanced around at the compong people present. No objections. "Come then, nuh?"

Akeem grinned and jumped down. He came over and looked
at Goat. He crouched beside the camel. He palped her flank, low
on her body. Goat snapped at him and caught him on the side of
his hand. "Shite!" Akeem cried out. He shook the bitten hand and
sucked away the blood. "Ah, girl, I know," he said. "Tha hurts
something frightful, nah true? We'll have thee better again soon."
To Cuffee, he said, "Gie her enough to overflow my hand," he said.
"In a full bucket of cool water. Then give her two more buckets of
water, an' she will take them."

Cuffee nodded. "Soon come." He ran off to get the saleratus.

Veycosi gave Goat's flank a tentative pat. Her skin twitched,
then rippled, belly-deep. She moaned. Veycosi pulled his hand away.
He remembered Thandy and Kaïra, still standing there. "Kaïra,
give me the bowl, please." She'd spilled most of the groundnuts as
she ran, and spilled even more in handing the bowl over.

Akeem watched her, his lips curled up in distaste. "Blackheart
Man ate her soul," he said.

"No such thing," Veycosi told him, offering Akeem the bowl
with what was left of the unshelled groundnuts. Akeem took a
handful, slipped them into his sleeve.

Kaïra plopped herself down right at Goat's head. Veycosi
reached for the girl. "No, picken! She will snap!"

Goat did not. She put her head in Kaïra's lap. Kaïra didn't appear to notice.

Thandy said, "Don't make her bite."

"I will watch her." He bade Kaïra shell and eat some of the
nuts. As an afterthought, he specified exactly nine of them. The girl
complied. Goat showed no interest in having any, even though they
were close as her own muzzle. She must be very sick indeed.

Cuffee came back out with a tin bucket full of water. He told
Akeem, "I dissolved the saleratus in here."

By now, poor Goat was too ill to protest much as Akeem used the hem of his robe to wipe the slimy froth from her mouth, then poured the medicine and the two buckets of water down her throat while Cuffee and Veycosi held her muzzle. Once they'd done that, she groaned and laid her head back in Kaïra's lap. The two of them remained quiet like that a good while, till Goat commenced to belching in long, redolent eruptions. Slowly, her flank began to subside. "Now," said Akeem, "give her a small measure of castor oil or coconut oil."

Cuffee fetched castor oil. Akeem helped him feed it to the animal. Little more time, they could hear a rumbling from Goat's middle. "It's working," pronounced Akeem. "Good girl."

Goat sighed, rocked to her knees, and stood. Akeem had to scramble out of the way as the camel let loose a stream of pale, foul-smelling shite, and a fart stink enough to singe nose hairs. But her belly was almost back to its usual size, and she seemed more comfortable.

Veycosi had Kaïra take Goat's lead and walk her to the first fish pond and back. This she did, under Thandy's and Veycosi's watchful eyes. So it came about that Thandy agreed to let Veycosi and Gombey mind Kaïra for a while. She stuffed a pack full with Kaïra's clothes, toys, and books, and they tied it to Goat. "Kaïra," Veycosi said, "follow me, please." They walked to his house, Goat ambling along beside them. Veycosi kept a guiding hand protectively on Kaïra's shoulder, steering her around anything in her path. He paid no mind to the people tittering at him because he walked a camel rather than riding it. His thoughts were only for Kaïra.

Over the days, Veycosi's Reverie phantasms became nightmares, and the nightmares worsened. In them, the piche-imbued man's

face loomed large and leering. He chased Veycosi through the halls
of the Colloquium, cackling and brandishing a spear with which to
jook out Veycosi's heart. In some of the dreams, Kaïra and Tierce
sat on the floor, playing a game of cat's cradle, oblivious to Veycosi's voiceless screams for pity.

In those days he spent much of his time keeping Kaïra fed and
making sure she bathed herself and used the latrine. Gombey came
by frequently, but mostly the tasks fell to Veycosi, who would pass
the long hours by chanting to the picken the tenor parts of songs
of lost books found. Kaïra seemed less restive when she heard the
melodies. Oddly, Goat seemed to like them, too. She had taken to
following Kaïra as close as she could. Wherever Kaïra bided, there
Goat would rest also, crouching down in the position Jacob called
"kush." Sith she couldn't come into the apartment, when Kaïra
was inside, Goat would lower herself by her front legs and make
shift to crawl onto the porch. She looked so imperiously forlorn
there, making mawing sounds at the window, that Veycosi took to
leaving it open and flinging the jalousies wide. Goat would thrust
her head on her long neck in through the window and regard Kaïra
watchfully. And when Veycosi sang, she would rest her head on
the window ledge and moan softly, apparently with contentment.
Occasionally someone came by with a tale of Chynchin to recite
to Veycosi. Word had gotten around that he was looking for such.
His stack of table-books was growing. He had thought to spend his
time preserving the books of others, not making one himself.

Thandiwe visited them most evenings. Veycosi craved her company, eager to tell her any slight news of Kaïra's behaviour that
might at a squint be construed as progress. Thandy remarked on
how sweet and gentle Veycosi was with her daughter. There was no
more talk of unbinding their engagement.

Were he being honest, Veycosi would have to admit to himself that Kaïra was showing no change at all. The same slack jaw, the same blank gaze. Once, Veycosi bade her smile, but the rictus Kaïra contrived at that command was a terrible thing to see. Minutes later, when her expression hadn't changed and spittle was dribbling from her mouth corners, Veycosi had told her to relax her face again.

All told, Veycosi was satisfied to be in Thandiwe's good graces once more, and to be doing his best by Kaïra. But he was daily consumed by an unfathomable guilt, and when he tried to sleep come nighttime, he would spend his nights once more fleeing the Blackheart Man in his dreams, and would wake sweating and breathless, wound about in his hamaca, half-strangled in his own sheets. And always, his nightmare pursuer had the face of the broken-legged man the piche workers had dug up, with its sour, furious expression.

And it was nonsense. Veycosi was exasperated at himself for letting a fanciful childhood notion rule him thus. He determined to visit the piche soldiers where the guards had placed them, lining the plaza of Carenage Town's seat of government. He would look well and good upon the face of that particular man, and thus satisfy himself that the poor, hapless soul was only a human being like himself who had made the wrong choice and thereby met a horrible death a couple of centaines before.

He went early in the morning, when the sun wouldn't be too hot on Kaïra, and there would be fewer people out and about to gawk at the younggirl.

When they arrived to the plaza, Veycosi checked for the umpteenth time that Kaïra was seated solidly up high on Goat's back, and holding on well to the rein. For himself, he walked at Goat's head, holding her lead. He reached up and patted Goat's flank. "Good girl," he said. Then he turned his attention to the reason he had come here.

Such grim figures they cut. No wonder there were stories in the news now about people spying a tar-covered figure creeping around the town. The very thought made Veycosi's heart stutter, and he usually such a sensible soul. Poor sleep and fretting over Kaïra were keeping his mind uneasy.

He remarked upon one of the piche statues as he passed it; a soldier woman, half-fallen off her camel, which had apparently stumbled down onto its front knees. Were it an actual statue, it would have been comical. But these were two beings, petrified at the moment of their ignominious death.

A thump from the shadows over yonder; Veycosi started. A wooden bucket rolled out from beneath the legs of a statue. Then came giggles, and the sound of feet pattering away. Veycosi caught sight of the bottoms of muddy little feet in flight. "Ey!" he yelled. "Mash, allyou! Get along now!"

A mirth-filled face peeked from behind a wall; another from atop it. Veycosi shook a finger at them. They fled, laughing.

He retrieved the wooden bucket they'd dropped. Whiting had spilled out of it, at the foot of the statue the little devils had been sporting with. They had already painted *Mamapiche Grindle Crewe Before All* on the side of the hapless pitch camel, and had whitened the nose of its rider. Pickens throughout town were cresting a wave of excitement as their crewes prepared to compete for best float come Mamapiche Day. "Beg pardon, sirrah," Veycosi whispered to the rider. "You know how youth stay." The man on the camel had one arm flung out, the other grasping at his collar, his face straining as it had been when he'd died, as his nose and lungs clogged with piche. Nearby was a piche-mired donkey, its legs thrown every which way as it had done in its efforts to struggle free of the piche. Someone had propped it against a rockstone so that it would stay upright. Who the rass had had the bright idea of lining the Palavera avenue with such as these? Samra was right. Chynchin had triumphed two centaines ago; need they make sport of the Ymisen dead, too?

Veycosi spied the one he had come to see. He gasped. His heart commenced to stuttering in his chest. His hands trembled. But he would see this through. He clicked at Goat to recommence walking, and he led her and her indifferent passenger to the man's side. Standing in front of the unfortunate soul, Veycosi made himself as calm as he could. The man was in a crawl, reaching forwards. Veycosi crouched to examine him further. Perhaps the man had been vertical, trying to climb out of the sucking piche. He examined the man's face. Surely the nose of his nightmare apparition had been more peaked, the lips less full. This was just a man. A real one, not the product of Veycosi's imagination. His features marked him as Garfun blood. And now Veycosi noticed that the man's clothing was ancient Garfun, not ancient Mirmeki. What was a Chynchin man doing amidst this group of soldiers? Had he been their prisoner, then?

Someone up to Mamapiche japes had found a tattered jacket in the Ymisen style, turned it inside out, and sat it on the statue's shoulders. That was another possibility; that the man had been a turned coat, for true. Hadn't Yaaya mentioned someone such in her version of the tale?

The face wore an aspect of terror. In a moment of sympathy, Veycosi reached out and touched the man's cheek. The black gum shifted a little under his fingers. Under the warmth of the sun, the piche of him had softened till it felt like flesh against Veycosi's palm. It would harden again in the cool of night. Disturbed, Veycosi snatched his hand away. A small blob of piche from the figure had stuck to his palm. Not thinking, Veycosi wiped the hand on the chest of his robe, on the left side. Then recollected himself. Too late. The piche had already stuck to the fabric. "Damnation!" He tried to pull it off, but it wouldn't come.

"Pursuing a new area of study, I see." Veycosi jumped to his feet. It was Steli. He nodded to Kaïra. "Good morning to you, Kaïra." Steli didn't seem to expect a response, but the thing was well done; few nowadays treated Kaïra as though she were actually present. Veycosi had a surge of missing his stern but principled teacher.

Veycosi informed him, "Ymisen has banned me from her ship while so many aboard it are sick. I'm looking after my intended stepdaughter instead."

"So I see. That is good of you." For all he was giving Veycosi a compliment, his lips were pursed like he was sucking limes. Fair he was, but slow to forgive.

The sun was full hot now. "Kaïra," said Veycosi, "pull your hood on to protect your head."

Steli's eyes went round as Kaïra obeyed. "Your charge getting better, Veycosi?"

"Sadly no, mestre, much as I wish it. Is just that she will obey simple commands if I give them. Only me, though. She don't hearken to no one else."

Steli just gaped, lacking for words. Veycosi said, "I sorry to hear about your Yddyta."

Grief replaced the amazement on Steli's face. He indicated some healing scratches on his face. "She gave me these. I rather see she and Kaïra plotting their usual tricks together. Not the way they are now."

Veycosi nodded sympathetically. "Thandiwe told me they were bannas."

"And that is the first you knew of it?" Steli replied, sneering. "So little you know about your woman's child. You only paying her mind now that the Blackheart Man take her?"

Veycosi didn't respond to Steli's jibe because, to his shame, it was true.

"Yddyta had piche on her hands when she arrived back to our compong," Steli said. "And reeds."

Gombey's old alpagats had been piche-fouled along the bottoms when Kaïra came back wearing them. Filiang had told him she'd found reeds between Kaïra's toes when she was bathing her.

Veycosi said, "You don't believe that codswallop that is the Deser—the Mirmeki who did this?"

Steli shook his head slowly. "For a rarity, I agree with you on something. The Deserters don't have no reason to have done such a heinous thing. After all, it happened to their pickens, too."

Strong emotion blindsided Veycosi. He couldn't tell what exactly he was feeling, but he was trembling with it. It was happening frequently nowadays. Veycosi's blood was running too hot with chagrin to bide any longer. He pulled air into his lungs to steady himself and said, "I must be on my way, Steli. Give Hleb good day for me, you hear? And tell her and Thianis to take courage."

Steli glowered and stepped slowly back out of Veycosi's way.

Time was, Veycosi had been one of Steli's favourite pupils. But he'd squandered that favour on playing the fool.

He clicked at Goat and set about going back the way they had come. There were more people about. Some pointed at Kaïra and whispered to their companions behind their hands. Some nodded sympathetically at Veycosi.

Kaïra's brow was bedewed with sweat. Maybe there would be a water-cocoanut cart along the way, so he could get cool drinks for the three of them.

As he was about to exit the plaza, Veycosi turned to look one last time at the piche man down on his hands and knees.

The man's face was turned sideways. He was looking over his shoulder, right in Veycosi's direction.

Hadn't he been looking forwards before, in the direction of his own outstretched hand? And how did he now seem to be reaching towards the donkey propped on the rockstone?

Bile rose in Veycosi's throat. His skin pimpled, his mind so agitated that he couldn't rightly remember how the man had been placed before.

He swallowed his gorge and continued, shuddering, on his way. The rhythm of his steps eventually began to quiet him. He wished he had the benefit of Kaïra's observant eye, the child's readiness to talk about anything. He wished so much.

Instead, he and his two companions continued silently home.

Veycosi put the plate down at the end of his worktable, where Kaïra was sitting. "Kaïra, child, eat your lunch."

Kaïra commenced to using the pappadums to scoop up the channa-pease curry.

When Steli's wife, Hleb, came to Veycosi's apartment and begged him to see whether Yddyta would mind him, maybe he should have told her no. He did not. Instead he tried, and found that Yddyta, like Kaïra, did indeed obey his commands, once he kept them simple. Veycosi saw the look on Hleb's face progress from tearful through wonder to suspicion. But he told Yddyta to mind what her ma and das bade her, and that worked tolerably well. He would offer to do so for Thandy as well. Only not just yet. Kaïra was frankly a botheration in many ways, but it was a comfort to have her still body sitting calmly by while Veycosi reread his notes and wrote out each folktale of Chynchin as fully as he remembered it. The picken did wander some. Frighted Veycosi half to death the first time she went missing. But Gombey found her down by her favourite riverbank Mamagua-spying spot. She was just sitting and staring out over the water. Goat was with her. Veycosi tried to keep an eye on them, but between them they had wondrous luck at giving him the slip. That time, he and Gombey agreed not to bother Thandiwe with the story of Kaïra's escapade.

Veycosi remained curious about how the three witches might have drowned the soldiers in piche all those years ago. Goat's misadventure with the bread dough gave him the idea to try yeast dough, dyed black with chenette fruit. He experimented, badgering the Colloquium's mess for flour and yeast for each experiment, until he hit upon a dough mixture dense enough that one of Kaïra's clay marbles wouldn't sink into it directly he dropped the marble onto the dough. Then he borrowed from Gombey some of the tiny soldier figures he and the Carenage elders were using to plot battle strategy. He laid down a strip of the dough on his table and commenced to dropping the small figures onto it one by one. The dough did swallow them, at a creeping pace. That tallied with how all the stories described the soldiers' engulfment.

But once the soldiers were engulfed, what would have immediately hardened the dough enough for the villagers to dance on it right afterwards? Unless that part of the story were pure fancy. Would be a pity, because the bit about dancing added joy to what was otherwise a gruesome tale. Maybe they had danced *beside* the trench, rather than on it.

Too besides, where would the original escaped slaves have found enough flour and yeast to fill the trench, and enough dye to colour it? He considered grated manioc, mixed with water to form a slurry. He rejected both flour and manioc, sith both were staples.

The Chynchin inhabitation was new in those days, and settled upon a desert island even the Cibonn' had rarely visited. They produced barely enough food to feed themselves.

And he couldn't arrive at a tipping-point number of soldiers such that the next one he dropped onto the dough made it collapse and swallow all the half-mired soldiers at once.

Not to mention, wouldn't the soldiers have noticed all this trench-digging and trench-filling activity? So many questions he couldn't yet answer!

Getting drying dough off the tiny soldiers had been a wearisome piece of business.

Kaïra coughed, bringing Veycosi's mind back from its ruminations. Was the food caught in her throat? Veycosi started up to go to her, but then she was breathing clear again. "Drink three swallows of the water in the mug, picken."

Suppose the villagers hadn't danced right away on the piche or dough or what have you? Maybe the day's heat would have cooked the dough such that they were able to dance upon it later?

Veycosi pictured the villagers dancing on the crust of a giant loaf of bread stuffed with dead soldiers like so many pigeons in a pie. No, it didn't seem likely the crust would hold. It was all too fanciful to credit.

He was humming. Recently, he'd begun to come up with tunes to which to set the tales he was uncovering. The battle of the piche lake would employ an ostinato: a minor third, G to B-flat, with a four-note repeating phrase in an urgent, majestic style to quicken the blood. Slaps of the djembe to evoke the hoof-strikes of mounts. Chords progressing from G minor to E-flat to F major, back up to G minor . . .

The clinking sound of Kaïra's fingernails against the bowl brought Veycosi back to himself. The child had eaten all the food, but still kept miming the actions. "Kaïra, stop." Veycosi wiped food off Kaïra's mouth, using a corner of his robe. The yellow curry stain wouldn't come out, but he paid that no mind. He would have to remember to trim Kaïra's fingernails. They had gotten overlong.

He took Kaïra to the privy, commanded her to relieve herself if she felt the urge. But he didn't think to tell the picken to squat, so there was some cleaning up to do after that escapade, and new clothing to dress Kaïra in, and the dirty clothing to be brought to the washer's.

How long since he had just taken a stroll without people looking and pointing? How long since he'd checked in on the negotiations with Ymisen, or visited Ma? Since he'd gone anywhere without a blackhearted girl and a ragged camel traipsing along beside him?

Not so long, to tell the truth, but it seemed centaines. Nuh must be time for Gombey to come and take Kaïra from him for a day? Maybe tomorrow? Suddenly Veycosi longed to drop in on Ma and his das.

Every so often, someone would drop by to recount to him some story they had learned from an elderly relative or friend. Many were the same old stories everyone knew, but every so often, he'd get one with a new detail in it, or an entire tale he'd not heard before. He'd taken to combining versions to round them out.

He missed Samra something fierce. He'd been avoiding her, avoiding troubling feelings that warred with his love for Thandiwe. But now that he and Thandiwe were bonded solid again, was there any need? He would send word soon to ask her to call upon him and Kaïra. Beg her to help him transcribe his retellings of the tales he'd collected.

Veycosi and Liguanea, his ma, touched cheeks; right, left. As ever, Ma smelled of sugar and cocoanut and tabac. She stepped back, smiling. "You looking good," she said. "Your das are in the backyard."

Veycosi replied, "Come to see you, Ma. Took a chance that Da Kola and Da Woorari would be here, too."

"He and Woorari and the gardener hilling my yams for me."

Veycosi nodded and made for the door. He passed through Ma's back terrace with its polished red stone surrounded by herbs in clay pots. Then out onto the sandy dirt, through the gungo peas patch, the wiri-wiri bushes—bright with little, round peppers in red, green, and yellow—and the small stand of cacao trees. He spied a low-hanging pod, a little longer than the palm of his hand. It was ripe; a creamy yellow with a red blush on one side. He plucked it from the trunk of the tree. It was well fat. He could scarcely get his hand around it. He cracked it open between his two palms. He picked out the fat beans inside and sucked on the sweet white pulp covering them. When he was a picken, he was forever bedeviling Ma by picking the best cacao before she could ask the gardener to harvest them. He would suck the beans dry of pulp. He even used to eat the stringy white fibre that ran through the centre of the pod, joining the beans each to each, though Ma would try to frighten him by telling him it would tie up his insides.

Ma's pumpkin patch and her yam hills were on the other side of the cacao. Da Kola hadn't seen Veycosi yet. Too busy arguing with Da Woorari while Adam the gardener listened in and dug yam hills.

"We should never do it, man!" said Da Woorari to Da Kola. "Times too unstable right now. Adam, shore up that plant over ya so."

Adam chopped his hoe into the soil where Da Woorari had pointed and started scraping together a fresh mound of dirt. He said, "Mestres, wartime is the best time to take a chance. If goods get scarce here, your wares going to be in high demand."

"Who say we at war?" Kola replied. Then he saw his son. "Cosi!" Kola put down the cutlass he was using to chop yams into chunks for planting. He smiled and pulled Veycosi to him. They brushed cheeks. "Adam," he said, "go 'weh with your talk about war. My son and his co-husband going to send Ymisen packing, you mark my words!"

"Yes, mestre."

Woorari said, "Raise the piche and bury every last man jack of them."

"Certain sure, mestre."

Veycosi embraced his other da, too. To get them off the subject of obeah, he asked, "What risk you thinking about undertaking, Da K.?"

Quick as cullybree wings, a frown flitted across Da Kola's brow and was gone again. "We have a chance to get a big shipment of rice," he said. "Over in Sondhane far from Chynchin."

"Three weeks there, four back," Veycosi said.

Da nodded, looking pleased that Veycosi knew the travel times. Rare enough that his son paid attention to the family business.

Da Woorari said, "Nice quality, too. Real nice."

"But we would have to sneak around the Ymisen fleet," said Ma, coming up behind them. She took the stick of tabac from her mouth and spat. "They stationed at every port on the island now. They not letting anyone from Chynchin leave, and not letting anyone from the outside enter."

"So we under siege?" Veycosi asked, shocked. He hadn't known about this new Ymisen action. So he couldn't have left for Ifanmwe, even if the Colloquium would have let him. What a way those people were bunging up his life! Is because the sight of their ship startled him why he had dropped that precious book into the reservoir.

Da Woorari laughed. "Can you rightly call it a siege? Is impossible to starve out any compong in Chynchin. Everybody growing their own food right on their grounds."

"Too besides," said Ma, "half the Ymisen soldiers coughing and sickly. One small little Chynchin phthisic that would scarcely make one of our babies sneeze." She took the hoe out of Adam's hands. "You doing it wrong," she told him. She set about mounding the nearest yam hill herself.

Before this, Veycosi wouldn't have noticed how peremptory his parents were with Adam. He wouldn't have noticed how almost everyone in Chynchin who did hard labour for others was Mirmeki. He went over to the water bucket standing nearby with a calabash cup floating in it. He dipped some cool water out of the bucket and took it over to Adam, who was sweating from all the work he was doing. Adam looked a little taken aback. He muttered a shy thanks, drank from the cup, then went to return it. But Veycosi took the cup from his hands. "Let me do it," he said gently.

His das had continued the argument over the rice. His ma handed the hoe back to Adam without even self looking at the man, and leapt into the debate with her husbands. Adam recommenced hilling the yams. Near as Veycosi could tell, he was doing it exactly the same as Ma had been.

Da W. said, "People stockpiling rice. Any dry goods. Just in case war come with Ymisen."

Veycosi contemplated his parents trying to sneak past the Ymisen fleet with their guns and cannons, and his mouth went dry. "Is too dangerous to try to leave," he told them.

Da K. nodded. "And getting back in would be a whole other piece of business."

Adam was planting the yam rootstock now, though it was clear he was listening in.

Da W. brightened. "Suppose we don't leave, exactly? We just need to get out from under this Ymisen influence. Me and Liguanea and Kola could retire to the east coast. Bring you with us, son. Even your family-to-be."

Ma's eyes lit up. "They have a nice compong out that way, just outside of Ouragan. They know me. Is there my third offside grandma used to live. They would take us in."

Woorari cheupsed; a sucking sound of irritation through his teeth. "What difference it make whether we in Carenage or Ouragan? Is still Chynchin, and Ymisen still dey-bout. You can't run from dog inside he own yard. Cricket, talk some sense into them two, nah? If we going, we should go entirely away."

Impossible choices. Stay, and risk being at the centre of a war. Try to leave Carenage, and risk getting caught. Retreat to Ouragan, only to perhaps find they hadn't gone far enough, and war still overran them. Go off in search of trade, and discover they couldn't return. Veycosi bit his lips in indecision, then pulled a quattie-coin from his pouch and held it up. It was a little bent at one edge, with a small black spot there. He must have used it to cook down Reverie for smoking. "See this?"

All three nodded. Adam watched as he hoed.

"If I throw it up in the air and let it come down, what odds you give me that it will hit a rockstone when it land?"

Da K. looked down at the ground. "But of course it must," he said. "Koo how many little rockstones here-bout."

Ma chided, "After you never made Adam clear the ground proper before starting to plant." Her voice was stern as she gazed at Da K., but her eyes were soft. Made Veycosi feel lonely all on a sudden. Over Adam's protests, Ma said, "Cosi-boy, what you on about?" They all looked at him.

Veycosi told them, "If I throw this quattie up and it hit a rockstone when it land, you will stay here in Carenage Town until this Ymisen business settle. If it hit plain dirt, you can take your chances and leave." He knew quite well what the odds were. This way, they would be stacked in favour of keeping his parents safe.

Woorari asked, "Leave and go where? To foreign, or to Oura-gan?"

"If it come to that, I will throw the quattie again to decide."

He flipped the quattie into the air. They all watched. Dirt, or rockstone?

But they never saw the coin land. A small buzzing blur above them, then a flurry, then a fall. A bird was fluttering in the dirt at Veycosi's feet, one wing trailing where his coin had broken it. Veycosi stared at it in horror as he realised what it was. He'd never seen one not flying. "A cullybree," he breathed.

"Is what you do, Cosi?" said Da Woorari, his voice quiet with dismay. "Is what you bring on us now?"

"But it was accidental," he replied. "Allyou saw how it happened."

"Don't matter," said Adam. "You going to have to do a civic duty as compensation, Maas' Cricket."

"Another one?" Veycosi protested, forgetting that he hadn't told them about the nonsense with the reservoir and the old book, praying that the broadsides and street chantwells hadn't reached them out where they lived yet. "I in the middle of doing one now."

Ma crooked a curious eyebrow at him. "Oh, yes? For what infringement, son?"

Adam shrugged. "Is compensation or lockup."

"Hush your mouth," Da Woorari told him. "He don't have to do a rass. Who to know what just happened?"

The cullybree was flopping from its back onto its front and back again. A film of red was spreading on its snapped wing. Veycosi muttered, "I will know. I will take it and go do the gods-damned penance." He pulled his over-robe off and threw it onto the bird. It was bigger than he'd reckoned from feeling them zip by his face up high on Tsigan' Rock. More the size of a small hen than of a sparrow. He put his hands around the lump the cullybree made in his robe. He picked it up, gently as he might. It struggled in his hands. Spots of blood began seeping through the fabric. The day Ymisen arrived, a cullybree had nearly been winged through Veycosi's carelessness. It was as though that day had been a rehearsal for this one.

"Mind yourself, Cricket," said Ma.

"Maybe someone can mend the wing," he told them. "That's all really wrong with it." He turned the bird over in one hand and carefully peeled back the folds of the robe. The cullybree squeaked and fought. "Hush," he cooed to it. "Quiet, now. I going to find someone to help you."

"I know a good bonesetter," said Da Woorari. "I see her mend a mongoose leg bone once. Healed it like it never break."

"Shite!" Veycosi had the broken wing folded back on itself. The bird was writhing in agony, hissing softly as it opened and closed its wide, flat beak.

"Woorari," said Da K., "now is not the time to be telling mako stories, man. How in blazes a mongoose going to find itself to a bonesetter?"

Veycosi shifted his hand beneath the bird so he was holding it just by its body. It yanked its wings free, the broken one hanging like a twig. The bird convulsed, and he dropped it. "Fuck!"

The bird tried to fly. It managed to keep the air for the space of one breath, then it flopped to the ground again.

"Catch ee! Catch ee!" urged the others as Veycosi went after it. He fetched it up again, made shift to pin it against his body with his forearm so he could hold its wing still. It snapped at him, caught his little finger in its beak. He cried out and pulled his finger away. Now both he and the bird were bleeding. The cullybree hissed and

gasped, but it was fighting less. "Rest easy," he urged it. It lay panting along his forearm.

He'd never seen a cullybree up close before this, much less
touched one. Most people hadn't; Chynchin paintings and sculp-
tures of cullybrees came from imagination and hearsay. The bird's
feathers seemed brown, in the main; a type of dark cream tea colour. Hard to say for true, for with every movement it made, a
rainbow of iridescence shot across those feathers.

"The mongoose belonged to my friend," said Da Woorari. "The
bonesetter, I mean. She name Nagle. She catch the beast trying to
thief out her chickens. She startle it when she come upon it in the
coop that night, so it didn't see the rooster attacking."

"A fowl set upon a *mongoose?*" cried Ma. "Woorari, you too
lie!"

"By Mama-ji's tits, not one word of a lie!"

The cullybree was an oddment, as though a picken had mixed
up the pieces of different puzzles and put them back together
wrong. Bottle-gourd body, tapered and bulbous like that of a
doctorbird. Tall-pupilled eyes like a cat's, and yellow. Flat, wide
duck beak. Pointy blue-green tongue, curling in pain at the present.
Teeth set into its mouth. What bird had *teeth?* Blasted thing hadn't
pecked him, it'd *bitten* him.

"Is the rooster crack the mongoose leg," continued Woorari.
"Nagle fixed it up, and it tamed itself to her."

The cullybree gasped. Its eyes fixed a stare. Its head flopped
back, and its plumage dulled from chocolata shot silk to riverbank
mud. Just so, in Veycosi's hands, it died.

"Ee dead," he said quietly.

"Guarded her chicken pen from other mongooses from then
on," Woorari told them.

"The bird dead."

"You mean to tell me a mongoose went wild on its own kind?" Ma asked Woorari.

Woorari shrugged. "Nagle showed it compassion. Maybe its own kind never did."

"Look," said Adam. He pointed to the fallen quattie on the ground. It had landed delicately on its edge, and remained balanced that way.

Ma kissed her teeth in frustration. "How we supposed to interpret that? Go or don't go?"

"Me *say*," Veycosi shouted, "the bloodclaat cullybree gone and dead!"

Four pairs of eyes met his. He held the carcass out to show them, and sucked the bitten tip of his little finger clean of his blood.

"Rass," said Da Woorari.

Veycosi sucked salt and looked at the body in his hand.

One of its teeth fell out, into the bloodstained folds of his robe.

The petty court was a long, high-roofed stone building with open doors at both ends and hinged panes in the roof, propped open today to let some breeze in. The building was in the same government plaza as the Palavera, which was also the grand court house, where larger crimes were adjudicated and tried, whereas the petty court was where minor charges were heard and decided upon.

A high counter ran the length of the petty court. Behind it sat a row of court administrators, one to a station. They each wore the same style of over-robe in dark red with narrow yellow stripes. A queue of people stood in front of each station, waiting their turns.

As Veycosi and his da Kola entered the building, a woman standing at the station closest to them was saying to the guard behind it, "I tell you, is my place she take at the market! All the higglers know

Tituba." She patted her chest as she said her name. "Everybody know say my stand is across from Angelou the cobbler, between Salome and her baskets and Farida and—"

"Is lie she telling!" said the woman beside her. She had a piece of paper waving around. "I got that space from Farida! Look the proof here-so!"

"Over there," said Da. "That look like the shortest queue." They took the end of the line. Ma had given Veycosi a piece of old reed cloth to wrap the dead cullybree in. The bird already had a faint smell of corruption. Veycosi'd never seen anything decay so quick.

"You sure you want to do this?" Da Kola asked him quietly. "Adam and Woorari won't talk your business, you know. Ma neither."

Veycosi thought about it little bit. His finger was still tingling from the cullybree bite. "No," he replied. "Gombey is my oldest banna, and he started as a guard. I couldn't look him in the face and know I was hiding something like this."

Da grunted. They stood for a time in silence, shuffling forwards little bit each time the line moved up. The speech all around them blended into their own composition; quarrelsome rhythms trying to drown out the songlike tones of people pleading their own cases, the screeches of playing pickens running up and down, punctuated by the guards' brassy voices calling for the next in line. Taken as a whole, Veycosi began to fancy it all as the polychromatics of a single, complex voice in multiple registers, trying to tell him something . . . something. . . .

In the day, one dozes under river embankments and in dark, semi-submerged caves, waiting out the heat of the sky-fire.

At night, one hunts. There are hundreds of us. Our eyes glitter red in the dark. One thrills to the rush of water over scales, to the scent of frightened meat, the bunching of muscle, lashing of tail, to the crunch between fanged teeth as the prey's body breaks open— be it carapace, scales, or skin—releasing flesh tender or stringy, hot and meaty. The gulping down of salty lumps, lubricated by the prey's bitter ichors.

Most often, it is a solitary existence. We come together in mating season. We lay our eggs in joint nurseries, and one female elects to look after them and the hatchlings. In alone times, one wanders the river and thinks one's reptilian thoughts, and one is content. . . .

Finally it was their turn. When Veycosi unwrapped the bloody package, the guard's eyes got big for so. She knocked her chair over as she jumped to her feet. The noise echoed in the long hall. Everybody else hushed. All eyes were on him and Da. The man behind him in the queue looked over his shoulder. "Mama, spare us," he whispered. Loudly, he announced to the crowd, "I think is a dead cullybree he have!" Tongues started wagging, people staring. Somebody said, "Koo the badluckiness Maas' Cosi gone and bring on we heads this time." Veycosi cursed himself for having worked so hard to be a recognizable face in Carenage Town.

The guard spat for luck, then opened a low door in the counter and let herself out. "Oonuh clear the way!" she barked. "Now!" The pressing crowd cleared a path to Veycosi and Da for her.

She grabbed Veycosi by the upper arm and pushed him towards the open gate in the counter. Da Kola followed. She took them to a door in the wall behind the counter and opened it. "Inside with me!" she snapped at them. They scurried to follow her. She closed and locked the door behind them.

They were in a small room with couple-three small tables, a few chairs at each one. On each table guttered a smoky oil lamp. A guard in a brown robe was lounging in one of the chairs, reading a leaflet. He jumped to his feet when he saw them.

"Sit," their adjudicator ordered them. They took the two closest chairs. She went round to the single chair on the other side, thereby putting herself under the protection of the guard, who remained standing behind the chair.

"Is who do this?" she asked, jutting her chin at the bird.

"Me," Veycosi replied. "It was a mistake."

"Too right. Give it me. Quick."

Veycosi held the dead cullybree out to her. She took it reverently from him, though her nose skinned up little bit at the smell. She stood and went through another door, this one in the back of the cubicle. He couldn't glimpse the space beyond it. She had closed the door too quickly. "What she going to do?" he asked the guard. The man looked right through Veycosi like his father was a glass-maker, and remained at attention.

So they sat to wait. The room was narrow and dark, with only one little window high up in the ceiling. Veycosi reckoned they used these rooms for when a matter turned out to be more serious than petty court could deal with in public. That alarmed him. For now, though, they waited. Little more time, he wearied of sitting, so he stood. The guard drew his machete. "Sit," he said.

"I just wanted to stretch my legs little bit."

"Sit."

Da Kola yanked on the sleeve of his robe and pulled him back down into his chair. "Don't argue with the point of a knife," he said. So Veycosi sat, and the guard resumed his stance. Time and time went by. Still the other guard didn't return. Veycosi was nodding off in the airless room when the door opened again. Made him jump. The guard who had brought them there came in, carrying the dead bird in its cloth wrapping. She put it on the desk, sat, and pulled paper, quill, and ink out of a drawer in the desk. She scribbled on the paper, then asked his particulars: name, what he did, who could speak for him.

"Me," said Da. "I'm his father."

She filled it all in on her forms. "Now tell me the story," she said, glancing at the package on the table. "Is what happened?"

Veycosi told her.

"You break a cullybree's wing by throwing a quattie at it?" she said. She snickered, then went serious again. "One so-so quattie? You sure you didn't use a slingshot and a rockstone?"

Veycosi shook his head. "I was only trying to flip a coin. I wasn't fixing to kill it. I didn't even see it."

More scribbling. "Is not you kill it," she said. "Not your quattie, any road."

"I don't follow you," Da told her.

The guard looked up from her writing. "The break in the wing might could have killed it, yes. But stopping killed it quicker."

She saw she wasn't making sense to them. "From the moment they hatch, cullybrees can't stop quiet, or they will dead," she explained. "That's why they mate in the air. That's why they lay on the fly; drop down moss into a crevice until it soft, and then drop the egg on the wing. Most of the eggs break, but some always land safe. They can lie still so long as they ain't hatch yet."

"Swive me. Then come hatching time—"

"If the hatchling is goodlucky, the action of pecking free of the shell will tumble the egg out the nest. Maybe the egg will bounce off the cliffside into the air. If it high up enough when that happen, the hatchling will bust out in midair and fly free. From then on, it can't ever stop still again." She smiled. "And the badlucky ones that not high up enough; well, that's the beginning of Mamapiche Festival."

The yearly rain of bickle from the sky; mostly around Tsigan' Rock and any other high places where cullybrees had managed to lay their eggs. Broken shells yielded up fatty pink-yellow yolks, stringy whites, and some of them contained the real delicacy: unhatched cullybree chicks so small that three of them fried crisp scarcely made a mouthful. Chynchin people waited all year and laid bets on the date of that few hours on a single day when the eggs came down. When the rain began, everybody laid down work and play and ran out of doors with bucket, calabash, pan; whatever they could find to catch the broken eggs. Hatching night was the biggest feast night of the year. The pieces of shell were painstakingly picked out from the eggs, and any unhatched chicks were set aside to be cooked separately. They scrambled the eggs with butter and thyme and spread them out onto plates. They seasoned the chicks with sea salt, scotch bonnet pepper, and chardon beni, fried them whole, and bedded them onto the plates of scrambled eggs, with fried, baked, or boiled johnnycake on the side. Then it was time to feast. Out came the rumbullion, the jugs of bittersweet mobby, the ginger beer. You tore off pieces of johnnycake and used them to scoop up the egg. As to the birds, you ate them whole, tiny bones and all; they crunched like celery stalks. And next morning, the pickens, their bellies still round from gorging themselves the night before, would open the Mamapiche Parade with the floats they had been planning in camps out in the bush. Thandy swore there was even a river fish that only ate that one night per year when Mamapiche threw down her annual feast. Ate till it could scarcely swim, for that meal had to last.

"So," said the guard, "is the hoosegow for you."

Veycosi gasped.

Da asked, "You would really jail him over a mistake?"

"Mistake or malice, don't make no difference. Is god's bird."

"But I have a commission with the cacique. I have to accomplish it within the sennight." Macu and the Colloquium had set him no specific time, but this woman didn't need to know that.

She shrugged. "That is your lookout, maas'. Your sentence is ten days."

There came a stench of rot. Da had opened the cloth in which Veycosi'd wrapped the bird. "But somebody cut it open!" he said. Da held out the rotting bird and looked at the guard for explanation. Veycosi could see where someone had not only slit it from gullet to gizzards, but had gutted it too besides.

The guard smiled. "That's why your sentence is only ten days, not two complete sennights. The guards have it to say that a taste of cullybree heart will make your own heart strong. I can't kill one of the birds, but I didn't have to kill this one. You bring it to us dead already. I done grill it. Me and Daigle here"—she indicated the guard who'd been standing watch over them—"can each have a little bit."

Daigle grinned at Veycosi. "Thank you, maas'."

And then there was nothing to do but let himself be marched to the hoosegow. "Da!" Veycosi shouted as they led him away. "Tell Gombey and Thandy! Somebody have to look after Kaïra! And Goat!"

One was content, that is, until three of your kind tore a hole in the tissue of "what is," right in the place where one happened to be basking on the riverbank in the shade of a low-hanging branch. It was quiet, and sudden.

One became two, cleft in twain.

Two became carved stone, transported to the hilltop
overlooking the sea.

Thus did Chynchin acquire a new deity.

Sister, why you even bothering to try to tell him our story,
when humans haven't the wit to hear us?

Because is a fine game, this telling of tales. I only wish to
play, too.

As an invisible playmate? You mystify me. But suit yourself.

Chapter 6

THERE WAS A MAN *named Titen who often amused himself by hunting and eating cascadura and its eggs. Cascadura fish live in the pockets of water that pool in the crannies of hardened piche that is Mamapiche's body. Cascadura are Mamapiche's children, and thus tapu to eat. Titen knew this well, but loved the taste too bad.*

Titen and his spouses had six children, but Titen's favourite was the youngest, a sweet boy picken named Alexei. When Titen went hunting in the bush and brought home peccary and guinea fowl for his family, he would prepare the meat and set aside the choicest parts for himself and Alexei. As to his wife and co-husband and the other five pickens, they had to content themselves with gnawing on the tough pieces remaining.

But even Alexei didn't know of Titen's habit of marauding cascadura nests. That he did in private, hiding in the bush to light a fire on which to cook his prey. He would squat by the fire and consume fish and eggs and all by himself, gorging till belly full.

When Mamapiche learned how Titen thus defiled her body and her children by not sharing her bounty, she became enraged.

She disguised herself as Titen's wife and slayed Alexei. She cut out the boy's heart and, still in her guise as Titen's wife, fed it to Titen, claiming it was the tender heart of a young wild hog he had brought home from the hunt. After Titen ate the heart, Mamapiche revealed to him the gutted body of his dead son. She said, "Oh, blackhearted man, as you cut out my heart by killing and eating my children, so I have cut out yours by making you feast on your own child. Eat no more feasts in solitary, or I will compel you to slice out and eat the hearts of your remaining pickens."

Mad with grief, Titen took himself to the soft, hot centre of the Mother Lake and threw himself in. Mamapiche took him to her bosom, and there the Blackheart Man remains, keening and mourning and begging her forgiveness.

But when pickens are own-way and don't heed their parents, Mamapiche sends her Blackheart Man after them, to slice them open and devour the living hearts from their breasts. And while he does so, he weeps for his folly, and for his own lost Alexei.

The guard stopped in front of the barred gaol cell that was to be Veycosi's lodgings for the next little while. There were three other cells in this section, all empty. He had spied perhaps ten such units of four cells when he entered the gaol compong. "Just me one?" he asked the guard, who had opened the cell and was ushering him inside.

"Nobody else at this hour," the guard replied cryptically.

The cell was perhaps three strides across. Walls covered with white plaster. Two small windows, high up. No glass, just bars. They let in air and light and had wooden jalousies that could open and shut with a long string attached to them. No hamaca. Instead, a plastered clay sleeping platform built into the wall, with a thin bedroll on it. Veycosi put his table-book down on the bed. It was either there, or the floor.

The guard had stepped back outside the cell. He clanged the gate shut. "Breakfast at seven by the bell, lunch at one, supper at seven. You saw the mess hall on the way in. Don't be late, or no food for you. Garden duty from eight till one. Bread-baking duty from five till seven and last thing in the evening."

Two hours working dough at hot ovens. "Privy?"

The guard nodded in the direction of an empty chamber pot in the corner with a square of neatly folded muslin placed inside. "You clean that out yourself, daily. Pour the waste into the privy outside. You get three privy visits a day. You have to check with the guard on the way there and on the way back. You get one bucket of clean water per day, for washing and drinking." With that, the guard left Veycosi to his own devices.

To look 'pon the cell, Veycosi could almost imagine he was voluntarily entering into peaceful cloister, there to meditate and seek enlightenment. Early to sleep, early to rise, and healthful labour for a few hours each day. As privation went, this was well. He would have a few days' quiet to work on his notes. The inmate uniform of unbleached calico was stiff and itchy, but that seemed to be the worst of it.

Veycosi sat on the sleeping platform. He didn't feel like reading over his notes right now. And they had taken his paan away when he entered. Ah, well. He lay back on the bedroll and closed his eyes. He'd woken up early to get here. He could stand to finish his sleep.

—and leapt up, heart pounding double time, to the guard clanging his truncheon against the bars. Blasted man looked well pleased with himself. "Eight o'clock; garden duty!"

Veycosi had scarcely taken notice of the town bells ringing the hour. He let himself out of his cell. "Breakfast first?"

The guard shook his head. "You were late."

That, any road, solved the mystery of why the other cells had been empty. They had all been eating.

Veycosi spent the next five hours in the hot sun with his fellow inmates, picking gungo peas and prickly okra pods. Lunch was an indifferent vegetable curry and lumpen paratha; nourishing enough, but prepared without art. Exhausted, he then slept right through dinner and was awoken in the late evening to go and help prepare the yeast dough for the next day's bread. At least the kitchen let him have a couple of stale parathas, so he didn't go to bed hungry.

His window jalousies did little to keep the mosquitos out. It was not a restful night. One day completed; nine more remaining. He discovered that the gouges in his cell walls were where previous inmates had scratched off the days of the week to mark time passing. The walls got a new coat of plaster whenever the cell had a new inhabitant.

Two days later, after lunch, there came a commotion from outside the gaol house. People's voices yelling. Veycosi jumped and jumped for the high windowsill. Banged his jaw against the wall for his pains. Eventually he got good purchase and pulled himself up till he could glimpse the outside.

The returned pickens were standing outside the gaol, milling around with that empty-eyed look. Some of them had their parents with them. Gombey and Thandiwe were there. His heart clenched to see them. Thandy was holding Kaïra's hand. The girl didn't seem to notice her "big sister's" attentions. Veycosi counted heads. They were all there.

His arms were weakening from holding him up. He let himself fall. Landed with one foot in the food bowl the kitchen let inmates keep in between meals. One edge flipped up and barked him on the shin. He was hopping around and swearing when he heard someone say, "What you want?" The voice had the sonorous tones of a guard.

"Not what *we* want," someone replied. "Is the pickens. They all just started heading this way. We came with them."

"I think they looking for Cosi." Thandiwe's voice.

"Don't make mock," said the guard. "Those mooncalf pickens can't look for nobody." Then: "Wait! Hold that picken! Where they going?"

Little more, from down the corridor that led to the gaol cells, Veycosi heard a high-pitched scream, then the sounds of a scuffle. A woman's voice yelled, "Leave her alone!" A man's voice—his gaoler's, it sounded like—shouted for another to "hold the little devils fast." Veycosi almost rushed through his door. He remembered just in time that he was forbidden to open it unless to go and request the privy. Instead, he tried to push his face through the bars to see what was going on. But they were set too close together.

Two blackhearted pickens came rushing down the corridor, with that blind, jerky walk they all had developed. "Kaïra! Sem!" Veycosi called out. "Allyou pickens; come to me!"

They came, but not before his gaoler pounced on Saoirse and grabbed her up. Veycosi tried to warn him, but the bedeviled picken fetched the man a nasty bite to the meat of his arm before Veycosi could get the words out. The gaoler shouted in pain and let her go.

The other pickens came into view, trailing fretting parents and a couple of bruised constables. The pickens clustered at his cell bars. Veycosi had to order Daffyd to stop trying to cram himself in through them. He was well fat, and would only hurt himself in the trying. Veycosi reached his hands through the bars, touched Kaïra's peppercorn-curled head. He'd missed her so! Thandy gave him a wavering smile. Gombey looked sad. "All of oonuh," Veycosi said to the pickens, "be still."

They did so.

"You see that?" said one of the parents. "It's Cricket they need."

Veycosi winced at the hated nickname. Blasted broadsheets.

"Siani," said one of the constables, "you don't see that he's confounded their minds? He's drawing them to him. Some kind of witchery." He spat on the flagstone floor.

"No such thing as witchery!" Veycosi replied, exasperated.

"No?" said Thandiwe. "So now you making mock of the story of how Chynchin came to be?"

Like she wanted to have him incarcerated in this place forever. "*Maidell* Thandiwe," he said, deliberately addressing her formally, "I'm tracking down the truth of what they did, not chasing some fool-fool jack mulateer tale."

She scowled at that. Damn his runaway mouth.

"The pickens have to stay here," said a man from the crowd. He was regarding his own child like a viper he'd found in his privy. "With the man who made them."

"I didn't make them!"

"So why they obey you, then?"

"Don't be ridiculous," one of the constables burst out. "You can't have pickens in gaol."

"Tell the pickens that!" replied Gombey. The whole crowd fell to arguing, with the other inmates yelling their two shells' worth from their cells, and the pickens milling about in eerie silence.

He couldn't care for a pack of wit-flown pickens! Except for Kaïra. Maybe they would let her stay with him, in an empty guard-house? Would Thandiwe allow that?

A warm liquid splashed the top of Veycosi's foot. He looked down. Kaïra had wet herself.

"Damn it," Veycosi muttered. He went and got the cursed food bowl, held it high, and dashed it against the ground. The shards flew and the remains of thin gravy and rice went everywhere, but the racket made everyone hush. "Pickens," he said, "those of oonuh who need the privies, let the constables take you."

"Your battyhole," said one of the constables. He kissed his teeth. Five of the pickens began to shamble towards the sound. The man backed away, shaking his hand no, a look of disgust on his face.

"Teilheith," said a father of one of the pickens, "that's your own cousin you're looking at like she's dogshit beneath your shoe."

The constable's face only hardened. One of his fellows stepped in front of him. "I will take them," he said.

"Thank you," Veycosi replied. As they wandered away, he called after them, "And let him bring you back here afterwards!"

There was wet spreading all down the front of Kaïra's boubou. Veycosi rubbed her little knobby shoulder, not knowing whether the child got comfort from it or no. "I'm going to need fresh water for cleaning these pickens up," Veycosi said to the constables. "And some more of that delightful congee we had to break fast and for midday meal. Though beg you see if you can't find little bit of meat in the pot this time. Growing pickens need their strength."

He addressed himself to the parents. "Oonuh could bring back some clean clothes for your children, please? I don't know how long we going to be here."

Teilheith glared at him. "Going to need to get permission for all this," he said.

"I should think so. Only don't take too long. Wouldn't want it to get back to Macu that her officers of the law are making Chynchin's next Mamacona go hungry."

Thandy began to cry. It sounded more like relief than sorrow. Gombey pulled off the danshiki he was wearing, removed Kaïra's wet clothing, and dressed the girl in it. It swallowed her up. Its hem reached well past her knees.

Teilheith watched the proceedings with a sneer of disgust. He said, "She's not going to be Mamacona now. Not with her senses fled."

Gombey stared him down. "I have faith in Veycosi. Our daughter will waken. All these pickens will."

The other parents didn't look so certain. It was making Veycosi's heart ache, but he had to side with them. He wished to the depths of the ocean that this business had never happened. That it hadn't caught him up in it somehow. That if it needs must have happened, that it hadn't blackhearted Kaïra.

The badly healed scar set up a fierce aching just then. He tried to shake the cramp out of the leg, bent to rub it. "What you doing?" Thandy asked him.

"Don't fret," he told her. "It's just the old caiman bite."

"What old caiman bite?"

Like this business had her losing her wits, too. She knew the story well. Gombey frowned at him. "They treating you well in here?"

"Passable."

Two constables brought the pickens back from the privies.

Until the other guards got back with word from their cacique, Veycosi had to bide there at the jailhouse. So there the pickens bided with him. And their parents, and any other relatives and friends who'd happened to come along. If he'd thought one blackheart picken was a handful, looking after eleven was like to drive him insane. Not to mention shepherding their kin. When one of the guards returned a few hours later with the cacique's decree that he had served sufficient time for killing the cullybree and could be released, Veycosi could have kissed her. So he returned to his room at the Colloquium—the fact that they let him continue to live there gave him hope he would be reinstated—and for the next few days, he visited the homes of all the returned pickens and showed them how he'd been minding Kaïra, and he gave the pickens such commands that would keep them well. Use the privy when they needed it. Eat when they were fed, but only enough to ease their hunger. Kaïra was able to return to Thandy most days, though sometimes she stayed with Veycosi, or with Gombey. Veycosi should have been relieved to no longer have the constant burden of looking after the girl, but he kept forgetting and setting out meals for two on days when Kaïra wasn't there. And Goat was especially irritable on those particular days, too. She bit and grumbled.

Kweku's wife, Matilda, thumped two mugs down onto the table, a mickle heavier than necessary. Veycosi frowned. She usually wasn't this sullen.

No matter. He turned to Androu. "Now," he said, "you going to taste a real rum." Veycosi'd been there minding his own business, nursing a mug and enjoying his new freedom, when the man had appeared out of the shadows and invited himself to Veycosi's table. Veycosi had decided to let him stay. He could gloat at the failure of Androu's nutmeg ploy.

Matilda lifted an eyebrow and flounced away. Veycosi faced off against Androu across the table. When Androu had lived in Chynchin, someone such as he would have a hard time being served so fine a rumbullion as this. Veycosi told him, "Matilda only bring this out for her best customers, like me. She age it five years in piche-charred oak. Go on, take a sip. I want to see the look on your face when you experience true grace."

Androu lifted the mug to his lips.

Veycosi thought, *Yes, you bastard. Wipe that smirk off your face.*

Androu's Adam's apple bounced as he drank a draught of the rum. He coughed and put the mug down. Now it was Veycosi's turn to smirk. "Too rich for your blood?" he asked oilily. He knocked back a swallow from his own mug. The raw liquid struck the back of his throat and burned its way down. What the blast? This wasn't cask-aged rum! This was raw high wine, fit only for the disgraced!

He put the mug down carefully, trying to control the anger rising in him, but Androu must have seen his face. "Look like the both of we in shame," he murmured. "That is the low grade of rum that's served to Mirmeki in rum shops in Chynchin, unless they be run by Mirmeki ourselves."

Veycosi exclaimed, "But I'm not to be treated like this! I'm doing Macu's business, and I'm looking after the blackheart pickens!"

"With maybe just a mickle more pride than is seemly, nah true? Thinking about how much that one act would shore back up your acclaim in Carenage?"

Veycosi's breath caught and burned in his throat. His mouth worked, but he said nothing. He would have liked to shout at Androu that he was being unjust, but it would be an untruth. Truth could sting as hot as lies.

Androu's expression softened into pity. That was worse. "Never you mind, countryman," he said. "This blasted place. You can't even self shit in your pot, but everybody going to be ssu-ssuing next day about how much night soil you make to fertilize the cane fields, and whether you should eat more next time so as to produce a bigger load."

Veycosi couldn't help himself; he was giggling well before Androu had finished his tirade. And noticing again how comely the man was when the wary look wasn't on his face. The moment didn't last long, though. Androu, changeable as a ratbat in flight, was already scowling again and looking around to make sure no one else had heard. Veycosi rolled his eyes. "Nobody paying we mind, banna."

"Don't you believe it." Androu signalled to have beer brought to their table as well. He said to Veycosi, "A lowlier drink, more suited to my palate." He nodded his thanks to the server who brought the flagon over. "And you didn't hear what I was just saying? Is Chynchin's way of making sure such as I stay unfortunate why I left here in the first place."

Veycosi grunted. "To go bide with our enemies." He jutted his chin in the direction of two men who had just walked into the tavern. Ymisen from their dress and pallor.

The men looked hesitantly around at the comess of the rum shop. One of the servers breezed by them. Then another. Then a third. The men didn't greet a single one of them, just waited imperiously to be served. Veycosi snickered. "Look at those wretches."

To his surprise, Androu chuckled as well. "They don't know how to comport themselves so that people show them welcome. You see the kind of people I live among?"

"And yet you keep trying to betray us to them."

Androu looked sidewise at Veycosi, warily. Veycosi continued, "But I thwarted you this time!"

Androu laughed his bitter laugh. "A-true, sirrah. With luck, you might well best me at this game."

"This is no sport!" Veycosi hissed in frustration. "People might die over this thing you calling a game. So what it is you want with me any at all?"

Androu sipped from his mug of disgrace and grimaced. "You ever taste a beer on ice?" he asked.

"Ice? No, never." He could scarce imagine ice. Water so cold, it thickened to hardness. "And please not to sidestep my question like that. I not stupid."

"Too right," Androu agreed. "You not stupid at all. And that is what I want with you. In Ymisen, they float small chips of ice in beer before they drink it. When you swallow, you feel the coldness sliding down your throat, warming slowly till it reach your belly. Such a refreshment to the body, even on a cold day." He took another sip of his beer. "One thing I never missed was warm Chynchin beer. Like spittle."

Veycosi pushed his mug away into which he'd poured himself some of the beer. He suddenly had no taste for it. He worked harder to imagine deep cold. Was it like being up in the mountains come nighttime, with no heavy blanket? A drink cold like that? And this ice, like little crystalline rockstones. Only they floated, Androu had said. And, held in the mouth, melted away again into mere water. The man was a despoiler, spreading his own dissatisfaction till those around him felt it, too, and wished their lives were otherwise. Resented what they had, thinking it spite that the world hadn't granted them more. "What colour?" Veycosi asked.

Androu looked perplexed.

"Ice," said Veycosi irritably. "What colour?"

"Oh. Mostly clear and a little murky. Like poor quality glass. Sometimes it have bubbles trapped in it."

Veycosi's mind was running riot, trying to make a picture, to imagine chips of cold crystal, floating. To feel them on his tongue. "And you still ain't answer my previous question."

Androu laughed. "After I can't charm you with my wit, nor my cooking, nor what I know of science. Prithee, what left for me to try?"

The innuendo made the tips of Veycosi's ears get warm. "Never you mind that. Answer me."

Androu leaned in closer. There was a bead of sweat running down his neck. "The thing about ice," he said, his grin evil, "is that is hard. When the lakes freeze over come wintertime, you could walk out on them for miles. They don't freeze all the way down to the bottom. Water under there, and fish. But protected. The ice is like a wall between them and us.

"But come more time, the season will change. Warm season will come, and the thing that was so staunch a barrier will melt all away.

"Chynchin is open for the taking," he continued. "Truth come in like summer and melt away all your protection. For I come to find out the thing allyou liars in the Colloquium been hiding for two hundred years. Oonuh don't have no magic."

"Yes, we—"

Androu slammed his mug down onto the table. "Don't lie to me!" People were looking. He lowered his voice. "I don't lie to you. I don't lie to nobody, about nothing. Do thou speak me true, my friend."

"We have cannon," Veycosi said. The bead of sweat had slid down Androu's neck to become trapped in the hairs of his chest. Veycosi imagined licking it off. "And muskets. And we can fight."

"Yes, yes. But what you don't have is martial strategy. That was the witches' real magic, but allyou never learned the lesson. How to command an army from a distance. How to break your opponent's nerve by killing many at a single blow. Cosi, I tell you, we going to overrun Chynchin like a dog overtaking a rat."

"Swive me," Veycosi muttered. Shite. Now he was the one speaking in innuendoes. His ears got warmer.

Androu swallowed more of his drink. "But," he said, "you could stop it."

"Me? Just me? How?" Veycosi's belly knotted, protesting the warm rum sloshing around in it.

"No, not just you, you prideful beast. Persuade the Colloquium to make Tierce a Fellow."

"What? I can't do that! Nobody can." Something was tickling at the back of his mind. He pushed it away.

Androu continued, "If allyou make ir an honorary fellow, ee will stay in Chynchin."

"To rule it, you mean."

Androu smiled. "No, in peace. As far as the word of Ymisen goes, any road. The heir not interested in statecraft. As much as possible, ee will leave Chynchin to her own affairs. If the Colloquium lets ir study there, ee will order ir flotilla to leave."

"Why ask me, a disgraced postulant? Why not make that part of the negotiations between Chynchin and Ymisen?"

Androu sighed. "I advised Ser to do so, but ee is stubborn. Ee wants to be offered a fellowship freely, on ir own merits, and on the strength of the offering of the rare book ee brought. Ee won't listen when I tell ir one must ask in order to receive. So here I am, asking you whether you can make it happen that the Colloquium invites Ser to join it."

Veycosi took another swig of the beer while he thought about that. There was something about making Tierce a Colloquium Fellow . . . why that sounded so familiar? He wiped his mouth with the back of his hand, then looked up to see Androu watching him hungrily. Softly, Androu said, "There is another remote possibility, you of the beautiful doe eyes."

Between the beer and the reluctant compliment from his enemy, Veycosi was having trouble concentrating. "And what is that?"

"Chynchin don't have juju, so I've been told, and I believe the source. Is only stories the highborn of the Colloquium been using to keep the rest of we subdued. I already tell Ymisen that allyou won't stand in their way. You can't."

"You said that already."

"But mayhap I'm mistaken. What they don't realise is that Chynchin *is* juju."

What the backside? "I don't follow you," Veycosi said. "No difference between the two."

Androu shook his head. "Man from the country of false magic, the real juju right here so all around you, and you can't see it even when you self breathing it."

"Talk sense."

"I always try to, though it has netted me no small amount of bother. Look you; in Chynchin, a dropped watermillion might bounce."

Veycosi shrugged.

"In Ymisen," he went on, "even if you could get a decent watermillion that wasn't soft on the outside and slimy on the inside from the long travel on the ship to get to us, if you drop that watermillion, it going to smash at your feet. Every time."

Veycosi snorted. "Not every time. Nothing could be so fickle as to have nought success, every time."

"True that. So let's say that once in a very infrequent while, it might be possible for a watermillion to bounce. But if it did happen, t'would be so rare that the Crucian fathers would be proclaiming it either a miracle or the devil's work, and the broadsheets wouldn't cease mentioning it and wondering over it for months. You know what the word 'fickle' mean in Ymisen?"

"Our two countries speak versions of the same language, Androu."

"In parts. What it mean here in Chynchin? When we—when *you* say it, what it mean?"

" 'Fickle'? You only trying to distract me again."

"Not a bit of it."

What all this had to do with saving his country from being conquered? "It mean 'governed by fate.' "

Androu nodded. "That is to say, 'fated'?"

"Yes, yes! Destined to happen."

"In Ymisen, it mean exactly the opposite. It mean inconstant. Took me a devil of a long time to realise it." Androu grinned. "Didn't help my courting, I could tell you that!"

Veycosi hadn't thought that Androu might have wed in Ymisen, might have pickens and spouses waiting for him to come home. Or one spouse; a wife. Veycosi had heard Ymisen folk married in twos, not threes. What a strange place it must be!

But Veycosi didn't care about Androu's wedded or unwedded state. No, he didn't. Not one rass. He was sure of it.

"Veycosi," said Androu, "the only body seriously trying to find the secret of the witches is you. And you just might succeed, because even though Chynchin people lost the magic, it didn't go far. It right here-so." He smiled, ever wily. "And you, my soul"—Veycosi's traitor heart swelled briefly at the endearment—"are tenacious as a pack of dogs at the hunt. I fear the fox won't long elude you."

Androu's accent wouldn't be still; sometimes Chynchin Mirmeki, sometimes high-flown Ymisen. "So," he continued, "I watch you day and night. Now you know."

Androu took no pleasure in Veycosi's company, then. Mama-ji, what in all the seven seas to do with an honest spy? Veycosi asked him, "And if you come to find out I've succeeded?"

Androu looked grim. "Well, so I will as is my duty tell that pink, blustering fellow Gunderson on the Ymisen ship, and he will inform Ser, and we shall see what we shall see."

"And if I don't suss out the secret of keeping Ymisen at bay, then we lose Chynchin to oonuh anyway?"

Androu nodded. "To Ymisen, any road. I frankly can't say how much I am Ymisenian."

"But you really would betray us to those dogsons?"

"I would."

"What the rass Chynchin do to you, that you hate it so? Even being Mirmeki could scarce turn anybody so stoutly against their own land!"

Androu fixed Veycosi with those blue eyes. "My land, is it? My portion is somewhat wanting, then. Someday soon I will show you what Chynchin did to me and mine. What it is still doing, all you Cibonn' and Ilife with your airs and your two-faced ways."

"But I—"

"Yes, you too, for all you pretend different."

"What the devil you mean by that?"

"Ah, lef' it," Androu said. "Shouldna have said aught. Beg pardon, sirrah."

Veycosi wasn't going to let it pass, though. "What. Did. You. Mean?" he insisted. "Don't tell me you turn coward when you turned your coat?"

The fury on Androu's face was like flame busting out from dry kindling. "Do not speak me such," he said.

"Don't call you what?" Veycosi answered. "'Coward,' or 'turncoat'?" "Deserter" was a bad enough word to use for the Mirmeki. Veycosi knew full well that "turncoat" was even worse. He'd spoken it on purpose, and of Androu at least, he knew he'd spoken it true.

Veycosi didn't even spy the motion. Suddenly, Androu had twisted Veycosi's wrist behind Veycosi's back, held down low between the two of them so that none in the rum shop could see. Veycosi picked up the mug to dash it against Androu's face, but he twisted his wrist farther. Veycosi winced.

"Very well," Androu growled in Veycosi's ear. "Since tha asks it so nice, I'll spit out the words I politely swallowed. Will't be still while I do?"

The lock on his wrist was slowly wrenching Veycosi's shoulder from its socket. "Yes," Veycosi grunted.

But Androu didn't leave go. "True that. I think you will be still, while I have you like this. My friend, th'art no better than thy fellows. For all thy fine ways with our folk, tha keeps one of us on a leash."

Who—? "*Samra?* You mean Samra?" The words came out choked through pain, while the rum show talk rolled merrily all around them. Veycosi could have cried out for help, but pride made him loath to do so.

To his surprise, it was Androu who broke the hold. Veycosi hissed in pain. He set about massaging his screaming shoulder.

Androu regarded him with . . . was that remorse? "Did I do damage?" he asked. Veycosi only glared at him. "Let me see," said Androu gently. He drew closer, went to lay a hand on the shoulder he'd so recently abused. Veycosi pulled back. Androu lifted the hand in an appeasing gesture. "Truly, not an attack this time. Remember, I do not lie."

Frowning, Veycosi let Androu touch him, ready to spring away to safety at any time.

Androu palped Veycosi's shoulder, making him wince. "Ah, my lad," murmured Androu, "beg pardon." He began massaging the shoulder. The pain eased. Androu leaned closer so that Veycosi could hear him above the din of the place. He smelled of rum and beer and cinnamon. "True, your words angered me. But only a very knave makes his temper the excuse for setting upon another."

"Exactly so," Veycosi growled. He moved away from Androu's soothing hand. "And I don't make Samra to spend time with me." He didn't trouble to tell Androu that he had sent Samra away from him, or that he was considering inviting her company again. He wanted to first hear what the man had to say about their connection.

Androu looked downcast. "And here again, I fear I must say the thing as I see it. I doubt not but her bondage is sweet. Tha' seems a gifted sort in that wise. 'Tis a sort of bondage nonetheless." Veycosi began to contradict him, but Androu continued, "If she returned to her studies she would soon surpass you, you know, an' she feared not losing her only friend at the Colloquium."

"That's a lie!"

"Some private matter between you two?" boomed a voice from just above their heads. "That you sit as close as brothers to have your parley?"

Veycosi shifted back guiltily in his chair. Androu never moved. "Just getting to know our friends, sirrah," he said lazily. "Or soon-to-be friends, I should say. Does that not seem wise to you?"

It was the Ymisen functionary. Veycosi glanced up at him, and, never mind the tenseness of the mood, had to bury his head quick in his empty mug to hide a snort of laughter.

Gunderson was sporting a vast robe, dyed near-indigo, that was clearly new and shoddily made. It had been hastily embroidered with gold thread and medallions of bark lace. The lace was already fraying, and the dye patchy. The straggling lines of embroidery around the edges of the robe read, in Djuka script, *Bussa me rassa; what a ugly massa.* Doubtless Gunderson thought the garment he'd commissioned said something else. Around his neck was a heavy gold chain, from which swung a gaudy soutien-seins. He hadn't understood that its purpose was to display a woman's breasts. It sat crookedly on his teta-free chest. On his head was a hat woven of cocoanut-palm leaves. It suited him fine, if you discounted the two holes in the brim that told you it had been made for a don-key. The Chynchin youth with him was weighted down with woven baskets, the kind you found in the market, made of red reeds from the riverbank. Plus a wood statue of Mamapiche, nearly tall so as the youth himself. And a pile of scratchy camel-hair blankets. And about twice ten of the little tinning toys some of the Mirmeki pickens made from old kerosene oil cans. At a table behind the functionary, a doxy was sitting on the knee of one of the Ymisen sailors. She spied the functionary and let out a whoop of merriment.

Biting his lip, Androu said, "An' it please you, sirrah, do join us. The rum here is most fine." From an angle the functionary couldn't see, Androu winked at Veycosi, then signalled for more to be brought to their table.

The functionary frowned. "I think not," he replied. "Strong drink and caution do not mix."

Androu nodded. "You know best, sirrah." Matilda bustled up with Androu's order on a tray. Her eyes got big and round when she took in the sight of the functionary. She discreetly ducked her head to pour rum into their mugs, but Veycosi could see her smiling and shaking her head.

Androu said, "Give you good walk, then."

The functionary grunted a surly reply and lumbered out of the rum shop. The youth with him struggled to keep up in his wake and to balance the while all the this-and-that the man had doubtless purchased. The instant they were beyond the door, the whole rum shop erupted in hilarity. "'What a ugly massa'!" said the doxy. "I know that hand! Is Calliope from down the market who embroider that!"

"Wai! Ugly for true!" shouted Matilda. She motioned for Androu to move over so she could sit beside him on his bench. She removed her spectacles and fanned her face. "Mama-ji, I ain't laugh so hard since last year's Pantomime!" She regarded Androu. "Mestre, wha mek you work for such a stupid man?"

He pursed his lips. "Better than being bound to a clever one," he replied.

Her belly laugh rang through the rum shop. "True words. For

those, you get the good drink." She motioned to a serving boy, who brought two heavy glasses and poured them well full of cask-aged rum. Matilda unclipped a smaller mug from her waist, took herself a tipple of the rum, and toasted with them. She knocked back her drink, nodded to them both, and went off to serve another table.

Androu raised one eyebrow. "This is indeed a silken rumbullion."

Veycosi peered at him over the top of his glass. "Like your friends don't like you back." Such satisfaction it gave him to say those words!

"Ah?" said Androu distractedly. "Which friends?"

"Nah the Ymisen people, man? The ones you come over here with?"

Androu stood. "Come. I give you a ride home, *friend.*"

He clapped Veycosi on the shoulder he had very nearly unseated a few minutes before. Veycosi winced. "Very well."

They drained their glasses. On their way out, they stamped their marks in Matilda and Kweku's book as the bouncer held it out to them, then stepped outside the rum shop to where lines of carriages waited for custom, many of the drivers dozing with their caps over their faces. They hailed one up, got inside. The horse made a brisk enough pace.

Androu turned to him. "Lemme tell you how it went, this thing of moving to Ymisen. Took me two years to battle my way up from cook to steersman. Had to learn to read their script first, and to navigate. Scarce nobody wanted to have dealings with a swart Chynchin witch."

"Swart? You?"

"Me same one, yes. Next to most Ymisen people, I'm dark. At least I was until their weak sun leached me of colour till I was white as them."

"And a witch?"

He gave a grim chuckle. "That's the thing. Didn't you see how the soldiers were flinching steady when they made land? Not the sailors, for plenty of them sneak their way into Chynchin before, even though Ymisen law forbids them. In Ymisen, they have it to say how all of Chynchin full up of witches and fey folk."

He leaned in closer. "The devil of a thing is, outside of Chynchin, that not far from the truth."

"Now you just making mock."

"Nah. Chynchin people good lucky too bad. Ymisen people don't like to play at cards with we. The polisi quick to escort we out from the racetrack and the cockfights, for a Chynchin person honest as the day is long will still win out more than a clever rogue."

"Chuh. That sound like fairy story."

"Maybe. Seem true to me, though. From what I see. Anyway, from steersman I made land on Ymisen. Got a work as a tallymaster in a bullet factory. Found a side line; swiving the mayor's wife. Tiralee, tiralah, one thing and another, and I end up a tallymaster for the Crown. When I used the books to trace a swindle that had been going on for years, I get appointed minor advisor to the Crown. All that took four years. Then from minor advisor to chief advisor, that was six more."

"So if them trust you so well, why they didn't make you the ambassador to Chynchin, instead of that man?"

"What, give a foreign witch that much power? Only born citizens of the land get those plums. So they send me with him to advise him. Some days, I swear I have to advise him how to draw breath and when to wipe his arse."

That surprised a bark of laughter out of Veycosi. "I know some pickens like that. And yet you stay there rather than coming back home."

Androu nodded. "For now. Sometimes I think more because is easier to stay on the road you started on than to switch tracks. But in truth, friend, it can be cold there in many more ways than one." The passing lamplight threw shadows over his visage. "Yet I do know that there, I can make some modicum of a way for myself. Here, my way was already set the minute I was birthed between the knees of a Deserter woman."

His face got solemn. "Please forgive our little set-to back there. It was my fault."

Veycosi waved the apology away. "Nah, man. Is me who first insulted you." He found he had indeed forgiven the man. Something about hearing his struggles was making fellow feeling easier. They were on opposite sides of the political manoeuvrings of their two countries. But for tonight, they were two men sharing strong drink.

The carriage pulled up outside the postulants' apartments of the Colloquium and stopped. Androu, mercurial as ever, seemed cheery again. "I suppose this is where we must say good night. Give you good walk, Veycosi."

Veycosi found he wasn't ready to leave Androu's company. "Will't have one more drink with me? For the road?"

Androu glanced at him sidewise, then nodded. "For the road."

Once in Veycosi's apartment, of course the verbal sparring continued. Androu jestingly tried to shame Veycosi for the sumptuousness of his living quarters. Veycosi teased Androu when he discovered the man thought he'd seen the Blackheart Man sneaking around town.

Drunken as they both were, words gave way to pickenish shoving and giggling. In fact, Veycosi was smiling when he playfully threw the first actual punch. Androu's smile became all teeth. He blocked with his two palms, stopping Veycosi's fist cold, a nose from his chest. The muscles in Veycosi's upper arm bunched painfully with the force of the uncompleted blow. Androu laughed, thrust his face in so close that the warm yeast smell of the rumbullion on his breath entered Veycosi's nose. Veycosi could feel his nature rising.

There was a heat flushing Androu's face as well. He blew Veycosi a kiss. "Ah, then. Are we wrestling, or tussling?"

Mischief made Veycosi say, "Which would you rather?"

Androu snorted. "Challenge me, would you?" On a sudden he laced his hands behind Veycosi's neck, pulled Veycosi's face down and brought his knee up same time. But as the knee rose, Veycosi shifted and twisted his torso to one side. Falling, he pushed on the side of Androu's raised knee, moving the leg as easily as opening a door. Androu stumbled. Veycosi hit the floor and rolled under him, sweeping him off his feet with the force of his body. As Androu fell to his hands and knees, his robe kilted up to show those strong legs.

"First point mine!" crowed Veycosi. He slapped Androu's upturned rump, made to stand. He didn't manage to get fully to his feet before Androu launched into a flying tackle and wrapped his arms around Veycosi's waist. Veycosi just had time to spy the grin on Androu's face before Androu shoved him down onto his back and straddled him, pinning Veycosi's shoulders with his knees. A sweet, sweaty muskiness rose warm from Androu's calico breechclout. Veycosi needs must breathe in the stiffening aroma. He hoped his moan was too soft for Androu to hear.

A drop of sweat fell from Androu's forehead into Veycosi's mouth. Veycosi tasted the salt. Veycosi wrenched his left arm free and tickled Androu's belly. Androu flinched away from Veycosi's digging fingers, reared back. Veycosi brought his knees up and thumped Androu good on the back with the fronts of his thighs. Androu got a look of surprise. Air rushed from his lungs with an

"Uh!" sound. He mock-glared at Veycosi, rose to a crouch. Before Veycosi could stop him, Androu dragged the hem of Veycosi's robe up over his head, trapping his head and arms. Veycosi shouted and tried to jackknife free, but Androu slapped his belly, hard and open-handed, and now it was Veycosi struggling for air.

Androu punched Veycosi's thighs back down to the ground. A weight settled on either side of his arms, which were jammed against his ears. It pulled the robe tightly across his face. He couldn't break the hold. His own helplessness inflamed him deliciously. "Let me up," he pleaded through the taut fabric. "I'd rather kiss you than fight you."

"Oh, my lad," Androu replied, his voice slow and thick. "There's kisses and there's kisses."

Veycosi felt Androu's weight shift, though still pinning him. Then a warm wetness trailed down his chest, and kept going downwards. Androu's tongue. Dogson was kneeling, his knees at either side of Veycosi's face, and leaning forwards to bring his face close to Veycosi's belly. Veycosi convulsed, not to get away, but to get closer. Androu must have been able to see Veycosi's cockstand plain as day, a mere handspan from his face. The thought only made Veycosi harder. When Androu yanked Veycosi's breechclout aside so his cocky sprang free, Veycosi nearly jetted there and then.

Androu slapped Veycosi's cock to the side. The shock of combined pain and pleasure made Veycosi's voice shrill when he cried out.

Androu growled, "Ee-hee. I know is this you been hiding under there for me."

With his arms snarled and his face muffled by his robe, Veycosi could only moan. In the tropical heat, his covered face had already sprung water. The salt of his sweat stung his eyes. Every breath he snuffled in smelled of Androu's musk. Picturing his own indignity, feeling the air on his exposed prick; his excitement peeled away the

remaining tatters of his disdain for Androu, revealing to both of
them the desire it had been concealing. "Please," he begged, even
as Androu's hot mouth sucked his prick in, even as Androu clawed
away the fabric between his own stiff cocky and Veycosi's face and
stuffed Veycosi's open, pleading mouth with said stiffness.

Veycosi struggled to do the job as well as he knew he could,
to suckle with his tongue, to relax his throat. He gagged a little,
but Androu thrust his cock in deeper, sliding it into his windpipe
and quelling the reflex. Veycosi whimpered, not quite in protest.
In response, Androu pressed more of his weight down on Veycosi's body, granting him no respite for his wide-stretched jaws, his
bruised throat.

Androu left off his own insistent sucking to ask, "Is this well?"

Veycosi grunted yes.

"Or shall we stop?"

Veycosi made shift to grind out an emphatic "Nuh-uh!" around
the tumid flesh blocking his throat. Though he would at some point
need to breathe again, he let the fight go out of him, the better to
concentrate on the rapture hardening his nipples and making his
hips buck.

Androu laid his mouth on Veycosi again, an almost unbearable
wet friction. And Androu now commenced to slowly sliding his
cocky in and out of Veycosi's mouth, now far enough out to let him
snatch a little breath, now so deep Veycosi's cheeks bulged with
trapped air and his nose was stoppered from the inside. The world
became this, only this. Androu took to stroking hard and fast, more
deep than shallow now, less opportunity for relief. He pushed in
until Veycosi's nose was crushed against the crisp hairs on the man's
belly bottom. And remained there, enthusiastically sucking and
licking Veycosi's prick the while. The sensations of pleasure and
privation warred in Veycosi's body, filling him up.

Abruptly, Veycosi's lungs had reached their limit of starvation. Suddenly he was struggling for air, the lack of it intoxicating even as it made his blood pound in his ears and in his prick in Androu's wet, almost biting mouth. Veycosi's arms were still trapped by the winding cloth of his robe. He tried to protest, but could only make wet mewlings around Androu's full flesh. His body began to convulse. And still no air! Stars began to explode behind his eyes. He was close, so close. He didn't care anymore if he fainted quite away. Androu began working harder and faster on Veycosi's cock, a sweet, aching friction as Veycosi tipped over the edge of consciousness. Only then did Androu lift his haunches and let his prick slide from Veycosi's nearly slack jaws. Veycosi took a great, roaring breath in and exploded into Androu's hardworking mouth. Androu swallowed and gasped and swallowed, his arms around Veycosi's hips. Androu began making snorting noises as Veycosi's spunk, too much to swallow it all, trickled out his nostrils. But the bastard held on until Veycosi was spent, a sodden, grateful rag of a man lying on his own floor with another gasping man's head on his thigh. Relishing the sleepy, sated song of his blood in his veins, Veycosi said, "This was my reward for discussing supposed Chynchin state secrets with you?"

Androu drawled, "I am originally of Chynchin. It comes to me that I don't give a rat's hairy ass about spying out its secrets."

"Since when?"

"Since its sweetest secret opened to me."

Androu kissed his thigh, high up on his leg. Veycosi shivered. His blood was already rising again, and he could feel against his cheek that Androu was still hard. "Wipe your nose," he said to Androu. "And lie back."

Samra found them the next morning, slumped in Veycosi's hamaca, drunk from their sport, and reeking of spunk and sweat. They never heard her come in until she was standing in front of them, arms crossed and an unreadable look on her face, Goat peering in curiously over her shoulder. Veycosi opened his sore-jawed mouth to explain, though he had no idea what he'd say.

Whereas sleepy-eyed Androu opened his arms in welcome towards Samra. He smiled. "Maidell," was all he said.

She kissed her teeth as though exasperated. Cut her eyes at them. Started unlacing her dress.

There was, barely, room in Veycosi's hamaca for three. Though their enthusiastic fossicking about did eventually split the hamaca along its bottom and send them tumbling to the floor.

They laughed, tangled in each other's limbs.

It had been warmer these past few days. It usually got that way leading up to rainy season. Datiao flexed his fingers. More and more of the piche had been leaching out of the dead soldiers his chantson was sustaining. Datiao had even begun falling asleep at night. He would wake, panicked, in the morning, and count the minutes till the sun melted enough of the piche off his face that he could resume the chantson.

One of the little musket girls had regained enough movement to scout the town for him and report back at fore-day morning, when most of Carenage was abed. She'd located Acotiren!

Today was the warmest yet. Datiao found he could slowly turn his face up to the blessed sun, as he had done days ago to stare at the man who had caressed his cheek. All around him, the dead were slowly stretching their limbs, snail-like.

His broken leg had healed. His donkey slowly turned its head to look at him.

Datiao nearly laughed out loud. Today. They would go and find Acotiren today, and he would reap her soul.

He moved his donkey forwards to the head of the line of not-statues. In between whispers of the chantson, he hissed their orders to them.

Chapter 7

I T WAS TOO WARM a night to be indoors. So Gombey and Veycosi set up outside, on Veycosi's front porch, while Thandy took Kaïra to the privy. Veycosi carried two stools and his desk out onto the porch, and his notes, and a kerosene lamp to see by. Goat was tied beside the low stone wall of the porch, bedded down for the night with her legs folded under her. She watched them disinterestedly as they came out.

Veycosi had told Gombey about his dalliance that morning with Samra and Androu. He'd made it out to be a thing of mere pleasure, though to his alarm, he'd been having impossible fancies of more. But that could never be. Androu was Chynchin's enemy. However this Ymisen offensive turned out, Androu would be returning thence. Too besides, Veycosi was already betrothed.

Gombey had raised an eyebrow when he heard Androu's name, but then had chuckled and slapped Veycosi on the back, congratulating him on such a delightful way of ferreting out Ymisen's secrets. Veycosi, remembering the confidences Androu had given him in the rum shop, reassured himself that that was really what he was about; being Chynchin's spy. But then should he not let Samra in on the ploy? And Macu? What a comess his life had become!

Some of the students were playing an informal game of batey out on the green, just out of sight. Ymisen had let it be known that they would consider any more rodas an act of war, so the students were back to their usual evening entertainments. The laughing and banter was a pleasant backdrop to the night.

Thandy slipped into Veycosi's room and came back out with the plate of food he had prepared for Kaïra; some roast breadfruit left over from lunch. Gombey got into the hamaca Veycosi kept strung out there, and lifted Kaïra into it. "Wai!" said Gombey. "What a way the picken getting heavy."

"My girl is growing up," Thandiwe replied. She pulled the other stool over and sat on it so she could hold the plate. Veycosi had put a cup with palm oil in the centre, and arranged pieces of roast breadfruit in a circle around it.

Gombey sighed. "Yes, is true."

"Kaïra," Veycosi said to the girl, whose eyes were tracking the firefly lights flickering over the grounds of the Colloquium. "Kaïra, your daddy and ma going to feed you some breadfruit. Eat it. Stop when you not hungry anymore."

Veycosi knew Kaïra was hungry. Had finally marked that the child's belly'd been rumbling. For how long? Mama-ji, what had happened to these pickens?

Goat sighed. She stretched out her long neck and lipped some hops off the bundle near her. Veycosi wouldn't let her have no more beer, but hops wasn't harming her, and she seemed to like the taste. At the sound of Goat's chewing, Kaïra turned her head to look at the animal. Whereas she hadn't give any sign that she'd heard Veycosi's instructions.

How in blazes I could be jealous of a camel?

Gombey dipped a piece of the breadfruit in the palm oil and held it to Kaïra's mouth. Still staring at Goat, Kaïra took a bite, and, like Goat, started chewing. Gombey's face was grim as he watched his daughter-to-be. "Thandy, what we going to do? This not Kaïra. She not inside there. How she going to become the next Mamacona? She won't be able to do her duties!"

Thandy only shook her head grimly. "It will be all right. If she—if she don't get completely better . . ." Her voice broke. She recovered, though. "If she need help to do her assigned tasks, she will be given it, as Chynchin does for those who are injured or halt."

Veycosi had been watching at Kaïra carefully. "Whatever happens, that is still Kaïra, for certain," he pronounced eventually.

"How you mean?" asked Thandy.

Veycosi said to them both, "Tell me what Kaïra is like."

Gombey replied, "You mean, what she *was* like."

"I do not. Just tell me, nuh?"

Gombey put another piece of breadfruit into Kaïra's mouth. He thought little bit. "She made friends easy."

"And is still true," Veycosi said. "Look how many people care about her now. Some of them she didn't know before this. Truth to tell, even that blasted camel like her better than me."

Thandiwe leaned forwards and wiped Kaïra's mouth with the edge of her sleeve. Gombey pressed his lips together and looked down at the ground.

Veycosi said, "Banna, I know you too good. That is the aspect you get when you fighting not to disagree with somebody."

"Hmm," Gombey muttered.

Thandiwe said, "She was curious, always curious." She looked at Veycosi, smiling a little. "You know what she used to say the most often, Cricket?"

"Easy. 'I went to see.'"

"But eh-eh! How you guess that?"

Veycosi chuckled. "Didn't need to guess. I know Kaïra."

Thandy's face fell again. "Well, then you know she not like that no more."

"You sure?" Veycosi racked his brains, searching for some way to give his love the lie. Ah. He knew what to say. "Then why she only wandering about the place all the time? Kaïra still like to mix herself up into everything. Was driving me to distraction before Goat started following after her everywhere she go."

"*Goat?*" said Thandy indignantly. "Is a cow camel you have minding my child?"

"Nah, man!" Veycosi raised his hands for calm. "I not leaving Goat to watch after her." *Not when I can find them wherever they gone, any road.* "Is more the other way around. Kaïra is the one minding Goat. Too besides, she going to be my daughter, too." A little while ago, Veycosi would have felt a quickly suppressed dismay at that thought. Tonight, he got up from his stool, went over to Kaïra, and gave her a kiss on the forehead.

They all four sat companionably for a time, the adults chatting of this and that while Veycosi wrote his notes out. This was how it would be when they were wed. It was comfortable, and sweet. It was well.

Cookie wandered by with a flagon of hill beer, as she was wont to do of an evening sometimes. Veycosi invited her in. She poured them each a measure.

Another figure was coming along the pathway. It was dark, but Veycosi's heart thumped; he would recognize the sway of that walk in his sleep. He said, "Koo Samra dey." A small headache was coming upon him. He had yet to tell Thandiwe about his tryst with Androu and Samra. Didn't rightly know what to say. He'd begged the two of them and Gombey to keep it quiet. Androu had nodded, looking amused. Gombey was holding his tongue, but he said only for a sennight. Samra had quietly agreed, but Veycosi noticed that since then, she'd been a shade cooler, more formal with him.

Goat belched as Samra went by her. Thandiwe's face held no expression Veycosi could read.

"Evening, Goat," she said. "Evening, Kaïra, Thandiwe, Gombey, Mestre Chef. How do?" She didn't say Veycosi's name.

"You know how it go," Gombey replied. "We deh-deh."

Samra hugged Kaïra's unresisting form, then regarded her worriedly. "No change?"

Veycosi hastened to reply, "None," before Thandiwe could. That would compel Samra to acknowledge his presence. She gave him a distant nod and accepted a mug of beer from Cookie.

Kaïra must have been full. She had stopped responding when Gombey held the food to her mouth. Thandiwe had the plate balanced on her knee. She smiled coolly at Samra, pursed her lips, then seemed to come to a decision. She reached and grasped Samra's hand. "Welcome, sestra."

Samra touched her forehead to Thandiwe's. She helped herself to a piece of the breadfruit. She finished eating it before she said, "Thandiwe, how things with you?"

"Yes, Siani Thandiwe," came a voice from the path. "How goes it with the lovely intended of Messrs. Veycosi and Gombey?"

It was Androu, approaching Veycosi's front porch, with the Ymisen heir in tow. They all stood and made their genuflections to Tierce. "Highness," murmured Veycosi. Tierce beamed at them all, but strangely, more so at Veycosi. What was that for?

At the sight of Androu, Samra had brightened. "Good eve to you!" she chirruped.

"And a better one for seeing both your fine faces," Androu replied, looking pointedly at both her and Veycosi. Veycosi felt the heat rising to his cheeks. He reminded himself he had done nothing wrong.

This night, Androu was wearing a white gauze robe. Sensible, in this heat. It fairly shone in the darkness, making his skin seem more swart than it was. And his blue eyes bluer.

Veycosi offered the heir his seat. Androu calmly watched the proceedings, with a small smile on his face. Or a smirk. He remained standing outside. But Veycosi was beginning to get the measure of the man. That snide expression often masked uncertainty. Androu didn't know whether he was welcome. "Come in then, nuh?" Veycosi said to Androu. A part of him was cautious, though. Even after what had gone between them, Androu might still be playing his spy's game. People had it to say that a duppy could only harm you in your own house if you invite it in.

Androu nodded his thanks and came under the porch roof. "Thank you, friend, for showing welcome to this commoner." He sat on the low porch wall beside Cookie and gathered his robes about him. Strong man's hands, he had, used in grace. A combination to which Veycosi was partial. And the benefit of which he had recently experienced. He quickly suppressed a memory of kissing Androu, both of their mouths smelling of Samra, who was lounging splayed and blissful between them.

"Highness," said Thandy, glancing sidewise at Veycosi, "you would like some refreshment? I sure our host can fetch you something."

Androu translated. Tierce shook ir head no. "Tell them," ee said to Androu.

Androu schooled his face. From what little Veycosi knew of the man, he grated at being commanded so. Nevertheless, he simply said, "The heir thanks you for your hospitality, but ee don't wish to interrupt your gathering for too long. Ee just wanted to give Veycosi the good news first. It should be in the broadsides by tomorrow morning."

Cookie asked, "What good news?"

Before Androu could reply, Tierce blurted, "We thank thee. Such . . . such honour." Ee inclined ir head to Veycosi.

What was this?

Androu said, "You are to be quit of me—of us—soon. Except the heir, of course. Ee will command the fleet to return to Ymisen."

"That's wonderful!" Thandiwe exclaimed.

Gombey was more reserved. "The heir does our nation a kindness," he said, bowing to Tierce. "I'm curious to know what caused this sudden change of heart."

The increasing unease Veycosi'd been feeling for days suddenly bloomed into a dread so profound it was all he could do not to run screaming from his own home. He wanted to tell them all to shut up. Someone was about to say something so abominable that Veycosi felt he would do anything not to hear the words. And the worst part: he feared the words would come from himself.

Androu drawled, "Maas' Veycosi, th'art a right scallywag. You never told me the other night that you'd already received permission for the heir to be made a postulant of the Colloquium."

Tierce nodded eagerly. "Yes," ee said, "I study here now. Astronomy."

Veycosi's gorge rose. The others were gaping at him. "But I didn't," he said. "It was just a demonstration of the cerem—"

On the other side of the porch wall, Goat levered herself to her feet. The shadowy bulk of her towered over them. She blew out a breath through her elastic lips and grumbled. To Veycosi, it sounded like "Awake, yet asleep." She looked directly at him. Caiman eyes.

. . . and suddenly, all the events that Veycosi had hidden from himself flooded back, overwhelming him.

"Oh, gods," Veycosi groaned. Too much Reverie. That was where those two missing days had gone. "Ee believed me? I only meant it in sport. I thought ee understood."

Then Veycosi realised the full import of his recovered memory. He leaned over the side of his porch and vomited yeasty beer. "It was me," he wailed miserably. "I hurt the pickens."

Cookie said, "You lie! Please tell me you lie, Maas' Cosi."

He shook his head. "I didn't mean to do it! I tried to make them go away safe. I told them not to let anyone get in their way . . ."

". . . and they followed your order to the letter," muttered Cookie. "I only know one trance that make people obedient so. Maas' Cosi, you give those pickens a strong dose of Reverie?"

Gombey clutched Kaïra to him. "What? Cosi, you really went and did something so reckless?"

Thandiwe stood. The plate and bowl in her lap crashed to the ground and broke into shards, spreading palm oil everywhere. She rushed to take Kaïra from Gombey, gathered the child protectively to her bosom.

Tierce was asking Androu to translate. Androu, his eyes wide, said, "Hush a moment please, Highness. Begging your pardon. I ain't hear the whole story yet."

"She had been screaming for three days," Veycosi mumbled. He could scarcely bear to look at Thandiwe.

Androu frowned. "Who?"

Gombey said, "I remember this. He's talking about Liguanea.

His mother. Happened when we were youngboys. Cosi, what this have to do with you dosing pickens with Reverie? How you could commit such a folly?"

Miserably, Veycosi continued. "I was nine. Ma was trying to birth my sister."

Samra said, "You have a sister?"

"No, I don't." He took a trembly breath. "By the third day, Ma no longer had voice to scream. She was only making a hoarse, wheezing sound. Horrible. And pushing, and straining, and bleeding. Midwife was doing all she could, but the baby wouldn't born. My das were out of their minds with fretting. On the first day, I had prayed to Mamagua for help for Ma. On the second day, I prayed to her twin sister, Mamapiche. Nothing. On the third day, Ma went into convulsions for a short time. And still the labour wouldn't progress. The midwife couldn't stop the bleeding. Ma got pale, her breathing shallow. She was dying.

"I went to the Upper Piche. I was desperate. I prayed to the Blackheart Man."

Cookie said, "The Blackheart Man? That fancy tale to scare misbehaving pickens?"

Veycosi nodded. "The very same. I had occasion to be told that story plenty times when I was a youngboy. So I was terrified of the Blackheart Man. I believed he could do anything to which he put his mind."

Thandy's eyes were wide as she listened to Veycosi's secret story. Samra's attention 'pon Veycosi was avid. Androu looked interested, but, as ever, noncommittal. Cookie just looked distracted, as though her thoughts were somewhere else. The heir was frowning in concentration, trying to follow Veycosi's Chynchin speech. And Gombey already knew how this went. Veycosi continued:

"I begged the Blackheart Man to do what he must to save my

ma. But as I thought about it, I realised I should offer him something in return, something that would be precious to him.

"I knew from the fairy story that he was cursed to rip out pickens' hearts. I reasoned that but for the curse, he fain would stop doing such evil, if he could. So I offered him myself. I told him that if Ma lived, he could have my heart, and I would become the Blackheart Man in his stead."

"Cosi!" Thandiwe's accusing gaze split his heart open, for what she was about to hear would turn her kindly heart from him, likely forever. She would never hold him in esteem again.

"Ma lived. Sometime that night, a still, dead little girl baby slid from her. The midwife tried, but couldn't revive my sister. She said the picken's heart had cracked under the strain of Ma's hard labour. But nine-year-old me thought he knew the truth. I was certain sure the Blackheart Man had heard my prayer, and taken the baby's heart.

"So that meant I knew what would happen next: the Blackheart Man would come and make me honour my promise. I would become the Blackheart Man, setting him free.

"For sennights I waited, in fear and dread. All that time, Ma was recovering, and the milk from her unsuckled tetas was making them hard and painful until it dried up, and she and my das were grieving the lost child. Me, I just felt guilt. I was convinced I was the reason Ma had survived, but in achieving that end, I had caused a picken to die—my own sister! And now I was going to pay for it forever, unless I could convince some other hapless soul to take up the awful task of murdering more pickens like myself."

Gombey said, "But it wasn't your prayers that caused Liguanea to live, and there was no Blackheart Man to come for you! I kept trying to convince you."

Veycosi nodded. "You did. But I didn't believe you. Sennights of nightmares, of waking up screaming. My parents thought it was because of what I'd witnessed Ma go through.

"Months and months went by. The Blackheart Man didn't come to claim me. And I grew little bit older and wiser, and I finally understood that the Blackheart Man was just a tale. He couldn't answer prayers, sith he didn't exist. He couldn't come and force me to take his place."

Cookie's attention was with them again. She said, "What this have to do with the blackhearted—excuse me, Androu and Samra—pickens?"

This was the part Veycosi had been dreading. The thing so awful he had pushed his recent deeds out of his mind till now. He was shaking, but he continued, small-voiced.

"The day the piche army came out of the tar, I went with Yaaya and Samra to see them. And I saw the one that was different from the others. The one wearing Chynchin clothes."

"Datiao," Cookie said softly. "Is Datiao him name."

Gombey asked, "How you know that, Cookie?"

"Never you mind. Seems I know some things."

Veycosi pressed on, suddenly in a hurry to get this tale done, to end the agony of waiting for the boom to fall. "I recognized him! Is the Blackheart Man, come for me! I been seeing him in my nightmares since I was a youngboy!"

Gombey rolled his eyes and kissed his teeth in impatience. "Don't talk nonsense, Cosi."

"Is not nonsense, and I will prove it to you. In any case, some nights ago, I was taking heir Tierce to the piche on a trumped-up story that I was going to initiate ir as a postulant to the Colloquium—"

Samra glanced sideways at Tierce, who'd clearly recognized ir own name. "And ee believed you?"

"Ee so badly wants to study with us there, and I reasoned if ee felt ee had been permitted to join us, ee might send ir army away. I reasoned to myself that I was merely doing Macu's bidding."

Androu said, "And would *merely* thereby get to claim credit for saving Chynchin, and be covered in glory, and acclaimed by all, nah true?"

Veycosi cast his eyes downwards. "Ah true," he muttered. "By the time you suggested that course, I'd already had the idea myself. I thought your ruse sounded familiar. I just didn't remember I had accomplished it days before, the night of the boulay ceremony. I took the heir somewhere secluded to have the sham ceremony. When Kaïra asked to come with, I said yes. I was feeling chagrined that I'd been overharsh to her some days before. She brought her whole crewe.

"I had stolen away some Reverie, as we students all do. I brought some with me, and we all trekked to the outskirts of town, on the hardened edge of the Upper Piche. I told Tierce what Reverie was, and ee and I were sharing it in my mock ritual as the pickens watched. . . ."

"Is all right?" Tierce asked. "For the children to be here?"

"Please let us stay!" Kaïra pleaded.

Veycosi gathered the pickens around him. "You going to behave?"

They chorused, "Yes, maas'!"

Tierce looked doubtful. The pickens shifted uncomfortably. Kaïra gave Veycosi a desperate look. Veycosi gave in. "All right. But"—he shook his finger at them—"a single peep from any of you, and I sending all of oonuh home one time. You understand?"

Kaïra's young friend Tubang got half a yes out before the rest shushed her. Solemnly, they all nodded their agreement to the bargain.

Veycosi smiled a reassurance at Tierce and continued mixing the bouffe. How much nutmeg powder to add? Three pinches? Yes, something so. And a measure of the tincture. That looked like the right amount. Veycosi stirred the mixture and tasted it. It was so bitter it made him shudder. Perfect, if a mite strong. "Is time," he said. "Now, pickens, this is serious business. So oonuh keep silent."

They nodded, elbowing each other in their excitement. Yddyta let out a nervous giggle, then clapped her hand to her mouth to quiet herself. Tierce leaned forwards, ir face eager and gleaming with perspiration in the half dark. What a way these people sweated! If their race had had any colour to their skins when their gods had created them, belike their forebears had sweated it all out of them. Veycosi chuckled at his own joke. Must remember to tell that to Gombey next time he saw him.

Veycosi poured the mixture into the chalice. It bubbled little bit. Had it done that all the times he'd mixed it before? He couldn't remember.

Never mind. He held the chalice up turned towards his attentive audience. The bitterness from that one little taste of the bouffe was numbing his tongue. His whole mouth inside felt prickly, then it felt nothing at all. He laughed, and it was as though someone else was moving his lips. His tongue was a senseless flap of flesh. Strong bouffe. This was going to be a good batch.

Veycosi went over to Tierce and held the chalice to ir lips. Ee skinned up ir face at the first taste, but took two good swallows. Ee sat back onto ir heels, then ir buttocks slid sideways to land ir sitting on the ground, ir legs crooked at an uncomfortable angle. Veycosi asked, "Th'art aright?"

Tierce nodded sleepily. The blue part of ir eyes was all black.

His turn next. Steli had told him that the mestre leading the ceremony often only mimed drinking from the chalice. Especially if they were in heavy demand to conduct plenty Reveries that day. Veycosi realised how much he missed the daily rituals of being a postulant; how much he would miss them if they never allowed him back. He might never be granted a true Reverie ceremony. So now here before him was Tierce, a sham aspirant to the Colloquium of Fellows, unwittingly undergoing a sham Reverie. Veycosi envied even that.

He wasn't going to mime a rass, then. For a few hours, his spirit would wander free in the lands of the gods, as though he were one of them. On impulse, Veycosi drank down more of the draft. Four good swallows it was, even with the moiety he spilled from his insensible lips. Veycosi thanked Mama-ji that his mouth was too numb now to taste the bouffe. The room began to swirl around him. Veycosi laughed and sat on the ground lest he float away, as the walls were now doing. The numbness spread upwards to his cheeks and eyelids, and downwards to his torso. It was crawling down his arms when Veycosi heard Kaïra's voice asking him, "Cosi? We could taste little bit of the bouffe? Just one small-small little bit?"

Veycosi felt such warmth towards the pickens in that moment. Why deny them this same feeling of well-being? He held the chalice out to Kaïra. Then he fell onto his back. As the Reverie took him away, he heard Kaïra doling out sips from the chalice to her bannas: "One a-quattie, two a-quattie . . ."

In his Reverie, Veycosi witnessed the birthing of the island that would become Chynchin, leaping up above ocean level on a swell of volcanic outpour millennia before the Cibonn' people first found and then ignored it for being too barren to inhabit. There was nothing but scrub grass and parched earth at the time. But the occasional ship that found itself storm-wrecked on the island left behind stuff that went wild and somehow thrived: ginger, chickens. He witnessed the birth of Kaïra to young Thandiwe and her astonishment throughout, for she truly had lain with no man yet. He vowed to cease disbelieving her. Perhaps he would even remember his revelation and his vow after he came out of the intoxication of Reverie.

Then the revelations turned dark. He was standing on the Upper Piche, so near its centre at the Mother Lake that the bottoms of his alpagats were warm and sticky with it. The Mother Lake was roiling, slow and inexorable as a belly cramp. A face appeared in it, a face of liquid piche. Its features were those of the piche soldier that had startled him. Veycosi tried to step backwards, to come away from there, but his piche-mired alpagats nailed him to the spot.

The lips of the apparition moved. You promised, *it said.* It is time. Free me.

Thick as piche, terror rose up to clog Veycosi's throat, overwhelm his mind. He managed to choke out, Not me! Don't take me!

Who, then? The pact must be honoured.

Veycosi lifted his head, dragged open his heavy eyelids. He pointed at Kaïra. She will take my place. She loves the gods.

The face of the Blackheart Man sank back into the piche, and all was well again.

Veycosi floated on dreams, for how long, he didn't know. The retching of one of the pickens brought him back to himself a little. All the pickens were holding their bellies, grimacing in pain.

"No!" *Veycosi shouted. The sound echoed through his head. He couldn't get a thought clear in his befuddled brain, except this: he had made a mistake. The pickens shouldn't have been here. In his current state, he was unable to look after them. They needed to be with their kin.* "Oonuh go home this minute!" *Veycosi ordered them. His words came out slurred.* "Straight home, and don't stop for any reason. You hear? Mind me, I say!"

Twelve pairs of inscrutable eyes turned Veycosi's way. Then the Reverie tide washed him fully again into the world of phantasms, of

*dark light and half-seen wonders that became the whole of his world.
One of the gods greeted him there in the wilderness, in the form of
a giant caiman of piche standing upright on its hinders. She opened
her long mouth in a smile of welcome. His heart swelling with love,
Veycosi opened his arms to embrace Chynchin's sacred mother.*

"*Mamapiche,*" he said.

Thandiwe shoved Veycosi. He lurched backwards. "You gave the
pickens pure Reverie!" she cried. "*You* poisoned Kaïra!"

The hurt and anger on her face made Veycosi's stomach knot
up all over again, so strongly he felt he might be sick. "Thandiwe,
Gombey, I sorry! Kaïra, I sorry!"

"You mad?" said Gombey. "I know you thought Kaïra was
plenty bother, but I didn't imagine you could be so careless." He
rushed at Veycosi and spat. The spittle ran a cold trail down Veycosi's cheek. "How you could betray us so, Cosi? Betray me, and
Kaïra, and Thandy. And all for sport!" He stood up and pulled a
sleeping Kaïra from Thandiwe's arms into his own. "She not spending one more night here with you."

He and Thandy left with Kaïra. Samra glared at Veycosi and
followed them.

"Well," said Androu. "Quite a pass you bring us to."

Tierce asked, "It was . . . untrue? No studying?"

Androu shook his head. "Not at the moment, Highness."

Tierce made a sound halfway between dismay and hurt.

Veycosi moaned, "How I could hurt pickens like that? Poison
them and not even self remember?"

"Some of us forget more than that already," Cookie told him.

The courtyard had gone quiet. A group of men turned the corner, heading for Veycosi's porch; pale Ymisen men in crisp woolen

uniforms, each one sporting a musket and a sword. They moved in lockstep. "That dog!" said Androu. "What the devil he think he's doing?" He drew his back up straight. "Highness, I'm sorry. I fear Advisor Gunderson is showing his true face. He never intended to fall in with your will to peace."

The heir stood to face the soldiers, ir face proud and grim. Androu took Veycosi's hand. "Do thou flee to somewhere safe," he said. "Off island, if you can. Take Samra. Ymisen's invading."

"What, now?"

"This instant."

The soldiers marched up to the porch. Their leader called a halt. "Tierce, overthrown heir to the crown of Ymisen," he barked, "your refusal to invade Chynchin as agreed upon has been deemed treason against the godly nation of Ymisen. We are charged with taking you into custody."

Tierce nodded; more a slow, musing nodding of the head than agreement. Ee stepped forwards and held ir wrists out for the chains. "What news will you tell the cacique?" ee enquired.

"She is expired at our hands," the captain replied. "As of this hour, we hold the seat of their government."

Androu made a strangled sound. "I am a poor engineerer," he said. His colour was high, his words sharp-clipped. "I thought to master my master. Fuck!" He kicked the porch wall, making the building shudder. "I was the one who advised them to take her," he told Veycosi. "Said it would mean a clean, quick victory, that with Chynchin's principal cacique imprisoned, all of Chynchin would fall into their hands like a full mango."

The shards of Veycosi's destroyed world went still and cold around him. "You had them kill Macu?" The smell of Androu's skin was still in his nostrils, the imprints of his hands on Veycosi's thighs.

"No, blast it! They were to keep her in high state, see to her every need but freedom. A golden cage, *I said*!" His voice rose to a shout. "Not this! Not twist her neck like a guinea fowl . . ." His angry outburst trailed off when he saw Veycosi's face. "Ymisen was never one to appreciate subtlety," he told Veycosi. "My love, I am so sorry—"

Veycosi's head was pounding. "No matter. Seems I turned my coat to match yours."

Androu's smile was bitter. "A thankless way to get you some company, you must grant. At least I never intended to lead others to murder. You had every intention of offering up Kaïra to a phantasm to assuage your fevered mind."

Which was worse? In the moment, Veycosi couldn't rightly say. "Just get away from me."

Androu looked like a kicked hound. "Very well. I must in any case accompany these jolly lads."

The squadron marched off with Tierce and Androu, both bound.

Cookie creaked to her feet. "Oh, Black Mother," she whispered. "I thought we'd bought us more time than this." Her speech was different, the accent antique. "Maas' Cosi, beg you a borrow of your camel."

"Goat? If you like," Veycosi replied distractedly. "But for what?"

"Thank you."

"Be careful," he said. "She's mean."

Goat pricked up her ears as Cookie came over. She snapped at Cookie, but Cookie confidently tapped her soundly on the snout. Goat shrank back and let Cookie untie her lead.

Goat unfolded herself to her feet, towering over little, frail Cookie. Goat yanked her neck to pull the lead out of Cookie's hand. "Hold!" barked Cookie. "Set!"

And swive him if the bad-minded beast didn't crouch down, though she mawed her vexation.

"Good Goat," said Cookie. She reached her hand out.

"Mind yourself," Veycosi warned. Goat could take Cookie's finger off with one good crunch.

"Give me my flagon, please."

Cookie poured a little beer into her palm and offered it to Goat. Goat gave Cookie's hand a delicate sniff, then lapped the beer up. Cookie smiled. "Good girl. There'll be more of that, but not too much." Cookie scratched Goat's flank for the space of couple-three breaths. "You going to let me ride?" she asked. Slowly, she clambered aboard Goat's back. Goat remained still. Cookie leaned over and patted Goat's neck. "She not the Goat I once knew, but I bet you she can be as fleet of foot when she have a mind to be. Up, girl."

Goat rose. Cookie used the lead to turn Goat's nose towards the road.

"Where you going?"

"To the Palavera. To see how bad things are."

As Cookie got settled, a heavyhearted Veycosi asked, "Cookie, you know what you doing?"

"Not Cookie. Not no more. Something cleared centaines of fog from my mind as you told your tale. It comes to me who I am. I name Acotiren. Take your lover's advice, Cricket. Get far away from this mess." And little, frail Cookie tamped her heels twice into Goat's flank, hard, and took off at a gallop.

Acotiren?

Veycosi tossed the rest of the roast breadfruit into a satchel. He had to warn Gombey and Thandiwe. And his parents!

As he was sneaking out of the apartments via a back way, he saw Kaïra, walking stiff-legged towards him. How had she gotten away from her mother?

Veycosi grabbed the younggirl up. In her hand, Kaïra held a torn, bloodied rag; a scrap from the robe Gombey had been wearing that evening.

Veycosi crouched in a hibiscus bush beside the road at the entrance to the market, shaking as he wept silently, holding Kaïra's hand. Bodies, mostly Chynchin bodies, lay bleeding on the path. A group of Ymisen soldiers meandered around them, occasionally jamming bayonets into the people lying there, to make sure they were well dead. Some of them weren't, and cried out as they expired from the bayonets' stabbings.

The market was on fire. Plumes of smoke rose from divers parts of it. And screaming. People were trying to flee from there lest they be burned, but Ymisen soldiers were blocking the way, shooting and stabbing. Hamstringing horses and camels as they tried to gallop through the blockade. A fleet man on a bicycle nearly managed to swerve past one of the soldiers, but a staff jabbed through the spokes of his front wheel jammed the wheel, stopping the bicycle dead. Its back end reared up, sending the man flying. Another soldier ran him through with his sword while the man was still in the air.

The wailing from the market. The grunts of people dying in the road. The screams of the injured. The screeching of maimed beasts. Spilled and broken goods that the soldiers kicked out of the way. It was all horrible beyond comprehension. And the smell rising from the road. Of blood let out from its proper home. Of shit from sliced-open guts. Veycosi had to cover his own nose and mouth, as much to block the smell as to keep in his own whimpers. He wished he could cover his eyes and ears, too. He gave thanks that Kaïra's wits were too dulled to take in the scene that lay before them.

With a war cry, a troop of Carenage Town guards a-horse and camelback charged the blockade. Behind them ran a second wave of Carenage citizens with muskets, bows, heavy-duty slings, machetes, swords. Some pelted rockstones.

The guards' volley of shot mowed down many of the Ymisen.
The citizens began picking off the rest. And now Ymisen blood was
also making of the road a river. Ymisen soldiers cried out for mercy
as they expired. The remaining ones exchanged fire. A Carenage
woman fleeing the market with her child in her arms got caught
in the crossfire. Child and mother, awash in red, collapsed to the
ground and lay still.

Now that the Carenage defending force was close enough, the
hand-to-hand combat began. Bayonets, swords, machetes, and the
swift dancing brutality of capoeira turned deadly. Veycosi would
fain have rushed to aid the defenders. His stones shrank within him
at the thought of taking a blow, or a life. Yet the muscles of his legs
knotted, rehearsing a fight stance. His arms were ready to block, to
push, to punch. For a brief measure, he contemplated telling Kaïra
to remain in the bush while he ran out to join the fight. But the
thought of a stray arrow or shot striking the younggirl . . .

So he whispered to Kaïra to crouch down low, and the two of
them scurried from bush to bush, away from the skirmish that was
only one of many playing out all over Carenage Town this day.

And how fared the rest of the country? Surely the small Ymisen
fleet that had accompanied Tierce was not enough to take on the
whole nation? Was the council sending word to the other islands
in the archipelago? Would any of them come to help? Some were
still owned by Ymisen. Forbidden to set foot on Chynchin soil. But
suppose those ones sent forces to swell the Ymisen ranks?

Statecraft. Warcraft. Mama-ji, what a pass they had come to.

He and Kaïra had to take side paths and scrabble through middens at the backs of shops and people's compongs. Veycosi was in
his own country, yet he had to slink like any stray dog to hide from
the Ymisen forces. Kaïra was slowing him down. Veycosi prayed
Ma and his das had received pigeon news of the invasion and were

making themselves safe. How they were to do that, he had no idea. And what had befallen Gombey? Was Thandiwe safe? And Samra?

Androu was right; the Ymisen regiment had numerous horses, but not a one of the soldiers used a camel. And he had yet to see a woman Ymisen soldier.

Veycosi had no idea where he was going. In the turmoil of his mind, he lost track of where he was. He came around the side of a building and found to his horror that he had led them to the avenue at the end of which was the seat of Carenage Town's government.

Cookie was standing in front of one of the piche statues; the one on which the pickens had written. Dead soldiers lining the avenue in front, live ones swarming the Palavera just beyond.

Something was wrong with what he was seeing; with the piche soldiers. "Stand still, please, Kaïra," Veycosi said softly. He talked to the child with all the courtesy he could now, though it wouldn't make up for all the times he hadn't, or for giving her and her bannas leave to drink potent draughts of Reverie.

Cookie wasn't moving. That was part of the strangeness. She was staring up into the face of the statue, but with no expression. And she was more still than the dead. No, not quite; her knees were slowly giving way under her. And still she looked up at the statue. Veycosi didn't dare call out her name. First he had to know is what was going on.

Slow and molasses-thick, the piche was dripping off the limbs of the statues, and their musket-runners, and their mounts. What the rass? It wasn't that hot a day, for all that Mamapiche season was nearly upon them. Veycosi took one small step closer, peering at the smothered soldiers. He probably lost some years of life right then, for one of them lowered her arm, normal as any living person might. Veycosi's whole body went cold.

But the statue's forearm fell to the ground, and he managed a

bitter, small chuckle. The arm had already been broken off when
she had smothered, he supposed. And now the piche had melted off
it, and it had come dislodged.

Then the piche soldier woman took a step forwards. And so did
another of the statues. Sense fled Veycosi. Only for an instant, but
when wit returned, he found himself crouching behind a butterpot
bush by the side of the road, clutching Kaïra in his arms. "Mama,
save us," Veycosi whimpered.

The piche soldiers, black and wrinkled as raisins, were all moving towards the one that held Cookie in its gaze. Some walked, one
or two on stumps of limbs. A few crawled. Horses cantered, on
four legs. Three, if that was all they had left. One even hopped,
monstrously birdlike, on two. Cookie sank a little lower towards
the ground. The piche soldier on his donkey—when had he climbed
onto the beast?—bent his head to keep his eyes on hers. His lips
were moving, Veycosi could see now.

He had to get her away from that horror. Nobody around but
him to do it. "Kaïra, stay here," Veycosi said. No, that wouldn't
work. For if he told Kaïra to bide, the picken would bide right
there-so even if danger came and Veycosi wasn't there to save her.
What to tell her, then?

Cookie was down on one knee now, her face contorted, her
trembling arms held out towards the dead soldier. The others of
the duppy regiment were gathered around him, staring blankly
at Cookie. Not so different from the blackhearted pickens in that
way. Two hundred years their flesh had clung to them. Did it smell
of rot, or of asphalt? And how he could stand against so many,
risking attack from the living soldiers as well?

Blast Kaïra. Stopping to think about her was making him stop
to think about saving his own skin so that he might protect her.

Master Tar was climbing down off his broken donkey, slow as

molasses, with the jerky movements of someone learning to move again after years abed. He was muttering the while.

Desperately, Veycosi told Kaïra, "Just don't let anybody see you." Then, looking around first to make sure he wasn't seen, he stepped out into the road. He looked back to give Kaïra a specific direction to crouch down behind the butterpot bush.

The picken wasn't there. Frantically, Veycosi did a quick glance around. And there Kaïra was, right where he'd left her, standing in plain sight not three paces from him. But if he turned his gaze away, he had to stare hard to make Kaïra out again when he looked back at the place where he knew she was. Veycosi's scalp prickled. Younggirl was standing right there-so, wearing a bright orange boubou, but discerning her was like spying out a stick insect in the branches of a bush. *Don't let anybody see you.* Is precisely that Veycosi had said, and the benighted bloody picken had found a way to make her body obey. Veycosi's skin went cold same time as a high giggle tumbled out from his mouth. His body began to tremble. "Good girl," Veycosi stage-whispered at Kaïra.

He'd best mind what he told the picken to do from now on.

Master Tar the Chynchin turncoat was down off the donkey now. He began a herky-jerky walk over to Cookie, still muttering. What was addling him so, that he must keep whispering to himself? Though of course he must be addled; whatever organ housed his senses would have given itself up to the piche centuries ago. So much hatred on his face, and Cookie staring intently upon that face as into the eyes of a beloved. "I soon come back, Kaïra," Veycosi muttered. He charged forwards.

Master Tar's attention was fixed only on Cookie, and all the other duppies were mesmerized by whatever it was that was going on between the two. That allowed Veycosi to reach to her before they noticed. But the instant Veycosi was among them, best believe they took note. Master Tar stumbled back in surprise, nearly took a fall. But his broken thigh straightened up. Veycosi could have sworn he heard it snap back to wholeness again. "Cookie," Veycosi said. "Get up."

Master Tar made to pull his machete from his belt, but it was fouled by piche, and held fast. Veycosi took Cookie by the arm and raised her to her feet. She came up like he'd dragged her from sucking mud; slowly at first, then almost a tearing free as she looked away from Master Tar. Suddenly, she shoved Veycosi away. The piche-tarnished sword that sliced the air between them told him why. The dead soldiers were on the attack. In a manner of speaking. One of them was trying to load an ancient musket. She—perhaps a she—was having a time of it, what with the unnatural angle at which her broken arm was bent. Three more with swords were coming for Cookie and Veycosi. Cookie turned her back against Veycosi's, the better to face down the danger from two sides. Mama. Veycosi hoped she could hold her own little bit till he could get her and Kaïra away from here.

The soldiers all looked less piche-logged than before. As the tar dripped off them, Veycosi could see a cheekbone here, the curve of a shoulder there. And they were walking straighter, exempt the few with missing limbs. A clumsy band, for true, but getting more able with every passing moment. How so, *more* able?

"Yer rass, Datiao!" Cookie said. He could feel from her motion against his back that she had bent over. It seemed she was lifting something into the air. Veycosi heard the thump as she brought it up hard against another something. He chanced a glance back. She'd fetched a big rockstone up against her attacker's head. The soldier's skull barely gave under the rockstone. His head only made a small creak, like a stuffed leather ball. Veycosi leapt around to Cookie's side. The man sliced at Cookie just as Veycosi kicked his feet out

from under him with a desperate Tiger Tail sweep. The soldier top-
pled. He landed along the blade of his own machete, then rolled
onto his back. He had a fearsome gash in his belly, but the lips of the
wound were tanned and insensible. Black oozed from between them.
"After we done kill oonuh oncet!" shouted Cookie. "You want I must
do it again?" Her speech had become ancient, from an earlier time.

More of the duppy soldiers were advancing on Cookie and
Veycosi. A grisly musket boy poured shot into the barrel of a blunderbuss that now gleamed of metal, not glistening tar. The officer
wielding the blunderbuss rounded on them. Danger behind. Danger before. Veycosi opened his mouth to shout to Kaïra to go find
safety. Best he could do, for he would soon be dead more than the
ones all around them.

"Did you see the whoresons run?" came a voice from down the
road leading to the Palavera.

Veycosi swallowed his shout. It was the Ymisen soldiers. The
ones who had been sacking the Palavera. Some were walking, some
riding. One was still laughing when he stepped in among the piche
soldiers. One of his fellows grabbed his arm and pointed at the duppy
soldiers. The first soldier screamed. The living soldiers all staggered
back, their pale faces gone even lighter. With a bang, the duppy blunderbuss sprayed them with shot, and now they were all screaming.
It was almost a relief to see blood spraying from wounds, not piche.

More Ymisen soldiers, hearing their fellows yell, charged into
the fray. Cookie leapt back into the attack, so what could Veycosi
do but follow? She yanked a bag of shot from a surprised musket
boy and swung it, bola style, at the nearest Ymisen soldier, who just
happened to be a living Ymisen one. Got him good across the forearm. He went down, grunting in pain from a cracked arm bone.

Mama's tits. Three sides fighting on the same battleground: living soldiers against dead soldiers and Chynchin; Chynchin against

dead soldiers and living; and a black guard of dead soldiers determined to take down any person alive. Chynchin had a way to do things in threes, but this was beyond imagination, even for it. And near as Veycosi could tell, the piche soldiers were winning this particular skirmish. Ymisen soldiers were lying dead or dying all around, and the air reeked of blood.

Veycosi swiped up the broken-armed soldier's sword and promptly sliced off a lock of his own hair with it; he had the blade facing towards him, not outwards. A piche duppy and a living soldier both leapt for him at once. When their bodies crashed together, that was all that saved him from the buckshot fire from behind them. The piche soldier flew apart. A piece of her scored Veycosi's face. The living soldier fell to the ground, air gargling out from his ruined throat with a sound Veycosi hoped never to hear again in life. The man landed on his back. His face and most of his neck had been torn away by the scattershot. Veycosi swallowed his gorge back down, then had to roll out of the way of a cantering three-legged camel with no lower jaw. Its rider was still glued along its side with piche. No time to catch his breath; a living soldier swung at Veycosi with his sword. He felt the tip of the blade scream along his ribs. Then a rockstone came flying out of nowhere and smashed the soldier's knee for him. He howled in agony and went down. Veycosi looked for his saviour. Cookie. The old woman had a good eye, and a better arm. She grinned at him, a battle-crazed rictus. Veycosi nodded to her, then saw two piche soldiers creeping up behind her. He pointed and shouted a warning, but they were too close for her to escape them. Veycosi began to run. Before he could reach her, they had seized her. She fought but couldn't win out against the strength of two. They began carrying her towards Master Tar, who was sitting his donkey again, a little removed from the fight. "Cookie!" Veycosi screamed. He was too far away. A stiff-legged musket picken swung a blunderbuss at him by its stock. Veycosi leapt aside, tripped as he did so. He fell full weight onto the musket picken. It felt like landing on someone who had been filled with rockstones. The picken stopped moving, but the sticky piche on its body was making it hard for Veycosi to rise. And the two black-guard soldiers had already delivered Cookie to Master Tar, who was regarding her evilly. "Cookie, look sharp!" Veycosi screamed again.

Goat came bounding out from somewhere behind a wall of one of the buildings. She kicked and head-butted her way over to Master Tar.

And for an instant, the whole black guard froze still as stone.

Master Tar's donkey got a look at the gleam in Goat's eye and began to sidle away, with Master Tar kicking its side to urge it back into position. Goat bit down on the head of one of the soldiers hold-ing Cookie and came up chewing. Cookie elbowed the other in the gut, which didn't seem to stop him, for he had no air to be forced out his lungs. But it did startle him long enough for Goat to raise a leg and ram him so hard that he raised up into the air and slammed down to the ground. Then she trampled him. He wasn't moving plenty after that, though his half-headed fellow was stumbling around, groping at the air. Veycosi would have preferred to fight his own way through to Cookie, but instead he slunk and crawled and hid behind bodies, piche and flesh both. Stealth must win when strength could not.

Goat kushed down low, folding her front legs, then her back. Cookie climbed aboard, and Goat stood. "Goat!" Veycosi called. "To me!" Would she, the blessed old brute?

Cookie didn't wait to find out. She picked up Goat's lead from off her neck and pointed her Veycosi's way. Piche soldiers that were between him and Goat scattered as best they might out of the way of her trampling feet and her cudgel of a head.

Then there was a single shot and Cookie cried out and twisted in the saddle. Ymisen reinforcements had arrived. Cookie nearly top-pled off Goat's back. She grabbed hold of the pommel of the saddle with one hand and hung on. There was red seeping through the sleeve of her robe. This new lot of living Ymisen soldiers well outnumbered the black guard, and their weapons were battle-ready. After their first astonishment at seeing an army of the dead, they waded in with a will.

"Fall. Back." It was a terrible voice, gummy and hoarse. Master Tar was speaking the first words aloud for two centaines. "Now," he said, a strange, flat roar. In between each loud-spoken word he muttered still. The piche soldiers began to beat a retreat. Master Tar didn't wait for them. His donkey bore him stickily away.

Goat clattered up to Veycosi. Cookie's face was grey. "Climb up," she said weakly. A shot flew past Veycosi's ear. Somehow, he clambered onto Goat's back behind Cookie.

"Head that way!" he told her, pointing to where Kaïra should be. Veycosi's heart panged for his country, but he couldn't study that right now. Mama-ji, but he hoped the girl was safe. Cookie flicked the reins with her good hand, and they were off.

"Shoulda never taught his rass the chantson," Cookie raged. Vey-cosi didn't know how long he, Cookie, and Kaïra had been travel-ling, dodging skirmishes. Long enough that they had dismounted Goat to give the poor beast some rest. Veycosi held Kaïra's hand. The girl stumbled along beside him.

"That Datiao," said Cookie. "Didn't trust him from the start. He always thought he one knew best."

She was raving. But he had to admit she'd acquitted herself better in the fight than he would have thought possible for some-one her age.

But then she sat down abruptly on a nearby rock, panting. Her complexion had greyed and she was holding her injured, bleeding arm. "Cookie," said Veycosi. "How do? You need that bandaged?"

She took couple-three breaths before replying. "Acotiren," she said. "I name Acotiren."

So she hadn't left off the fancy of being one of the witches. "Of course," Veycosi answered. "Acotiren."

She cut her eyes at him. She'd had too many years on this earth to think that Veycosi believed her. Plenty years, but not so many as she imagined. He helped her tear a strip from the hem of her robe. He bandaged her arm with it. "I found my soul case," she told him.

"Awoah? Good. Wish I could find mine." Veycosi looked down the road they were on. Androu's apartment was still some furlongs away. Maybe it was far enough away from the town centre to be peaceful. Would they ever get there? The pickens milled around him vacantly. They had shown up one by one. Veycosi couldn't think how they had found him. He stood. "We have to keep on, Cook—Acotiren."

"Is Datiao have it," she said.

Veycosi took her other arm and helped her, groaning, to her feet. "Who have what?" He was only half listening to her. He did a quick tally of the pickens; all there, miraculously. He bade Goat kush, then sat the two youngest on her back. They were so light, she might scarcely notice their weight. What those poor children must have had to do to get safely to him made him feel the horror of his crime against them anew.

"Datiao," Cookie replied. "The one you call Master Tar." She spat to one side. "You didn't see he had something in his hand?" Veycosi had bade Goat to stand again. Now he patted the camel high on her wither to indicate she should start walking. She began moving. With a sigh of determination, Cookie got to her feet and started along the road again beside him, the pickens following.

"I was too occupied with seeing the dead walking," Veycosi replied, "to note what decorations they were carrying."

She cackled at that. "I take your point," she said. "But it was my soul case. Is that giving him life. Him and the rest of the soldiers. You saw how he was starting to mend?"

"Yes, that I did mark." What a tale! He could almost be convinced she truly was Acotiren from long-ago times. After all, they had just been attacked by soldiers from that time.

He clicked his fingers for Goat, who had fallen behind when she'd spied a patch of honey grass. Contrary brute cropped one more leisurely mouthful before she deigned to resume ambling along behind them. But he wasn't going to leash her anymore. Would have been sorry repayment for her buying him and Cookie their lives just now.

Cookie stopped again, put her hand on Veycosi's shoulder for support. She held her side and gasped.

"Is it your wound?" he asked.

"No. Little scratch like that will scarce bother me."

"What, then?" She was sweating; that light, insensible sweat that the sick sometimes got.

She replied, "Have to get my soul case back from Datiao."

"Or what?"

"When he drain out all my soul from it, he and the rest will be hale again, and I will be dead."

Chills walked like fingers across Veycosi's shoulders and upper back. "Goat," he said softly. "To me, I said." Goat wandered up to the head of their straggling party, trying hard to look as though she'd just happened to come where Veycosi had commanded her. He put his hand on her flank. She bent her head to have her ears scratched. He did so, though briefly. They could find themselves in the middle of a skirmish anytime. Goat gave a groan of pleasure.

"Old girl," Veycosi said to her. "Kush." She grumbled as she did so, but she knelt. "You going to ride with these two pickens," Veycosi told Cookie. She didn't demur. He helped her onto Goat's back, behind the little ones. He could swear the woman he'd pulled away from Master Tar had been plenty more heavy.

"Up, Goat," he said. Goat rose. Veycosi adjusted the satchel with the roast breadfruit pieces and his hooking so the strap was crosswise about his body. And on they went in silence.

Strange to see the day go about its business around them: the little lizards sunning themselves on the pleasantly whitewashed walls around the compongs they passed; the stray dogs scratching in the middens for scraps. Chynchin was lost and Veycosi the scapegrace who'd tried to sacrifice his own daughter, and still it was a day like any other.

"Cosi?" said Cookie. She was Cookie, damn it.

"Ah?"

"What you did with the soul cases?"

"I don't follow you."

"Yours and the pickens'. Where you put them, lad?"

Veycosi stopped dead in the road. The pickens drew to a halt with him. He looked at all their little necks. Not a one of them wearing a soul case. He tried to hearken back to before the pickens, turned heartless, had all returned. Had any of them been wearing soul cases then? He sighed. "I don't remember," he confessed. The memory was lost in the haze of his recent Reverie excess.

A cullybree winged by overhead. It shat on Veycosi's shoulder. Cookie raised an eyebrow. "Bad luck," she said.

Chapter 8

THE DEATH OF THE WITCH ACOTIREN

AS TOLD TO VEYCOSI BY COOKIE, LATTERLY
SELF-STYLED ACOTIREN, MASTER CHEF
TO THE COLLOQUIUM

THE OBE ACOTIREN WATCHED *the soldier woman, who had collapsed onto her knees now, her scream hiccoughing into sobs. While the army was becoming tar beneath the feet of the villagers, Acotiren had pushed through the crowd and fetched her fearless grandchild from the first branch of the mango tree. He'd fallen out of it thrice before, but every day returned to try again. She hitched him up onto her hip. He clamped his legs at her waist and fisted up a handful of her garment at the shoulder. He brought the fist happily to his mouth.*

Acotiren's face bore a calm, stern sadness. "Never you mind," Kima *heard her mutter in the direction of the grieving woman. "What we do today going to come back on us, and more besides."* Maridowa *glanced at the obe but said nothing.*

Then Acotiren produced her obi bag from wherever she had had it hidden on her person and tossed it onto the pitch. Mother

Letty started forwards. "Tiren, no!" cried Mother Letty, her face anguished.

She was too late to intercept the obi bag. It landed on the road. It was a small thing, no bigger than a guinea fowl's egg. It should have simply bounced and rolled. Instead, it sank instantly, as though it weighed as much in itself as the whole tarred army together.

Maridowa was dancing on the road and hadn't noticed what was happening. It was Kima who saw it all. Acotiren pressed her lips together, then smiled a bright smile at her grandchild. "Come," she said. "Make I show you how to climb a mango tree."

Tranquil, as though she hadn't just tossed her soul case away to be embalmed forever in tar, she turned her back to go and play with the boy, leaving Mother Letty kneeling there, tears coursing through the lines on her ancient face as she watched her friend go.

In less than a year Acotiren was frail and bent. There was no more climbing trees for her. Her eyes had grown crystalline with cataracts, her hands tremulous, her body sere and unmuscled. One morning she walked into the bush to die, and never came out again. But by then her daughter's child, Acotiren's fifth grandchild, was so sure-footed from skinning up gru-gru bef palms and mamapom trees with his nana that he never, ever fell. Wherever he could plant his feet, he could go. His friends called him Goat.

"Goat?" Veycosi asked as he finished scribing the tale Cookie had told him. He was sitting on the floor with his back against the divan on which Cookie was resting. "They called your—her grandson Goat?" He was getting so used to Cookie's fancy that she was the saviour witch from ancient times that he was starting to think of her that way himself. He lay down his stylus and massaged his cramped fingers. He stood to stretch, glancing as he did so out the window of Androu's vacated apartment. Goat was cropping her way through someone's abandoned callaloo patch. Veycosi hoped they were far enough away from the city to have some time to rest.

Cookie—Acotiren, whoever she was—flapped a tired hand at him, like waving away a fly. "I see where you're looking, but no, Cricket. My grandson didn't come back as no camel." She kissed her teeth and lay back on the divan. She closed her eyes. Her eyelids looked thin and dry. Her eyeballs shifted around beneath them. She was weakening as Veycosi watched.

He checked on the pickens, who were lying on the floor, nodding off in a knot beside the divan. Some of them were already asleep. The others blinked slowly and blankly, staring at nothing. So tired they looked! He bade them sleep, then returned to his position on the floor, knees pulled up, back against the side of the divan. He never realised war could be boring so. Sitting and waiting for tragedy to find you, terror became a background roar, and you found you still had to continue with the daily tasks of life.

"If you went dead then," he asked Cookie, "how comes it you alive now?"

A small smile. "Who say I went dead?"

Veycosi sighed. "All the stories say."

"The stories say I went into the bush *half*-dead. They don't tell you the rest."

"But now you going to tell it me?" This was a tale that would make any griot line proud to adapt. If Cookie gave him leave, he would scribe it into his book of tales of Chynchin. Were there to be no more Chynchin after today, maybe someday someone would find his book of tales and revive the nation again. In song, at least.

He picked up his book and stylus again.

"True I was sick plenty bad when I went into the bush," said Cookie in a whispery voice. "Took almost all my strength to make my way. I wanted to go in deep enough that nobody wouldn't look for me."

"Why?"

"I know not," she replied. Sometimes her speech sounded archaic for true. "I was like to a very dog on its last legs. I wanted nothing more than to find a quiet hole where I could make my transition to the next life in peace."

Cookie continued, "I reached to a massive old poui tree in the middle of the bush. Never been so far in before. Like me, the tree looked half-dead. It was lightning-chewed. The branches on one side were black and leafless all the way to the top. Charred in places. The other side was in full bloom. Pink flowers topping it like a fancy hat, and more dropping to make a carpet on the ground. The tree had been blasted nearly the whole way down to its roots. Right at the base was a hollowed-out place, lined with the pink of fallen poui blossoms. It made a pretty seat just wide enough to hold my rump." She cackled. "I used to have plenty more rump to fill out my clothes them-there days."

"So you went and sat inside the tree?"

"Fell into it, more like. Rainwater had collected in the base, under the flowers. Got my arse a wetting for my pains. The water chilled me. I started shivering, but I didn't care for none of that. My eyes were going dark. I was dying for lack of my soul case."

"But it's just a bauble!" Veycosi protested. His fingers tapped the place on his neck where his soul case usually hung. "People don't waste away when they lose theirs!"

She shrugged. "Things happen different to me. Is how I knew from small I was a witch."

"What you did after you sat down in the tree?"

"I died," replied Cookie. "Nothing. Blackness. Then I slept."

"You died, *then* you slept?"

"Ah-hah. Backwards. Like I was backing out of death into sleep, and thence to waking again. Felt so refreshed when I woke!" She cackled again. "All those long weeks preparing for Ymisen to come a-rousting, wasn't plenty sleep to be had. I had to pass away in order to get some rest." She smiled and shook her head.

One of his fingernails caught on the stylus and tore. He swore. He nibbled the torn piece of nail off his finger and spat it aside.

"I didn't know my own self," said Cookie. "I looked down at my body. I was wearing a robe that was rotting off me. The poui tree I was sitting in had calved; a shoot was growing from its base that had risen up green right between my knees and was heading for the sky. I got out of the tree. I didn't know it then, for at first I disremembered who I was, but there were no more cataracts in my eyes. No more rheumatism in my joints. My hair was tall all the way down to my feet. But gone white all the way through."

She was quiet some little while, then she gave a gasp. Veycosi looked up from his work. She was sobbing quietly. "If I'd been myself, I would 'a known from the hair," she said. "Would 'a guessed is what had happened. All those decades had gone by while I slept!"

"And after that?"

"I made my way through the bush. Didn't know where I was going. Ran out of bush eventually. There was no encampment anymore, but a whole rassclaat town. People saw me stagger out near naked. They gave me clothes.

"Nobody there to know me, Cricket! Nobody to recognize me. I was beginning to remember who I was, but when I saw my face in a mirror, I didn't want to believe that was myself. I had wasted away so till I never got my form back. Letty, dead from since. I went and saw her grave. Maridowa still alive, but near witless. She knew me, a-true. In her own way. But who would pay mind to a mumbling old woman?"

"How long?" Veycosi whispered.

"Fifty and three years!"

"You slept away a whole lifetime?"

"Close to. People didn't believe I was Acotiren. They thought I was some old dotard as mad as Maridowa. I asked after my grandson. 'Metata,' I said. 'Is where Metata dey?' Finally somebody heard me who knew our family. 'Oh, you mean Goat!' he said. 'Gone buccaneering years now. Nobody know if he quick or he dead.'"

Acotiren wiped her eyes dry with the heels of her hands. "At least he found a work where the climbing was always good. Me, I learned not to try to convince people who I was. Witches were old-time story to them. I became Cookie."

"A hundred and fifty years ago?"

She smiled. "Ah-hah. Is like my body forget how to die. From the time the doors of the Colloquium opened, always been a Cookie there. Always been me."

"And no one," he asked skeptically, "realised you weren't aging? Weren't passing to the next life?"

She shrugged again. "I don't know why not, Maas' Cosi. From that day when we three witches opened some kind of door wide to change the fate of Chynchin, this place have pockets and occurrences of the uncanny that can't be explained. Maybe one of them hovering around me, like a cloud."

Veycosi had no reply to that. He cast an eye over the sleeping pickens. The smaller ones had instinctually curled into the body warmth of the larger ones. He realised they might all be feeling chilled after their sweaty forced march. The pile of them lying there didn't take up plenty room. His hooking might be big enough to cover them all.

Groaning to his feet, he fetched his satchel from the hook by the door. He opened it and pulled out the crumpled fabric. He shook it.

The missing soul cases clattered to the floor. The noise woke the pickens, and Cookie. The pickens remained where they were, sith he'd given them no commands. Cookie saw where the noise had come from. "So that's where you put them," she said.

What was that trickling sound from the other side of the table? Oh, swive him. How long since he'd herded the lot of the pickens out to the privy? He would deal with the soul cases in a bit. He bade the pickens come and stand near him. "We have to make haste," he told them, though he knew they wouldn't reply. He couldn't see any danger from out the window, so they went outside to where the privy was, and he told them one by one to relieve themselves if they needed to.

A flash of sunlight dashed into his eye. He looked up. From here, he could see one of the seventy relay towers that girded Chynchin. Reflected firelight pulsed from the very top of it. A daytime signal to tell the neighbouring towns they were under attack!

How long would it take them to muster to Carenage's aid, though?

When he got back to the room, Cookie had drifted to merciful sleep. She was snoring a little. Cookie? Acotiren? She would have it to say they were one and the same. But Cookie was who he'd always known her to be, so Cookie it would remain. For now.

Maitefa was shivering. Poor wight was only wearing a light shift, after all. Veycosi wrapped his scarf around her, sari-wise. The sun had begun its march down to the horizon but was still visible in the sky. Veycosi lifted Maitefa into his arms and took her out to the backyard, where she could get warm in what remained of the sunlight. Her indifference made her awkward to hold. He had to instruct her to put her arms around his neck. This was the same picken whose agility and quick thinking had bested a capo mestre many times her size. Water brimmed over from Veycosi's eyes. He longed to see her responsive again, in even the smallest way. "Look, Maitefa," he said, pointing up to the sky. "Koo the cullybrees."

Maitefa's eyes obediently followed where Veycosi was pointing. The cullybrees were flying lower. It was close to hatching time.

There came a disorganized tromping of feet along the road, around a bend where he couldn't see. Veycosi's heart dropped into his belly. He pulled Maitefa into a crouch with him behind a large euphorbia bush. Who was coming? Carenage Town citizens, fleeing the two armies?

Then he heard the never-ending syllables of Datiao's repeated chantson, spoken loud and ungarbled from a throat now cleared of piche.

Mama-ji!

Veycosi hustled Maitefa back inside, only to find Cookie looking in even worse shape than before. "It's the tar army!" he told her.

"Oh." She looked resigned. "He find me, then."

"We have to leave!"

"I can't run, son," Cookie said. She closed her eyes. "Too weak. Mek them come. You take the pickens and go."

No *time*! The thump and scrape of the duppy army had reached the gate. Veycosi looked around wildly. He couldn't lead eleven tired pickens on another forced march.

The duppies were coming up the walkway. Veycosi could hear the wheeze of terror in his own throat.

He was nimble. Maybe he would have to leave the rest to their fate. In his wit-flown need to survive, he half made to run.

Then he saw Kaïra's dull gaze, looking not at him, but through him. No. He would not abandon that child again. None of them. He picked the spilled soul cases up, slipped Kaïra's over her head, then put on his. He gathered up and threw the rest of them willy nilly at the other pickens. He didn't know what else he could do for them. "Put them on!" he yelled. He didn't know whose was whose, but he hoped against hope that some of them would touch their rightful owners and return their wits to them. Maybe then they could run to safety.

Of course, nothing happened. Cookie had just been spinning tales after all. But she was his charge now, just as the pickens were.

He scurried to gather all the pickens in front of Cookie's divan. He put himself in front of them and her, to fight the duppies off as best he might. To finally face the Blackheart Man that had come out of the piche in search of him.

The door slammed open. The piche soldiers entered the doorway a-tromp and advanced towards them. Their sulphurous reek filled the apartment. Their awfully broken, piche-infused bodies made his skin crawl. Pity for what had happened to them lived side by each with terror for what they could do to him.

Datiao's face was livid with triumph. He advanced upon Veycosi, muttering the chantson the while. The soldiers were plumping up. Still sere, but no longer merely dried skin stretched over brittle bone. As Master Tar worked his obeah, their bodies were trying to quicken back to life. With slight success that Veycosi could see, despite their having filled out little bit. Their wounds, bloodless, still gaped open. Other than Master Tar's, their broken limbs had not reset. Missing body parts had not regenerated. The soldiers' expressions—those with faces left, any road—bore no malice, just sadness. Some of them stared only, pleadingly, at Datiao. That one man's drive for revenge was keeping them all bound in this nonliving life.

They brandished their weapons but seemed loath to use them.

Veycosi moved towards them, waving his hooking as though it were a net and the duppies so many lobsters he might entangle in it. He looked ridiculous and he knew it, but he couldn't think of anything else to do. "Stay back!" he shouted. Blasted pickens began following. The soldiers would overrun them to get to him! "Remain behind me, pickens!" he ordered them. The duppy soldiers, those that had eyes remaining in their heads, rolled them nervously in the direction of the pickens. Seemed even the dead found the children uncanny. Or perhaps they had enough wit left to hate the thought of killing pickens.

Behind him, Cookie rasped a breathy laugh. "Duppies and all fear the Blackheart Man," she said.

Him. She meant him. They were looking at him. Muttering the cantrip in between his orders, Master Tar barked at his men to fall to. Looked like they feared him the more, for they rushed immediately at Veycosi and Cookie. Veycosi managed to entangle two of them in his hooking and push their cracked-leather bodies to the ground, only because their bodies were too broken to be nimble. Then a keen thread of fire burned along his side. He cried out and fell to his knees. One of the dogsons had come up beside him and scored him with her knife. He threw his hand up against her next blow. Cookie grunted. Her two feet landed on the floor in front of Veycosi, and now it was she shielding him. Master Tar shouted. From Veycosi's place peering out behind Cookie's hem, he saw Master Tar dash forwards and elbow his soldier to the ground before she could strike Cookie a blow. "Mine! *Mumble*," he cried out. "Acotiren *mumble* is mine to kill!"

Acotiren. He knew her to be Acotiren. She'd been telling the truth.

"But is me you want!" Veycosi blurted. He rose, legs trembling, to his feet. He had already proved himself able to steal the hearts of pickens. He must be able to do worse than that. Cold with fear, Veycosi made his legs move forwards to face Datiao.

Datiao turned his gaze from Cookie-who-was-Acotiren to Vey-cosi. The duppy took a rasping breath. "Who *mumble* you?"

Veycosi didn't understand. "Is me, Veycosi," he said. "I begged you to save my mother all those years ago. I said I would take your place, and now you've come to fulfill your bargain."

Datiao frowned. "Don't know *mumble* you. Acotiren *mumble* is my *mumble* prize." So saying, he shoved Veycosi aside with the flat of his machete.

"In your dreams," Cookie told Datiao. Veycosi could think of her by no other name. She rested her hand on his shoulder. "Cricket, you deh-deh?" The gesture was meant to be one of comfort, but he could tell she could barely stand. She was leaning with all her weight. The pressure intensified the pain in Veycosi's side till it roared like the surf, but he made shift not to cry out. He was only wounded. Cookie was dying from Datiao's obeah.

Master Tar lifted the heel of his outstretched palm to his lips. The palm was pink, its life lines clean. He was really a fine figure of a man, for one dead over two centaines. He smiled like a very demon and blew a sulphur-heavy breath at Cookie. Cookie staggered. The long exhalation stank of tar, then cooled to simple human warmth. He'd blown the last of the corruption out of him and into Cookie. "Cinder," he said, "in your eye." No muttering this time. Cookie coughed, gave a death rattle of a breath. Her knees began to give way. Datiao seized her by the neck of her robe, yanked her briskly to her feet, as though she weighed no more than ash. Veycosi didn't try to stop him. Mama-ji forgive him, but he didn't even self try. She was their buffer. Dead, he couldn't help the pickens. Is that he told himself, any road.

Datiao smiled the loving smile of a yawning crypt at Cookie. He opened his free hand. A thing lay on his palm. It was round and black, no bigger than a pigeon's egg. Weakly, Cookie reached for it. Datiao batted her hand away. "Not yours," he said. "Not any-more. Your soul, your life? Mine now, Acotiren."

She groaned. Datiao closed his endmost three fingers over her soul case. With pointing finger, he tipped Cookie's chin up so that her two eyes made four with his. His look 'pon her was attentive as a lover's. When he had her gaze, he commenced to stroking the side of her face with the obi bag. She jerked in his grasp, began to trem-ble. "Give me the rest," murmured Datiao. "Every last little bit. All your life for all those times I died."

The piche soldiers had found their voices. They were keening in low, breathy moans, the sound punctuated by the dripping of bitumen quitting their bodies and falling to the floor.

Cookie's breath huffed out of her. Her head slumped against Datiao's hand. Her body went limp. Datiao cried out in triumph, let her crash to the ground. Veycosi broke her fall best he could, though it tore at his wound little more. He turned her over to see her face. It was slack. No breath, no heartbeat. She was dead.

"Mine," said Datiao again. He put her soul case to his lips and with a dreadful, gulping effort swallowed it. The last of the grey-ness left his face. He breathed in, examined his restored hands and arms with a self-satisfied look. "Good. Now I going to—"

Then he screamed, "No! You can't—!" He backed away from Cookie's body, started muttering the chantson again, frantically. "Stop it!" he said, his voice gone high and strange. His eyes were wide.

The piche soldiers began making noises even more tortured than before. Datiao grabbed his throat. He heaved and heaved, chanting and pleading the while.

Then, weirdly, he laughed, his voice higher than it had been.

And just so, the piche soldiers fell back into petrification, every one. They dried and blackened, writhing like slugs thrown onto the fire. The cordwood sound of piche soldiers tumbling was all around. As Veycosi watched, their petrified husks crumbled away, leaving only piles of soot on the floor. Datiao gave another high-pitched shout, staggered towards Veycosi. Veycosi slid Cookie's knife from its scabbard and clambered to his feet to face Datiao.

Datiao stopped. He felt his own body, his face with his hands. He looked mazed. He stared at Cookie's body. "I . . . dead?" he whispered. To Veycosi's grief, Cookie, like the piche soldiers, began also shrinking, blackening into a husk, crumbling into ash.

Veycosi rushed Datiao, though the pain tore through his side like the bite of a rusty blade.

"Cricket, no!" Datiao cried out. It was Cookie's voice. Startled, Veycosi slipped in his own blood, crashed hard onto the heel of his free hand. The jolt sang pain through him. He near fainted away from it.

Datiao kicked the knife from his hand, knelt beside Veycosi. "Cosi-boy, don't dead, now," he said. "Let me bind that wound." He put his hands on Veycosi, who tried to scramble from his grasp. "Cosi, is me," said Datiao. "Is Acotiren."

"You killed her," Veycosi told Datiao. Tears started from his eyes. "You happy now? Please, just leave the pickens alone. They can't harm you."

"Datiao didn't kill me! You don't understand?" Datiao tapped his own chest. "This is me, Acotiren!"

Veycosi was nearly insensible. He couldn't defend himself against Datiao, couldn't fathom what he was saying. He could only gape dazedly at the man.

Datiao looked at his own hand, its fingertips red with Veyco-si's blood. He turned it front and back. It was like he'd never seen his hand before. "He swallowed me," he said. "My soul case. He put my soul inside him, and it pushed his out." He gave Veycosi a shaky smile. "Datiao gone, Cosi. He gone for good this time."

"You not Cookie, blast you! You making mock." Veycosi couldn't hold his head up any longer. He lowered it to the floor. Datiao had won. Veycosi had been no help at all, no saviour. The pickens, Chynchin; all were lost.

Datiao started tearing the hem of his robe into strips. "Wai! Thought I was strong before! What a thing to have a man's sinews!" He began to wrap Veycosi's wound. "I will prove to you that I am Acotiren," Datiao said. "One night I catch you and Thandy making woo outside in the back of the kitchen when you thought everybody was gone. Was only me left, checking that the bread was rising proper for the next morning's meal. I gave you each a tulum sweetie from the kitchen and sent you on your ways."

It was true. That was a thing a devil duppy from beneath the earth probably wouldn't know. But Cookie would.

Datiao's hands were gentle, but impartial and quick. He handled Veycosi like Cookie would cube meat for the pot. "The old war done at last," he said. "We still have the new one to fight, though. . . ." He closed his eyes. His features settled into a mask, a duppy of the old Acotiren's. "Two rassclaat centaines, but finally the blasted gate we opened that day is closed."

"You?" Veycosi asked. "You closed it?"

"Or something like that. Maybe because I swallowed my soul case. Ease up your right side little bit there so I can wrap your wound proper."

Veycosi's ear for sound recognized those speech patterns, the turns of phrase. This *was* Acotiren, his Cookie, in Datiao's body! A wild excitement filled Veycosi's breast. He half sat, wincing at the burning in his side. "So you're going to save us!" he said. "I knew something would!" Is lie he was telling. He hadn't known anything of the sort. He'd hoped he would win the day. But that victory wasn't for him. Chynchin really was juju, after all. He'd found Chynchin's actual hero.

Acotiren frowned at Veycosi. "Nah me," ee said.

"Don't make jest; of course, you. You going to stop this invasion, just like the three of you did before. You going to magic Ymisen into the ground, nah true?"

"I—" Acotiren's man's voice broke back into an old woman's. Ee swallowed. "Hold still and let me finish tie this bandage."

But Veycosi pushed ir hands away. "No! Now is not the time to mind me! You have the whole of Chynchin to save!" He rocked to his feet. The sting of the knife slash was merely spice to the stew of pain that action brought him. He grunted. Tried to pay it no mind. "Come on, nuh? What you need me to do? I going to do it, whatever it is."

"You can't do nothing, Cricket," Acotiren said gently. "I can't do nothing. Not anymore."

"But you must! Only you know how!"

Acotiren walked over to the front door and opened it. Ee looked up. "I thought so." Ee turned to Veycosi. Ee was smiling. "Come see, nuh?"

"You only have to use the same juju as before," Veycosi said, pleading. He struggled to stand. He limped to ir side and looked where ee was pointing.

Backwinging as though they were seagulls, thousands of cullybrees were calmly landing, on tree branches, on rooftops, on the ground, everywhere the eye could see. More followed, in waves. They chirruped at each other and jostled and pecked for space. "But they can't do that!" Veycosi said. "They all going to dead!"

Acotiren narrowed ir eyes and scanned the mass of cullybrees.

"I don't think so, you know. They not magic anymore. Chynchin rejoining the world." Ee giggled and pointed. "Look at those over there. They already learning how to walk."

Ir voice kept switching registers, almost like a youngboy's when he got old enough his piss start to make froth.

And ee was right. The cullybrees were trying out their legs, taking shaky steps. One tripped and tumbled from a rooftop, taking three of its fellows with it. Two righted themselves midair and took wing. One fell to the ground, rolled, and came to its feet. It shook its head, ruffled its wings, and took a few more steps. None of them looked to be burning up in their own heat. "What happening to them?" Veycosi asked.

"The gate shut, Cosi son. No spell-casting chantsons going to work in Chynchin anymore; no more than in the rest of the world, any road."

"I remember your—Master Tar's chantson, though," Veycosi replied wonderingly. "Years of griot training in instant memorization."

"The chantson is ongle words now. And his name was Datiao," Acotiren reminded him. "We three witches created that chantson expressly for him, to protect him as he spied on the Ymisen soldiers for us. After he went into the piche, he turned its use to his own ends."

Came a noise behind them. Veycosi and Acotiren turned. The pickens were calmly exchanging soul cases, fastening the correct ones around their necks. "We," said Kaïra, "got our soul cases back before the gate shut."

Caiman eyes. They had caiman eyes. Veycosi shuddered. Kaïra watched at him calmly, then said to Maitefa, "Feeling better?"

"Yes," Maitefa answered. "Faster. Like mongoose."

All the pickens laughed at that, so Veycosi supposed it must have been a jest of some sort. Not one he had followed.

Overcome at seeing her enwitted again, Veycosi snatched Kaïra up into his arms, though his wound made him wince. The picken made a startled sound. "Child," Veycosi said, babbling through tears. "My Kaïra! I did this thing to you—to all of you! Through my own cravenness."

"Yes," Kaïra replied. She pushed Veycosi's arms away. "I remember that now. We all do."

Veycosi's sobs grew stronger. "I know. That can't get forgiven."

Little Yddyta spoke up at that. "Coin," was all she said.

Acotiren shot Veycosi a quizzical look. Seemed ee couldn't follow the pickens' train of thought, either.

Kaïra said, "Yddyta mean you will have to earn your forgiveness with your future actions." She looked to Yddyta for confirmation. She nodded.

Chastened, Veycosi answered, "Yes. So I will."

Acotiren looked bemused. "Cricket, your children are plenty gracious."

"They not my chil—" Veycosi regarded the pickens, who were now in a huddle, chatting, it seemed, about their Mamapiche float. At least, he thought that was the matter of their discussion. They were conversing rapidly, talking over and under each other in branched chains of associations that made Veycosi dizzy.

Had he not been feeling so chastened, Veycosi would almost have been amused. For all the maturity of thought of which they were apparently now capable, they were still pickens. At the moment, they had more of a thought for Mamapiche revelry that now might not happen than they did for Ymisen's attack on Chynchin. In a way, they *were* his pickens. He had made them . . . this. He knew he would continue to look out for them until or unless he could deliver them safely to their parents again. And he would face whatever punishment Carenage chose for him, if Carenage survived.

Now the flock-in-flight flow of the pickens' chatter seemed to have turned from who would fashion their paper-over-balsa masks for the festival to the relative viscosities of piche and water. "I wot," whispered Acotiren, "that now you've dissolved the sinews of their minds, they can remember everything they ever heard since they quickened in their mothers' wombs."

Could they? It was only conjecture. And if true, would not exactly be a blessing. Some things were best pushed to the corners of one's memory. He must find some way to mend the pickens. And he must get his family and his intendeds safely away from this attack. Mentally, he glossed over who exactly his intendeds now were. They seemed to be shifting in his heart's mind, and now was not the time to think on such things. He must somehow turn the tide of this war, for Chynchin's sake. And find a second copy of the book he'd damaged. He would make full restitution. He would—

—try to do it all. Headstrong, and all on his own. As ever.

The thought landed on his shoulders with the weight of a cullybree touching ground for the first time; he was doing as he was ever wont to: planning his affairs so that all the attention and the glory would accrue to him.

Veycosi gave a rueful laugh. "Evidently," he said to Acotiren, "this chirping cricket has some lessons to learn."

"No doubt," that worthy replied in ir now-this-now-that voice.

"First, these pickens need to be kept safe. Please help me, Acotiren?"

"Certes. The battle will be focused in the centre of town. And don't forget you're wounded. You could stay here and mind them."

Veycosi nodded. "Yet I need word to go to their families, if any still . . . live."

Acotiren crooked an eyebrow at the table. "I not sure how we would achieve that right now in all this comess."

"Mestre Veycosi?" Sem was plucking at Veycosi's sleeve.

"Yes, picken?"

"Beg pardon, but we not going to stay here with you."

Veycosi said, "But you will! All of you. Is not safe for you out there!"

Yddyta regarded him expressionlessly. "And we were safe before in your care?" She spoke older than her years.

Veycosi could feel his ears reddening, a shame-knot tightening in his belly. "I not going to let anything happen to you again!"

Tubang spoke up this time. "This is war. We can help."

Acotiren said, "Pickens, you must heed your eld—"

But Sem was already talking over ir. Ee said to the rest, "The main ship."

Kaïra laughed, a free, childlike sound that Veycosi realised he'd been missing. "Yes!" she said. "And the piche! Their cannon!"

They all put their heads together, nattering away, a diminutive war council. Veycosi told Acotiren, "This will keep them occupied until we know what is what in Carenage Town."

"Come then, nuh?" said Maitefa eagerly to her bannas. "What we waiting for?" Her colour was high, her eyes bright. She showed no sign of the languishing that had been plaguing the pickens before they came back to themselves.

The pickens swarmed towards the door. Acotiren, ir eyes wide, first made to block their path, then had to step out of their way lest ee be trampled.

"Wait!" Veycosi shouted.

Kaïra stopped and turned towards him. The other pickens made haste, dodging bumbling cullybrees. They leapt, ran, or somersaulted over anything in their way. And the while, they were trading back and forth: "Me for the carts!"

"And me!"

"My ma's boat!"

"Allyou have to stay here!" Veycosi told Kaïra. "You only pickens, you going to get hurt!"

Kaïra nodded. "We might." Her gaze on Veycosi was bright, cold, knowledgeable. Veycosi had the urge to go still, to small up himself so Kaïra wouldn't see him, wouldn't smell him out, would glide right by and hunt out other prey. "People get hurt," she said. Then her face went cheerful. "If you see Ma and Da Gombey, tell them I all right for now. Tell them fate willing, I see them again soon." She turned to set off again, then hesitated. She turned back. She said to Veycosi and Acotiren, "You could help. We need someone to handle the Ymisen force inside the Palavera." She took off without waiting for an answer, shouting for her bannas to wait for her.

Acotiren swore. Ee dashed outside, sprang onto Goat's back, and galloped off after the pickens. Naught for Veycosi to do but wait, nurse his injury, and fret. How were his intimates faring? His parents? Mama-ji willing, they were too far out of town for the invasion to have reached them just yet. And what about his betrotheds? Was Gombey hurt? Could he and Thandiwe ever forgive Veycosi for what he'd done to Kaïra? In their place, he wouldn't. His soul ached for the loss of them, whether it be through war, or through his betrayal. Gombey's parents? Did they still live? Thandiwe's mother? Samra, who surely would never speak to him again?

And Androu, whose chosen masters had had him arrested. Who knew what they were doing to him now? Gods, gods. So many beautiful souls that could be lost to Ymisen's greed! And him out here, able to do nothing! The dogsons would have first taken the Palavera, Chynchin's seat of government. Veycosi gave thanks that at least the blackhearted pickens did not aim to go there, where the Ymisen force would be the strongest.

The Palavera, which had remained high and dry when Veycosi had blown open certain outlets of the dam.

And round and round went his unstilled mind, till he was near dizzy with fretting.

Little more, Acotiren returned, looking vexed. Ee slid down Goat's side to the ground and came to the outside stoop, where Veycosi sat.

"I lost them. They separated and sped away like mongooses. Couldn't catch a one of them in the dark."

"I can't understand them," Veycosi told ir. "Their minds working too fast."

Acotiren nodded. "Eventually, everybody meet something they can't fathom. Even you."

"But is what do them?" Veycosi asked ir. "And what they think they could do?"

"I don't know. Come. I will put some water to boil. I going to make manioc dumplings stuffed with skellion. Plenty manioc and skellion growing in the kitchen garden."

"I have to find those pickens. Their parents not going to forgive me if any harm come to them."

"And you not going to be any help to them if you too bassour-die with hunger to think straight. I see a rabbit hutch out back. You know how to skin rabbit, right? And pick me couple limes off the tree to dress it with, so the flesh don't taste rank."

Clearly, ee hadn't left behind a centaine and a half of being a master chef when ee'd sloughed off the old Acotiren's body. But Veycosi had had a thought. He still had a part to play!

"Mestre Acotiren, beg you stick a pin in that notion. Mama-ji know, I want to taste the meal you planning, but right now I have to get up to Tsigan' Rock."

The climb up the hill in the dark was a chancy one. Veycosi gave thanks for Goat's sure-footedness. He prayed there would be no rain. If the phosphorus he'd loaded into Goat's pack were to get wet, the explosion would reduce him and Goat both to paste on the instant.

He tried to drive from his mind the covert trip around the outskirts of besieged Carenage Town to collect the ingredients he needed. Even from the edge of town he could hear the boom of musket fire. The smell of spent powder and blood made him cough, quietly as he could. He heard cries of agony and, at one point, rapine grunts and the victims crying out in pain, begging the Ymisen soldiers to stop. He glimpsed dying, broken bodies. What right had he to be safe up here, climbing up this hill far from the troubles below? He should be down there, fighting. But he kept reminding himself that he was doing as Kaïra asked. Part of someone else's plan this time, not haring off half-cocked on his own. But the plan of pickens? If he thought on it too much, the weight of the folly of it all made his breath stick in his craw.

The quiet up there beside the newly mended reservoir, away from the terrible sounds of war, was a blessing. He got Goat's pack off and scurried around the reservoir, closing all the sluices except the one leading to the Palavera. He marvelled at Acotiren's healing skills; his wound pinched and ached, but much less severely than it had a few hours before.

Once back at Goat's side, he set about by moonlight assembling the bombs. He couldn't risk working by lamplight, lest Ymisen soldiers see the flickering light and come to investigate. As he laboured, he tried to do the math in his mind. How many bombs did he need? Plenty more than three. But he didn't have enough of the variables, and he was too anxious to be able to keep all the sums in his head.

Midway through the twenty-second bomb he nearly leapt out his skin at the whipcrack sound echoing over the bay, as of Mamagua's vast tail slapping the water. Goat snorted in surprise and threw her head up.

Then the bay exploded into crashing sounds and explosions of light, giving false dawn to the fore-day morning sky. Veycosi looked down into the bay. Only two of the Ymisen warships could still be seen, and those were holed and on their sides, sinking fast. Looked like the other three had already sunk. The light of numerous bursting cannon showed that the water of the bay was full of jetsam and floundering human bodies. Veycosi gave a silent cheer for the doughty souls, whoever they were, who had contrived that feat. It would be a key blow to the attacking Ymisen force. Lines of caimans were already arrowing over to investigate. They preferred river water, but would venture into the sea if lured by much tasty prey.

Now it was time for him to do his bit. He quickly filled the pack with the rest of the bombs he'd made and threw it into the reservoir.

A wet drop landed on his shoulder. He touched it. Slimy. He looked up, and a small egg cracked itself open onto his forehead, spilling wet eggstuff and a tiny, writhing bird body. He dashed it off his face onto the ground. More and more were falling from the sky.

The eggs were hatching. The season was turning, and Mamapiche time was upon them. Ordinarily, today would mark a huge feast in Carenage Town. It was the only day when it was permitted to eat cullybree, and only the eggs and hatchlings that didn't survive their maiden leap into the sky.

No time to think on that. Veycosi ran towards Goat. She would get them to safety before the bombs blew.

But his headlong dash in the dark must have startled her. She leapt away from him. He called out to her, trying to calm her with his voice. Farther down the hillside, she stopped and stood still. He would have made it to her, had he not slipped on egg slime and fallen.

The world went a roaring white, and Veycosi knew no more.

Chapter 9

GOAT'S SONG

L ONG AGO. MY DESERT *clan was enslaved, brought to this land, and made to bear burden. To walk unshod over harsh ground that cut our foot pads. We hold in regard those of you who treat us well, who rub our feet with cocoanut oil and wrap them in soft cloths. We deign those of the two-legs who do not overburden our backs, who rub behind our ears, who feed us sweet grasses. But in our dreaming souls, we sail, broad-beamed, across the desert, and its sands are warm against our solidly spread toes.*

Veycosi's ruse the night of the battle had worked. The pressure of the water he had bombed in the reservoir had exploded through the pipes at the Palavera, flooding it and collapsing the roof. More than half the soldiers occupying the building had perished: drowned, or crushed, or both. A few of the Carenage Town elders, too. It was some comfort to know that Steli had survived. Yaaya had not yet been found, be she quick or dead. Veycosi rather thought the latter, and he grieved for the hawk-eyed old woman with the strong sense of mischief.

"*In the end,*" Acotiren sang softly as Bokor Zunaiya put a fresh bandage on Veycosi's stump, "*it was the pickens who accomplished most of it.*" Veycosi tried not to be too obvious in how he gnashed his teeth against the pain, how he clutched the sides of the cot he was lying on in his room at the gaol infirmary. Here he was again, incarcerated.

"Shh, shh," Zunaiya said soothingly. "Soon done." Her touch was both firm and swift, with the practised deftness of one grown seasoned over decades in one's chosen calling. Her manner was brusque, but not uncaring.

Tailor-sitting around him on the floor, five of the blackhearted pickens watched gravely. The surviving remainder hadn't visited him, and who could blame them? But as to Yddyta, Gza (remorseful Gza, too young to have a death on her hands), Daffyd, and Maitefa, while Veycosi was abed healing, they invariably gathered around him. Some of their parents tried to prevent them, but a picken was slippery as a worm. They found ways to wriggle away from their homes to come to him. The council had given the gaol infirmary permission to let the pickens in, though they weren't to eat from him while they were there.

"You healing well," the bokor told him. "In a fortnight or so, you can be up and about on crutches."

"May it be so," Veycosi murmured.

"Good day to all," said a voice from the open doorway.

Veycosi recognized it immediately. He lifted his head. "Gombey! Banna!"

And so it was. Moving gingerly, the newly conferred replacement cacique of Carenage Town came closer. He pressed his hand against his flank as he walked. His forearm was bandaged, and there was a healing scar along the side of his face that came so close to his eye that Veycosi felt his bladder clench at the sight of it. Gombey looked Veycosi sternly up and down but said nothing. Veycosi reached a hand to his friend. "I'm so glad you're alive! When Kaïra came to me with that piece of your bloodied boubou in her hand, I thought . . ."

Two of the pickens were bringing a stool in for Gombey. Not responding to Veycosi, he went and sat carefully in it. He took a leather flask from his sleeve, uncorked it, and had a swig.

After a space of uncomfortable silence, Acotiren picked up ir chant again: *"And not just the few blackhearted ones, either. Many others fell in with them, for by nature, every picken is a blackheart in some wise. Eldritch creatures they are, with eldritch ways of looking at the world. Until age tames them, all pickens are wild."*

Zunaiya chuckled in amusement at the line. Veycosi was especially proud of having written that bit of wisdom. It felt both true and in some wise false, as many good axioms do. He looked to Gombey, but that one's expression hadn't changed.

Veycosi's right foot had healed, though lacking its two largest toes. Bokor Zunaiya had made an odd-smelling poultice for reducing the scarring. She was having wooden toes carved for him, with a leather strap to hold them on. But his lower left leg was gone from just below the knee. And he was serving time for the poisoning of the pickens, which had led to "grievous bodily harm" to themselves and others. For the gravity of his crime, they would have put him in a locked cell this time. But he needed care the day long, so the infirmary it was for him. Any road, he was in no position to make an escape. Nor did he desire to. The punishment was more than just.

Zunaiya began massaging the thigh muscles of Veycosi's damaged leg. She had told him it was necessary, lest the muscles shorten and the chopped bone end break through the flesh. It was all Veycosi could do not to cry out. He hissed pain through clenched teeth.

Gombey's brow furrowed. Was that pity? If so, Veycosi did not wish it.

Acotiren halted the chant and regarded him with sympathy. "I sorry, Cosi."

Veycosi essayed a smile, knowing full well no one was convinced. "Needs must. Beg you please, resume the tale? It distracts my mind. And the pickens love to hear you chant their story."

Acotiren nodded and took the story up again in ir melodious double-tongued voice. After nearly two centaines of being a mestre of the culinary arts, Acotiren had decided to take advantage of ir new vocal range by training up as a chantwell. Once ee had accomplished ir apprenticeship, the griots would be falling over themselves to write arrangements for ir. Especially since ee brought to the enterprise ir own previously buried knowledge; the chantson that ee irself had helped write, and that doomed Datiao had chanted under the piche for two hundred years, waiting his chance for ill-appointed revenge. Veycosi had incorporated the sense of it into the tale he was writing of how Chynchin had won free. Acotiren was chanting that selfsame tale right now.

"Picken bush radio spread like wildfire,
Pickens of the Mirmeki joined them,
And pickens of the fisherfolk,
And others."

Acotiren switched into the chromatic scale as Veycosi had composed it, to signal a moral about to be delivered:

"Pickens care not for race or creed,
Pickens care not for status,
Until adults teach them they should.

Pickens that day showed all of Chynchin
What its true face could be!"

Allegro now, the chant picked up tempo to match the excitement of the story. Veycosi intended this section to be accompanied by a sole djembe, patting out a stolid syncopation. This was Veycosi's first time hearing his version of the history in the voice of another. It was fascinating to hear the results of his own efforts. Acotiren was learning ir newfound craft well.

"Solid balls they rolled from molten piche,
Big as cannonballs from molten piche,
They hardened in the cool night air."

Veycosi had gotten the story from the pickens themselves, once he was recovered enough to have visitors. The way they told it, overnight, the fisherwomen's pickens rowed out to the five Ymisen warships. Because many of the Ymisen had the phthisic bad, the pickens had been able to sneak past them. In between coughing fits, few noticed the tiny shadows of pickens in the dark, creeping towards their cannon. Swift blades and arrows put paid to those few. The pickens replaced as many cannonballs as they could with the piche bungs, for bungs they were. Rolled into cannon still warm from previous firings, the balls melted and gummed up the works. Thus were ships vanquished by their own backfiring cannon.

Acotiren sang:

"Unlikely? Yes, But forget not that the world is an unlikely place,
The pickens rose up in the night, black as piche,
And sank the Ymisen ships."

Veycosi had composed a triumphant, swelling phrase for the next part:

"*Mamagua clasped the soldiers to her raging bosom,*
As her sister Mamapiche had done two centaines before."

The pickens looked around, smiling, at each other. This generation of Carenage pickens might never tire of hearing the tale of how they themselves had saved Chynchin the second time around. They even freed the deposed Ymisen heir, for they had marked how ee cared for Chynchin. They reasoned, should Ymisen come a-calling again, Chynchin might use Tierce's goodwill as a bargaining chip.

Veycosi imagined the next bit of the story as an interlude:

"*The cullybrees helped, too, for their eggs hatched that night,*
Egg slime and egg yolk raining from the skies.
The streets were slippery with it,
Chynchin people, accustomed to the annual bounty,
Can skate around in it without falling,
But the feet of the Ymisen soldiers slid out from under them,
And Carenage easily captured the fallen soldiers."

"*Mamapiche fed us as Her season of reign began,*
We brought out our bowls and buckets,
We caught broken eggs falling from the sky,
In the midst of mourning and destruction,
We fed on Her bounty,
We gave thanks for Her bounty."

Veycosi was sad he'd missed the egg feast. It might have been the last one, now that the cullybrees could lay their eggs in nests like natural birds.

Sweat had broken out on his forehead as he writhed under Zunaiya's ministrations. Acotiren wiped his brow with a cloth. Veycosi thanked ir. He sighed and closed his eyes, remembering that night. The rain. The darkness up on Tsigan' Rock. The dull thump of explosions in the harbour below. It was a good thing the pickens had let Tierce loose, because ee in turn liberated Androu, and it was those two who found Veycosi up on Tsigan' Rock, semi-conscious and half-dead with blood loss from the lower leg he'd blown nearly to bits in his explosion. Somehow, he'd managed to tie it off with string from his hooking. Else he might have bled to death right there. They later told him that Goat, only a few scratches on her, had crouched by his side the whole time. It was Androu and Tierce who hoisted Maas' Veycosi up unto Goat's back and carried him screaming down the hill to the bokor surgeon Zunaiya. That worthy had kept him insensible through the operation by having Acotiren regularly drip stupefying mafeisan mixed with wine down his throat. Else Veycosi might have woken in the middle of the amputation, screaming and thrashing around with the agony of it.

Veycosi could still sense the missing leg. It itched and ached something fierce. The surgeon said the feeling should pass with time, if he were lucky. Ah, well. Chynchin had ever been an overly lucksome place. Though perhaps it was more like to the rest of the world, now that the cullybrees had landed. It could be that "fickle" now meant in Chynchin what it meant everywhere else.

Veycosi hadn't yet finished setting the rest of the story to song. Acotiren had chanted all there was so far. Ee stopped chanting and spoke instead. To Veycosi's chagrin, ee said, "And let we not forget the achievement of Maas' Veycosi here, who so ingeniously contrived to flood the Palavera with a high-pressure wave of water bombed out of the reservoir into the Palavera pipes. The main Ymisen force had stationed itself there, and he caught them entirely by surprise."

Veycosi felt himself blushing. "It was a small thing, compared."

Acotiren smiled. "As these pickens here well know, size and significance have no inherent correlation to each other. The squadron leader drowned in that first burst of water. At once, the old Mirmeki men who spend their days in the Palavera listening to and arguing with and reasoning on the decisions made there took advantage of the situation. They come from the same warlike tradition as Ymisen, after all—"

"But," piped up Tubang, wriggling with eagerness to put her mouth on the story. She was a little Mirmeki child of about nine. "But though Ymisen enslaved our forebears and made them into Mirmeki, Chynchin is our home, too."

Acotiren's grin grew bigger. "So it is, picken! More for your people's ill or their good, if truth be told. But go ahead, picken. Tell us what the men did."

Then followed a knock-on tale, shyly told and with much backtracking and hesitation once the picken had eyes on her, of the old men the squadron had mistaken for helpless and had thus bound in a corner and ignored. Of how they slipped their bonds and turned on their would-be captors. Of turning the ropes that had held them into whips and slings. Of how, despite some of the elders sadly never leaving the field of that battle alive, the remainder bested the Ymisen in the Palavera.

"Is true," said Zunaiya, now rubbing cocoanut oil into the flap of skin she had neatly sewn over the amputation. "We rise up and submerge Ymisen for a second time, two centaines later. And right now, though, all Carenage healers have plenty plenty custom. So many injured, so many dying."

Veycosi marked the rhythm to her words and told himself he would write them down later.

Zunaiya released Veycosi's thigh and leaned back, stretching out her shoulders. "How does that feel, Maas' Veycosi?"

Veycosi's smile was likely a fearsome one. He was trembling. "I . . . it is well, siani," he lied through gritted teeth. "I thank you." He was panting. This treatment left him daily exhausted, as though he'd done hard labour. So many times he'd nearly begged Bokor Zunaiya not to lay hands on him again.

With some effort, Gombey rose to his feet. He stumped over to Veycosi's side and handed him the flask. "White rum," he muttered.

Astonished, Veycosi accepted the flask, Gombey grimly waving his thanks into silence. While Gombey bade the pickens move his stool closer to Veycosi's bed, Veycosi had a good swallow of the rumbullion. The familiar burn of the spirits was not so much a comfort as it was a promise of future oblivion. He felt a tear start down the outside corner of his eye. He dashed it away with the heel of his hand.

Gombey noticed, though. He leaned over and put his hand on Veycosi's shoulder, which nearly made more tears start. Veycosi sniffed them back.

Gombey took his hand away. His voice was rough when he said, "We put Ymisen's tail between its legs. We have a new pact now. They give us raw iron, we give them nutmeg and processed piche."

Ever curious, Veycosi asked, "What to stop them from overrunning us with a full-size army next time?"

Gombey held out his hand for the flask. He took a dram, swirled it around in his mouth before swallowing. He looked at the floor and spoke quietly, as though to himself: "The further arrangement is that Ymisen will have limited access to Chynchin. Two hundred of their citizens can make landfall here annually, so long as they going to study or do research at the Colloquium. And they have to leave when they done. Tierce is the first Ymisen student admitted. Ee promised Ymisen ee would return there after graduation to be its ruler."

They passed the rumbullion back and forth for a space. Acotiren and Zunaiya each had a taste. The pickens began a clapping game. The spirits were taking effect; Veycosi felt pleasantly muzzy. His muscles unknotted. Zunaiya cautioned, "Not too much of that now, Maas' Veycosi. If it sicken you tomorrow morning, you won't thank yourself."

Reluctantly, Veycosi refused the flask the next time it came around to him. The drink had lent him courage, though. He touched Gombey's knee to get his attention, and, his voice catching, asked, "Samra?"

"Samra will have her Sept within the month. I ordered it. It opens the way for more Mirmeki to study at the Colloquium."

"Huh. So simple, so easily achieved."

"Yes, once power had the will to make it so." Gombey's lips quirked. "Strange. Soon as it was a decree from the cacique so there could be no retaliation from within the Colloquium, three Colloquium Fellows stepped up right away. Status within that institution makes for an excess of caution, nah true?"

Veycosi grunted in agreement.

Gombey said, "Androu remains in Chynchin. He will be a while recovering from his injuries. Speech comes a mite slowly to him nowadays." Gombey's grin was a wry one. "But his words are no less sharp. He fought staunchly for our side, so he cannot return to Ymisen."

This time, Veycosi let the tears quietly come, thinking on everything he could not undo. So much ruin he had caused! Add to it all the heart's ache of the two blackheart children who hadn't survived their pickens' war campaign. Sudharshan and Saoirse. He was a chantwell-in-training. He would make sure their names were never forgotten.

Seeing Veycosi's sorrow, Acotiren turned to the pickens. "Come, young 'uns. Maas' Veycosi need his rest."

"But he's already reclining," protested little Yddyta.

"Nevertheless, we going. Cricket, today I am to be tested in sight-reading, and I must supervise the luncheon meal for my plaza. We making agouti stew. And manioc dumplings stuffed with skellion. I will have one of the students bring you some."

"So I finally going to taste those dumplings. Yes, you go 'long, friend."

Acotiren herded the pickens out, and Zunaiya started collecting up her things as well. As the pickens left, Daffyd cheerily called out, "Oteng! Good walk! You going to see him?" Veycosi didn't recognize the young voice that responded in the affirmative, and Gombey was blocking his view. Who was Oteng?

Zunaiya had looked up when she heard the name. She smiled. "Ah, Maas' Veycosi, here's a young visitor you haven't seen since your mishap. I think I should remain a little longer."

Gombey stood and leaned over Veycosi, revealing Thandiwe, who stood in the doorway behind him with a boy beside her.

Veycosi didn't recognize the child. He tore his gaze away to pay mind to Gombey, who took Veycosi's hand in two of his. "I have to take my leave. Early day tomorrow." He touched his cheek to Veycosi's; one side, then the other. He murmured, "This is not forgiveness, you realise. You may never have that from me."

Veycosi's heart broke. But he replied, "I know. But you giving me grace. I accept that for the generosity it is."

Gombey nodded and turned to Thandiwe and the boy, who

embraced him warmly. Thandy said, "Family supper tonight, so don't work too late. Lev is currying mutton."

So. Veycosi's jealousy of *her Lev* had proved in some wise prescient, if misplaced.

Gombey limped away. Veycosi didn't resist the bite in his voice when he spoke to Thandiwe. "My replacement is a Mirmeki man, then? Not too long ago, you used to call them 'those people.'"

Her expression was cold. "Perhaps I'm learning that the man who honours my child also honours me."

That smarted. Pridefully, he retorted, "May your former intended at least ask how Kaïra fares?"

For some reason, Bokor Zunaiya chuckled. Thandiwe scowled at Veycosi and protectively threaded her arm through that of the boy with her. "Well, I would have forbid him to come see you, but I know he would only manage it by himself. At least this way, I'm here to protect him."

Confused, Veycosi frowned up at this Oteng. The face was strangely familiar. Was he one of Kaïra's bannas? He thought he'd finally learned to recognize them all.

Oteng said, "I longed to visit you sooner, to tell you everything happening with me. But I still sometimes wake up screaming. Nightmares about that night with the Reverie, and everything after."

He took a step closer to Veycosi's bed. Thandiwe barked, "Kaï—Oteng, step away from him. Remember what I told you."

"I remember, Ma. But look at him. He can't do anybody anything right now." Oteng's face took on a tender expression. "Too besides, I remember what he did afterwards, how he looked after me and my bannas. How he tried to do right. Cosi, your leg hurting too bad? You going to get a fake one? When they letting you out of gaol?"

The spate of questions washed over Veycosi too quickly to answer, all delivered in the breaking voice of a boy just becoming a man. Veycosi knew that overeager manner. He propped himself up on his elbows and regarded the child's features well. Noted the early fuzz of hair sprouting on the chin, but also the way the boy's eyes and mouth resembled Thandiwe's. And Kaïra's.

Briefly, Veycosi wondered whether Thandiwe had a son or brother whose existence she had been concealing. Or perhaps the boy was a cousin? Then another thought dawned. He had thought he was getting used to the scalp-tightening sensation of his world overturning yet again. "I—*Kaïra?*" he whispered, his mouth dry.

The child looked abashed. "I forget I look different now. Yes, is me."

Zunaiya chuckled. "Well, lad, you have changed a mite in a couple brief sennights!"

Veycosi boggled. Had Thandy had a change of heart? Was she dressing the girl up as a boy to spare her becoming Mamagua?

But Kaïra's shoulders had broadened. Her upper lip had the shadow of a mustache. And there was no doubt that was a pubescent boy's breaking voice. "What is this?" Veycosi asked.

Zunaiya, a satisfied look on her face, sat back down on the edge of Veycosi's bed. "Maas' Cosi, you may want to take up your writing implements. I think this story will make a wondrous addition to your collection." She rested her hands in her lap and waited for Thandiwe and the Oteng boy to take up the tale.

Sestra, why you think Chynchin did that trick twice?

Trick?

The boy Oteng. The man Acotiren.

The boy was never a trick. Merely a mickle belated. That bokor suspected what he was immediately he hatched forth from his dam twelve years ago.

And the man?

Her? This land merely helped her triumph over her enemy. Perhaps as a means of healing the damage to Chynchin that she and her two fellows had wrought much earlier by making magic. The two results may look the same, but they proceed from very different origins. The natural world is infinite in space and time. One must expect some repetition.

Ah-hah. Well, there is another thing I wonder.

And what is that?

If Chynchin is restored to what it was, why are we still here? We were changed at the same moment it was.

Who knows? The natural world does not answer to us.

THE TALE OF CHYNCHIN'S FIRST MALE TWINNING CHILD

FIRST RELATED TO VEYCOSI OF THE COLLOQUIUM
BY KAÏRA, NOW NAMED OTENG, OTENG'S MOTHER,
THANDIWE, AND SIANI ZUNAIYA, BOKOR OF CARENAGE
TOWN, WHO WAS PRESENT AT KAÏRA'S BIRTH

Parental instinct woke Thandiwe that morning, to the sound of her daughter softly moaning.

Thandiwe was out of her own hamaca in an instant, and at her child's side. Kaïra had recovered from being poisoned by that vile Veycosi, but she was strange now, thoughtful and standoffish. Thandiwe had strung Kaïra's hamaca beside her own, the better to keep an eye out for her daughter.

Kaïra groaned and clutched at her belly. "Ma," she whimpered, "it hurts."

"Let me see." She pulled Kaïra's boubou up. There was a red and angry lump below Kaïra's belly button. Thandy reached to touch the lump. Kaïra howled and twisted away from her hand. From even the brief touch, Thandiwe could feel how warm the swelling was. "Mama-ji," she murmured. Was this because Cosi had poisoned her? Thandiwe called out to wake her own mother, Filiang. After some minutes, a bleary-eyed Filiang, her hair in night-plaits, came to see what had happened.

Kaïra was sweating and pale, her body burning up with fever. Little more time, she was no longer talking sense, only tossing back and forth and muttering pieces of words. Thandiwe and Filiang tried to give her mobby to drink, to bring the fever down. But Kaïra wouldn't swallow. And the swelling kept growing bigger. When the skin over it began to crack, Thandiwe sent for the doctor.

Filiang said, "Maybe she making a baby?"

Thandiwe shook her head. "Not like this."

For her part, Kaïra knew none of what was happening. Her belly had been paining her, yes. It had been for a few days. But she paid it little mind. She and her bannas had a children's war to coordinate. Plus, her mind had been in fugue for some days, disjointed by the overdose of Reverie. She had come back to herself to find Chynchin's cullybrees touching down, and a living and a dead army making havoc in Carenage Town. Everything was different. Her thinking, too. She and her bannas could follow each other's half thoughts and finish each other's sentences. Why did everyone else think so slow? Then the danger and excitement of the children's battle, and the recovery of Chynchin, with so many dead, so much destroyed. A world overturned. What was a little bellyache, to that? She remembered climbing into her hamaca that night, wincing a little. Falling asleep dreamless. She did not remember the pain that made her call out for her ma.

The woman standing just inside Thandiwe's door with her doctor bag was middling in age and in height, wearing a dark pai-jama and matching tunic, their weave uncharacteristically plain for a woman of Sindhu blood. She wore earrings, but no rings, necklace, or bangles; nothing that could get in the way while she worked. That is, she dressed as surgeons of the bokor class did: in whatever fashion they pleased, but the garments were simply styled and in dark colours that hid bloodstains until the garments could be washed. A surge of alarm swelled Thandy's throat. "You're a surgeon?" she asked the woman. "Does my Kaïra need cutting, then?" In the time it had taken the woman to arrive, the crack on Kaïra's belly had split apart farther. There was little blood, just glimpses of more flesh inside the wound. Thandiwe's mother, Filiang, was sitting with the semi-insensible girl to make sure she didn't pull at it.

"Siani Thandiwe," the bokor replied. "You don't remember me?"

Thandiwe stared at her. Her features were familiar. The calm set to her posture. The long, slim nose that had broken and healed back a mite crooked. The ironic set of her mouth, which Thandiwe somehow knew could on a sudden turn to a wide, warm smile. "Siani Zu . . . Zunaiya?" Thandy asked.

And there was that smile she now remembered. "Exactly so!" said the bokor. "You going to let me in?"

"Oh! Of course!" Thandiwe stood aside. Zunaiya entered, alert and looking around. Zunaiya had been one of the bokors present when Kaïra was born. It had been their job to assert whether she was, in fact, a twinning child.

Just then, Kaïra called out, "Ma? Where you deh?"

"Coming, Kaïra!"

Zunaiya said, "I presume that's my patient?" and headed in the direction of Thandiwe's sleeping room, Thandy trailing after her. Over her shoulder, Zunaiya said, "We been keeping an eye on the little one from since she born."

"Who, we?"

"The bokors who confirmed she was a twinning child."

Kaïra was awake, tossing her head back and forth and blowing out little breaths. Filiang held one of her hands, trying to comfort her. Kaïra's face was twisted in pain. "What happening to me, Ma?"

"I don't know, my love. This siani is a bokor. She knew you when you were born. Maybe she can help you." Thandy knew her smile was tight. She wasn't fooling her child.

Zunaiya approached the hamaca, resting her doctor bag at the picken's feet. "Hello, Kaïra. What a way you turned out comely! Let me have a look at where the pain is."

When Zunaiya lifted the boubou, Kaïra looked down at herself and exclaimed in horror. "Is what that?"

Thandy and Filiang only gaped, speechless. A lump of fleshy skin was protruding from the wound. Zunaiya nodded. "Exactly what I thought." She patted Kaïra's cheek. "Don't fret, picken. You going to be all right. The pain should be less soon. The fever likely going to come down by itself. Things progressing the way they should."

Kaïra, tears streaking her face, wailed in confusion, "What things? What progress?"

Then she writhed in pain and cried out as the wound opened out little more.

Thandiwe's heartstrings ached to hear her picken in such agonies. And Zunaiya was smiling! What kind of monster could be happy to see a child in such straits?

Kaïra whimpered once, softly. Then she looked down at her belly and gasped. "Ma," she said, "look, look!"

Zunaiya's grin grew even broader. "All my days as a healer," she said to Kaïra, "I only ever see this once before. I just never thought it could happen to a twinning child. You, sweetness, are even rarer and more precious than we knew."

She made space for Thandiwe and Filiang to see. Filiang gave a soft scream. For herself, Thandiwe couldn't remember what she was thinking at that moment.

Pushing out of the crack in Kaïra's belly was a boy-sized cocky and balls. Her mind a torrent, Thandiwe looked to Zunaiya for an explanation.

Zunaiya sighed happily. "Your daughter is now your son," she said, as though that made all clear.

And Kaïra laughed, like the weight of the world had been taken from her.

———

"I decided to take the name 'Oteng,'" said the picken. "It sound fine, nah true?"

Veycosi was having trouble keeping up with his notes as the three people recounted him the story. For one thing, it was so wondrous that he was entirely absorbed and kept forgetting to write. For another, an excitement had begun welling up in him the instant he realised what had happened to Kaïra-that-was. It tickled at his insides like tabac smoke, till he had to let it out. He clasped the

picken's hand between his two. "So now you don't have to be the
next Mamacona! You can be what you want!"

A silence fell around the room. Oteng's face darkened and he
cast his eyes downwards. "Is so I thought, too. But Siani Zunaiya
say I still have to do it."

Thandiwe scowled at Veycosi. "My . . . son was born with a
responsibility. Unlike you, he hews to his."

"Yes, Ma," said the boy. Didn't she mark how disconsolate the
prospect made him? Were Kaï—Oteng his, he would be petitioning
all and everyone to get the child released from this career he had
not sought and did not desire. Veycosi understood how a youthful
Thandiwe, knowing herself with child, might seize upon a fanciful
story to make her life more exciting. Women's wombs quickened
every day. In Chynchin, it was a matter of rejoicement when it happened. Just not of such renown that there would be dancing in the
streets.

But to have a child who would become a god; now *that* was a
thing of which people would take note. Fair enough. Yet Thandy
was a mature woman now, and still seeking to achieve fame by foist-
ing an unwanted life onto her child. Veycosi still missed Thandiwe
something awful, though now he was thinking there might be an
advantage to not marrying himself to one such as she. He couldn't
disdain her overmuch, though. Hadn't he committed his own acts
of overweening folly, thus bringing harm to those he loved? One
thing was clear: Thandiwe loved her child fiercely. She was a better
mother than he would have been a father.

He dragged himself out of his melancholy thoughts by asking
Bokor Zunaiya, "How did all this come about?"

"Because we have no other," she replied. "On the day Oteng
was born, my fellow bokors took the child from Siani Thandiwe
to examine him, so we could confirm or deny whether he was a

twinning child. And in truth, Oteng was identical to his mother in every way. I marked, though, that the child's privates were of uncertain sex. Mind you, no two sets of privates are identical. But this variation was out of the ordinary."

At this, Oteng looked abashed. Zunaiya smiled at him. "Apologies, lad; I not making mock, merely avowing that you are truly unique. That is a beautiful thing."

Zunaiya continued, "I was the oldest of the lot of bokors assigned this task. In my decades of work I'd heard of this kind of thing, had even witnessed it once; a boy who looked to be a girl until his nature came down at puberty. But all our knowledge told us that since the child was Siani Thandiwe come again, an eventual boyhood was impossible. We all know Chynchin is home to the unlikely, though. So we decided to confirm her as a twinning child, but to keep an eye on her. If the twin goddess had chosen to make the next Mamacona a boy, who were we to gainsay her?"

Thandiwe made a noise of satisfaction at that. Oteng said nothing.

And then Veycosi knew what his true penance should be. His heart beat fast when the idea came to him. Would he be ready? Would he be allowed? Mama-ji, please say he would.

Jolting Veycosi out of his thoughts, Thandy said, "Is time we leave."

He gasped. "So soon? I have a favour to ask you and Oteng."

That was the wrong way to word his request. He knew it immediately the words poured forth. Sure enough, Thandiwe snapped, "We have nothing more to give you, and nothing we owe you. Oteng, come away."

"Thandy, please listen to me. Just for a minute? I don't want to, can't, ask forgiveness. I know that. I just want to do what Mamacona would want."

Thandy's furious eyes met his. "You lie. You have no faith."

"A-true," he replied, "I don't." He mentally berated himself. He was botching this. She needed truth from him, not wiles. He tried again. "But I don't need faith in gods to know what I need to do now."

"You know is not me you betrayed," she growled, "but this boy. This trusting picken who never did nothing but love you!"

Tears were never far from Veycosi's eyes nowadays. "I know."

She took Oteng by the hand and began walking away. As she pulled him along, Oteng said, "Ma, please hear what he have to say? For me? Please?"

She stopped, looking down at the hard tile floor of the gaol infirmary. Veycosi didn't dare hope. Thandiwe remained so for some seconds, her back to Veycosi. He could hear her sniffing back tears. Then she dashed her hand across her eyes. She didn't turn to face him, but muttered, low, "State your piece."

He explained what he wanted to do, while Oteng, precious Oteng, Mamagua's son Oteng, looked then at Veycosi, then at his mother, his face alighting with wonder. Once he'd laid everything out, Veycosi said, "I will be out of here in time for the Mamapiche parade. If the council says yes, then it is arranged. Will you let me do this?"

Oteng agreed immediately. Thandy took longer, but when she finally admitted to herself Oteng's true feelings about his coming fate, she let the decision be his. In that moment, she was utterly beautiful in her love and care for her child.

"Thank you," said Veycosi.

Sleep was scarce that night. The usual phantom pain, certainly. But it remained largely in the background, muted by the foment of his mind as he conceived and refined the plan the way he wanted to present it to the council. If they agreed, he would free Oteng.

It was Tierce, flush with the joy of being a student, who found in the Colloquium's archives the sources Veycosi needed, copied down the details and drawings, and brought them to him in the gaol. Two of the inmates were women of the fisherfolk, handy with sail-mending needle skills. They were given the duty of cutting and sewing prototypes at one-fifth, one-quarter, and half size. The pickens took these and launched them from the trees around the gaol. They all fell and burst apart. Veycosi recollected that the last time he had experimented this way, his calculations had been so wrong that he'd nearly burst the reservoir open. His heart lurched into his throat then; a similar mistake this time would mean death.

Tierce seemed affronted when Veycosi explained his dilemma the following day. "Why wouldst thou not ask one's . . . my help?" ee said. "I am studying the stars, look you."

Veycosi frowned, not seeing the relevance.

Tierce rolled ir eyes. "I must almost daily do calculations of the movement of objects in space."

Of course. So that was another aspect of his plan he needs must give over to another. It chagrined him until Tierce showed him ir scale drawings. He had to admit was a comfort to know he had company in his endeavour.

A new half-size prototype, loaded down with a rockstone, made the trip successfully, to applause from the inmates working that day in the gaol's farm.

———

There you have it; Acotiren consumed Datiao and her own soul case, thus pushing shut the gate between the real and the numinous, the gate that occasionally creaked open a smidgen to let the two commingle for a space. That was normal. It was only in Chynchin that for two centaines the gate had gaped open wide enough to make the place a locus of the uncanny. No more, though. This country is like any other now. Obeah may work sometimes, but mostly not. Acotiren will live and die now, like any other human being. A dropped watermillion probably will not bounce, but will crash to the ground and burst open, dashing its sweetness to be crushed underfoot.

And apparently we the twinned god persist, as gods do anywhere there are people whose faith brings them into reality.

In addition, do forgive my sister. In her frustration at your deafness to us, she played a Mamapiche trick on your memory. You were never attacked by a caiman. You have no caiman scar on your foot. No matter, though, sith you no longer have that foot.

"Remember, lad," said Jacob. Goat was kushed down. He patted her saddle. "She going to come up on her back legs first, then her front ones. So she going to tilt down, look you, then straighten out as she lifts up. Put your hand on the tarfa in front of you, and keep that arm straight."

The peak above wasn't the highest point on the mountain range, but it stuck out the farthest. It suited Veycosi's purposes well. The stone Mamacona sisters stood on the hill farther above; the same place where they'd ever stood, calmly overlooking a Chynchin so changed, Veycosi marvelled that they still cared to remain there, rather than leaping off into the sea that was Mamagua's domain.

Veycosi regarded the frame of wood and fabric on Goat's back that was the saddle. "Maybe I should just climb the hill myself."

Jacob gave him the blankly knowing look of one who'd raised an own-way child. "As tha will't, lad. But Goat and I will come alongside."

So off they went. Veycosi struggled with each step, trying to handle the weight and discomfort of his new peg leg. Behind Veycosi, Gilead, Maitefa, Daffyd, and Oteng struggled under the floppy weight of his latest folly. Gza trailed along beside them, alternately carrying and dropping four long lengths of rope and four of supple bamboo. Veycosi could have had Goat tote the lot for him, but the pickens had begged and reasoned with him until he let them.

One of Veycosi's crutches slipped in the shale. Down he went, with a cry. That had *hurt*! Maitefa and Oteng dropped their burden and ran to him. "No, don't help me," he told them. "All is well." Jacob just looked on calmly. Veycosi managed to clamber upright. He resumed the torturous climb.

The second time he measured his length in the hillside dirt, Oteng came and knelt by his head. Gently, he said, "I did the sum. At your rate of progress, it going to take you almost three hours to get to the top. Parade will finish long since."

Veycosi was sweaty with the effort. His fine new boubou was smeared with dust. He'd scraped the palm of one hand. The ache at the base of his stump had progressed from sullen to insistent. Oteng said, "If you ride Goat, we will reach in fifteen minutes. Enough time to break fast and get set up." Then he held an arm out to help Veycosi stand.

It was the adultish reasoning that unnerved the most. With a grumble, Veycosi let the picken help him. Oteng bade Jacob and Goat come over. It needed almost the whole party to get Veycosi securely onto Goat's back. He hadn't reckoned on how challenging it would be to grip the saddle with one lower leg gone. He nearly slid off a few times, but did finally find the trick of it. They continued up the hill, with Jacob guiding Goat by her lead. The camel stepped smartly today. Maybe she liked the new foot wrappings.

Jacob had informed Veycosi that camels' feet were suited to deserts, not the rocky hills above Carenage. So then, by way of apology for taking her up into the hills in her bare feet the night of the battle, Veycosi had had her feet shod in lengths of soft woven canvas.

The day was a fine one; light clear as glass, the sky blue, the sea breathing calm and deep. Fishing boats dotted her breast. Fewer than usual; boats had been stove in during the skirmish.

The Colloquium had agreed that under the circumstances, this history he was recording counted as finding a new tale to equal the worth of the book he'd drowned in the reservoir.

Pain occupied much of Veycosi's life nowadays. His stump hadn't yet built up enough callus. It frequently chafed to rawness where it rubbed against the heavy wooden leg Bokor Zunaiya had had carved for him. The itchy ache in his phantom leg was, for some reason, worse at night. He would wake weeping from it and reach for Ma's bitter tea brew, which she left in the jug by his bed. He'd rather have slept in a hamaca, but the shape and movement of one currently made his injury ache intolerably. Ma and his das had taken him back in so they could look after him while he was recovering. He daily thanked whatever gods might be that they had decided to take that ocean trip after all. They had even convinced the yardman Adam and his family to join them. Their timing had been perfect. Now they were back with stores of rice that war-riven Carenage needed.

When Veycosi reached near the top, he saw that Gza had fallen behind. "Oteng, please help Gza fetch the sticks and rope the rest of the way."

Oteng went to do that. He took precisely half the burden; two bamboo rods and two lengths of rope. They joined the others, who were already laying Veycosi's hooking out on the ground, smoothing it into the basket shape he'd hit upon, and laying out the four large triangles of closely woven silk that would complete the assemblage. Each trying to shout over the other, they fell to discussing last week's batey match, the merits of each goal, of each player. They were demonstrating by kicking a rockstone to and fro. Seemed they all remembered the game play for play. They were perfectly normal pickens, never mind the excess of logicality to which the blackheart pickens were prone. At least, Veycosi hoped that was so.

Jacob helped Veycosi to dismount. Veycosi sat on a nearby rock and massaged the knots out of his thigh.

Daffyd broke away from the other pickens and came over to him. "Maas' Veycosi," he said, "you have anything to eat?"

Veycosi's answering smile was a wry one. "Not for me to give you food from my hand. Not after last time. Don't fret, though. Bickle coming for us." He had been watching Tierce and Acotiren, who were racing each other up the hill towards them, laughing and taunting each other as they came.

He sighed. He would never again be that nimble.

Yet here he nevertheless was, on the hillside too.

The two arrived, sweat-shone, panting, and happy. Acotiren opened up the leather bag slung over ir shoulder and shared out the accra cakes ee had brought. Ee offered three of them to Goat, who as ever was crouched close to Oteng. The animal lipped the accra cakes delicately up from Acotiren's hand.

The pickens squatted on the ground at Mamagua's tails and ate. Daffyd said, "We need aught to drink."

"You know where the spring is," Veycosi told them. So then they palavered about who would go and fetch water for them all. At first they felt it should be the one who'd done the least work. But then they decided it should be the one who best loved to give service. Sem, puffed up with pride like a crapaud in mating season, hied irself off to the spring to get them all a drink.

When Sem returned, everyone drank from the calabash ee'd brought back, then poured the remainder over Mamacona's tails with a prayer. "Oteng," Veycosi said, "you see my pipe?"

"Look it here." Oteng took the pipe and the pouch with the makings out of the panier on Goat's back and handed them to Veycosi.

Veycosi had had plenty of time to think about himself while he was recovering from the accident. Androu had the right of it. Veycosi had wanted to be congratulated. Thanked. Adored. Damme, he worked hard to do the right thing. To treat every somebody like a cacique, born into a family of rulers. But in his heart of hearts?

Hot up here on the mountain, in the bright sunlight. Far below him, the sea wafted up its salty smell; Mamagua's cunny, ever birthing life. He was grateful there were no more bodies and parts of bodies bobbing in her near the shore, though the river docks in Carenage Town were still being strained free of the dead.

He had wanted their gratitude. Androu's. Samra's. All their ilk, if he was to be truthful with himself; all who'd been born into an unfair station. He had wished them to recognize when he treated them as equals. But especially those two. And swive him, some deep part of him still quietly craved that.

Veycosi wanted Androu to understand that no somebody but Veycosi would ever treat him with such regard. He wanted Samra to know is only him who would ever understand her. Yet he knew it wasn't true, and he hated himself for the wanting.

He opened his pouch. Shook the contents out into the palm of his hand and looked at them. He had dried snakeroot leaves. He'd crushed the dried leaves to a powder, which he mixed with some gratings of his favourite Reverie—now somewhat scarce in Chynchin, sith so many of the nutmeg orchards had been destroyed—soaked in kumaka pod water, and dried again. Smoking it gave a pleasant, slurry cast to the world and to one's dealings with it. Tended to block one's water for most of a day if one weren't careful. Uncomfortable, that. But the muzzy, temporary conviction that all would be well had been worth it to him often, especially in these last few days.

Chuh. Veycosi brushed the bouffe and kindler off into the dust and slung the pipe out over the side of the mountain. It bounced once, high and spinning end over end. Then he didn't see it again.

As he went to slip his purse back into his sleeve, he felt something small and hard still inside it. He reached inside it and pulled out the cullybree tooth he'd been carrying all this time.

He wanted the world to be awestruck by him. He wanted praise. To be patted on the head and given a treat, like a monkey on the leash when it does its one trick.

Only for the monkey, the trick is outside its nature. Whereas fair dealings were something that any person should be able to receive from any other, nah true? Even a babe in arms would hold out its chewed-over biscuit to share with another, for the simple joy of seeing the other eat.

And that same babe would dash its little fists in fury against its mam's cheek if she didn't give it what it wanted.

He didn't know the answer. He only knew he wanted their regard. To rass with their love, if they would only fear losing his! Was he so wrong in that? *Me ain't know*, diplomatic Acotiren would probably say. But Veycosi did know.

A fat cullybree wandered by, pecking at ants in the dirt. So quickly they were getting used to being ground-tied!

He could hear from Carenage below the beginnings of the parade music. His cue. He found he was trembling.

He held up the cullybree tooth from his purse. It was crenellated like a horse's tooth, but smaller. Some things were magic, and some people tried to *make* magic. And Veycosi? Which he was?

He looked out on the sea that went forever, to places he had never been. He could be a being who entered a ship that set sail upon that sea. He could be soon, now that the Colloquium had reinstated him. If he wanted it. He wasn't sure he did. But perhaps to expand his new métier of being a collector of living histories.

Yet even doing something so unremarkable as stepping onto a ship, he would be part of the flow of the miracle that makes a sea to be, and a world, and beings to sail upon and live in it. Was the existence of this world miraculous, or simply natural? Was there a difference?

Ah, he didn't know shite. Except this: sometimes the world was wondrous, and you found it was bearing you up where by rights you should be sinking.

"Oonuh ready?" he asked the three adults and the pickens. The latter joyfully asserted that they were; Acotiren and Tierce, too. Jacob seemed less certain.

Acotiren helped him get into his costume and fasten the mask. Then, holding Acotiren's hand and struggling against the wind, Veycosi moved right to the very edge. He dug his heel in as his belly curdled within him and his fearful stones pulled themselves into his body. It was such a long way down. Here was where everything had begun, with him hanging off the edge of this cliff.

"Is all right, Cricket," said Acotiren. "Not going to let you fall."

Dry-mouthed, Veycosi managed a chuckle. "A-true. I plan to take care of that myself."

The pickens and Tierce were holding the kite aloft. Tierce functioned as anchor by wrapping the fifth, longest piece of rope around ir body. The kite's four large triangles of silk had been bound together by their long edges, with the bamboo as struts. In configuration it

was a type of cone with square edges. Jacob was on one knee, holding the basket down on the ground. The pickens had attached it
to the kite by the four ropes. The kite tugged playfully at the rope
holding it fast. If all went well, that line would tether Veycosi to
solid earth. Jacob, Tierce, and Acotiren would be the ones primarily
controlling it. The pickens wanted to help, and so they would. His
life would in part be in the pickens' hands. That seemed meet.

Still holding tight to Acotiren, Veycosi grasped Jacob's shoulder
and climbed into the basket.

Now both Jacob and Acotiren held the basket.

"Now?" yelled Oteng.

"No! Not yet!"

He put the cullybree tooth into his mouth. Like a piece of chalk,
it drew water from his tongue and stuck there a little. He pretended
it was one of Thandy's crabstones and crunched down on it. Bit by
bit, the dry crumbs worked their way down his throat.

He knew there were those who cared about him. Some of them
managed to do so even though he'd wronged them grievously. He
didn't deserve such grace. And he knew there were those about
whom he cared.

It was time. His heart was trying to beat its way out his chest,
but he was going to do this thing.

He took a deep breath in, then out. "Now!" he called out.

Jacob and Acotiren released the basket. Everyone held on to
the rope while Tierce unwound irself from it and took hold with ir
hands. Slowly, they paid the rope out. The man-kite leapt into the
air to the limit of its tether. It pulled the basket off the ledge with it.
Veycosi yelped as he found himself jerked off the cliff onto the air.
The basket swung in tight circles. Veycosi closed his eyes. He hung
on as tightly as he might and prayed he would be able to hold his
breakfast down.

"Cosi!" yelled Oteng. "It's working!"

He made himself open his eyes. The air had filled the kite. The air bore him up, as it once had done with the cullybrees.

The wind made Veycosi's eyes water and his nose sting. It was glorious. He shouted a huzzah at his companions on the hill, and they jubilated back at him. Goat swung her ears back at the sound, but otherwise ignored them all, thinking her own camelish thoughts.

He was swinging out high over Carenage Town. He could see it in the act of rebuilding itself. Below him, the Mamapiche parade was snaking through Carenage Town's high street, accompanied by the cacophony of ululations and the beating of old, blackened iron pots with dull, overused machetes, their flat colour symbolizing Mamapiche's tar nature. Doubtless the crowd had already noticed the lack of the lead float, which should be bearing Oteng. They had doubtless also noticed the lack of Oteng himself, and were wondering when he would show up to be taken to the Mother Lake and dipped inside it to emerge as the embodiment of the trickster Mamapiche.

Veycosi yodelled and pointed down towards the parade. That was their signal. With a halloo and a hullabaloo, Oteng and his Mamapiche crewe began running down the hill, dragging Veycosi in his kite along with them. This was their float. Goat loped along behind them.

Veycosi's belly flipped with the downwards motion. So it had felt when as a picken he would dive from one of the fisherwomen's ships into the sea. He was grateful for the breeze that swelled over and past him; this black clothing was devilishly hot!

Chynchin needed the blue waters of Mamagua that flowed through it, yes. That was life, and sustenance. But it also needed the black vein of piche. That was Chynchin's heart. Chynchin's fierce, black heart was its engine.

Chynchin needed its Mamapiche, and that was to have been
Oteng. And he, Veycosi, had been intended to become Oteng's da.
Had in his soul in fact done so, even though his troie with Than-
diwe and Gombey was undone.

The parade had stilled. Veycosi could see the upturned faces
of the crowd below. Little more, and he would be able to make
out their features. His entourage, dragging him ever downwards,
kept up their bellowing. Among them, Oteng met Veycosi's eye,
grinning joyfully. Veycosi grinned back. He double-checked the
security of the belt around his waist. Yes, the caiman tail should
hold. He slipped the mask onto his head. It had a speaking cone
built into its snout, extending inwards towards his mouth. That
would let him join the shouting without deafening himself inside
the mask. One-handed, he held the mask secure against the wind of
his downwards descent.

A da could sacrifice himself to set his picken free. People of all
nations understood this. Certainly the council of elders had when
he told them what he meant to do. Steli had even given him a grave
nod. Thus it was that Veycosi, Chynchin's own Blackheart Man,
would become Mamapiche in Oteng's place.

The pickens and the three adults were on level ground now,
running pell-mell to head off the parade. They had to keep moving
quickly, in order to keep his kite aloft until they could land it in its
rightful place at the head of the parade.

Veycosi began his own ululation, joining his voice with the
crowd's as he swooped down onto the parade; his first hijinks as
Mamapiche's Blackheart Man.

ACKNOWLEDGMENTS

My profound thanks and blessings to the following: Cathy Thomas and her amazing working group of women writers; my beta readers, who were so generous with their time, their deep knowledge, and their general cheerleading; my editor, Joe Monti, and the whole team at Saga Press, who created and are getting the word out about the beautiful and beautifully edited artifact that is this book, both hard copy and digital; artist Tarajosu, whose cover image makes me gleeful every time I look at it; my agent, Donald Maass, who's been my stalwart since my very first novel.